ALSO BY JACKIE ASHENDEN

The Tate Brothers

The Dangerous Billionaire
The Wicked Billionaire

The Nine Circles series

Mine To Take
Make You Mine
You Are Mine
Kidnapped by the Billionaire
In Bed with the Billionaire

The Billionaire's Club e-book series

The Billion Dollar Bachelor
The Billion Dollar Bad Boy
The Billionaire Biker

Available by St. Martin's Press

THE UNDERCOVER BILLIONAIRE

JACKIE ASHENDEN

This is a work of fiction. All of the characters, organizations, and events portrayed in this novel are either products of the author's imagination or are used fictitiously.

THE UNDERCOVER BILLIONAIRE

Copyright © 2018 by Jackie Ashenden.

All rights reserved.

For information address St. Martin's Press, 175 Fifth Avenue, New York, NY 10010.

ISBN: 978-1-250-12283-4

Our books may be purchased in bulk for promotional, educational, or business use. Please contact your local bookseller or the Macmillan Corporate and Premium Sales Department at 1-800-221-7945, ext. 5442, or by e-mail at MacmillanSpecialMarkets@macmillan.com.

Printed in the United States of America

St. Martin's Paperbacks edition / March 2018

St. Martin's Paperbacks are published by St. Martin's Press, 175 Fifth Avenue, New York, NY 10010.

10 9 8 7 6 5 4 3

To the wonderful ladies of the House of Ashenden. Touchable Tush Tuesday's is a constant inspiration.

ACKNOWLEDGEMENTS

Thanks to my editor, my agent, and the rest of the lovely people at smp.

Also to my support crew—you guys are the greatest.

CHAPTER ONE

Wolfgang "Wolf" Tate's three favorite things were, in no particular order, fighting, fucking, and blowing shit up. Sometimes he was sad he couldn't do all three things together, but then blowing shit up while fucking was not only dangerous, but stupid. Fighting and fucking, well, he wasn't averse to that.

Kidnapping, though, did not rank highly. In fact, kidnapping wasn't featured at all, yet here he was, standing in Olivia de Santis's bedroom at four in the morning, ready to put his hand over her mouth and haul her up out of her bed and over his shoulder.

He didn't want to do it, he just didn't. But fucking Cesare de Santis, her father and Tate enemy number one, had denied Wolf's perfectly reasonable request to hand her over just days earlier, leaving him with no choice but to go grab her himself. She was a vital part of his takedown plan, which was why he was in her bedroom, watching her still, small figure sleeping deeply under her white comforter, preparing to take her with him by any means necessary.

The woman in the bed sighed and turned over, a bar of dim light from a gap in the curtains illuminating her face.

Wolf let out a silent breath, taking a second simply to look at her, because it had been a long time since he'd seen Olivia de Santis in the flesh, over ten years, all told. He'd been eighteen, ready to enlist in the Navy, and she'd been sweet sixteen and never been kissed. Yeah, a sweet kid, he remembered that clearly, and she still was, given the emails he'd received over the years from her. Though at twenty-eight, not a kid any longer.

It was probably a dumb thing to watch her like this, since every second he stayed in her room was another second he could be discovered, but shit, he wanted to look at her. The photos she'd sent him didn't really convey the changes since that brief moment outside her father's study, a week before he'd left to join the Navy.

They'd met when Wolf had been seventeen, the first time de Santis had invited him into his house, celebrating the fact that Wolf had agreed to work for him in secret, turning traitor on Wolf's own family, the Tates. Olivia had been fifteen, a quiet, self-possessed young girl, who'd viewed him with suspicion initially—understandably since their families were enemies. But over the course of that year, Wolf's frequent and secret visits to the de Santis mansion had meant they'd run into each other quite a lot in the library outside her father's study, and slowly her distrust had melted away and a certain friendship had formed between them. It shouldn't have worked. She was shy and quiet, and frighteningly intelligent, while he was loud and brash, and certainly not known for his brains. Yet for some reason it did. And when he'd left to join the Navy, she'd stayed in touch, emailing him regularly while he responded where and when he could.

Her face had matured, losing that teenage roundness and revealing a small, determined chin and slightly upturned nose. She had the same rosebud mouth he remembered and the dark, de Santis winged brows, but she'd missed out on the rest of the showy de Santis good looks. Not pretty, yet not unappealing either.

Not that it made any difference what she looked like.

He wasn't here for fucking. He was here because of his dead father's last letter to him. A letter given to him two weeks ago at the meeting with his brothers at Leo's alehouse, a military bar.

A letter containing a promise. The same promise his father had always made him—if Wolf completed the mission he'd been given, he'd finally, after years and years of hope, get to meet his mother. Because Noah had finally located her. Unfortunately, with Noah being dead and all, Noah wouldn't be able to be there for the happy reunion, but if Wolf completed his mission, he'd be sent his mother's location.

It was all Wolf had ever wanted ever since he'd been small. A family. A *real* family. And that letter . . . fuck, that letter was promising him that at last.

His father. His mother. Him.

All he had to do was kill Cesare de Santis.

Easy. No problem. He'd been training for that his whole goddamn life. It was going to mean a few sacrifices along the way, but his father had always told him that. *"Nothing worthwhile comes without sacrifice, Wolf,"* his father had said. *"Nothing worth fighting for is taken without blood."*

Wolf had accepted that the way he'd accepted everything his father had told him. Because he knew a secret that no one else knew.

He wasn't the foster son everyone thought he was.

He was Noah Tate's real son.

Not that his father ever treated him that way. He'd told Wolf early on that he couldn't afford to be a real father to him, not while the de Santis threat was hanging over their heads. But that if Wolf would do what he was told, become the weapon his father wanted him to be, then when it was all over, he'd get the family he deserved. Noah could finally acknowledge him.

It wasn't that Wolf wanted the company or his father's

billions. Money had never meant anything to him. No, all he wanted—all he'd *ever* wanted—was for his father to tell the world that Wolf was his son. And then they'd find his mother.

But none of that would happen unless Wolf killed the man who threatened the entire Tate legacy. His father had been clear. Until Cesare was dead, Noah couldn't risk bringing Wolf's mother out of hiding and he couldn't acknowledge his son.

Unfortunately Noah's death had changed things. He wouldn't be able to formally acknowledge Wolf now, but he'd told Wolf that his name was on Wolf's birth certificate. So even if his father wasn't around to see it, once Wolf had completed his mission, he would have all the proof he needed to show everyone that Noah Tate was actually his father. After he'd killed de Santis and gotten his mother out first.

Sacrifices. Yeah, Wolf was okay with sacrifices to get what he wanted.

Even if that included sacrificing his friendship with Olivia de Santis.

A twinge of regret hit him at the thought, but he shrugged it off. It was what it was and how he felt about it made less than no difference at all. She had access to Cesare's schedule and he needed that if he was going to make a successful hit. The guy's security was insane and Wolf had no intention of getting himself killed, not after all the years he'd spent waiting for his reward. It was why he hadn't taken out de Santis when he'd met him in his limo a couple of days earlier. All this had to be done without it being traced back to him, to anything Tate in fact.

Which meant that becoming familiar with Cesar's schedule, his movements every day, was a must. And the only person who had access to that was Olivia. Oh, she wasn't going to want to give him the information willingly, not given how protective she was over her father, but he'd figure a way around that. He'd get that information by any means necessary.

Sacrifices and all that shit.

Moving soundlessly, he went around the side of the bed and crouched down beside it. He'd wondered whether he should have had a backup in case Olivia resisted, a rag soaked in chloroform or something, but in the end he'd decided that was too fiddly. He preferred to keep things simple. If she didn't want to come with him, there were a few ways he could make her—without unconsciousness being part of the deal.

Still sleeping deeply, Olivia made another small sound and turned over onto her side so that she was facing him, nestling her cheek down into the pillows. One small hand had crept up to curl beneath her chin. She looked like a child, fast asleep and dreaming of fairies or whatever magical bullshit it was that children dreamed of.

That twinge of regret hit him again, which was annoying. Christ, it wasn't as if he was going to do anything to her. He was only going to pick her up and take her away where he could get what he wanted from her without interference. Once he'd taken Cesare out, then he'd let her go. He just had to be careful not to let slip any of his plans. Of course, she'd probably guess in the end that it was him who'd killed her father—she was a smart girl after all—but if he was careful, she wouldn't have any evidence pointing to him.

Or there were other ways to keep a woman quiet that didn't involve death or violence. He knew a few. If it came to that.

He just had to make sure that kidnapping her wouldn't blow his cover with de Santis. It was irritating that the night he'd told de Santis he wanted Olivia in return for taking out that arms dealer, de Santis had told him she was already promised to someone else, someone very powerful and very dangerous. He'd argued for de Santis to break the agreement, give Wolf a little something in return for fourteen years of being a Tate spy, but it soon became clear that de Santis wouldn't. Or couldn't, at least not without serious repercussions.

The man she'd been promised to was in the Defense Department, an alliance that de Santis needed in order to keep his gun-running on the down-low.

Wolf had had to make a small adjustment in his plans after hearing that. It was yet another reason the guy had to die. He'd been subverting good American sailors to do his dirty work for him, and Wolf couldn't let that go.

He was a SEAL through and through. Loved his team. They were the family he'd never had and he'd defend them with his life, and the thought that de Santis had used one of them to sell his weapons on the black market had made Wolf want to break something. De Santis, if he had his choice. And shit, he'd take down de Santis's Defense Department contact too.

Hence the kidnapping.

Olivia wasn't going to like it, but that was too bad. He was on a mission, a mission he'd been working toward for fourteen years, and nothing was going to get in his way.

Wolf laid a hand across her mouth and held it there, then leaned in and whispered in her ear. "It's me, Liv. It's Wolf. Don't scream."

She didn't immediately move and he wasn't surprised. As far as she was concerned, she was sleeping in her own bed, in her father's very well protected Upper East Side mansion, and probably the last thing she'd be expecting was an old friend come to kidnap her.

He waited patiently, keeping his hand where it was, over her mouth, feeling her warm breath against his palm. She gave another sigh, murmuring something and trying to turn over, her long dark lashes fluttering. But she must have realized something wasn't right, because her lashes fluttered yet again then slowly lifted, her eyes dark in the dim light of the room, staring blankly at him.

He stared back as sleep began to clear from her gaze and realization hit.

Right on cue, her whole body stiffened, her eyes going wide with terror, her mouth opening under his hand, all ready to let out one hell of a scream.

"It's me, Liv." He pitched his voice low and hard to cut through her fear. "So don't scream. I'm not here to hurt you."

She ignored him, her hands shooting out from underneath the comforter, her body twisting, trying to get away.

Fuck, he didn't need this shit. He'd thought she'd take one look at him, recognize him, and then be cool about it. Sadly it didn't look like she was cool about it at all.

Cursing, he firmed his hand over her mouth and moved so he was leaning over the bed, using his weight to pin her to the mattress, stop her thrashing around and making noise.

She made an outraged squeaking sound, twisting like an eel, and he could feel her begin to draw her knees up to her chest in a classic self-defense move, all ready to shove him away with her legs.

Fucking hell. Perhaps he should have bought the chloroform after all.

Sure enough, she shoved at him hard, and maybe if he'd been a smaller, weaker man, that would have worked. But Wolf had spent ten years in the Navy, eight of them as an elite SEAL, and no one had ever defeated him in hand to hand, let alone a small, bookish woman who happened to be his friend.

Gently, because he was a big guy and she was *very* small in comparison, he eased his weight over her, pinning her entirely so she couldn't move no matter how hard she tried. Then he lowered his head so his mouth was near her ear. "For fuck's sake, Liv," he hissed. "It's Wolf. Calm the hell down."

She struggled a second longer, then stilled. Her breathing against his palm was frantic and ragged, and he could smell a soft, sweet scent. Strawberries or something. Had she always smelled like that? He couldn't remember. The important thing, though, was that she wasn't struggling anymore. Perhaps she'd finally realized who he was.

"You going to be quiet now?" he whispered. "Nod if you are."

She gave a jerky nod.

"Good. Okay, here's the deal. I'm going to take my hand away and then I'll tell you why I'm here. But no screaming, understand?"

Another jerky nod.

Wolf raised his head and looked down at her. The light was dim, her features indistinct, but there was no mistaking the wide darkness of her eyes staring up at him. Yeah, she was still scared, wasn't she?

Slowly, he took his hand away from her mouth.

"Get off me, you asshole," Olivia de Santis gasped on a rushing breath. "You're crushing me to death."

Huh. Maybe she wasn't so scared after all.

He shifted, easing his weight off her, moving to sit on the side of the bed.

She scooted away from him until her back hit the headboard, her hands gripping the comforter and pulling it after her, holding it in front of her like a shield.

A long moment passed where she simply stared at him and he wasn't sure whether she was scared or shocked or pissed, or a combo of all three. Not that it mattered. He didn't have time for explanations, not until he'd gotten her to the safe house.

"What are you doing here, Wolf?" she asked at last, her voice slightly shaky. "I mean, how did you get in? The last I heard from you—"

"I can't explain now," he interrupted, glancing at the door. "We have to get out of here." Was that a footstep he heard? He knew the security de Santis had on the mansion inside out. He also knew that since his brother Van had rescued their adoptive sister Chloe from de Santis's clutches not two weeks earlier, de Santis had doubled said security. Which meant at least a couple of guards would be out in the house somewhere.

"What do you mean we have to get out of here?" Olivia glanced at the clock on the nightstand. "Oh my God. It's four in the morning. What on earth are you—"

"Now, Liv." He stood up, grabbed the comforter, and jerked it out of her grip. "Come on. We'll go out the window. Don't worry, all you have to do is put your arms around my neck and hang on."

She didn't move, staring at him with wide eyes, obviously in shock. She was wearing the most ridiculously prim nightie he'd ever seen—long and white, with a high neckline and lots of little buttons. Very Olivia and no doubt really fucking annoying when it came to climbing out of windows.

"Well?" He frowned at her. "What are you waiting for? Let's go."

"You're kidding right?" She drew her knees up to her chest and wrapped her arms around them. "I'm not going anywhere. Not until you tell me what the hell you're doing in my bedroom."

Shit, he *really* didn't have time for this. Should have brought the damn chloroform.

"I'll tell you, I promise. But we need to leave before someone discovers I'm here."

Her expression turned concerned all of a sudden. "Are you feeling okay? Something's not wrong is it?"

Jesus Christ. She thought he was sick.

Rapidly losing what little patience he had—and he never had much to start with—Wolf leaned down and circled his fingers around her upper arm, holding her firmly. Then he jerked his head toward the window. "Out. Now."

Olivia blinked.

Then she opened her mouth and screamed.

It was clear to Olivia that Wolf Tate had gone stark raving mad. Not only was he in her bedroom when the last email she'd had from him had mentioned being in Wyoming for his father's funeral, but he was also trying, for no good reason that she could see, to get her to escape out the window with him. That was after lying on top of her, all huge and muscular and frightening the living daylights out of her.

That wasn't the Wolf she knew. The Wolf she knew was a quiet, respectful, and genuinely nice guy, not to mention way more intelligent than he often thought he was. He was her friend. And friends didn't sneak in through windows trying to get her to come with them.

She probably shouldn't have screamed, but she was still muzzy with sleep, not to mention struggling with the shock of him being right there in her room, in the flesh, after ten years of nothing but email contact. And when he'd taken her arm in one huge hand, his long fingers holding her gently but firmly enough that she couldn't get away, screaming had been instinctive.

Except the scream ended up muffled, vibrating against his palm as the other huge hand clamped itself over her mouth instead.

His face was suddenly inches from hers, the color of his mismatched eyes muted in the dim light of the room. "Don't even think about it," he growled menacingly. "And if you bite me, I'll bite you back, understand?"

Olivia snapped her teeth together with a click, only just

missing his skin, fighting to remain calm as adrenaline pumped hard through her system. Fear and shock and anger tangled themselves together inside her, along with a familiar, wild thrill of excitement.

He's back, her stupid brain kept singing. *He's back. He's back. He's back!*

She glared at him, trying to get her feelings under control and pay attention to the situation at hand, trying not to simply stare at him, study the lines of his face to see how he'd changed, find the young man she once knew in the hardened Navy SEAL standing in front of her now.

He'd sent her a couple of photos of himself while he'd been on base and on deployment. One of him in uniform when he'd graduated as a SEAL and one of him standing in front of a tank with a massive gun cradled in both arms. She hadn't noticed the differences ten years in the Navy had made then, but boy did she see them now.

He'd always been tall—six five to her five five—not to mention broad, but somewhere along the way, he'd filled out too. And how. Massive shoulders, arms that could lift a small car, a heavily muscled chest that strained the black cotton of his top and the worn black leather of his jacket. But that wasn't all. Back when she'd known him, his features had been unformed, giving him a bland kind of handsomeness. But they weren't unformed now. The years had sharpened them, making his jaw hard and his nose a blade. Giving him high cheekbones and broad forehead. A man's face. Rough and battered, with lines at the corners of his eyes and around his quite frankly beautiful mouth. And to top it all off he had a short, dark Mohawk that made her want to run her hand through it, see if his hair was as soft as she suspected it was.

God. He was even more gorgeous now than he'd been at eighteen.

Stop staring at him, you idiot. He's got his hand over

*your mouth don't forget. Anyway, weren't you supposed
to not be in love with him?*

There was that. What had started out as a teenage crush
had gradually, over the years they'd corresponded, deepened into something more. Something that wouldn't ever
be returned—she knew that too. He'd never felt about her
the way she'd felt about him.

Not that it mattered right now. Not when he was standing there with his hand clamped over her mouth muttering something about not wanting to be discovered and how
they had to escape out the window.

There was an intent look in his eyes, and it suddenly
hit her that he was in fact serious. That he did indeed want
her to go with him. Right now.

Olivia opened her mouth to tell him he could take his
hand away and explain just what the hell was going on
when his gaze snapped to the door of her bedroom. He
gave a soft curse, then before she quite understood what
was happening, he removed his hand from her mouth and
slid one hugely muscled arm around her waist, picking her
up and slinging her over his shoulder like she weighed
nothing at all.

Too shocked to say anything, Olivia stared at the
ground, trying to figure out why her world had upended
itself and what exactly she was doing draped over one of
Wolf's massively powerful shoulders.

But she didn't have time to puzzle it out because he
clamped one arm around her legs, holding her still, and
then he was moving over to the window.

Her heart rate skyrocketed as she heard him pull aside
the curtain, and she twisted, trying to see what was going
on. "What the hell are you doing?" she demanded breath-
lessly. "Put me down!"

He didn't answer, but then the world tilted yet again and
there was cold air swirling up underneath her nightgown.

And when she looked down, she found herself staring into the darkness of the garden that lay at the base of her window. A garden that was a good three floors down.

Dizziness caught at her, a scream building in her throat.

Dear sweet baby Jesus. Wolf had actually climbed out of the window and now there was nothing between her and a three-story drop but empty air and him. She closed her hands reflexively onto the black leather of his jacket, the scream escaping as a hoarse cry. "Wolf!"

"Yeah, yeah, I know." He didn't even have the grace to sound concerned. He just sounded irritated. "Just don't struggle and you'll be fine."

There was a sickening drop, his shoulder abruptly pushing hard into her stomach, and she gasped, shutting her eyes so she didn't have to see the ground rushing up to kill her.

But there was no impact, only another couple of drops and then one hard bounce. And then it felt like he was walking, and fast. She opened her eyes again, and this time she saw the sidewalk reassuringly under his feet. It would have been a relief if she hadn't been held over his shoulder like a sack of flour.

With an effort, she got her tight jaw to work. "Y-You can put me down now."

"Nope." He was jogging, and she had to swallow hard as the dizziness hit her again, the movement bouncing her against his back. "Nearly there, though."

Olivia barely had time to wonder where that was before he'd come to a sudden stop and she heard the sound of a car lock beeping. Then she was pulled from his shoulder and bundled into the back of the car.

She sat there for a second, too stunned to move, her brain struggling to accept that she wasn't in her cozy bed anymore and that the man she'd been friends with for over ten years had apparently kidnapped her. Then, as the driver's door slammed shut, she pulled herself together and reached for the door handle.

Only to find herself sliding across the seat as Wolf pulled away from the curb in a screech of tires. She squeaked, scrabbling to hold onto one of seats in front of her as he made another hard turn, making her slide the other way.

His gaze met hers in the rearview mirror, a passing streetlight illuminating his different-color eyes, one green and one blue. "Put your fucking seat belt on."

Her heart was beating far too fast and for some reason she wasn't nearly as terrified as she should be. Or as furious with him.

Great. Just great. He's kidnapping you and all you can think about is how exciting this is and how wonderful it is that he's here.

Was she? Was she really that stupid?

That was up for debate, but not putting on her seat belt simply because he'd ordered her to, really *would* be stupid. Especially since he was driving like a maniac.

With shaking hands, Olivia grabbed the seat belt and clicked herself in, still holding onto the seat in front since even with the belt she kept sliding around. "Are you ever going to tell me what the hell you're doing?" she demanded, hoping she sounded strong but knowing she probably didn't.

"Yeah." He made another screeching turn, zigzagging through what little traffic there was with all the casual expertise of a race car driver. "But not until I get you somewhere safe."

A bubble of some sort of emotion caught in the back of her throat. Perhaps it was finally panic? If so, she was probably due.

"I was safe in my bedroom," she pointed out, clutching hard onto the cheap vinyl.

"You were. But I wasn't." Wolf kept looking in the rear-view mirror and not at her. Was he checking to see if they were being followed?

"Dad probably wouldn't have liked you being in my bedroom at four in the morning, no. But it's not like—"

"I promise I'll explain it all when we get there," he cut her off, scowling. "But could you just shut the fuck up for two seconds? I need to lose this tail."

Nice. She didn't remember him being this rude.

Olivia opened her mouth to tell him exactly what he could do with his damn tail, but then the car swerved and swerved again, then accelerated, and anything she'd been going to say went completely out of her head as death in a head-on collision loomed large in her future.

She bit down on yet another scream as a garbage truck pulled out directly in front of the car and she braced herself for impact. Except again, there wasn't one. Wolf simply put his foot down, swerved around the truck, dodged a motorcycle, made a hard left down an alley then another right, cutting across a main street and narrowly missing yet another truck, before ducking into yet another alley.

By that stage, Olivia had had enough.

She closed her eyes and laid her forehead against the seat in front of her, praying to whomever would listen to get her out of this in one piece. Oh yes, and maybe save Wolf too, though she wouldn't mind if he suffered an injury as payback for scaring her half to death.

She didn't know how much time passed, but finally the sickening lurches of the car stopped and she realized that in fact the car had stopped too.

There was a moment's silence broken only by the ticking of the engine. The driver's side door opened then slammed shut, the sound echoing weirdly, and another door opened, cold air rushing into the car and making her shiver.

"Liv?" Wolf's rough, gravelly voice, much harsher and deeper than she remembered. "We're here."

She swallowed and lifted her head, glancing out the windows of the car.

"Here" appeared to be an underground parking garage.

Wolf was standing at the open rear door of the car, staring at her, massive arms crossed over an equally massive chest. And despite having been kidnapped from her bedroom at four in the morning, not to mention barely surviving the car journey from hell, a small bubble of joy exploded in her chest.

Now that there was more light and she wasn't being hauled around over his shoulder, she could see he wore what looked like a black thermal with a black leather jacket thrown over the top, worn jeans, and heavy black boots. The fabric of his thermal clung lovingly to his broad chest, highlighting every superb muscle, while the denim of his jeans clung to his lean hips, pulling tight over powerful thighs.

She couldn't stop staring.

Ahem. He kidnapped you, don't forget.

Olivia took an unsteady breath and attempted to pull herself together. She really should be yelling at him, not staring like a lovestruck teenager. It was shock, definitely shock.

His straight dark brows lowered, mismatched gaze narrowing. "You okay?"

Swallowing, she tried to unclench her hands from the seat she'd been clinging to, a shiver sweeping through her. God, it was cold. Really, really cold.

"F-Fine," she said, deciding to ignore the tiny stutter. "If you could call being woken up at four in the morning, tossed over someone's shoulder, carried down the front of a building, then driven by a maniac into an underground parking garage 'fine.'"

"Yeah, I get it. I know this is a hell of a surprise, but I wasn't given much of a choice. Come on, get out of the car. You look like you're freezing your tits off."

Very carefully, Olivia did not look down at her chest, even though she was, literally, freezing her tits off. She didn't like not being in control, really, *really* didn't like it, and being kidnapped—no matter that her kidnapper was a friend—was the very definition of not being in control.

It was very important that she get some of it back.

"I'm not going anywhere," she said clearly. "At least not until you tell me what the hell is going on."

Wolf made an impatient sound, his boots scraping on the concrete as he shifted on his feet. "I'll tell you upstairs. It's too cold down here and you're only wearing . . ." He paused, his gaze dropping down to her nightgown. "What is that? A nun's outfit?"

"Habit," she corrected automatically. "A nun's outfit is called a habit."

"Outfit, habit, whatever. You're cold. So come on, let's go."

"And I'm not wearing a nun's habit. It's my nightgown."

"Liv. Seriously. I don't give a shit what it's called. You're shivering and you need to get warm."

She *was* shivering. But she also wasn't getting out of this car until he told her what the hell was going on. Sure, she might get hypothermia, but she had to draw the line in the sand somewhere. He wasn't going to have this all his own way. Had he been this pushy ten years ago? She couldn't remember.

"Well, I don't give a shit about shivering or being warm," she said, consciously mimicking his flat tone. "I'm not leaving the car until you tell me why I'm here."

He was silent a moment, glaring at her, letting her know in no uncertain terms that he was very unhappy with her little ultimatum. Then finally he said, "Okay, one last time. Are you going to get out of the car?"

Olivia folded her arms, more to stop herself from shivering than anything else. "Does it look like I'm going to get out of the car?"

"In that case you got three options. One, you stay here and spend the next few hours locked in the car. Two, you come upstairs with me willingly, where there's a bed, a bath, where you can warm up and also get a couple of hours' sleep. Three, I pick you up and throw you over my shoulder again and take you upstairs whether you fucking like it or not."

Okay, *now* she was starting to feel angry about the situation—and about damn time. She wasn't going to let him get away with shocking her like that, with absolutely no explanation whatsoever. Friends didn't do that, they just didn't.

She met his gaze and lifted her chin. "I believe I'll stay here, thank you very much."

CHAPTER TWO

Olivia was sitting in the back seat of the car, wearing nothing but that stupid white cotton nun thing, her arms folded and her determined chin set at an angle that told him she wasn't going to be moved come hell or high water.

He remembered that about her. She could be stubborn when she wanted to be. Very, very stubborn. Not that she ever made a big song and dance about it. She simply dug her heels in and refused to budge, like a fucking mule.

She kind of has reason, dickhead.

Well, sure. But hadn't he told her he'd explain? He just wanted to go where it was warm and comfortable, and more importantly, where they wouldn't be disturbed.

Shit, the longer they were out here in the parking garage, the more likely it was that they would draw attention. And after they'd been tailed fairly determinedly from the de Santis mansion, Wolf wasn't prepared to risk it.

The bolt-hole he'd brought Olivia to—a hotel—would only work if they hadn't been spotted going in, and the more time ticked by, the closer it was getting to regular working hours, which meant hotel employees would be around and the chances of running into them would be higher.

He had to move her and he had to move her now, not dick around with things like explanations. Mainly because he hadn't had a lot of time to think about what kind of explanation to give her.

Strategy had never been his thing—he left that to the smart guys—and tended to go off of instinct and what was happening in the here and now. He'd just hoped that a decent explanation would occur to him once he'd gotten Olivia safe, and that hadn't happened yet.

Which looked like he was going to have to settle for option three.

Gonna draw attention even more if she screams.

True, but that couldn't be helped. He'd simply have to encourage her not to scream.

Muttering a curse under his breath, he stepped up to the car, bent, and reached inside, grabbing her hips.

"Hey!" she protested, her hands flashing out and slapping hard against his chest. Her normally calm voice had gone all breathless, and the harsh light of the garage was washing all the color out of her skin, making her look even paler than normal. "I said I wanted to stay here."

"Yeah, well, I changed my mind. Option one is not an option any more." Firming his grip on her, he began to pull her out of the car.

"Wolf, stop it!" The hands on his chest pushed hard, and suddenly there was a knee pressing against a very important part of his anatomy.

He could easily have avoided that knee. Could have pulled her from the car as easily as an oyster from its shell. Could have trapped her hands, tossed her over his shoulder and carried her to the service elevator he was planning on using with absolutely no problem at all.

But he didn't. Because as he stared into her white face, it hit him like a bullet hitting Kevlar that this was Olivia. The girl he'd first met the day he'd been invited into the de Santis mansion, who'd become his friend, the first he'd ever had.

His father encouraged the friendship, telling him that getting as close to de Santis as possible included getting close to those he loved, including his daughter.

Wolf hadn't expected to like Olivia though. He'd thought she'd be a spoiled brat, a society princess with a massive trust fund to go along with her massive sense of entitlement. But she hadn't been that way at all.

She'd been wide-eyed and earnest. Interested in him, his thoughts and his opinions, in a way no one else ever had been. As if he had something worthwhile to say. She treated him as though he was smart, and since he'd always been told that wasn't where his strengths lay, he'd liked that. Probably far more than was good for him.

He'd liked her.

He also hadn't expected that she'd stay his friend throughout the years he'd been in the Navy, training hard to follow his brothers into the SEALs. Apparently not minding the sometimes months of silence when he was on deployment, providing him with some contact, with a re-minder of real life, when war had made it feel like the world had gone to hell.

Now though, the world hadn't gone to hell and it was just Olivia he was holding, and there were other things starting to impinge on his consciousness. Such as the warmth of her curvy little body soaking into his palms where he was gripping her hips, and the faint scent of strawberries. The very slight hint of pink through the sheer cotton of her ridiculous nightgown, right about where her nipples would be . . .

A shock went down his spine, and before he could second-guess what the fuck he was doing, he'd let her go and was backing away from her, his heart beating oddly fast.

Olivia's deep blue eyes widened, obviously as surprised as he was that he'd backed away. And for a second, he couldn't seem to look anywhere else but at the cotton of her nightgown, almost as if he was trying to see that hint of pink again. And maybe if he looked lower, he'd see—

Fuck. What was wrong with him? This was Olivia, the girl he'd befriended. Whom he'd never been attracted to, not even once.

You've been on deployment a long time.

That was true. Six months and then he'd had to take bereavement leave because of his father's death. He'd told his brothers he'd cut it short, that he'd gone back to base after all the director bullshit had gone down with Tate Oil. But he hadn't. He'd actually spent the last week or so holed up in New York, pretending to be de Santis's loyal soldier-boy, the way his father had insisted all those years ago.

But there had been no time for women. Not even a night. Christ, six months of celibacy was a long time. It had to be that making him react to her. It wasn't because he was suddenly attracted to Olivia, no fucking way.

Pissed with himself and rapidly losing patience with this entire damn situation, Wolf scowled. "Get the fuck out of the car, Liv. And FYI, you don't want to mess with me, not right now."

She blinked, and a moment passed when he thought she wasn't going to get out and he realized he didn't know what he would do then. But at last she let out a breath and pushed herself out of the car, smoothing down that stupid night-gown and pushing her long, straight brown hair behind her ears. "Okay," she said, all calm now. "Let's go."

Without thinking, he reached out and grabbed her arm, reluctant to let her follow him in case she decided to make a break for it. And again that weird shock shot down his spine. But this time he gritted his teeth against it and held on, turning toward the door that led to the service elevator.

She stiffened as his fingers closed around her, which pissed him off for no good reason.

She has every right to be pissed off, given the way you've been hauling her around.

Yeah, and he didn't need his fucking conscience showing itself right now. Not when he had very important shit to do.

Olivia came with him obediently enough, and luckily the service elevator was already at their floor so they were able to get in the moment he hit the button.

"Can I ask where we are?" Olivia said as the doors slid shut.

He went to the pad near the door and quickly typed in the code he'd been given. It would take them to the right floor without stopping. "A hotel. The James."

He could have taken her to his other little bolt-hole, but he didn't want *anyone* to know about that, which left him having to find somewhere else to take her. He didn't own property in New York, unlike his brothers, and he'd been debating the merits of simply taking her to some low-rent motel in Brooklyn. The security of places like that was always a worry, though, so it wasn't ideal. But luckily one of his SEAL buddies—a guy he trusted implicitly—came from a rich family of hotel owners and had offered him a room in his family's hotel off the books. Of course Jase thought Wolf was bringing in a girl on the sly to have a sneaky couple of days with, he didn't actually know it was because Wolf had kidnapped the daughter of Cesare de Santis and was now preparing to interrogate her. Jase might have given him a different answer if he'd known that.

"The James," Olivia echoed. "Okay."

Wolf stepped back from the number pad as the elevator jerked and began to rise, running his gaze over her again. She was standing near the back of the elevator car, her arms crossed, looking very calm. But he didn't miss the fact that she was shivering slightly.

Shit. Of course she'd be cold. She wasn't wearing any-thing but that damn nightie thing, not even any shoes. He glanced down at her naked feet, frowning. The elevator was pretty much bare metal, which must feel icy against her skin.

His training had inured him to physical discomfort, so he shrugged out of his jacket without a second's hesitation and put it around her shoulders. It was huge on her, the hem reaching mid thigh, but at least it would be warm.

"Thank you," she said, and given that she didn't pro-test, she must have been really fucking cold. "You're a very thoughtful kidnapper."

He leaned back against the wall of the elevator beside her. "And you're taking all of this very well. Apart from the thing in the car."

She lifted a shoulder. "What's the point in making a fuss? I'm hardly likely to go running off now, am I? Not when I'm only in my nightgown. And besides"—she leaned back against the elevator too, mirroring his stance—"it's you. I mean, I don't know why you're kidnapping me, but you're hardly likely to be sending my finger back in a matchbox to my father in return for ransom money."

It shouldn't have annoyed him that she was treating all of this so matter-of-factly. Yet for some reason he *was* an-noyed. Christ's sake. He was a motherfucking Navy SEAL, who'd kidnapped her from her bed in the middle of the goddamn night. Shouldn't she at least have the decency to be a little terrified of him? Yeah, they were friends, so it wasn't like he was a complete stranger to her.

But still. She didn't *really* know him. In fact, given all the secrets he was keeping, both from his own family and from her, he might as well be a stranger to her.

A tight feeling clenched in his chest at the thought. Al-most as if he'd regretted all the lies he'd told her. Stupid to feel that, though. His father had warned him of the dangers of letting himself get attached, and so he'd tried very hard not to. It had been difficult, though. Especially when she'd been genuine.

Dammit. He shouldn't be thinking about this. He didn't have time.

"How do you know I don't want your finger?" he said instead. "I might have the matchbox all ready to go."

Olivia shot him a glance that told him she was in no way frightened by anything he might say to her. "Sure you do."

She wasn't taking this at all seriously, was she? Which was great when it came to making sure she was secure, but not so great when it came to interrogating her on de Santis's schedule. She'd want to know why he was asking her, and if he told her the truth, there was no way she'd give it up without a fight, friend or not.

Cesare de Santis might be a criminal, but Olivia loved him. She wouldn't want to see him die. And that was going to make getting the information he wanted out of her somewhat problematic.

That thought did nothing for his temper.

He scowled. "Don't get comfortable, Liv. You're here for a reason."

"Obviously I'm here for a reason. Otherwise I wouldn't be here at all, right? And I presume it wasn't simply because you were in the neighborhood and thought you'd come and say hi."

There was amusement in her voice that worked its way under his skin, needling him. She used to tease him in a gentle way all those years ago—to make him smile, she'd said—and he'd found it cute. Mainly because people were afraid of him, intimidated by his size and his manner, and their first reaction was to get out of his way. Not Olivia. That she had the gumption to tease him at all, had been . . . refreshing.

He did not find it refreshing now.

"No," he said flatly. "It wasn't because I was in the neighborhood. And you should be a whole more fucking concerned about that than you are right now."

One corner of her rosebud mouth turned up in a smile. "Okay I hear you. I'm shaking in my boots."

Jesus Christ. Was the woman actually humoring him? Just what the hell did she think was happening here?

"By the way," she went on, clearly having no idea how deep the shit she was in went. "I appreciate all the effort you've put in to bringing me here, believe me. But if you'd wanted to ask me something, you could have just put it in an email." That smile of hers seemed like it was begging him to join in on the joke. "No need to kidnap me in the dead of night and stuff."

A long moment passed where Wolf wondered what the fuck he was supposed to say to that, because anything he *did* say at this point was going to change things between them quite profoundly. And he was pretty sure that once he started asking her questions about her father, she wasn't going to find this half as amusing as she apparently did now.

He stared down at her, unsmiling, letting her know that this was as far from a joke as it was possible to get. "Just what the fuck do you think is happening here, Liv?"

Her gaze flickered at his tone and she pulled nervously at his jacket. "You wanted to speak to me? I don't know why you went to all that fuss in order to do it, but I guess you have your reasons."

"And you're not curious about them at all?"

Her dark, winged brows lowered. "Of course I am. But you told me you were going to explain. So that's what we're doing now, yes? We're at this hotel and then you're going to explain why I'm here, and then you're going to drop me back home."

If only it was that simple. But if it was that simple, she

wouldn't be here. She'd be still tucked up in bed, blissfully sleeping.

"Yeah," he said, because that's all he could say. "Sure. That's exactly what I'm going to do."

The elevator stopped with a jerk, the doors sliding open.

Wolf put out a hand to hold her there then stuck his head out to check the hallway. It was clear.

He jerked his head toward the doors. "Out."

There was a crease between her eyebrows, but she didn't hesitate, stepping out of the elevator and into the hallway.

The place was a typical five-star hotel, with thick dark carpeting and white walls, all noise swallowed by the dense hush of luxurious furnishings and expensive sound-proofing.

"Follow me," he ordered, moving down the hall, taking a look at the numbers on the doors. Olivia walked silently beside him as he went right down to the end before finally finding the right room number.

The door was held open by a small stack of towels, just like Jase had promised him, so all he had to do was walk right in.

He gestured for Olivia to go in first and it wasn't until the door had shut behind them with a heavy thump that he let out a breath he hadn't realized he'd been holding.

Okay, phase one of his plan had been completed, thank Christ. She was here. And since he'd lost that tail, he was pretty sure no one had discovered where they'd gone, which meant she was secure. Now it was time for phase two.

He followed Olivia down the short hallway and out into the room proper, which appeared to be a massive corner suite, with huge windows that looked out over Central Park. The living area was all clean white walls and a thickly carpeted floor in dark charcoal. There was a sectional sofa near the windows with a low glass-topped coffee table nearby stacked high with magazines. The decor and furniture looked expensive and luxurious, the colors in muted silvers and grays and whites, presumably to call attention to the view of the park directly in front of it.

Then he noticed that there was an ice bucket beside the sofa with champagne chilling in it, and on the coffee table were a couple of champagne flutes, plus a basket of what looked like special food. Candles had been lit—scented, by the smell of vanilla lingering in the air.

Wolf had never been a romantic kind of guy, so points to Jase for trying to set the mood. Unfortunately romance was *not* what Wolf was here for.

"Wow," Olivia murmured as she went over to the coffee table, glancing down at the gift basket and the champagne in the ice bucket. "I . . ." She stopped then turned to glance at him. There was something glowing in her deep blue eyes, something . . .

Oh shit. Did she think that all of this was for her?

"It's not what it looks like," he said shortly, before she got the wrong idea. "This isn't a date or anything."

An expression crossed her face, though it had gone before he could figure out what it was, and she turned away. "No, of course not. I didn't think it was."

Fucking hell. That's exactly what she'd thought, wasn't it? Which meant . . . Yeah, he didn't want to think about what it meant, especially not when getting romantic with Olivia de Santis figured exactly nowhere in any of his plans.

Mentally cursing Jase, Wolf moved over to the minibar. There was a counter with one of those fancy-ass capsule coffee-making machines on top, and if there was one thing he really needed at four—no five—in the morning it was a coffee. Strong and black and sweeter than hell.

"You need any caffeine?" He pulled out a mug from the shelf above the machine and put it down on the counter.

"No, thank you."

She sounded more subdued than before, so he turned to check that she was okay. She'd sat down on the sectional sofa, perching right on the edge of the seat, her hands clasped around her knees, fingers interlaced. It was still dark outside and the recessed lights of the hotel room were soft, but even so, he could see the shadows beneath her eyes. She was looking tired now.

Perhaps he should leave interrogating her until after she'd had a couple more hours of sleep.

"You want to go to bed? Get some more shut-eye?" He nodded toward the bedroom. "We can talk later if you like."

She shook her head. "I need to get back home by . . ." Reflexively she looked down at her wrist as if there was a watch there then pulled a face and glanced around the room. "What's the time?"

"It's five o'clock." He turned back to finish making his coffee, putting one on for her anyway since she was going to need it. Especially when he told her that she wasn't going home. That she'd be staying here until he'd iced her dad.

"Oh, in that case I'll need to be home probably by seven." She sighed. "God, do you think anyone saw you carrying me down the front of the building? I'd hate to worry Dad."

"No one got a good look." There had been that tail after he'd put her in the car, but maybe that had been his paranoia talking and he'd imagined it? Whatever, definitely no one had seen them enter the parking garage, that was for sure.

When the coffee was ready, he dumped some creamer into Olivia's cup then went into the minibar and got a small bottle of Hennessy. Dividing the brandy between the two cups, he then picked them both up and turned, coming over to where she sat and putting the cups on the coffee table.

The crease between her brows deepened. "Thanks, but I said I didn't want one."

He reached out and grabbed one of the armchairs, dragging it over to the coffee table and sitting down. "You may not want it, but you're going to need it."

"That sounds ominous."

Okay, now it was time to get serious.

Wolf met her gaze. Held it. "Liv, you're here because I need some information. And I'm afraid I'm not letting you leave until I have it."

Olivia was conscious that her heartbeat had suddenly picked up speed. Odd, because he hadn't said anything particularly scary. Apart from the not-letting-her-leave part, but he surely couldn't be serious about that? He could be quite a funny guy when he wanted to be, and she loved his quiet sense of humor, so maybe it was some kind of elaborate joke?

Then again, even if he wasn't kidding, didn't he know that if he needed help with anything, she'd give it? There was no need for all of this . . . kidnapping stuff.

She kept her fingers interlaced around her knees, numb fingertips and toes beginning to warm up. She was very conscious of his jacket around her shoulders, the heavy weight comforting. It smelled of something smoky and dark, a cedarlike scent, along with the scent of leather, and she liked it very much. It smelled like him. Like Wolf.

He was across from her, his massive body sitting slightly forward, his elbows on his knees, his fingers clasped between them, the expression in his gorgeous eyes curiously intent.

She gave a little laugh then wished she hadn't since it

sounded nervous in the heavy silence. "You're not going to let me leave? Okay then. Guess I'd better tell you what you want to hear."

He didn't smile. "Drink your coffee. You're not going to like what I have to say."

For the first time since he'd pulled her out of her warm, cozy bed, a small, cold thread of doubt wound through her. She hadn't had time to be worried about what he was going to do with her, and then when she had, in the car, she'd actually felt calm. Because this was Wolf, her friend. Whom she'd been emailing for ten years, and whom she knew wouldn't hurt her.

Wolf, whom she was in love with and had been ever since she was sixteen. All this had to be a joke.

Except he wasn't smiling now, and he wasn't laughing. His roughly handsome face was utterly serious, that long, generous mouth set in a hard line. His jaw, darkened with five-o'clock shadow was tight, and there was a glitter in his eyes that made that thread of doubt tighten.

And it came to her suddenly that ten years of emailing didn't mean you actually knew someone.

Needing caffeine stat, Olivia reached for her coffee. He'd put cream in it, which was annoying, and when she took a sip, she nearly choked.

"Oh my God, what have you spiked this with?" she demanded, eyes watering.

"Brandy." He reached for his own cup and took a sip, sadly without choking.

"Why?"

"Like I said. You're going to need it."

Again, there was no smile, pulling that thread of doubt even tighter.

She took another sip of her coffee and didn't choke this time, conscious of the fiery burn of the alcohol as it slid down her throat. Conscious also that she was alone in a

hotel room with Wolf Tate, and that no one else knew she
was there.

*And he's not going to let you go until you give him the
information he wants. Not forgetting that.*

No need to panic though, and she was very good at not
panicking. Her father was always telling her how much he
valued her cool head, so there was no reason to lose it now.

"Yes. You keep saying that. I suppose you'd better tell
me why."

Wolf took another swallow of his coffee, the cup tiny
in his huge hand. "You have access to your father's schedule, right?"

"I manage his diary, yes."

"And his email?"

She frowned. Why would Wolf want to know that? "I
have access, yes. Why?"

"Because I need information. Your father has a lot of
fingers in a lot of pies, but there's one in particular I'm interested in. He's got a contact in the Defense Department
who's been looking the other way while your father oper-
ates a nice little gun-running business through the military. I want evidence of their relationship."

That didn't make any sense to Olivia. Why would Wolf
want that? Wasn't Wolf supposed to be working *for* her
father? At least he had been for over the last ten years.

Still, that was beside the point anyway. Her father didn't
have any secret government contracts, so what on earth
was he talking about?

"I don't know what you mean." She put her cup down
on the coffee table. "Dad doesn't run guns. He never did.
And he certainly doesn't have Defense Department contacts these days. He stepped down as CEO of DS Corp a
year ago. He's retired now, as well you know."

The truth was that her father hadn't really retired, he'd
been forced out by his four sons, something she still hadn't

forgiven her brothers for. Not that they cared. Not about their father and not about her, either.

But she was okay with that. They apparently didn't know what family loyalty meant, but she did. Her father might be estranged from his sons, but he had her at least.

Wolf drained his cup and put it down with a click. "What I know is that he's been dabbling in foreign weapons sales. And not just plain old stock standard rocket launchers and shit like that, but experimental weaponry. He's been using the military to find buyers, and like I said, he's also been paying certain government officials to look the other way while he does it."

Olivia almost smiled. That was . . . crazy. In the past her father hadn't exactly been squeaky clean, but that had been years ago. He was retired now, spending his days seeing old friends and doing the odd charity function, going out to the golf course and generally enjoying life. He had a few business interests on the side that she helped him take care of, but nothing at all like what Wolf had just described.

"Where did you hear this?" She made no effort to hide her surprise. "Because wherever you did, it's not true. I mean, you've been working for him for ten years, Wolf. You should know better than that."

He should. Wolf had come into the de Santis fold at seventeen, after her father had offered him support and asylum from Noah Tate's violent rages. She still remembered the first time she'd seen him, a glimpse through the doorway of the library as he'd been shown into her father's office.

His presence in the de Santis household had been a secret, since everyone hated the Tates and her father hadn't wanted it known that he'd extended an olive branch to Noah Tate's youngest adoptive son. But no one had known she'd been in the library—no one tended to notice her anyway—and so she'd seen him. An impossibly tall, impossibly broad young man already at seventeen, with a black eye and a swollen jaw.

Excitement was rare in her sheltered life, and fascinated both by the rare glimpse of her family's most entrenched enemy and by the bruises on his face, Olivia had taken to hanging out in the library just in case she saw him again. And sure enough, the following week at the same time, she had.

Then the week after that, Wolf had been shown into the library to wait since her father had an earlier appointment, and she'd hidden behind the door so no one would know she was there. And once the door had closed, there she'd been, alone in the library with one of the evil Tates. It had been frightening, yet thrilling at the same time. Certainly the most exciting thing to have happened to her in all her young life.

He'd been studying the bookshelves, but the moment the door closed he'd noticed her, his gaze coming to hers almost instantly. She'd felt it then, like a lightning bolt hitting the center of her chest, a sizzle of electricity, a connection. It had knocked the breath completely out of her and it was only afterward that she'd taken in that not only was he gorgeous, but he had the most amazing eyes she'd ever seen, one a deep dark blue, the other an intense leaf green.

He'd been surprised to see her, obviously not expecting anyone to be in the room, and had been even more surprised when she'd introduced herself. She'd babbled something about the book she was reading—a collection of Greek myths that she loved—not expecting him to know what the hell she was talking about or even be interested. But he *had* known. He'd asked her what her favorite myth was, so she told him it was Hades and Persephone. And then he revealed that his favorite was Theseus and the Minotaur. And then they'd had a long discussion about all the different myths, and it had been amazing—and probably the longest conversation she'd had with anyone ever about stuff that she liked.

She'd seen him regularly after that, hanging out in the library whenever it was his time to see her father. He'd never talked much about his family to her, only a few mentions here and there of his brothers. Definitely not about his father. But she already knew about that thief Noah Tate and what he'd stolen from the de Santis family. And that Wolf had come to Cesare for help in taking Noah down.

So yes, ten years, and Wolf was asking her these . . . strange questions? It didn't make any sense.

Wolf's gaze held an expression she couldn't decipher. He said nothing, leaning back in his chair in a long, lazy sprawl. He ran an impatient hand through his short Mohawk, making her own palm itch to touch it, gazing at her with that impenetrable look on his face.

"So I guess, if you have access to his diary, you're still your dad's personal assistant, right?" he asked eventually. "I mean, that's what you told me in your emails."

Huh. Another strange question. She'd told him that a long time ago.

"Yes. Like I said, I arrange his diary, help him out with his business interests, that kind of thing."

"Right, right." He tilted his head, staring at her, making her feel like a bug under a microscope. "What do you know about Daniel May?"

An uncomfortable feeling twisted inside her. Daniel was a business contact of her father's, one whom her father had encouraged her to be friendly to. She'd even gone out on a date with him, after Cesare had encouraged it. Not that it had been very successful. Daniel seemed to be a nice enough man, if quite a bit older than she was, but he'd spent the majority of the date answering phone calls, which was a bit off-putting.

But what did that have to do with Wolf?

Maybe he's jealous?

Olivia looked down at her hands, her heart rate speeding up. What a stupid thought. Of course he wasn't jealous. After the embarrassing slip she'd made when she'd seen the candles and the ice bucket, his very definitive reaction had certainly put to rest to any fantasies she might have been entertaining that he felt something for her.

"Daniel's just a friend of Dad's," she said, the uncomfortable feeling digging deeper. "I don't know why you're asking me these questions."

Needing to move, she got up from the sofa, grabbing the empty coffee cups and taking them over to the coffee station. "Sorry I can't help you, Wolf. I'd really love to sit down with you and have a chat, but it's probably time for me to get back."

There was no answer.

She turned around.

He was sitting in the armchair, long legs stretched out in front of him, one hand still scrubbing through his hair in an absent movement. The long sleeve of his thermal had pulled up, revealing a flash of color on the tanned skin of his wrist. She blinked. Was that a tattoo?

Before she could get a good look at it, however, he dropped his hand then pushed himself out of the armchair. He didn't speak, moving down the short corridor that led to the door of the room.

She followed along behind him, expecting him to open the door for her. But he didn't. Instead he stopped in front of the door and took his phone out of his pocket, then waved the room card in front of it, before swiping it through the card reader. The phone beeped and he typed something into the screen.

Nothing momentous happened, though she had no idea what she was expecting.

He turned around.

She was standing in the middle of the hallway, and it was quite narrow and he was very, very tall. And very, very broad.

He took a couple of steps toward her, his gaze holding hers, towering over her. Making her feel small and fragile. It was exciting and she didn't know quite why, her heart beating very hard inside her chest.

The heat coming from his heavily muscled body was making her mouth go dry, and the dark, spicy scent of cedar was heavy in the air around her. And all she could think about was how much she wanted to put out her hands and lay them against the hard wall of his chest.

She'd never touched a man like that before. Never wanted to. Her heart had always and would always belong to him, that would never change. It didn't matter that he'd never given any sign that he felt the same way about her. It made no difference at all to her poor heart. It beat for him and him alone.

Olivia stared up into the deep blue and green of his eyes, suddenly overcome by his nearness.

"You might wanna get out of the way," he said, all rough gravel and sand. "I need to take a shower."

Heat rushed into her cheeks. Had he caught her staring? Great, second time this morning she'd made an ass out of herself in front of him.

She swallowed, smoothing her nightgown reflexively to cover her embarrassment, then stood aside. "Then you'll take me home?"

"Yeah, sure." He went past her, disappearing through the double doors that led to the bedroom.

Once she heard the bathroom door close, she leaned back against the wall and took a couple of deep breaths, trying to get her racing heartbeat under control.

This whole morning had been one weird thing after

another, and her getting all weak at the knees and being
ridiculously female in his presence was the icing on a really
strange cake.

She wasn't usually this . . . flappable. In fact, she didn't
let much get to her at all, because her father preferred it
when she was calm. Maybe it was only that she was tired.
She had been woken up at four in the morning after all.

It's not tiredness. It's Wolf.

Olivia sighed. Okay, of course it was Wolf. It was Wolf
and the ridiculous torch she'd been carrying for him for
years. And seeing him again for the first time in years. In
which case, him dropping her home as quickly as possible was probably the best idea, before she could make an
even bigger idiot of herself than she had already.

Pushing herself away from the wall, she glanced at the
door.

There was no need to leave now, not when he said he
was going to take her home, but she found herself moving
toward the door anyway. Reaching out to test the door
handle.

It was locked.

CHAPTER THREE

Wolf shrugged out of his clothing and stepped into the white marble shower, sighing as the hot water streamed over him. He shut his eyes and turned his face into the flow, trying to get his mind to calm the hell down, because it was too full. Too full of everything.

He couldn't work out whether Olivia genuinely didn't know anything or whether she was playing him. Given that she'd always seemed pretty open and honest in her emails, it was difficult to believe that she was playing him. Then again, it was also difficult to believe she didn't know anything.

She was a smart woman. If she was her father's PA, she was bound to handle more than his diary and his supposed "business interests." And she certainly had to know that her father was sketchy as fuck. She couldn't be totally oblivious to his true nature, surely? Maybe once, when she'd been sixteen. But not now.

The other option was that she was protecting the ass-hole. That somehow she'd sensed that his reasons for wanting the information weren't good ones and she was trying to make out like she knew nothing.

Ah fuck, this was turning into a piece of shit. He'd thought keeping her here would be easy, that he'd feel fine about it, but as it turned out, he didn't like it.

Then again, his feelings about the situation were irrel-
evant. He wasn't going to be able to get to his mother until
de Santis and his other sketchy cronies had been taken care
of, and quite frankly nothing else mattered but that.

Not Olivia and certainly not his own pussy-ass scruples.

His father had taught him that the weaker feelings were
vulnerabilities and that in order to be strong enough to
complete his mission, he had to strip them all away.

*"You're a sword, Wolf. You're my sword. And there
cannot be any imperfections in your blade, understand?
I don't want you to shatter at the first blow."*

Yeah, and he wasn't going to shatter. He would be flaw-
less. He would do his father proud.

Unfortunately though, it looked like getting the information he wanted from Olivia, without telling her the
truth, was going to be difficult. And that left him with only
two options. He threatened her, or he tried some other way
of getting it out of her.

Christ, he didn't want to threaten her. He'd never been
the kind of man who hurt women, but threatening them
wasn't much better. And she was supposed to be his goddamn friend.

*You fucking tool. Remember. The only easy day was
yesterday.*

He scrubbed his hands over his face. This would have
been easier if he'd done what his father had told him and
not gotten attached to her. But then he'd always felt a little
protective toward her. Ever since the day he'd first seen her
in the library of her father's house, small and wide-eyed.
She had a book clutched to her chest and she'd stared at
him as if she'd never seen anything like him in all her life.
He'd thought she'd be afraid of him, since people tended
to be.

So when this little girl started babbling on about the
book she was reading, totally not caring that her family's

THE UNDERCOVER BILLIONAIRE 41

enemy was standing in the same room. Talking to him and asking him what he thought as if his opinion was worth listening to, he hadn't been able to help responding.

Not many people knew it, but he liked reading, and myths were his favorite—and he didn't get to talk about books with anyone at the Tate ranch.

Things had snowballed from there. Every time he'd had a meeting with de Santis, Olivia would be in the library, so he'd often turn up early to talk with her. He liked that she didn't seem to care who he was, and was quite happy to talk about whatever she was reading at the time. She was happy to talk about anything else too, especially anything that interested him.

Early on, he'd decided not to talk about his own family with her, because he had too much to hide and Olivia was way too perceptive. So he'd asked her questions about hers instead, intrigued despite himself. It was clear the de Santis family were pretty fucked up, but he liked hearing about them all the same, because a part of him envied her them.

Plus, listening to her was way easier than having to lie all the time about how Noah Tate was a violent asshole who beat his children and that Wolf had come to de Santis—Noah's enemy—for help because he didn't know who else to turn to.

De Santis had lapped it up, and even though Wolf tried not to talk to Olivia much about it, it was clear she did too.

When Noah had heard that Wolf had met Olivia, he'd told him to keep cultivating that relationship—in case it turned out to be useful. So cultivate it he had. But even so, he'd never been able to shake the feeling that lying to her was wrong. Strange that it had never bothered him with anyone else, only her.

Wolf turned off the shower and wiped a hand across his face to get the water out of his eyes. He was reaching for a towel when there was a soft, timid knock.

"Yeah?" He stepped out of the shower, giving himself a quick dry with the towel.

"Um, it's Olivia," she said unnecessarily from the other side of the door. "I thought you should know that the hallway door is locked somehow. I can't open it."

He'd wondered how long that would take her to discover. He'd hacked the swipe card and lock with relative ease, making it so he could lock the door from the inside and unlock it only with a special code.

"Gimme a minute," he said. "I'll check it when I get out."

"Okay. I'll wait out here."

He slung the towel around his waist, extracted the burner phone from the pocket of his jeans, then backed over to the bathtub and sat down on the edge of it. He stared down at the screen, his mind turning over and over.

There were too many things to think about, too many threads he had to tie up. He didn't know what his two older brothers were up to, and after what had happened with Lucas a couple of days ago, they were going to be really, really pissed that he'd seemingly disappeared.

He didn't want to have to talk to them about anything, not given all he was hiding, but he had to make sure things were okay. He wasn't as close to them as he'd once been—he couldn't, and still be the weapon his father wanted him to be—but they were still his brothers.

Two days earlier, he'd shot an arms dealer who had been going to kill the chick Lucas had been protecting, the widow of one of Lucas's SEAL team buddies. It was a mission de Santis had given him, because de Santis hadn't wanted anyone left alive to incriminate him with his sketchy arms deals. Wolf hadn't had a problem with it—especially given the fact the asshole had been holding a gun to Grace's head—and de Santis had told him he'd handle the fallout, but Wolf wouldn't mind knowing whether Grace had recovered and how his brother was.

Gritting his teeth, Wolf forced himself to key in Van's number. Talking to his oldest brother was easier than talking to ice-cold Lucas, even though, as a SEAL commander, Van tended to be a bossy prick.

He answered on the second ring, his deep voice full of suspicion. "Who the hell is this?"

Of course. Burner phone. Van wouldn't be able to recognize Wolf's number.

"It's me," Wolf said.

"Wolf? Where the fuck have you been?" Van sounded pissed. "I've been trying to call you for the past two goddamn days."

"Yeah, yeah. I know. I should have gotten in touch sooner."

"Damn right you should've," Van growled. "You using a burner?"

"Yeah. Is your phone secure?"

"Should be. What's going on? You still pissed at me about Chloe?"

Wolf let out a silent breath. His oldest brother had gotten together with their adoptive sister, which had shocked the hell out of everyone, and Wolf still didn't really know if he was okay with it. Though quite frankly Van's relationship with Chloe was the least of Wolf's problems right now. Not that he wanted to get into the rest of it. There was too much to say, too many secrets to reveal, too many lies to unmask, and he couldn't face it. Not over the phone at least.

"I want to know whether Lucas and Grace are okay," he said shortly.

"They are. And the press have been framing it as a random hit. Drugs. No one has been able to identify you. But shit, Wolf. What the fuck is going on? Lucas told me there's no way you could have known what was going to go down with Grace, which begs the question as to why you were there in the first place."

Wolf scowled at the white marble wall opposite. "I can't tell you."

"What? What do you mean—"

"I just fucking can't. End of story."

There was a silence down the other end of the phone.

"Need help?" Van asked at last.

Wolf's jaw tightened. Van was a commander through and through—no man left behind and all that crap. And if one of his brothers needed help, then he was the first to offer it. "No," he said, because getting Van involved was the last thing he needed. "I'm dealing with it."

Van snorted. "Yeah, of course you are. Look, whatever's happening with you right now, you're still a director at Tate Oil, and since Chloe and I are in Wyoming right now, I need you to handle the shit that's going down. Lucas is—"

"I can't," he interrupted, knowing this was going to sound like a bunch of pussy bullshit, but dealing with Tate Oil was not high on his list of priorities right now. He'd never wanted to be a director in the first place and pretty much all he cared about was getting rid of de Santis, finding his mother, and claiming Noah as his father.

That might upset things in terms of Van's inheritance since his adoptive brother, as the official Tate heir, had inherited the whole of Noah's fortune. But Wolf wasn't looking to unseat Van as the true heir. He didn't give a shit. He only wanted what little of his family remained.

"What do you mean you can't?" Van demanded. "You agreed to be a director. That means you signed up to—"

"Text me the details and I'll see what I can do," he interrupted yet again because, short of hanging up, he couldn't see any other way out of this conversation.

Another silence.

"Fine," Van said, even though Wolf was clear that it wasn't fine. "But deal with your shit or man up and get some help, because either way, I'm going need you on board with Tate Oil. There are things you need to know about de Santis."

Wolf gritted his teeth. He knew already what things Van was talking about. Not that he wanted to reveal what he knew right now, not when he was pretty sure Van's response would be a military interrogation that would put their SEAL training to shame. "Yeah, yeah," he said, trying to sound like his old give-no-fucks self. "Whatever you say."

His brother exhaled on a long breath. "Wolf, I know it was hard on you when Dad died, but—"

Oh, *hell* no. He wasn't having *that* conversation. "Sorry bro, shit's going down. Gotta run." And before his brother could respond, Wolf disconnected.

Okay, one shitstorm handled. Now on to the one currently standing outside the bathroom door.

Right on cue, there came another knock. "Wolf? I really need to get going soon. I don't want Dad getting worried about where I am."

Tossing the phone back on the vanity, Wolf stood up and ditched the towel, pulling on his underwear and jeans. Then he picked up his thermal in one hand while opening the door with the other.

Olivia was standing right outside and as the door opened she gave him a tentative smile. Then it faded, her eyes widening as they dropped down the length of his body. She blinked and looked away fast, obvious color rising into her cheeks.

Well, shit. He knew enough about women to know what that meant.

An odd feeling shifted in his gut, and it wasn't the annoyance with the situation that he should have been feeling. It was almost as if he liked her reaction, which was weird because Olivia was his friend. He didn't actually want her.

You could use that, though.

The thought streaked brightly through his head before he could stop it, and his immediate instinct was to dismiss it because he'd already spun her way too many lies to count, and pretending he was into her was just wrong. But the thought stuck in his brain like a thorn.

Olivia was blushing furiously and smoothing her hair, her attention on the wall behind him. In that cotton night-gown, her dark hair down her back, her cheeks red, she looked ridiculously young and fresh-faced. Like a school-teacher or a governess or something.

He studied her a moment, the beginnings of a plan forming in his head.

She had access to information he needed and if he wasn't going to threaten her, he had to figure out another way to get it. If she wanted him, that would certainly give him a lever he could pull. It would mean lying to her, pretending he was into her, but he was running out of options. He needed that intel.

Anyway, it's not like your friendship with her is real anyway. You were doing it for Dad, remember.

More feelings shifted around in his chest, uncomfortable feelings. Almost like denial. It made him want to growl. Sure, he liked her and didn't want to hurt her, but he had a mission objective and nothing could get in the way. He had no room for soft emotions like regret and denial.

Anyway, fuck, he was a double agent and lying was what double agents did. So using her reaction to him in order to get more information out of her wasn't doing anything worse than he'd done already, right?

Something whispered in his head that it *was* worse, but since he couldn't afford to listen to that voice, he didn't.

Being a SEAL meant ignoring a whole lot of uncomfortable shit anyway, both mental and physical. And he hadn't survived the training because he was a pussy who let things get to him. Hell no, he'd survived because he had what it took. The right stuff, endurance, mental fortitude or whatever crap you wanted to call it. He had a mission, and for him and for his father, the ends justified any means.

She gave him a quick glance, as if afraid to look at him too long. "Those are some tattoos," she said, her voice breathless. "When did you get those?"

So she liked the tattoos. But then women often did and he was shameless enough that he enjoyed the attention. Especially when they offered to lick them.

He glanced down at the ink on his chest and arms. "Over the years. Got some on deployment, some back at base." He met her gaze purposefully and held it. "You like 'em?"

She blushed even harder and looked away, pushing a strand of hair behind her ear, not that it was loose, and cleared her throat. "They're very nice."

Hmmm. Interesting. She more than liked them, that was clear. Good. He could use that if he was going to go ahead with the plan that was already pretty much a done deal in his head.

A honey trap. With him being the honey.

"Anyway," she went on, awkwardly clasping her hands across her stomach. "The door to the hallway is locked and I can't seem to open it. And I really need to get back home. So if we're done here . . . ?"

Right, so how to play this. Telling her the truth about his mission was impossible, which left him with having to figure out how to keep her here in a way that wouldn't scare her off and give him some time to get this seduction plan into place.

Maybe telling her that this wasn't a date had been a mistake.

He gave her one of his loose, easy smiles, one that usually

had the chicks creaming themselves, and tossed his thermal over the bed beside him. "Must be something wrong with the door. I'll take a look at it in a second. But hey, where's the rush?" Her gaze had come back to his and he held it again, making sure that smile was firmly pasted across his face. "Don't you want to sit down and catch up?"

He was smiling at her. For the first time since he'd picked her up out of bed and carried her out of the window, he was smiling. And God . . . it was the same glorious, lazy, sexy smile she remembered from years ago. Like a sunrise slowly creeping over the horizon, banishing shadows and promising warmth.

Dear heaven. You're a lost cause.

Oh yes, she was. Totally. Her poor heart was turning over and over inside her chest and there was nothing she could do to stop it. Especially with him standing there wearing nothing but a pair of jeans, all sculpted muscle, tanned skin, and tattoos.

Dressed, he was a warrior. Undressed, he was a god.

Heavily muscled shoulders and chest; hard, corrugated abs; powerful biceps. A sprinkling of dark chest hair. Just . . . a perfect male specimen designed specifically to send female hormones haywire and primitive responses crazy. Strength, virility, a hunter who would keep his mate and their children in food for the cold winter. Who would protect them against anyone who wanted to harm them.

Pull yourself together, you idiot. It's like you've never seen a naked man before.

Half naked. And of course she had. On TV and in movies. Which she supposed didn't count, but still. That had been her choice. Dating had never featured highly in her life and she'd been more than happy with that.

She blinked, unable to look away from him and those mesmerizing tattoos. On his chest was an eagle with outstretched wings and a trident behind it, along with a curling, black tribal-looking design that circled one pec. There were stars there too and some writing she couldn't quite make out. But that wasn't all. On his right bicep was another tribal-looking design with lots of jagged edges that wrapped around his elbow, spearing down along his long, muscular forearm. There was what looked like a skeletal frog incorporated into the design, which was odd. His left arm was a riot of color in what she guessed was an Asian design, with water and a dragon and, oddly enough for such a masculine guy, flowers. The dragon's tail trailed down and curled around that forearm too, which must have been the hint of color she'd seen earlier.

He wore a chain around his neck, and hanging off it, right between his pecs, were . . . dog tags. Those were his dog tags, because he was military. Holy God, why was that so damn sexy?

You're staring. Stop it.

She blinked yet again. He'd said something, hadn't he? What was it? Oh hell, she was being ridiculous. He was just a man and the tattoos were just ink. Nothing that warranted this response. Sure, she'd been in love with him for years, but this was bordering on stupidity.

With an effort, Olivia got herself together, though it was difficult with him smiling that beautiful, sexy smile, amusement glittering in his blue and green eyes.

What if he knew why she was blushing and staring? What if he guessed that she was finding him absolutely to die for?

You think he hasn't already?

Her blush got even hotter. Oh yes, he'd guess all right. It's not as if a man who looked like that wouldn't know when a woman was attracted to him. Which was downright embarrassing. Especially when he didn't feel the same.

This time she forced herself to hold his gaze and tried to get her heart rate under control. "What did you say? Sorry, I missed it."

His smile was devastating, making it abundantly clear to her that he knew exactly why she'd missed it. "I said there's no rush. Why don't we sit down and have a catch-up?"

Olivia ignored the heat in her cheeks and pretended she'd never been caught staring openly at his body. "A catch-up? Oh, but didn't you want some information?"

He lifted one of those massive shoulders. "That can wait. I'd like to hear all about what you've been up to first."

Oh, right. That seemed a bit odd after he'd been so very serious and insistent about the fact that he wanted information from her. Then again, they hadn't seen each other for ten years and it would be nice to talk to him.

So he kidnapped you out of your bedroom at four in the morning, drove at breakneck speed to get here, hustled you up to this room, demanded information from you and now is perfectly happy to kick back and "catch up"? You don't think something's a little off?

That *was* all a bit strange, but then again, that was Wolf. She hadn't seen him in so long, and if he wanted to talk, then she wanted to talk too. Yes, she did want to get back before people realized she was missing from her bedroom, so they wouldn't have long to chat, but . . . Well, when was the last time she'd sat down and had a chat with a friend? She didn't have many friends to chat with, period.

She swallowed, trying to get some moisture into her dry mouth. "Okay. But I can't stay long."

"Hey, it's five thirty in the morning. No one's gonna know you're not there." He nodded toward the door to the living area. "Let's go sit down. Don't know about you but I could do with another coffee." Another flash of that toe-curling smile. "Unless you want to go for the hard stuff and crack open the champagne?"

She could feel her own mouth starting to turn up at the corners, giving him a smile in return, because she just couldn't help it. "Nice idea, but no. It's a little early in the morning for me."

"Are you sure?" One straight dark brow lifted. "Looks like expensive French shit. Be a shame to waste it, right?"

She didn't normally drink. Sometimes she'd have a glass of wine with a meal, but mostly she stuck to water. Her mother had been the big drinker in the house and, after seeing where that had led, Olivia had steered clear of alcohol. "I'm not much of a drinker," she said. "What with Mom and everything." He knew about her mom and her eventual suicide when Olivia was thirteen. She'd talked to him about it on and off over the years.

A frown creased his forehead. "Yeah, but you're not your mother, Liv. I've told you that before. One little sip isn't going to turn you into an alcoholic."

Of course she wasn't her mother. She'd spent the last fifteen years of her life making sure she wasn't her mother. "I know."

"Yeah, right." He moved past her, heading toward the bedroom doorway. "Come on, let's go sit. You have a sip of mine and see what you think."

She followed him, trying not to notice the way his jeans hung low on his lean hips. Or the play of muscles on his beautiful back. Or that he had yet another tattoo inked down his spine and between his shoulder blades. An intricate black design of arrows and spirals, shooting up and outward. It was beautiful, just beautiful.

What did they mean, all these tattoos?

She wanted to touch them, trace the outlines with her fingers, learn the history of each one . . .

Perhaps you shouldn't sit down and chat with him. Especially since you can't seem to function when he's around.

Annoyed with herself, Olivia pulled her gaze away from him. She needed to stop acting like she was fifteen again. She was twenty-eight, for God's sake. Sure, she was as in love with him as she'd ever been, but that was no excuse for acting so starstruck.

In the living room, she sat down on the couch again while Wolf headed to the ice bucket. He picked up the champagne bottle and ripped off the foil, undoing the bit of wire over the cork, then positioning his fingers under the cork in preparation for easing it out.

She hunched her shoulders unconsciously, waiting for the pop.

He noticed and grinned. "Relax. You wouldn't believe how many times I've popped champagne corks."

"Oh really? I thought you were more of a beer guy."

"I'm a beer guy, too. But champagne goes nicely with . . . other things." There was a wicked glint in his eyes, which did nothing to ease her heart rate, making her wonder what "other things" champagne went nicely with. But she felt too self-conscious to ask, so she said nothing, merely watched as he popped the cork then splashed some of the fizzing liquid into one of the flutes.

"Fucking hell," he muttered as he dumped the bottle back into the ice bucket. "It's pink."

She couldn't help grinning. A massive SEAL warrior holding a delicate crystal flute of pink champagne was a sight you didn't see every day.

Wolf raised the glass to his lips and took a sip. Frowned. Then he shot her a glance from underneath his ridiculously long, thick lashes. "Want to try some?"

He meant the champagne, of course he meant the champagne. But that's not where her brain had gone.

"No, thank you," she said, unable to keep the prim note from her voice.

He gave a soft, rough laugh. "Seriously? Not even a taste?" He took a couple of steps toward the couch, his massive form towering over her, before dropping fluidly into a crouch in front of her holding out the glass. "Come on. Live a little."

He was so close, his body only inches away from her knees, and she could see the writing on his tattooed torso. It looked to be some kind of prayer, not that she was going to study it too hard, because having him so close was doing things to her that she didn't want him to see.

Her palms were sweaty where they were clasped in her lap and her pulse was going haywire. The movement had set his dog tags swinging, and she couldn't seem to tear her gaze from his chest. He hadn't dried himself off properly and there were a few drops of water beading his skin, one of them slipping down his left pec . . .

Actually, on second thought, maybe she did need a sip of wine. If only to make her mouth less dry.

"Okay, okay." She took the glass from his hands, careful not to accidentally brush his fingers with hers, because if that happened she'd probably spill it all over herself—or worse, him.

He grinned, staying in that distracting crouch and interlacing his fingers between his knees, watching her.

The champagne was icy and delicious on her tongue, not too sweet, yet with a yeasty aftertaste she liked very much indeed.

Wolf raised a brow. "You like?"

"Yes, actually I do."

"Excellent." He rose to his feet again, his movement smooth. "You keep that glass and I'll get myself another."

Olivia knew she should protest, that drinking a whole glass of champagne at five in the morning probably wasn't a great idea. But she was still feeling dry-mouthed. And anyway, it was good to have something in her hands to fiddle with.

"So," she said as he picked up the bottle, "I was sorry to hear about your father. I mean, I don't know whether you're grieving him, especially considering what he did to you, but I just wanted you to know that I'm sorry. And that if you want to talk about it, well, I'm here."

Wolf didn't say anything immediately. He finished pouring himself a glass, then turned and sprawled down in the armchair he'd been sitting in before, putting the glass on the floor beside the chair. "Yeah, thanks." There was no discernible emotion in his voice, but that meant nothing. People grieved in different ways and she wasn't one to judge.

"Do you . . . want to talk about it?" she asked hesitantly.

He let out a breath. "No. No, I do not." His mouth curved in another smile. "I'd much rather hear about you."

She could feel herself starting to blush yet again. Yes, she had to get that under control. He was her friend, nothing more.

Glancing down at the glass in her hands so she didn't have his glorious naked chest right in her face, she rubbed her thumb absently up and down the stem of her flute. "You know everything already. My emails were pretty self-explanatory."

"Sure, but I'd like to hear it from you. You went to college, right? I mean that's what you always told me you wanted to do. But you didn't end up studying history, you said."

She remembered those conversations they'd had in the library. About the future and their dreams for themselves.

She'd always wanted to go to college to study history, while he'd always been clear that he wanted to join the Navy and become a SEAL like his brothers. Then he'd find himself a wife and settle down, because he wanted a family of his own.

"No, not history in the end. I studied business because Dad said it would be more useful, and since he was bank-rolling it . . ."

"But you were into it, weren't you?"

"To be honest, not to start with." She raised her glass and took another sip of her wine, letting it fizz on her tongue. "But I enjoyed it in the end. And Dad was right, it *did* end up being useful." She might have regretted not doing some of the history papers she'd wanted, but the business subjects hadn't been uninteresting. And she was good at them.

"What happened after that?" He cocked his head, giving her a look she couldn't decipher. "How were those intern-ships?"

After completing her degree, she'd had some intern-ships at different companies, all part of her father's plan for her to start working at DS Corp.

"Oh, those were great. It was an excellent experience and the perfect opportunity to expand my skill base. I worked with some fabulous people."

He gave one of those soft, gravelly laughs. "Man, you sound so corporate."

"I guess I am pretty corporate these days."

"Apart from your nun nightdress."

She smiled, unable to resist the glint of amusement in his eyes. "I find wearing a pencil skirt and heels in bed a bit uncomfortable."

He laughed again and reached over the arm of his chair for his glass, holding it between long fingers as he studied her. "Yeah, no joke. So how come you're still living at home? I thought you would have moved out by now. Got your own apartment, all that shit."

There was nothing judgmental in his tone, so she didn't know why she felt defensive. Or why she felt the need to explain herself. But she did all the same. "I didn't want to move out. Dad is all alone in that house, and when he stepped down from DS Corp last year, he needed someone to take care of him. Especially since my brothers weren't interested." Not when they were the ones who'd engineered his "retirement" in the first place.

If Wolf heard the defensive note in her voice, he didn't show it. Instead he took a sip of his champagne and watched her from over the rim the glass, his gaze vaguely unnerving in its intensity.

She felt awkward all of a sudden, which wasn't what she wanted to feel right now, not with him. "It's fine," she said, trying to cover it. "I like living with Dad. And hey, I get all my meals cooked and my laundry done. It could be worse."

"Yeah, right. I hear you."

"What about you?" Time to turn this back on him. "I guess you can't talk about your missions and stuff, but . . . is the Navy all you hoped it would be?"

He gave a slow nod. "Definitely. I mean, the training was shit and probably the hardest thing I've ever done, but being part of a team . . . It's awesome knowing they have my back, no matter what. And I have theirs. It's a family, you know?"

She nodded, even though she really didn't know. The de Santis family had never been like that, or if it had, she wasn't part of it. She was the youngest and the only girl, and had been pretty much ignored for most of her childhood. Her brothers had had their own issues, but once they'd taken down their father, she'd pretty much decided that she didn't want to have anything to do with them. In fact, the only person who'd been on her "team" had been her father.

But only after Mom died.

Yes, but what did that matter? He was on her side now and that's what counted.

"That sounds pretty amazing." She took another sip from her glass. "So you kind of got the family you always wanted, huh? Must be nice to have that after all the stuff you had to put up with." She'd seen the bruises Noah had given him. It had made her ache for him.

He gave her one of his slow-burning smiles. "Yeah, you're right. It is amazing. I'm heading back to base once my bereavement leave is over. Gotta support my buddies."

A pinprick of disappointment stabbed at her, which was silly. He would never stay, not now that he'd found his family. So she would enjoy his company while she had it. "Of course you do. I mean, I have the same thing with my dad. He's my team and I have to support him."

"You're a good daughter, Liv." Wolf idly swirled the champagne around in his glass, studying her. "I hope he appreciates you the way he ought to."

"Thanks." Something warmed in her chest at his praise. She didn't often get it from her father—or from anyone, really—and she often told herself that she didn't need it. That she knew he loved her. "He does."

One corner of Wolf's mouth lifted. "Good."

The word sounded deliciously rough, making her want to shiver. She lifted her glass, taking another swallow to cover the response. If he would only put on his shirt all of this would be so much easier. "You must be cold," she said. "Shall I get your—"

"Tell me something," he interrupted, draining his glass and leaning forward in the chair all of a sudden, the flute held between his fingers, his dog tags swinging.

"What?"

His mismatched gaze met hers. "Are you seeing anyone right now?"

CHAPTER FOUR

Olivia's midnight blue eyes went wide.

Okay, it was a pretty personal question, but he thought they'd been friends long enough. And besides, it was extremely relevant to his plan. When he'd mentioned Daniel May earlier, she'd been very dismissive, so whatever her father wanted for her, she wasn't holding a torch for that guy, that was for sure.

But maybe there was someone else? Not that it mattered, not if her response to him was anything to go by, but it would be useful to know.

A wash of pink stained her cheeks. Obviously the answer to that question was likely to be "no." She'd been blushing nonstop ever since he'd taken his shirt off and now she was sitting on the couch in that awkward pose, right on the edge of it, as if she was getting ready to make a quick getaway. Nervous and that fucking virginal nightgown she was wearing . . . Yeah, he'd lay money on the fact that she wasn't seeing anyone.

In fact, he'd lay money on the fact that she'd *never* seen anyone.

"No, not right now," she said, slightly prim. "Why do you ask?"

"Just wondered." He glanced pointedly at her empty glass. "Another?"

She blinked and looked down at it, as if surprised it was empty. "Oh. Yes, that would be nice."

He got up and came over to where she sat, reaching out for her glass as she held it up, noticing that she kept her fingers away from his, as if afraid of any contact.

No, not afraid. Definitely nervous.

She gave him a strained smile as he took the glass, and it was obvious to him that she was making a very real effort to keep her eyes up and to not look at his chest. And he didn't think that was because she didn't want to look.

He turned to the ice bucket, pouring her another glass before setting it down on the coffee table in front of her.

"What about you?" she asked as he turned and went back to the armchair. "Are you seeing anyone right now?"

"Nah. I'm not looking for anything long-term. Not while I'm in the Navy." But once he had his mother back, he'd start looking for a special woman to share his life. Families, after all, didn't create themselves.

Her mouth twitched. "No, I don't suppose you are." She glanced at the ice bucket. "You're not having another glass?"

He leaned back in the chair and patted his stomach. "Gotta watch my weight."

As he'd hoped, her gaze went right to the place he'd patted then darted away again.

"I don't believe that for a second," she muttered, taking another sip from her own glass.

"Yeah, you got me. I'm very definitely a beer kind of guy." Also, he didn't drink when he was on a mission, especially not a mission as important as this one was. Her, on the other hand, well, he was quite happy to keep refilling her glass. Not that he particularly wanted to attempt a drunken seduction, but a drunken interrogation was an entirely different story.

"That does not surprise me." She smiled, sipping yet more champagne. "So, tell me about life as a Navy SEAL. Been on any dangerous missions?"

He couldn't tell her much about what he'd been doing since most of it was classified information, but he could tell her a few things—mainly about the grueling training he had to undergo to earn his trident. So he talked, and as he did so, he was conscious that though they hadn't seen each other for over ten years, it felt like no time at all had passed. That he was once again seventeen and back in de Santis's library, having one of those long, rambling conversations with de Santis's fifteen-year-old daughter who, for some reason, was interested in what he had to say.

He hadn't been attracted to her then, though he'd liked her very much. Mainly because she'd been fifteen and, though reasonably pretty, too young for him. His father had tried to get him to take the relationship to a romantic level since that was more useful to the mission, but Wolf had insisted they stay friends. No one talked to him the way she did, as if he was smart and had something worthwhile to say. Certainly Noah had never talked to him like that.

"I don't need your brains, Wolf. That's what your brothers are for. What I need from you is your strength."

He'd told himself he hadn't minded not being as smart as his brothers. That he didn't mind being his father's weapon. But there had been times when it had . . . rankled.

Such as when his father had refused to send him to the exclusive school he'd sent Van and Lucas to, instead sending Wolf off to a training camp where the focus had been on physical rather than intellectual skills. His father had said it was because he didn't have the book smarts, that his strengths lay in his physical achievements, and that was more important.

He'd tried not to care about that, but he had.

So yeah, having Olivia interested in his conversation and curious about his opinions had been a pretty cool thing and he hadn't wanted to mess that up by getting interested in her.

But the more he talked to her now, the more it became clear that she wasn't fifteen any more. She was a woman—hell, she certainly looked like one.

It was true that she didn't have the intense de Santis good looks the rest of her family did, but there were those expressive dark, winged brows and that very determined jaw. The famous de Santis eyes—midnight blue, like shadows—were also present and accounted for.

Yeah, she had strong, very definite features that held their own appeal. And then there was her body, not that he could see much of it under the stupid white virgin's robe she was wearing, but the slight hint of pink nipples was visible through the thin cotton and he could tell she was wearing white panties. Very cute.

Okay, so if he was going to use her reaction to him as a way to get information, then a slow seduction was the next logical step. And shit, he wasn't averse to the idea, now that he thought about it. Not at all.

A lousy thing to do to use her like this. Selfish even. But then she wasn't truly his friend, was she? Oh, she thought it was all genuine, and hell, he certainly thought of her a friend, but it had all been on his father's orders as a way to get closer to de Santis.

She was part of his plan and now it was time to put that plan into action.

He would kill Cesare de Santis, avenge Noah Tate. And then he would find his mom. Just like his father had promised him.

"Oh my God," Olivia was saying. "You carried fifty pounds for how long?"

"Twenty miles. Jogging." He grinned, enjoying the shock on her face. "And that was an easy day."

"That's . . . incredible, Wolf. I can't even imagine doing all of that and surviving."

Was it incredible? He supposed it was from the outside. But then his SEAL training hadn't been only about physical strength. It had been mental too, and that had been the part he'd struggled with.

His father hadn't wanted him to go into the SEALs, had wanted him to stay an enlisted man. Had told him he didn't have the aptitude for it, and besides, he was needed to keep working for de Santis. But Wolf had decided that he'd wanted this and wanted it enough that he'd argued with his father—the only argument they'd ever had.

Noah hadn't been keen, but Wolf had argued him around in the end by telling him that as a SEAL he'd be even more deadly than he already was.

"Lots of people didn't survive," he said, glancing at the liquid in her glass. It was almost empty. "The training is tough."

"You're telling me. What got you through?"

"Knowing that Van and Lucas got through. Fucking instructors kept telling me that my brothers got better scores than me, so I should give up right now."

"But you didn't."

"Nope. I'm not a quitter." It came out sounding more emphatic than he'd meant it to, but maybe that was a good thing. Maybe it was time she knew something true about him.

Yet Olivia simply nodded like it wasn't any big surprise. "Of course you're not. You never were."

He frowned, her acceptance making something uncomfortable shift inside him. "What makes you say that?"

"Oh, I just remember how dead set you were on joining

the Navy and getting away from your father. I know Dad offered you a job at DS Corp and a place to stay in New York, but you didn't take it because you were very definite about going into the military."

That's right. De Santis had offered him that. At the time, Wolf had been surprised by how much the offer had affected him. Noah had never offered him a position at Tate Oil, had never even mentioned one. And when Wolf had brought it up once, Noah had laughed and told him not to be stupid, that he wasn't the corporate type.

He'd always known that, but for some reason he hadn't been able to shake his own . . . discomfort at his father's response. Strange when he didn't even care about Tate Oil. But then, he *was* Noah's son and he'd thought that maybe his father would have wanted him following in his footsteps.

Apparently not.

Then he'd found out that the offer from de Santis was for a janitorial position. Because of course Cesare didn't want him working at DS Corp at a corporate level. What he'd wanted was for a Tate to be cleaning his toilets. It shouldn't have felt like another kick in the teeth, even though he'd thought he'd gained de Santis's trust by then, but it had.

He wanted to tell Olivia the exact nature of the job, since he was pretty sure she hadn't a clue, but he wasn't ready for that discussion yet. It would lead to some unpleasant truths that she didn't need to hear, at least not before he'd gotten the information that he needed out of her.

"Yeah, I'm not the corporate type," he said, parroting his father and not liking the way it sounded for some reason. "Guns and smashing the shit out of things is more my style."

Olivia gave him a look. "Is it? That's not what you used to tell me."

He didn't like that look either, didn't like it at all. "It is now. You want some more champagne?"

She glanced down at her once again empty glass and surprise crossed her face. "Oh, uh . . . maybe not." Her head lifted and she looked around the room distractedly. "What's the time? I should be getting home."

Shit. He needed her to forget this stupid time pressure.

"Relax," he said calmly. "The sun hasn't even come up yet."

Olivia turned and glanced out the windows. "Oh, true. Well, still, I probably shouldn't have any more." She yawned, putting her hand over mouth.

He frowned, noting the dark circles under her eyes. She looked exhausted. Maybe his seduction plan could wait.

Are you kidding? Take advantage of someone's weak points, isn't that the first rule of interrogations?

That uncomfortable feeling in his chest twisted again, his own point of weakness. Letting her sleep would be a stupid idea and yet . . .

You can't get all pussy-ass now.

Wolf nearly growled. Did it matter if he let her get an hour or two of sleep? Hell, if she was well rested, she might take to the seduction even better than if she was sleepy.

You're lying to yourself.

Yeah and that fucking voice could shut the hell up. If she wanted some sleep, he'd let her sleep. It was probably the last time she'd have anything like peace, that was for sure.

"Tired?" he asked out loud. "Perhaps you should take a nap before you go home. It's a work day after all."

Leaning forward, Olivia put her glass on the coffee table before sitting back against the couch and yawning again. "Maybe I should." She gave him a small smile. "Getting kidnapped at four in the morning takes it out of a girl."

"I'm not sorry." He wasn't and not only because of his mission, surprisingly enough. He'd enjoyed this little interlude, especially after the past few weeks since Noah died. Just sitting here, talking to her like they used to.

Her small smile widened. "I'm not sorry either."

That feeling in his chest shifted and he put his hand on his heart, rubbing absently at the ache there. Her gaze followed the movement of his hand, lingering there before darting away again.

She cleared her throat. "Maybe a nap wouldn't hurt."

Wolf kept his hand where it was and sure enough, she glanced at his chest again, as if she couldn't help herself. "Feel free to use the bedroom. I'll wake you in say, twenty minutes?" He wouldn't wake her. He'd leave her to sleep for however long she wanted to and figure out how to deal with her inevitable freak-out later.

"That would be great." She pushed herself off the couch then paused, and this time looked right at him. "Thanks for the chat, Wolf. It's really nice to see you again. And I mean that. Really nice."

That made him feel weird too, because when she found out the truth of why he was here, she wouldn't think it was so nice. Yet right now her expression was very open, very honest. And it was clear she meant every word.

The only person in his life who'd ever been genuine with him, and now he was going to use her.

He rubbed at his chest again, trying to get rid of the weakness that was eating away at him. Because it didn't matter if she'd always been honest with him or not. His father's death needed avenging. And then there was his mother . . .

Anyway, he wasn't going to hurt her, only seduce her. And he'd make it good for her. Sex was something he was very, very good at indeed.

"It's nice to see you too," he said, meeting her gaze and

holding it, wanting her to know he was genuine about this at least. "I've missed talking to you."

She looked embarrassed and pleased at the same time, which he found oddly appealing. "Oh, me too. Email really doesn't cut it."

There was a moment's awkward silence, which he made no effort to break since he wasn't the one being awkward and he kind of liked that she was. Even though he had no idea why.

Olivia clasped her hands together. "Well, okay. I'd better take that nap then."

"Yeah, go on. I'll wake you in twenty."

She gave him a smile then turned and headed toward the bedroom.

He watched her, rubbing at the ache in his chest that refused to go away.

Olivia woke up dry-mouthed and muzzy, and with the beginnings of what felt like a major a headache. For a long moment, she lay on the very comfortable bed, staring up at the ceiling, trying to figure out where she was, because she definitely wasn't at home.

Then slowly a memory filtered through, of being kidnapped by Wolf. Of the hotel room he'd brought her to and . . . Oh God, the two glasses of pink champagne she'd polished off.

Great. No wonder her mouth felt like the bottom of a birdcage.

Sighing, she turned over onto her side and contemplated getting up. Then caught a glimpse of the clock on the nightstand. And the time displayed on it.

Oh shit. It was ten a.m.

She sat bolt upright then pushed herself off the bed, having to pause a moment to catch her breath as a wave of dizziness hit.

Hell, what had she been thinking? Drinking at . . . what? Five in the morning? That wasn't like her, even given Wolf's distracting presence.

And speaking of, why hadn't he woken her up? He'd told her he was going to give her twenty minutes.

Annoyed, Olivia strode to the bedroom door, then stopped.

Wolf was standing in the living area—still shirtless, damn the man—looking down at a hotel trolley that had a number of plates with silver covers sitting on top of it. He was in the process of lifting one of the covers to reveal a stack of very crispy bacon and sausages. The smell hit her almost as soon as she saw the food and yet far from making her sick, she was conscious that she was, in fact, very hungry.

Still. Ten a.m. Her father would be beside himself.

She opened her mouth to ask Wolf why he'd let her sleep so long, but he forestalled her.

"I called your father," he said without looking round. "I told him you were taking the day off. He wasn't happy, but he's okay with it. So why don't you sit down and have some breakfast?"

She frowned, her head still a little fuzzy. "You called Dad?

Replacing the cover on the plate, he turned and gave her a lazy grin. "I thought you could do with the sleep, so I gave him a call."

Olivia didn't know what to say. She'd been expecting all this time to rush home before her father realized she was gone, and now . . . well. There was no rush. And she could have the whole day off.

An uneasy feeling shifted in her gut and it wasn't the wine this time. She didn't take weekends and she very rarely took a vacation, mostly because she never knew what to do with herself.

Managing the household and her father's social and business engagements, plus handling his financial investments and a couple of his side projects, was a busy job and she liked it. It made her feel useful and she knew her father appreciated it hugely, which she also liked.

But she wasn't sure she liked having a day to simply sit around in a hotel room with Wolf.

"Okay," she said slowly. "But I'll just have breakfast, if you don't mind. I really do need to go home. Dad might not mind me having the day off, but I have a ton of things to do that can't wait."

Wolf was silent, his smile fading, leaving an indecipherable expression on his face. Then he turned back to the trolley. There were a couple of clean coffee mugs on it, plus a big stainless steel pot that had to contain coffee.

He picked up the pot. "There's another reason I want you to stay." Carefully he poured the steaming black liquid into the two mugs. "You know how I said that I didn't want to talk about Dad's death? Well, I changed my mind." Putting down the pot, he glanced at her again, and this time there was no smile on his rough, handsome face. His eyes glittered with something she couldn't quite place, whether it was anger or grief, or a complicated mixture of the two, she didn't know. "I think maybe I do want to talk about it."

Her heart clenched. He wasn't an easy man to read, she remembered that from years ago. Most of the time he was laid back and relaxed, and but there were times when that chilled-out exterior would drop and she'd catch a glimpse of something else behind those mismatched eyes of his. Something that looked a lot like anger.

She didn't blame him if so. Noah Tate was a bastard of the first degree, and the way he treated Wolf made her sick. But since Wolf never talked about it, she'd never pressed, mostly because she'd only been fifteen and hadn't known what to say to him.

She wasn't fifteen now though, and the thought that he finally wanted to talk to her about his father made her throat constrict painfully.

Olivia moved away from the doorway, coming over to where he stood. She looked up at him, barely aware of his half-naked body right now, her attention entirely on that strange combination of emotions in his eyes. "You know I'm here if you want to talk, Wolf. But there's no pressure if you don't, okay?" She reached out and touched his arm lightly in an unconscious gesture of comfort. Only to have the heat of his bare skin tingle against her fingertips, making her want to snatch her hand back again.

He didn't move and yet she saw something in his eyes flare, something that wasn't the anger or grief or whatever it was that had been there a moment earlier. And suddenly the air between them was full of tension, thick and electric and somehow confusing.

Seconds before, she'd forgotten he wasn't wearing a shirt. Now, awareness poured through her. Of how close he was. Of how tall and broad he was, and how fragile and small she felt next to him. Of his tanned skin and the fascinating designs inked into it. Of his dog tags hanging between his pecs, the metal shining as a ray of weak winter sunlight caught it.

He smelled good, of cedar and leather, with a musky, masculine undertone that was all him.

Olivia swallowed. This was wrong. Wrong to be feeling this while he was grieving and wanting to talk. Wrong to be so aware of him physically. He was her friend, nothing more and she really needed to get a damn grip.

She took her hand from his arm, hoping it looked like a measured movement and not because touching him was doing crazy things to her heartbeat. Only to have him catch her hand as it dropped, his long fingers wrapping around hers.

"Are you sure?" His voice was low and rough, the look in his eyes making the breath catch in her throat. "I know this has been a shock. Me basically kidnapping you and then taking you here. I just . . . want to talk to you. In person. And un-fucking-interrupted for a change."

Her brain was operating way too slowly and she couldn't think of what to say. All she seemed to be aware of was that he was holding her hand, making heat rise up her arm and into the rest of her body. A wild, restless heat that was totally unfamiliar to her.

She'd never felt this before, not even that last day in the library, when she waited there until after his meeting with her father, hoping desperately that he'd accept her father's offer of a job and sanctuary, and deciding not to leave until she knew what he was going to do.

Hearing her father's office door close, she'd darted into the hallway to find Wolf standing there with his hands in the pockets of his jeans and his normal easygoing smile nowhere to be seen. She'd seen the anger in his eyes then, loud and clear, though all he'd said was, "I'm sorry, Liv. I can't stay. I'm enlisting tomorrow."

She'd been so disappointed, trying not to burst into tears in front of him and failing. He'd taken her in his arms— he'd only ever touched her one other time—and given her a hug, whispering to her that he was sorry, but it had to be this way.

And she . . . well, that hug had been the most confusing thing to ever happen to her. There had been something about the heat of his body and the feel of it against hers, about the strength of his arms holding her, and the warmth of his breath in her hair that had made her pulse race. Made her shiver for reasons her sixteen-year-old self couldn't fathom.

But now . . . she knew what it meant now.

She swallowed, resisting the urge to pull her hand away

from his. Not wanting to give herself away more than she already had.

Oh come on. He already knows. You've never been very good at hiding how you feel.

She looked away, letting her hand rest in his and trying not to pay any attention to her racing heartbeat. "Okay," she said, her voice sounding far more husky than she wanted it to. "Let's have that coffee then and we can talk."

But he didn't let her hand go. Instead she felt one long finger catch her beneath the chin, turning her head back to meet his gaze. "Hey, what's up?" he murmured. "You're blushing."

No kidding. She tightened her jaw and steeled herself to give him a steady, level look back, as if nothing was wrong, nothing at all. But that stare of his was mesmerizing. She'd always loved how he had one blue eye and one green. Heterochromia it was called, or that's what he'd told her when she'd asked about it once. Not that it mattered what it was called. She simply found it beautiful, that crystalline blue matched with the leaf green, the colors vivid through his long dark lashes . . .

His mouth curved. "Liv? You can answer any time."

Oh, right. He'd asked her a question and now she was staring at him like a lunatic.

A question he already knows the answer to, come on.

A wave of sudden annoyance caught at her, partly driven by her own helpless reaction to him, because yes, of course he knew. He must. He wasn't stupid, no matter that he always talked his own intelligence down, and neither was she.

"You know why I'm blushing already." The words were out before she could stop herself.

His eyes widened, which made a small part of her very satisfied that she could surprise him. Because really, she was getting tired of being the only one who was flustered.

She didn't like how out of control it made her feel, and come to think of it, she was starting to feel a bit peeved that she didn't rock his world in quite the same way as he rocked hers.

She stared back at him, making no move to pull away. There was no point now, not if he knew how he affected her anyway.

"Yeah," he said slowly, searching her face. "I guess I do."

"So why ask me then?"

He didn't let go of her hand and that finger under her chin stayed exactly where it was. Her heartbeat was banging like a damn drum in her head, and she wanted to pull away with just about every part of her.

But something small and defiant and stubborn held her still.

"Maybe I wanted to check something." The finger beneath her chin moved, trailing very lightly down her neck. Goose bumps erupted all over her skin and it was all she could do not to gasp or take a quick step back.

"Check what?" Shivers of excitement were chasing all over her skin and her voice sounded husky. And it annoyed her. What was he doing? What was he looking for? An admission that she was attracted to him? If so, why?

His finger paused in the hollow of her throat and she knew he could feel her pulse. And that it was fast. Too fast.

His gaze held hers, intense all of a sudden. "It's been six months since I've been with anyone, Liv."

Wait, what? Was that an . . . invitation?

No, it couldn't be. He didn't feel that way about her. He was her friend and he'd never done anything to make her think he felt anything more for her. She didn't want to go there, she just didn't.

Swallowing, she said, "I thought you wanted to talk about your father?"

"Yeah, well, maybe I changed my mind." His finger moved lightly on her skin in a gentle stroking motion, while his gaze dropped down to her white nightgown. "Maybe I want to do something else."

Something else . . .

Olivia jerked away from him before she was even conscious of doing so, taking a couple of steps back to put some distance between them. She was breathless, her heart raging behind her ribs, her pulse rocketing, and her skin strangely hot and tight. "I don't . . . know what you're talking about." Her voice sounded thick and unsteady.

Wolf stared at her. "You know what I'm talking about, Liv. I think we both know what I'm talking about."

"Yes, and I thought I was your friend." She couldn't get her breathing under control or her heartbeat. "Was that why you brought me here? To . . . to . . ."

"To what? Fuck you?"

She'd long gotten used to Wolf's filthy mouth, but hearing that word in conjunction with herself made a hot, electric thrill shoot straight down her spine.

He couldn't mean it, though. The whole thing was too weird. The kidnap, the hustling into the hotel, and then the strange questions he'd asked her. Not to mention the look on his face when she'd stupidly thought the champagne and the candles had meant something else.

She couldn't afford to believe he could mean it.

"No," she said, hating the way the word came out so shakily. "You don't want that. It doesn't make any sense. You said this wasn't a date."

The intensity of his gaze felt like it was burning right through her. "It's not. I never fuck on a first date."

Again that hot thrill, and this time moving lower, between her thighs. Her brain was going places she didn't want it to go, sending images she didn't want to see rioting through her mind. Wolf naked. Wolf touching her. Wolf fucking on the first date. Wolf fucking her . . .

"No," she repeated, shaking her head violently. "No."

There was a tense, heavy silence.

Then he was moving toward her, fast and fluid, and she only had time to stumble back a few steps before he was right there in front of her. He grabbed her hand and, before she could stop him, brought her palm flat to his chest, right over his left pec, pressing it down onto his skin. "You want me, Liv. I know you do. I can see it in your eyes."

She froze, what little breath she had left rushing out of her.

He's correct. You do.

But not like this. Something wasn't right. She could feel it.

He made no move to do anything else, merely held her hand against him, that intense uneven gaze holding hers.

The heat of his body was blistering. Hard, muscle. Tanned skin slightly roughened with hair. The steady, slow beat of his heart.

She'd been so good, so careful. She'd never imagined touching him, because she wasn't a masochist. It was bad enough being hopelessly in love with him let alone to fantasize about anything else.

But now she *was* touching him and it was . . .

No. No, she couldn't do this. It was too close to what she desperately wanted and it was becoming obvious to her that she was simply a convenient body. He didn't want *her*. If in fact it was actually sex he wanted in the first place.

She jerked her hand away from the furnace of his naked chest.

Only for him to take one step even closer, his other hand sliding into her hair, his big palm cradling the back of her head, his fingers pressing gently against her skull. Then before she could react, he lowered his head, and that wide, beautiful mouth was on hers.

Shock held her utterly still.

Wolf Tate was kissing her. Wolf Tate was kissing *her*.

If she hadn't been able to breathe before, now it was as if all the air in the entire world had been sucked away and there was no relief to be found anywhere.

His lips were . . . soft. She hadn't expected that. He was so hard everywhere else, and yet there was nothing un-yielding about the mouth brushing gently over hers. Nothing forceful. His breath was warm, and somehow she couldn't stop shivering as he brushed his lips over hers again, a butterfly kiss.

He made a sound, rough and approving, inhaling as if her scent was something he liked. Then his tongue touched her bottom lip, gently coaxing.

Wildfire was kindling in her veins, a rush of intense heat sweeping over her, scorching her.

She felt dizzy. This was her first kiss. With the only man she'd ever wanted it to be with. The only man she'd ever wanted to touch, ever wanted to have touch her.

It's not real and you know it.

Doubt was a small, hard kernel of ice sitting in her gut, impervious to the flames. There was too much that was strange about this whole situation, too much she didn't know, and she couldn't kick the feeling that Wolf wasn't telling her the whole story.

Which meant she couldn't give herself over to this kiss. She couldn't let him do anything more. Another woman might have thrown caution to the winds and take what she wanted, even if this was all she'd ever have, but Olivia wasn't that woman.

Her whole life was about caution. About watching and waiting, about thinking things through carefully. And as much as she wanted Wolf Tate, she'd already told herself she would never have him, not the way she wanted him. It was something she'd come to terms with long ago. Because he didn't want her. He wasn't in love with her the way she was in love with him, and if she let herself have this, only to find out that it wasn't real . . .

Well. She'd never recover.

He was holding her firmly, making it clear that she wasn't going to be able to pull away unless he let her. So she put a hand back on his chest again, steeling herself against the rush of heat, and let it rest there a second.

He made another of those rough sounds, his mouth opening on hers.

Olivia shoved. Hard.

It was like moving a mountain. Afterward, she knew he must have let her push him, because it was clear she didn't have the strength to move him if he didn't want to be moved. But right in that moment all she was conscious of was his hand slipping from the back of her head as he went back a step.

She didn't wait for his reaction, dodging past him and heading straight for the door of the hotel room. Time to leave. Very definitely time to leave.

Her heartbeat was racketing around in her chest, her skin sensitized, her mouth tender and feeling almost bruised, Olivia put her hand on the door handle and wrenched at it, desperate to get out.

But the door didn't open.

She pulled at it again, harder.

It remained shut.

"It's locked." A dark, rough voice behind her.

She ignored him, pulling futilely again at the handle, not caring if she broke the stupid thing, fear beginning to gather in the pit of her stomach.

"I'm sorry, Liv," Wolf said.

She whirled around, breathing fast.

He was standing in that short corridor, his massive form blocking out the light. Blocking out everything. All she could see was his eyes and the hard, implacable look in them. As if that soft, impossibly hot kiss hadn't happened.

"I can't let you leave," he said quietly. "Not until you give me what I want."

CHAPTER FIVE

Olivia was pressed against the door, the lovely flush dying out of her skin, leaving her face pale, her eyes huge and dark, staring at him as if he'd suddenly sprouted wings, horns, and cloven hooves.

Yeah, he could hardly blame her for that. He'd fucked up and he'd fucked up royally. He should never have mentioned wanting to talk about his father, that was for sure. It had felt wrong at the time, to use her sympathy and caring against her, but he'd been conscious that the longer he held her here, the more dangerous it was. De Santis would no doubt be moving heaven and earth to find her and eventually he would. And if he wasn't careful, de Santis would find out that it was Wolf who'd taken her.

He couldn't let that happen and potentially give the guy a heads-up about his intentions. He had to get that information and stat.

Being blunt and mentioning "fucking" hadn't helped either, he'd known that the second she'd blushed like a rose. Some girls got off on dirty talk, but he should have realized that Olivia wasn't that type. She didn't swear, for one, and for another, she'd gotten very uncomfortable when he'd asked whether she was seeing anyone.

Making her touch him had been a start, because he'd

seen something hot leap in her gaze the moment he'd brought her palm to his chest, but that kiss . . .

Yeah, that had been a very big mistake.

His last deployment in Eastern Europe had been nothing but hard and cold and shitty, and kissing Olivia . . . well, that had been the exact opposite.

Her mouth had been so soft and she'd smelled like strawberries, her hair a silky glory against his fingers. And all he'd been able to think was that it had been so fucking *long* since he'd touched anything this soft. Tasted anything this sweet. He wanted more, wanted to slide his tongue into her mouth and get a proper taste of her, grab her hips and pull her against him, feel the warmth of her body against his. So much so that he'd forgotten momentarily what he was supposed to do.

Until she'd shoved hard against his chest and he'd had to let her go.

He could have gone after her, and maybe he should have. Maybe he should have held her tighter and kissed her harder, slipped his hand under her nightgown and made her forget she'd ever resisted. But that fucking weakness in his chest, that feeling of reluctance, had stopped him.

Sex wasn't what he wanted from her. De Santis's schedule and that intel about Daniel May were the key objectives of this mission, and since he was obviously too weak to use sex against her, then maybe he'd have to use something else.

Tell your dick that.

Wolf ignored the thought. Of course he was fucking hard. First time he'd been close to a woman in six months, and his goddamn dick didn't know what to do with itself. Apart from the obvious.

But he'd mishandled things, blown his opportunity. He wouldn't force himself on her, and if seduction wasn't going to work, then he'd have to try something else.

Christ, if only he'd been a better planner, been smarter about this, then maybe he wouldn't have fucked up so badly. Too late now.

Either way, though, she wasn't leaving until he'd gotten what he wanted.

She had her hands pressed against the door as if she wanted to push herself right through it and out the other side, and he could see her obvious fear.

He was scaring her, which made that weak feeling inside him worse and pissed him off. Because fear was a useful tool if it was handled right.

Or you could just tell her the truth.

Sure he could. *"Hey Liv, your dad killed mine and my last orders were to kill yours so I can finally get my mom out of hiding. So if you could give me the intel on his schedule so I can plan a hit, plus get me anything you have on May so I can hurt that prick too, that would be great. Kthanxbai."*

Yeah. No.

"I don't know what you want," Olivia said, her voice breathy with what he didn't think was desire, not this time.

He didn't come any closer to her. He had to handle this with better care from here on out, and overwhelming her with either fear or desire would probably not go well. For either of them.

You know you can kiss her friendship goodbye from now on, right?

Another thought Wolf shoved violently from his head. He'd never had her friendship to start with, so why that should matter now, he had no fucking idea.

"Yeah, you do." He kept his voice neutral. "I asked you about your father's government contracts. And about Daniel May."

She straightened, her chin lifting, and he found himself

reluctantly admiring the way she was collecting herself, even though she was scared.

"I don't know anything about either of those things," she said with quiet dignity. "Like I told you. Any government contracts are with DS Corp, and Dad's got nothing to do with the company these days. And as for Daniel May, he's—"

"Your father is going to give you to him," Wolf interrupted flatly. It was time for her to learn at least some of the truth. She wouldn't believe him, not when she'd always been such a staunch supporter of her father, but if he could plant the seed of doubt in her head, then that was a start.

He was going to have to do something to stop her from going to the authorities and reporting him once her father was dead, he'd always known that. She was a loose end he couldn't afford to leave lying around. Another man would have dealt with that in a much more violent and permanent way, but that would never be an option for him. Not when there were plenty of ways to get her on his side.

She frowned. "What? What do you mean he's going to give me to him?"

Wolf thrust his hands into the pockets of his jeans, wishing his fucking hard-on would die because it was difficult to concentrate, especially when he kept getting glimpses of her pink nipples through the plain white cotton of her nightgown. And most especially when the cotton pulled tight over them and he could see that they were hard.

"I mean," he said through gritted teeth, "that your father has done some deal that involves you marrying that asshole."

Olivia blinked. "That's ridiculous. I went out on one date with Daniel, but only because Dad suggested it. He told me Daniel had lost his wife last year and was finding it difficult getting back into dating again, so would I help him break the ice, so to speak. It was a disaster and he never asked me again."

Wolf narrowed his gaze, studying her. It was clear she believed what she said and hell, maybe it was true. Maybe Daniel had lost his wife and was finding it difficult to get into dating again. But it was also true that Cesare had promised her to him, and had taken great delight in telling Wolf so.

"You're looking at more than a date next time," he said, letting her see the truth in his eyes. "Whatever he told you, you're going to be marrying Daniel May and he's not going to take no for an answer."

Olivia's frown deepened. Then her forehead cleared and she gave a soft laugh. "That's ridiculous. Dad would never do anything like that. I don't know where you heard about it, but that's not Dad's style. He's a traditionalist, yes, but he's not medieval."

Fuck. He was going to have to tell her more, wasn't he?

"I didn't just hear about it," Wolf said, looking straight into her blue eyes. "Your dad told me himself."

"But I don't—"

"Two days ago. I told him I wanted him to give you to me and he told me that he'd already promised you to Daniel May, and that May would be very unhappy with him if you were seen with anyone else."

Her rosebud mouth opened. Then shut. Then she walked forward, brushing past him to go into the living room without a word. Heading straight for the . . . oh *hell* no.

Wolf came after her, only just managing to grab the room's phone from the coffee-making station before she picked up the receiver.

She said nothing, merely watching as he ripped the phone from the wall then wrenched off the connecting jack so it couldn't be plugged in again without rewiring.

Dumping the now-useless phone down beside the coffeemaker, he turned and headed into the bedroom, because there was a phone there too and he wasn't taking any chances.

When he came back into the living room, she was standing near the windows looking out, her arms folded. She didn't look at him as he approached. "So I'm your prisoner now, is that what this is?"

"Yeah." Because there was no longer any point in prettying it up. "I told you I'm not letting you leave until I have the information I need."

"You didn't call Dad, did you?"

"No, I didn't."

"So he doesn't know I'm here."

"No."

She turned her head, a flame of pure anger leaping her deep blue eyes. "He'll turn this city upside down to find me. You know that, don't you?"

Wolf held her gaze. "Of course I know that. Why do you think I took you here? As far as the rest of the world is concerned, this room is booked for a newly married couple from Florida on their honeymoon."

"Why?" If the word had had edges, it would have cut him to shreds. "Why are you doing this?"

His body didn't flinch, though there was a part of him deep inside that did. That regretted what he was doing. That could see the cracks already running through their friendship get deeper with every word he spoke, the delicate structure of it beginning to shudder apart.

"Nothing worthwhile comes without sacrifice, Wolf . . ."

Their friendship had been nothing anyway. Not when it had always been built on lies. *His* lies. So did it really matter if it broke? Perhaps it would even be better, because then at least he wouldn't have to keep lying to her. It would hurt her, sure, but that couldn't be helped.

If you wanted an omelet, you had to break a few eggs, as the saying goes.

"Yeah, that doesn't concern you." He kept his voice cold and hard. If he was going to end this fragile friendship of theirs, he had to do it quickly, before he changed his mind.

"It doesn't concern me?" She looked at him incredulously. "You kidnapped me, Wolf. You want information from me and you're not going to let me go until I give it to you. Information about *my* father. So yes, I think it actually does concern me."

"You don't need to know why. All you need to know is that I want access to his schedule and the details about his relationship with Daniel May."

One dark brow rose imperiously. "I know nothing about May. And as for his schedule, what makes you think I'd give you access to that?"

He ignored her. "You're the one who manages your father's appointments, his diary. His business projects. You have access to his files and all his private documents. Even if you don't know about May, you should be able to find some record of his relationship with your father. Emails, shit like that."

Her lovely mouth hardened. "I told you. I don't know anything about it."

Was she lying? He couldn't tell.

Come on, asshole. You know she's not lying. She's the most honest person you've ever met.

"I want access to Cesare's schedule, Liv. Now."

"Why? What could you possibly want that for?" Her face was very pale, her eyes gone very blue. And beneath the anger in them, he could see something else. Something that made his chest hurt.

Pain.

He turned away from her, heading for the minibar fridge, suddenly needing something stronger than coffee.

Leaning down, he pulled it open and got out a mini bottle of scotch. Unscrewing the cap, he took a swallow straight from the bottle. The liquid burned going down, making him grimace.

Christ, she wasn't going to give him anything willingly, was she? She was way too smart. Smarter than he was. And now that he'd basically killed any chance of using the levers he had—their friendship and her desire for him— he had no idea what the fuck to do.

He should have planned this better. He was a fucking SEAL for God's sake. His father would have been embarrassed at what a fucking mess he'd made of the situation. But then that's why he'd given the company to Van, right? Because Wolf was the gun, the weapon in someone else's hand. That's what he'd been trained for. That's *all* he'd been trained for.

He wasn't a strategist or a leader. He never had been.

Wolf turned around and leaned back against the counter over the top of the minibar, taking another swallow of scotch, the alcohol glowing comfortingly in his gut.

Olivia stood by the window, bathed in the pale winter sunlight. She looked . . . fierce standing there, with her arms folded and those winged brows raised. Haughty even. Except the whole effect was undermined by the fact that the sunlight made her nightgown see-through and he could definitely see her nipples now.

His dick liked that very much indeed, and suddenly all he could think about was that damn kiss. Her mouth and what it tasted like. Her small hand on his chest and how it had felt. The instant flare of response he'd tried desperately to tamp down.

He'd never had a kiss like it and certainly hadn't expected his own intense reaction to it.

Jesus Christ. What the hell was going on with him? He was supposed to be impervious to all this kind of bullshit.

She's always been your weakness though, and you knew it even back then.

"If I let you go," he said into the heavy silence, trying another angle, "your father will give you to May. Is that really what you want?"

"No, of course not. But since that's clearly something you've made up or have misunderstood, I don't need to worry about it, do I?"

"Why would I lie to you about that?"

"Why would you lie to me about the fact that you called Dad? Why would you lie to me about wanting me?" Sarcasm edged her tone. "Forgive me if I don't believe everything you tell me, Wolf."

Frustration threaded through him, though there was nothing to be done about it. He *had* lied to her. In fact, he'd lied to her for years, so why should she believe what he said? There was no reason.

And now he'd changed things between them, altered the delicate balance of their friendship by first using her sympathy for him to get her to come close, and then her attraction to him for a seduction. Like trying to cut a wire on an unexploded bomb by chopping at it with an ax.

That's pretty much you all up, though, isn't it? You don't even know what subtlety means.

But that was old news and he had no time to rescue things. He had to get her on his side and fast. Desperate times called for desperate measures.

"Do you know why I was adopted?" His voice sounded strange in the heavy silence, and almost as soon as he'd said it, he wished he hadn't.

She frowned, the change of subject clearly catching her off guard. "No. What's that got to do with anything?"

Shit. Nothing to do but continue.

He drained the rest of the scotch then tossed the bottle away. Put the heels of his hands on the edge of the counter and curled his fingers underneath, gripping tightly to it. "Dad used to tell me it was because of my eyes. That he'd thought the colors were cool and different. That they made me special. He intended to adopt only me, but then Van piped up and told him we were a team and he couldn't take me without him and Lucas too. So Dad adopted us all."

"Oh. I'd never heard that before."

He smiled without amusement. "It's a lie."

"Oh," she said again, shifting on her feet, her frown deepening. "How so?"

"Dad didn't adopt me because of my eyes. He adopted me because my father was murdered by an enemy of his." It wasn't quite the truth, but near enough.

Olivia's mouth opened, but nothing came out.

"He adopted me because he wanted to make me into a weapon. A fucking guided missile that he'd launch at the right time, to blow the shit out of his enemy."

Her arms dropped to her sides, the frown disappearing from her face. "Wolf . . ." She took a step toward him then stopped.

No, he'd made a mistake. Again. Telling her this was wrong, because the more she knew, the more it would tie him to de Santis's eventual assassination. But now he'd started he couldn't seem to shut himself up. It was as if the truth was demanding to be let out to balance all the lies he'd told her. Like he was a fucking sinner confessing to a priest, needing absolution.

"Dad was simply waiting for the right moment to light the fuse."

She didn't say anything, simply stared at him.

"A couple of weeks ago, after Dad's funeral, all three

of us got letters from him. They'd been written before he died and were to be sent to us in case of his sudden death. You want to know what mine said? That my father was murdered." He shifted against the counter, forcing himself to hold her gaze. "It was the match to that fuse, Liv. And guess who my target was?"

She didn't understand why he was telling her this or what it meant. Clearly it was supposed to mean something though, because she could hear in his rough, gravelly voice the sharp bite of what sounded like pain.

He'd backed right off from her, leaning against the coffee-making counter, those long, strong fingers gripping the edge of it as he'd fall over if he was to let it go. That beautiful mouth was in a hard line, no sign now of those sexy, slow-burning smiles. His stubble-darkened jaw was tight, his massive shoulders tense, giving the impression of a powerful, leashed animal ready to explode into movement at any second.

The expression on his battered features was very definitely anger, but she could see, glittering in his eyes, the same pain she'd heard in his voice.

He looked like a man at the end of his rope, and dangerous with it.

A guided missile . . .

He'd asked her who she thought his target was, but she had no clue. She was too busy focusing on the pain in his voice. As if the father who'd beaten him had meant something to him. But that surely couldn't be right. Why had he come to her father then for support? For help? He'd wanted out, at least, that's what she'd always been told.

She swallowed, overwhelmed.

First the kiss and then him trapping her in the hallway, telling her he wasn't going to let her leave. The heat in his eyes and the note of rough sexiness in his voice had vanished utterly, leaving her in no doubt that all of it had been a put-on, a façade. A trick to get her to give him the information he was so desperate for. Information she wasn't going to give him—and couldn't anyway.

She'd been furious at him for that and still was, not to mention furious at herself for falling for it, for ignoring the doubt that had pulled at her. Hurt too, that he would stoop to using her attraction to him against her, to using their friendship too.

But getting carried away by anger or hurt, or anything else, would be a stupid thing to do. She had to shove all those messy emotions away and concentrate on the most important thing. Which was getting out of here and away from him.

She shook her head. "I don't know who the target was, Wolf." A part of herself—the part that wasn't furious with him, that was his friend and always would be—wanted to go to him, touch his arm, soothe his pain. But she stayed where she was.

Half an hour ago she would have trusted him with her life.

Now? Now, she wasn't sure she trusted him with anything at all.

"Think about it," he said curtly. "Dad only had one major enemy who was any threat to him."

There was only one person that could be. Cesare de Santis. Her father.

"No." She seemed to be saying that a lot lately. "That would mean that Dad had your parents killed. Which is quite patently ridiculous. Sure, he wasn't the most ethical person when he was in charge of DS Corp, but he wouldn't have people killed."

"How do you know? Do you have any proof that he didn't?"

"Do you have proof that he did?"

He shifted against the counter, and she tried not to watch the flex of his abs as he did so, angry with herself for even noticing. "Yeah. I do."

A stab of something sharp shot through her, making her shudder, like the first blow of an ax against the trunk of a tree. "You might think you have," she said quickly. "But whatever it is, you're wrong. Dad would never hurt anyone."

She wouldn't believe it. She couldn't. Her father was no saint, she'd always known that, but he'd never resort to murder. Just as he'd never "give" her to some man she didn't even know, the way Wolf was insisting.

Her father loved her. He needed her. He would never get rid of her.

Yes, he had his faults, but everyone did. At heart, he was a good man, she was certain.

Anyway, that was all beside the point. Wolf might simply be manipulating her again the way he'd manipulated her before he'd kissed her. Giving her a sad story, pretending he was hurt and trying to get her sympathy.

"You have no idea what kind of man your father is, Liv," he said harshly. "No fucking idea at all."

She pressed her lips together, not wanting to tell him he was wrong yet again, because it was obvious he wasn't going to listen. "You really expect me to believe any of this?" she asked instead. "You didn't kiss me because you wanted me, did you? And you didn't kidnap me to catch up. The only reason I'm here, the only reason you even touched me in the first place, is because you wanted that information and you didn't care how you got it."

His features hardened, a dangerous light glittering in his eyes. "Okay, if you want the truth, then yeah, that's exactly why you're here. Why I kissed you. I don't want you, Liv. I want what you know about Daniel May. I want access to your father's schedule and his email accounts. Because you know what else I'm going to do when I get them?" He pushed himself violently away from the counter. "I'm going burn his fucking empire down and him along with it."

Shock was a knife in her side. "Why? Simply because someone told you he murdered your father?"

"Yeah, exactly."

"No, that's insane. I mean, come on. After everything he did for you? You came to him, Wolf. You wanted his help and he gave it to you. He's done nothing but—"

"I came to him because Dad told me to. Because he needed a Tate on the inside of the de Santis family and thought I was the best bet." He was moving now, slowly walking over to her, stalking her like a giant panther, and she could feel fear kick hard in her chest. But she didn't move, shock deepening all around her. "Everyone underestimates me, Liv. Everyone thinks I'm stupid. But it's good, it means I can fly underneath the radar. So no one ever suspects, even your father." He stopped right in front of her, staring down at her, eyes glittering. "Even you."

There was a weird roaring sound in her ears and some part of her was dimly aware that she recognized the flame in his eyes now and it wasn't pain after all. It was anger.

Awareness filtered through her, of the tension in his posture. Of how he was holding himself so carefully, so tightly leashed. Not moving too fast, like a person with a headache not wanting to make it any worse.

But it wasn't because he was in pain. It was because he was furious.

"What do you mean, even me?" she asked stupidly.

"There's a reason I'm your friend, Liv. I was told to be. So I could get close enough to your father to take him down."

It didn't make any sense. None of it did.

She stared up at him, looking right into those furious mismatched eyes and his roughly handsome face. He wasn't the unformed boy she remembered. He was a man and there were scars on that face. One near his blue right eye and another on his jaw. Signs of experiences she never shared, things he'd done that she didn't know about.

He was supposed to be her friend, someone she knew well, and yet it was becoming very clear that she didn't know him at all.

Did you ever know him? Or did you just tell yourself you did?

"I . . ." she began thickly. "I don't believe you."

"Believe what you want." His mouth curled in something like a sneer. "It's all true. The only thing you need to know is that that fucking fuse is burning and your father is going down." Then before she could say anything, he brushed past her and headed toward the bedroom, slamming the double doors after him.

Olivia couldn't move, not for long seconds after the echo of that slam had died away. Eventually she moved over to the sofa and sat down, her legs shaking.

It couldn't be true. It couldn't. Ten years of friendship a lie. All those conversations they'd shared in the library, the sense that she'd found someone at last she could talk to, someone who listened to her the way no one ever had . . .

It was all a lie.

He hadn't been her friend because he'd liked her. He'd been her friend because his father had told him to. Because it had given him an inside to the de Santis family.

Grief twisted in her chest, stabbing deep into her heart, and then anger, roaring right behind it. Anger at him for the way he'd used her, and anger herself for believing him. She was supposed to be smart, supposed to be intelligent. And yet she'd been sucked in. One of those lazy smiles was all it had taken, the one that lit his eyes. One smile and she'd been his.

Something cool slid down her cheek and splashed on the back of one hand clasped in her lap.

Her jaw tightened. No, she couldn't do this. She couldn't sit here and give into grief and anger and recriminations. She didn't have time to examine all the implications either. Her most important priority now was getting out of here, getting back home, and getting away from him.

Olivia brushed another tear away, swallowing hard. Then she pushed all the pain and grief and rage firmly to one side. She'd deal with that later, when she had the time and space for it, but right now her number-one mission was to figure out how the hell she was going to get out of this hotel room and warn her father. Because he had to know that Wolf had somehow gone crazy and was throwing around wild threats.

Pushing herself up off the couch, she went down the short hallway and tried the door handle again. Still locked, dammit.

She stared down at it, frowning.

How had he managed to lock it from the inside? Clearly he had the ability to unlock it too since there were those trolleys of food sitting there indicating that room service had made a visit. So how had he done it?

It had to be something to do with what he'd done with the swipe card and the card reader since the lock still seemed to be functioning.

Puzzling it out, Olivia paced back down the hallway and into the living area again, pausing to stare at the big double doors of the bedroom that he'd slammed behind him.

Okay, maybe she could just ask him?

She didn't want to talk to him, she was still too furious, but she made herself go over to the doors and leaned in, trying to hear what he was doing. There was nothing but silence.

"Wolf?" She made her voice loud. "Full marks for taking me prisoner, that's really well done. But what if there's a fire? The door's locked from the inside."

There was no reply.

"Okay," she said to the door. "Thanks for your confession and everything, and for ruining the last ten years of my life, but I'm freaking out about the door. I don't particularly want to burn to death—"

"I can open it." He sounded pissed, his voice rougher and more gravelly than ever. "The lock responds to a code on my phone. I can get us out if worse comes to worst."

Ah, okay. So he *was* using his phone to control the lock. She had no idea how that worked, but if she could get hold of his phone and maybe figure out what code he was using, then she'd be able to get out.

Though, there was one small stumbling block to that plan.

He was six five of solid Navy SEAL muscle and she was five five of not very much muscle at all. He'd be able to stop her leaving without even breathing hard.

She cursed under her breath and paced the length of the living room, arms folded, her brain busy sorting through possibilities. What she really needed was to incapacitate him somehow, at least enough for her to get his phone and try the code. But how to do that?

Pausing, she scanned the room, looking for anything heavy that she might be able to use to hit him over the head with. But almost as soon as the thought occurred to her, she dismissed it.

He was a warrior, she was not. If by some miracle she even managed to hit him, she might not do it hard enough, or she'd strike a glancing blow and he'd get nothing but a bruised head instead of instant unconsciousness. Yes, and if that happened, he might tie her up. She definitely wouldn't get a second chance, that's for sure.

No, she couldn't hit him. She didn't like the thought of hurting him anyway, even though he was a complete bastard who'd ripped her heart into a thousand tiny pieces. She couldn't trust herself to go through with it. Which meant she had to think of something else.

She paced the room again, turning over more options in her mind, when her attention caught on the small, empty bottle of scotch he'd tossed onto the floor. He'd drained it and that wasn't the only thing he'd had to drink. There was the brandy he'd emptied into their coffee cups when they'd arrived here and then the glass of champagne. And that bottle . . . He'd emptied it quickly.

Olivia bent and picked it up, the beginnings of an idea forming in her head.

He must be tired, given it had been four a.m. when he'd come into her room. So he'd had to have been up even earlier than that. Not a lot of sleep. Then again, when he'd been talking about his training, he'd mentioned the fact that the candidates were used to operating on no sleep.

But what if she added more alcohol to the mix? He was a big guy, so he'd need a lot, yet he didn't seem to have any issues with draining that scotch. If she brought him more, he might drink that too.

Sadly, given his height and build and the size of the mini bottles, she didn't have enough alcohol to get him falling-down drunk. Especially if he wouldn't touch the wine. But would it be enough to get him to fall asleep? And if it was, how long would she have to wait for that to happen?

Letting out a breath, she moved over to the windows and looked out, her brain working furiously.

Staying here for too long was impossible, she *needed* to

get back home, tell her father what Wolf had been doing all this time, give him a warning—and as soon as possible.

"He killed my father."

Wolf's voice floated through her head, but she shoved it away.

She couldn't afford distractions, not now.

So, how to get a huge Navy SEAL to relax enough to lower his guard and fall helplessly asleep? Yes, that was the difficult question.

A memory filled her head, of an embarrassing kitchen conversation she'd had after coming downstairs one morning to find a woman dressed in nothing but one of her father's shirts, poking about in the fridge.

She'd been someone he'd picked up the night before at a function—mercifully she'd been a good ten years older than Olivia—and Olivia had ended up having the world's most awkward conversation with the woman. Especially when she'd started giving her details about her father she didn't ever want to know.

But one thing the woman had said was sticking in her brain, and for some reason Olivia couldn't get it out.

"Want to know my little trick for when you're done and they're still into it?" the woman had said, even though Olivia hadn't wanted to know. "Scotch and a blow job, honey. Get 'em drunk then give 'em a really good orgasm. It's more effective than a damn sleeping pill, honest." She'd then winked at her. "You'll thank me later."

It was later now and Olivia wasn't sure she wanted to thank the woman for putting that idea in her head. Because she had a horrible thought that though she could handle the getting Wolf drunk aspect, she wasn't sure at all about the orgasm part.

Breathlessness caught in her throat, her heart beginning to speed up.

Right, so even though Wolf Tate was a lying son of a bitch who'd single handedly destroyed their friendship within the space of a couple of minutes, her body apparently didn't care.

You could give him that orgasm.

The tightness in her throat constricted even further and she found herself staring at the closed bedroom doors.

She hadn't wanted to get closer to him before, not when she'd been sure he didn't actually want her—and she'd been right, he hadn't.

But . . . he hadn't been with anyone for six months if what he'd said was true. So maybe he'd respond to her? Maybe?

What about your heart? Your pride?

Too late for her heart and as for her pride, she'd sacrifice that without a second thought if it meant getting out of here.

Besides, there was no room for secret hopes and dreams, not now. Not that there had been any in the first place, but still. He'd given her the truth, torched their friendship to the ground, and now even that didn't matter anymore.

She knew exactly where she stood. He didn't care about her and he never had.

The pain of it cut deep, but again she shoved the emotion away, trying to view the problem objectively. Her inexperience was a serious stumbling block. She'd never seduced a guy before, but obviously she knew the mechanics. Knew that for a blow job you basically opened your mouth and. . . . sucked?

Logically that was the way to go, though. She wouldn't have to get naked, wouldn't have to worry about her virginity. All she had to do was put him in her mouth and make him come, and then with any luck, he'd go off to sleep.

What if he doesn't?

Olivia inhaled then let out another shaky breath. If he

didn't, then she'd have to think of something else, but this plan was as good as it got.

The only question now was how to broach the subject without making him suspicious? Because after she'd pushed him away so fiercely, he was going to guess that something was up, that something had made her change her mind.

Olivia stared at the bedroom doors for a long minute.

Then, her heart thumping, she moved over to the mini-bar and opened it, taking out a mini bottle of bourbon and forcing herself to approach the bedroom.

She lifted her hand and gave a soft knock. "Wolf? Can I come in?"

CHAPTER SIX

Wolf scowled at the sound of the knock and debated whether or not to tell her simply to go away. Because the last person in the entire world he wanted to see right now was her.

Especially given how spectacularly he'd blown up this entire fucking situation. Christ, if he'd ever needed any proof he couldn't organize a piss-up in a brewery, this was it. His plan—such as it was—had been badly thought out and poorly executed, and when things had gotten tough, he hadn't doubled down to get it done, he'd pressed the button and exploded it right in his face.

If his COs ever learned of it, they'd make him hand over his trident—and he would, without a second's thought.

He wasn't sure if it was even possible to fuck up more than he had already, but apparently, it was.

That truth had come out whether he'd wanted it to or not, and he hadn't been able to shut himself up, running at the mouth about how their entire friendship was a lie. That he'd only gotten close to her because his father had told him to.

He should never have said it, but he'd gotten so damn angry. Story of his fucking life. His SEAL training had been tough for precisely that reason, because he struggled to keep his feelings locked down and always had, no matter how hard his father had ridden him about it. But in the end he'd succeeded by burying them all beneath a fuck-you smile and a give-no-shits attitude.

Yet talking to Olivia, telling her the truth, had tripped something inside him and he hadn't been able to get a grip on the fury that had coursed through him. Fury at his father for dying before Wolf ever got the chance for the acknowledgment he wanted. Fury at Cesare de Santis for taking that chance away and for keeping Wolf's mother under threat, keeping him from the family he'd always wanted.

Fury at Olivia for believing it was all real when it wasn't.

Fury at himself for letting it matter and for not being able to lock it the fuck down when he should.

So much goddamn fury.

And he *still* hadn't gotten what he wanted out of her, and he didn't know what his next step was going to be.

"What the fuck do you want?" he demanded, staring at the closed doors.

"Are you hungry?" Her voice was slightly muffled. "There's all this food out here."

Why was she asking him that? Why was she speaking to him at all? After everything he'd said?

Ignoring her, he looked down at his phone, swiping through his list of contacts. Perhaps he should call Lucas. Talk to him about the evidence he'd collected on de Santis's gun-running operation, see if he had any links to May. Then again, maybe not. He didn't want Lucas to know what he was planning, and the asshole would definitely try to get that out of him.

Then fucking pull yourself together and stop sulking like a goddamn baby.

Yeah, he should. He really should. His COs didn't need to demand his trident; he'd hand it in himself for being such a pussy.

There was a soft click.

He looked up.

Olivia had come in anyway and was standing in the doorway. In that stupid nightgown, with her glossy dark brown hair down her back and no makeup, she looked as fresh-faced as a little girl. Except that little girls generally didn't have mini bottles of bourbon in their hands.

"What?" He made no effort to hide his bad temper. There wasn't any reason to after all, not now. "I'm not hungry."

"No, but are you thirsty?" She held up the bottle, coming over to the bed where he was sitting.

Bourbon. A mistake, given that scotch he'd just downed. Then again, why the fuck shouldn't he? Sure, he had to watch over Olivia, but it wasn't like she was getting out of here anytime soon, at least not by herself.

Hell, there wasn't much else to do but drink, at least until he could think of a better plan, so why the fuck not?

He put his phone on the nightstand and took the bottle she was holding out. Unscrewing the cap, he tipped his head back, taking a deep swallow. It was smooth going down, setting up a warm glow in the pit of his stomach.

Settling back against the pillows, he looked up at her.

She was standing beside the bed, her hands clasped loosely in front of her. There was a by-now familiar crease between her dark brows, and the way they flicked up at the ends made her look slightly wicked, now that he thought about it.

"Well"—he took another swallow of the bourbon, eyeing her—"you got something to say to me?"

Her gaze was direct and he couldn't tell what she was thinking. "I want to do a deal with you."

"A deal? What kind of deal?"

"I'll do something for you if . . . you do something for me."

He took another swig of the bourbon. "Yeah, yeah, that's usually what deals are. Christ, give me the specifics, Liv."

Her delicate fingers knotted as if she was nervous, yet there was a very determined slant to her jaw that told him she was going to do this come hell or high water. "I'll give you the information you want, if . . ." She stopped, then looked away from him. Color stained her cheekbones.

What the hell was going on now? He hadn't known what he'd expected when the truth about his double-agent status came out, but he'd have thought anger would be the least of it.

When he'd told her, she'd gone white and shocked looking, and he'd stormed off because he'd needed to get away from her and the pain in her eyes, the hurt that felt like a knife in his own soul.

He'd been prepared for her anger, yet it wasn't anger in her eyes now. It was definitely nervousness, which he didn't understand. What kind of deal was she trying to make with him?

"If what?" he prompted when she didn't say anything.

Olivia kept her gaze on the wall behind his head, remaining silent so long he thought she wasn't going to answer. Then she inhaled and her deep blue gaze came to his. "While we're being honest with each other, there's something you should know. I kind of lied when I told you that I didn't want you. The truth is . . . I do."

That wasn't a surprise. He'd known it the moment she hadn't been able to drag her gaze from his chest, and the kiss he'd given her, the way she'd remained completely still under his mouth, had only confirmed it.

"And?" He took another swig from the bottle, the

bourbon glowing warmly inside him, making everything seem a shitload better than it had five minutes ago.

Her blue eyes were dark. "I've actually wanted you since I was fifteen years old, Wolf. The moment I saw you."

It took a while for the shock to get past the bourbon in his veins, but when it did, all he could do was stare at her. "Seriously? But, you never said—"

"I didn't say anything because you were a Tate. You were the enemy. And then when you weren't the enemy anymore, I was too shy to say anything. I wasn't used to talking to people much, not people who were interested in me and I . . ." She stopped again, glancing away, her throat moving as she swallowed. "I didn't want to do anything that would stop you coming to the library."

Something twisted in his chest, a knife turning, scraping bone.

Jesus, why did that hurt? It made no sense. Their friendship hadn't even been real in the first place, so the loss of it shouldn't have hurt. Certainly hearing her tell him how she'd wanted him shouldn't.

Apparently though, it did.

He couldn't think of a word to say to that, but luckily, she went on without waiting for him to speak.

"So anyway, I wanted you. And I guess I still do. And since our friendship doesn't matter anymore and those conversations we had in the library are long gone, I thought now is as good a chance as any to get what I want." She glanced back at him again and her chin lifted slightly, her back straightening. Steeling herself for whatever it was she had to say.

You already know what she's going to say.

Yeah, he had some idea. For some reason it made his pulse begin to accelerate, his heartbeat sounding oddly loud in his ears.

She held his gaze this time, her hands twisted in front of her. "I want to give you an orgasm. A . . . you know . . . a b-blow j-job."

Holy shit. That was *not* the first thing he'd thought she'd say. Maybe another kiss or maybe she wanted to touch him again, but a blow job?

"You're kidding me," he said incredulously. "Now?"

The color in her cheeks blazed, a small blue flame of anger lighting her eyes, obviously not pleased with his re-action. "Yes, now," she snapped. "And don't look at me like that. You were the one who told me you hadn't been with anyone in six months." One brow arched. "Or was that yet another lie?"

Fucking hell. This was insane.

Shock seeped slowly through him. He'd kissed her and she'd pushed him away, making it very clear she didn't want to go any further. Yet now she was coming in here and telling him she wanted to give him a BJ? What the fuck was going on?

"Seriously?" he demanded, ignoring the question. "After you shoved me away before, *now* you suddenly want to suck my cock?"

Her chin lifted even higher, the look on her face becom-ing haughty despite her flaming cheeks. "I shoved you away because you didn't want me, you only wanted the informa-tion I had and apparently didn't mind seducing me for it. So now I've decided that since you don't care about me or our friendship, I'll take a little something for myself. You get to have an orgasm and the information you want, while I . . . I get to have one of my fantasies and then you let me go."

Christ, this was the last thing he was expecting. And it should have been a relatively simple thing to say "No, I don't want a blow job," because really, he couldn't take her up on it. Not after the things he'd said to her. Not after the way he'd hurt her.

And yet . . .

He couldn't stop looking into her serious blue eyes, because they were always serious. That was Olivia. A serious, earnest little thing, whose face had lit up whenever she'd seen him and whom he'd always looked forward to seeing, too. It had been wrong to let himself like her knowing that in the end he'd betray her, but he hadn't been able to help himself.

Even now, even in this fucked-up mess of a situation he'd created, he felt a kind of respect for her. That he'd been an utter prick to her and yet here she was, facing him down, taking something for herself despite everything he'd done. Finding her own way out of the situation and quite frankly doing it a hell of a lot better than he was.

Or maybe that was bourbon talking. Hell, he couldn't tell.

He let his head fall back on the pillows. "So lemme get this straight. You'll give me the information and in return I let you give me head."

"Yes." She gave a little nod. "That's right."

"Okay, first of all, a girl never needs to ask me if she can suck my dick because the answer will always be yes. And second, this sounds like a fucking one-sided deal to me."

"Why? We both get what we want."

"Sure, but I get the best of it, don't you think?"

"Do you?" The look in her eyes was suddenly sharp. "You don't want me, Wolf. You never did. So I can't imagine what you're getting out of it, barring an orgasm of course."

He hadn't wanted her, no. And he could see how that hurt her. But now . . . well, that wasn't quite the case. The thought of her lovely rosebud mouth closing around his cock. . . . A hot rush swept through him, all the blood in his body heading south.

But that was because he hadn't had sex for six months,

surely? Wanting her in particular, after all the lies he'd fed her, seemed wrong. Then again, could he afford to turn her down if that would give him the information about May he needed? If she gave him access to her father's schedule?

Yeah, tell yourself it's all about the intel.

He ignored the thought, turning his head on the pillow. "You really want to do this?"

She didn't look away and didn't hesitate. "Yes."

"After everything I said to you?"

"Yes."

He studied her, noting the color in her cheeks. She didn't look afraid. She looked . . . determined.

Sexy. Not.

"Have you ever done it before?" he asked, already knowing what the answer was going to be.

"No," she said, confirming his suspicions. Then she sniffed. "But I'm sure that won't be a problem."

Jesus. He was starting to feel a bit muzzy around the edges. He normally had a good head for alcohol, but he'd cut back while he'd been on deployment and it was becoming apparent that little sleep the night before, and a lot of spirits on top of a glass of wine, was a bad idea.

He blinked slowly at her, finding himself focusing on her mouth. It really was perfect. Full bottom lip, cushiony top lip, and as he knew from that kiss, so fucking soft.

Been a long time since he'd had a mouth like that one on him. A very, *very* long time.

She's inexperienced. She's your friend. And now you're going to let her give you a blow job. What the fuck are you doing?

He didn't know. But seeing as how she wasn't his friend anymore and this had been all her idea, he was starting to think that he might let her do whatever she wanted to him. After all, he sure as hell didn't have a better plan for getting that information.

He forced himself to look at her and not fixate on her mouth. "You want me to tell you what to do?"

"No." She continued to give him that haughty look. "This isn't for you, Wolf, understand? I'm taking this for me."

There was something in her eyes that made that knife scrape through him again, and he didn't know whether it was loss or grief of pain, but what he did know was that he'd been the one to put it there.

"I'm sorry," he said impulsively, the words a touch more slurred than he would have liked them to be. "I'm sorry I lied, Liv. I'm sorry I hurt you. You were never meant—" He stopped. She'd always been going to get hurt and he knew it.

She'd never had a friend, or so she'd told him. At least not one who listened to her the way he did. Locked away in her father's house, she'd always been heavily protected. The youngest and the only girl, she hadn't been allowed to go to school, being taught by an army of private tutors instead, everywhere she went being tailed by at least two bodyguards.

Her life reminded him a bit of Chloe's, his adoptive sister, but at least Chloe had the Tate ranch to roam around on. Olivia had nothing but her father's Upper East Side mansion. She hadn't seemed to mind though. She'd told him that she liked that her father protected her. It made her feel cared for, loved . . .

"Don't apologize." Grown-up Olivia's calm, practical voice this time, edged with sweetness. "I know you don't mean it."

"Bullshit," he muttered. "Of course I mean it. Hurting you was never the intention."

"But you knew what would happen if I found out." She was staring down at his groin now, a frown creasing her forehead, as if working out how to get started. "And you went ahead and did it anyway."

"Yeah, but—"

"You should stop talking now." Before he could respond, Olivia put out a tentative hand and brushed the front of his fly with her fingertips.

And all the breath left his body.

She heard it, the sudden hiss as she let her fingers graze the denim of his jeans, right down the front of his zipper. The material felt rough against her skin and she could feel the outline of him beneath it. Long. Hard. Getting harder.

She blinked and took her hand away, glancing up at his face.

He was laying back against the pillows, his massive, long body stretched out on the comforter, ankles crossed, still with his boots on. The snowy white of the linen somehow made him seem even bigger, even more dangerous than he already was. He'd put his black thermal on again and that combined with the blue jeans, black boots, and his coal black hair, all those dark colors standing out against the white, made him look . . . almost demonic.

Except for his eyes. Those special blue and green eyes. They were glowing now, and judging by the stain of color on his sculpted cheekbones, he was either starting to suffer the effects of the alcohol he'd been drinking or maybe her touch had actually affected him.

"Do that again." His voice was thick and gritty, full of sand.

You did affect him.

A surge of something that felt awfully like satisfaction filled her, but she shoved it away quickly. She didn't want to get into that. Didn't want to get into feeling pleased that she'd done something to him. This wasn't about him and his pleasure. This was about her and what she wanted.

When she'd first entered the room she'd tried to tell

herself that this was simply part of a mission she had to do, an operation to rescue herself, so there was no point in being nervous. She didn't have to enjoy it. She didn't even have to like it and that it was better not to, because it wouldn't ever happen again.

Yet he was laying there like a big lazy panther, and she knew that no matter how many times she told herself this was simply part of a mission, it was never going to be just that.

She wanted him. She always had. And okay, so he didn't want her, but what did that matter? She could take this moment for herself. She could savor it, enjoy it. And she would always have it, no matter what happened to her in the future.

New experiences were far and few between in her life, her father's protection being what it was, so why shouldn't she fully give herself over to this one? Why should she view it as a mission?

She hadn't been fully truthful with him though. This wasn't actually a fantasy of hers, mainly because she didn't let herself ever have fantasies about him, not when they weren't ever going to come true. But now . . .

Oh yes, now she could have this particular fantasy. And she could make it come true.

She lifted her hand, ran her fingers lightly over the front his jeans a second time. Again, he sucked in a breath, long, black lashes veiling the glow in his eyes momentarily. "Yeah, I like that. Do it again, baby. Harder."

"Baby." He'd called her "baby." She wasn't sure if she liked it. She wasn't sure she liked him ordering her around either, not when this was her fantasy, not his.

"No," she said and took her hand away.

His lashes flicked up, the heat in his eyes focusing into a narrow beam and straight at her. As if he could will her to do what he wanted with the power of his gaze alone.

It nearly worked too, her hand reaching out to him. But she stopped herself at the last minute. This wasn't for him and she didn't want him telling her what to do. She wanted to discover it for herself, explore him the way she wanted to. For once in her life please herself instead of someone else.

"All right, suit yourself." Wolf lifted his arms and put his hands behind his head. "But if you need some tips, just let me know." His lashes fell again and it looked for a second like he'd gone to sleep.

That was good, wasn't it? Maybe she wouldn't need to do this at all. Maybe if she remained quiet and didn't move, he'd fall deeply enough asleep that she could grab his phone without him noticing.

You don't really want to do this after all, do you?

She swallowed, realization hitting that now she was going to have to touch him again. Unzip his fly and touch him. Put her mouth on him. Make him come. It had been all fine in the abstract, but now that the moment was actually here . . .

Maybe she should have accepted his offer of instruction?

She stared at down at his body laid out on the bed, trying to think about how to begin, to approach it the way she approached some of the business problems she ran into with her father's various interests. Breaking something down into various, smaller tasks and concentrating on those, was the usual way she handled it, so maybe that would work here.

So first of all she needed to get his thermal off, because if there was one thing she wanted to do, it was to touch all that muscle he'd had on display. All those fascinating tattoos.

But should she get him to do it? Or should she just . . . get on him or something and push the fabric up herself?

Getting him to take it off was the most logical thing and yet there was a part of her that didn't want him to move. She wanted to do it herself.

Or you could just leave him to go to sleep. Because he probably will. The whole orgasm thing isn't really necessary and you know it.

Her heart was beating loud in her ears and her breathing was fast. No, it wasn't necessary. But she'd told herself it was a vital part of her plan because letting herself have things she wanted had always been very difficult for her. Especially things she wanted very, very badly.

You always lose them . . .

But she couldn't lose this moment and it couldn't be taken away, could it? Right now, she had it. Right now, she had him.

A brief moment of fear caught at her though she had no idea why, dismissing it before she could examine it too closely. Instead she studied him a second longer then, gathering her nightgown in one hand, she raised it up and climbed up onto the bed.

It was awkward, but if she refused the fear, she refused the embarrassment as well, arranging herself so she was kneeling upright astride his powerful thighs. He didn't move, but she could see the gleam of his eyes beneath his lashes—he wasn't asleep after all. He was watching her.

She sucked in a silent breath, her heartbeat getting louder. The denim of his jeans felt rough against the inside of her knees and he was so . . . hot. But then she'd felt how hot he'd been earlier, hadn't she?

Her mouth had gone dry. One thing to think about all of this, quite another to do it. To be kneeling over the man she'd been in love with for most of her adult life. The man she'd never allowed herself to fantasize about, because it was safer that way, easier to deal with.

If you can't ever have it, you can't ever be hurt when it's taken away.

And right now, no one could take this from her.

Olivia inhaled yet again, trying to get herself to calm down.

Okay, so don't think about the whole task, just the next step. What did she want to do now? Touch him . . .

Slowly, she lowered herself down so she was sitting on his thighs. She could feel the muscles beneath her tighten in response though he made no other move. God, again the heat of him shocked her. She hadn't expected to notice it or even that she'd like it. But she did. She really did.

Her skin tightened, goose bumps rising. There was a heavy sensation between her thighs, a kind of throb.

Desire.

She'd felt it before, sometimes at night, in dreams. Formless dreams that she never remembered when she woke up, but that left her hot and sweaty and aching. She didn't like to think about those feelings, so she always ignored them.

But she had the thought, sitting astride Wolf's prone body, that those feelings may not be so easy to ignore now. Not now she was here and he was beneath her.

Perhaps this wasn't such a great idea after all. Perhaps she should just get off him and leave him to sleep.

"Hmmm," he murmured, sapphire and emerald glittering under those long silky lashes. "Changed your mind already?"

There was something in his rough voice that crept under her skin like a burr. A kind of challenge. Or a dare.

It made her stiffen, a flash of irritation going through her. "I'm not afraid, if that's what you're thinking," she said curtly.

"Well, of course not." This time there was an edge of

amusement in his tone. "Olivia de Santis afraid of a little old blow job? Never."

He was mocking her now, which annoyed her. It also made her want to show him that she really *wasn't* afraid, which was puzzling when she'd already decided she didn't care what he thought of her. But somehow she couldn't let it go. He thought she was trapped here, he thought she couldn't escape.

She'd show him. She'd show six feet five of muscle-bound Navy SEAL who was afraid and who wasn't.

Olivia said nothing. Instead she reached down and pulled at the fabric of his thermal, sliding it up his body and under his arms, revealing all that beautiful, sculpted muscle, tanned skin, and vivid ink.

One corner of his mouth lifted, but she didn't want to look at his face, because that hint of a smile and the gleam of his eyes were doing things to her she wasn't comfortable with. So she looked down at his chest instead, reaching out her hands to touch him, placing both palms down on his pecs.

Oh . . . God. So hot and so unbelievably hard. Yet his skin was smooth, satiny, with the slight prickle of hair.

She swallowed, sliding her palms down his torso, watching the cut muscles of his taut stomach flex and release as she touched him. He felt . . . so good. Better than anything she expected.

Finally touching him, after all those years . . .

Her throat tightened and there was a part of her that wanted to snatch her hands away and run from the room, forget any of this had ever happened. But somehow she couldn't bring herself to do it. He was here and he was letting her touch him and, God, she couldn't stop.

She stroked him, mesmerized by the play of his abs, by his ink, by the rise and fall of his massive chest, the slide of the dog tag chain across his skin as he breathed. Hot. . . .

She couldn't get over his heat and how her fingers felt scorched, like they would catch fire at any second. And her heartbeat was so loud she couldn't hear anything else.

She'd never thought about touching a man like this. Never allowed herself to, not even Wolf. She'd loved him but always from afar, always from a distance.

But there was no distance now. He wasn't merely a new email in her inbox, with stories from whichever place he'd been deployed. Or even a name in the "To" line of one her own emails, pouring her heart out to him about what was happening in her life. He wasn't the memory of a tall, lanky boy who'd sat sprawled out in her father's library, listening to her talk.

He wasn't the guy in the photos he'd sent her, cradling a gun or looking hot in a uniform.

He was a living, breathing man who was lying right beneath her and she was touching him and it was real. It was *all* real. The hard heat of his body, the feel of his skin under her hands, the sound of his breathing . . .

This was the man she loved. And he was right here.

A small, cold current of fear wound through her.

Loving Wolf Tate had been easy, because he'd existed only in her head. In her memory and in her imagination, fueled by his emails and the very rare phone calls. Her love had been an abstract thing, composed of longing and excitement, and a thrilling sort of nervousness. It hadn't been physical, because she'd never let herself think of him like that.

Because it made you uncomfortable. It made you want, and you can't ever want.

A tremble went through her and she found herself staring at the harsh lines of his beautiful face. That mobile, perfect mouth. The gleam in his fascinating eyes.

And it came to her, very suddenly, that this wasn't safe any longer. He didn't exist in her head now, a construct she'd invented to channel all the love she had inside her into. A nice safe ideal to worship from afar without ever getting close.

But if she continued with this, she'd definitely get close. And if she did, something would change inside her. A door would be opened that she'd always kept safely closed, and all the desires and needs she'd been keeping locked away would flood out. Real desires. Real needs. With hard, sharp edges that would cut her to pieces.

She'd let herself want before. She never wanted to again.

Olivia snatched her hands away from him, fear a cold stone in the center of her chest. Abruptly all she wanted was to get as far away from him as possible, put some of that distance between them right back again.

Except Wolf must have realized something was wrong, because he sat up, and put his hands on her hips, large warm palms sliding down over her butt. Holding gently but firmly right where she was in his lap.

"Hey," he murmured, frowning, his gaze searching hers. "What's up?"

She had to fight to breathe, to not show a hint of her fear, because there was no way she could explain to him what the problem was. Not without revealing herself completely, and she couldn't do that. Telling him she wanted him was one thing, but telling him she loved him was quite another.

Do you love him though? Or did you only love the idea of him? You don't really know him after all.

The thought made her breathless and she couldn't stop staring at him, the familiarity of his face changing, becoming someone else's. A man with lines and scars, with experiences she didn't know about and maybe never would. A man who wasn't that boy she remembered, or the guy she'd imagined sending her those emails.

A stranger.

His frown deepened and he lifted a hand, brushing a strand of hair behind her ear, his fingertips grazing her skin as he did so, sending a shiver of reaction right through her. "You looked scared," he said quietly. "You know I would never hurt you, Liv. Never ever."

Her throat constricted and she couldn't speak, not that she knew what to say anyway. She simply wanted to get off him and get away. Pretend this had never happened.

But then you'll never escape.

Yes, she could. She'd just . . . wait outside until he went to sleep. Or ply him with more alcohol. Actually, that was a good start, wasn't it? She'd go get him something else from the minibar.

"G-Gin," she forced out. "Would you like some gin?"

His frown deepened. "Gin?"

"I could go and get some for you." She was achingly aware of his body underneath hers, of the firm press of his thighs against her butt, and the warmth of one palm resting on her butt cheek. All that insane heat he put out was soaking into her, making her skin feel tight and her mouth dry. Sending her pulse into the stratosphere.

And now he was sitting up, his chest was mere inches from hers, and it was like he was everywhere, surrounding her with heat and that dark cedar and leather scent.

It was too much for her. *He* was too much for her.

She wanted to push him away, but that would involve touching him and she'd already discovered what a bad idea that was.

He stared at her, obviously puzzled. "I don't want any gin. I thought you wanted to give me a blow job?"

"No," she said thickly. "I've changed my mind."

"Why? Did I do something you didn't want? Did I scare you?"

She couldn't look at him. Her heartbeat wasn't slowing

down and her fingers itched to touch him again, slide under his thermal and stroke his skin. Learn what it was like to touch a man like him . . .

No, God no. She couldn't.

"Liv?" One thumb and forefinger gripped her chin gently, turning her face toward him. "What's wrong, baby?" There was concern in his voice and she could see it in his gaze too.

And she remembered the day in the library when she'd been struggling with the anniversary of her mother's death, and he'd noticed she wasn't herself, and had asked what was wrong. There hadn't been any reason not to tell him, so she had and he'd pulled her into his arms and given her a hug.

She'd burst into tears, because no one had hugged her like that for years, not even when her mother had died, and she'd forgotten how good it was to be held. To be comforted and reassured.

It had been years since that hug, years since she'd seen that same concern and warmth in another person's eyes, because although she knew her father loved her, he was a cold man and he never showed it.

And she knew that if she didn't get up and leave right now, she'd burst into tears like she had all those years ago. All it would take was for Wolf to open his arms and hold her the way he had before, and the door inside her would burst wide open.

And she didn't know what would happen to her if it did.

"Let me go, Wolf." Her hands curled into unconscious fists. "Please, let me go."

CHAPTER SEVEN

He didn't know what the fuck had changed, but the distress in Olivia's lovely blue eyes was real and it made his chest hurt. He couldn't think where it had come from either, because she'd looked like she was into it.

Shit, *he'd* been into it.

Her slight weight pressing down on his thighs and the heat between her legs so very close to his aching groin had been a delight he'd never imagined.

He wasn't much into teasing or dragging things out when it came to sex. He was too impatient, wanting to get down to the business of orgasms pretty much straight-away—no fucking around, so to speak.

But the way Olivia had touched him—half hesitant, half eager—stroking him as if he were a work of art, had been one of the most erotic experiences of his life. And he'd be fucked if he knew why. All she'd done was touch him, for Christ's sake.

Yet there had been something about the feel of her fingers on his skin and the way she was sitting on him, about the prim, plain white cotton of her nightgown and the deep glow in her midnight eyes, that had turned him on like nobody's business.

The expression on her face had been so serious and yet there had been an element of wonder in it too, that had mesmerized him. Because what had been so wonderful about touching him? Plenty of women had touched him and never looked at him like that, not once.

But then everything had changed and she'd looked almost afraid, snatching her hands from him like he'd burned her.

"Hey, hey," he murmured, stroking his thumb over her chin in an unconscious soothing movement. "Where's the fire?"

But she only stiffened, jerking her head out of his grip and scrambling awkwardly up and off him.

"Liv." He made a grab for her and missed as she slid off the bed. "What the hell is wrong?"

But all she said was, "I'll go get the gin," before turning and leaving the bedroom.

He stared after her, surprised and not a little pissed.

Okay, if she wouldn't tell him what the issue was, then that was her choice. She certainly didn't owe him an explanation either, not after the way he'd treated her. But he really didn't like the idea that perhaps he'd scared her.

Kind of like closing the barn door after the horse has bolted and all that shit.

He sat back against the pillows and scowled, scrubbing a hand through his hair.

He hadn't been fine with scaring her earlier, no matter that fear was a useful tool and blah de fucking blah. And he wasn't fine with it now.

She was Olivia, and no matter that he'd destroyed their friendship, he still liked her. Still didn't want to hurt her.

And now you're pissed that she's not going to give you a blow job.

Yeah, that too.

He could feel the lingering warmth of her across his thighs, and the touch of her fingers on his chest, and his dick ached like a bastard. He'd never thought about her in that way before, yet now he could think of nothing else but having her lips wrapped around his cock.

"Fuck," he muttered under his breath, because the obvious conclusion was that he'd gotten impatient and scared her or something. Except he couldn't think of what it was that he'd done except tell her what he'd wanted a couple of times, then put his hands behind his head so he wouldn't reach for her.

Olivia appeared again in the bedroom doorway and waved the mini bottle of gin she must have taken from the minibar. "Here. Do you want anything with it? I think there was some tonic water, but I'd have to go check."

"I don't want any gin." He knew he sounded grumpy and sulky, but didn't give a shit. "I want you to tell me what went wrong."

She moved to the side of the bed and put the bottle on the nightstand. "I just . . . changed my mind, okay? Have the gin instead."

"What is it with you and the gin? Are you trying to get me drunk or something?"

Her cheeks colored and he could see by the way her gaze flickered that that's exactly what she'd been trying to do. "I just thought you might like some."

Yeah, right.

Not that it mattered if she was trying to get him drunk. It wasn't as if she could escape easily, not with the code to the door lock on his phone. Anyway, although he was tired and muzzy around the edges from the scotch he'd had, the sexual frustration she'd left him with was likely to keep him from getting any drunker.

"I don't," he said shortly. "At least tell me I didn't do anything to you."

Her gaze flickered again. "It wasn't you. It was me. That's all you need to know."

It should have been a relief to hear that, but for some reason, it wasn't.

"Okay. Good to hear." He folded his arms. "Maybe you could go help yourself to all that food. I need some time-out." He didn't bother to hide the pissiness in his tone, even though he knew it was making him sound like an angry little boy. He was tired and sexually frustrated, but what he really wanted from her was the truth. And she wasn't giving it to him.

It made him even angrier that he knew he had no right to demand it from her either.

The expression on her face was impossible to read, but he thought he saw something that looked like hurt flicker in the depths of her blue eyes. Then it was gone. "Fair enough," she said and turned, disappearing through the doorway, her white nightgown flowing out behind her.

Fucking pull yourself together.

Wolf muttered another curse, then despite his better judgment, already impaired by the other spirits he'd downed—not to mention the demands of his sadly ignored dick—he grabbed the bottle of gin off the nightstand and unscrewed the cap. Taking a healthy swallow, he reached for his phone and glanced down at it, sorting through the various emails he'd received, all of which were bullshit.

Five minutes later, he'd finished the bottle and his annoyance was fading. The warm glow already in his stomach glowed even warmer, and he couldn't resist closing his eyes for a second, his brain helpfully feeding him images of Olivia sitting astride him, looking at him with that hot blue flame in her eyes.

He liked that, liked it very much, and pretty soon he had fallen into a weird dream where she was constantly touching him, yet never getting any closer to the place he *really* wanted her to touch. And every time he tried to grab her hand and show her, he kept grabbing at empty air instead.

Consciousness arrived some time after that, along with a disgusting-tasting mouth, a headache stabbing him behind the eyes, and a hard-on that wouldn't quit.

Groaning, he groped around for his phone to check the time, because he'd been certain he'd been looking at it just before he passed out.

But it wasn't there.

Wolf cursed, forced his eyes open, and looked around on the bed. He seemed to have got himself tangled up in the comforter, but after a second or two of untangling, it was clear the phone definitely hadn't gotten caught up in the fabric. It wasn't on the nightstand either.

Shit. What the hell had he done with it?

Muttering more curses and scrubbing at his hair, he hauled himself off the bed and went out into the living area, only to find his phone sitting on the coffee table.

Weird. He could have sworn he'd had it in his hand before he'd nodded off.

Moving over to the coffee table, he picked the phone up and pocketed it, belatedly realizing that the room was strangely quiet. Not to mention empty.

He looked around, his headache pounding. "Liv?"

There was no answer.

What the fuck?

His stomach dropped away as he turned around a second time, searching the room again, just in case he'd missed anything. But she definitely wasn't there.

He went back into the bedroom, pushing open the door to the bathroom.

It was empty.

Growling, he made another meticulous, fruitless check of the entire hotel room, but she wasn't there.

Somehow, Olivia had gotten out.

Fury gathered inside him. How the *fuck* had she done it? The door had been goddamn locked from the inside, there was no way she could have unlocked it. No way in hell.

Unless she accessed the code on your cell phone.

Oh Jesus Christ. She'd asked him about the door, about how it had been locked, and he'd told her because she'd sounded worried about it. And there was no way could she have used that against him because she would have had to know his code. No one knew his code.

Yeah, so how the hell did she get out?

Snarling, Wolf grabbed his phone from his pocket and looked down at it, unlocking the screen with his thumb. The app he'd used to override the room lock was open.

Holy shit. She must have guessed his code.

Beneath the fury—mainly directed at himself for once again screwing things totally like the giant fuck-up he was—something inside him went quiet and still.

His code was the date Noah had adopted him, and for some inexplicable reason, she'd remembered it. How? No one knew that date except Noah and his brothers—and his brothers wouldn't remember, and Noah was dead.

You told her. Remember?

He blinked, staring down at the phone in his hand.

Fuck, that's right. One of those evenings in the library, talking with her while he'd waited for his meeting with de Santis, and she'd seemed very quiet, very withdrawn. So he'd asked her what was wrong and her blue eyes had filled with tears, and she'd told him that it was the anniversary of her mother's death.

She'd looked so sad and small that he'd pulled her into his arms for a hug before he'd even thought about it. Then she'd laid her head on his chest and cried silently, shaking. Her grief had shocked him, especially since she'd always seemed so self-contained, and he hadn't known what to say. He'd never had to comfort anyone before.

So he'd said the first thing that had come into his head,

about how his mother had had to give him up for adoption, because she was homeless and hadn't been able to afford to take care of him, how even though he didn't remember her, he wished he did. He didn't mention that his mother was still alive and that Noah was trying to find her. He'd simply wanted Olivia to know that he understood her feelings of loss. Then he'd babbled on about how he'd committed the date of his adoption to memory as a way of honoring her, and he'd said it out loud, sharing it with her as she'd wept.

He'd never thought she'd remember it. He'd never thought she'd even heard it. But she *had* heard and she *had* remembered.

And now he was well and truly fucked.

Shoving the phone back into his pocket, he headed toward the door, then stopped. There was no use going after her. She was probably long gone by now, back home to her father no doubt. She'd tell him what had happened, warn him that Wolf was coming for him, giving him a whole lot of time to protect himself and making blowing him away a hell of a lot harder.

"*Fuck!*" Wolf turned and kicked the armchair, which happened to be the nearest piece of furniture, shoving it into the coffee table and knocking that over too. Magazines spilled everywhere, the champagne flutes rolling onto the carpet.

He was very tempted to keep going, to pick up some more stuff and hurl it around the room, but that wouldn't solve anything. He had to pull himself together, calm the fuck down, and decide what his next move was going to be.

Taking a couple of deep breaths, he forced his tense muscles to relax, got his raging heartbeat under control.

His brain should have been thinking about May and figuring out what alternatives there were if de Santis knew he was coming, but all he could seem to focus on was

Olivia. On the distress that had crossed her face as she'd sat astride him on the bed earlier that morning. On how she'd remembered a date that he'd told her only once, years and years ago. On how she'd outsmarted him—her, the sheltered daughter of a weapons billionaire with no physical skills to speak of, getting away from a hardened Navy SEAL with eight years military experience.

He could almost admire it if she hadn't fucked with his plans so completely.

Let her go. You can't reach her now. De Santis will make sure she's untouchable anyway.

Wolf growled deep in his throat. So what was he left with? He needed that info on May to take that particular asshole down, and he needed de Santis's schedule in order to get around de Santis's own insane security. And he didn't have either of those things.

Which left him with only one option: taking Olivia back.

She'd have warned her father, no doubt about that, which meant his plan to take de Santis out while the element of surprise was still on Wolf's side was well and truly fucked. But maybe he could use Olivia as bait to lure de Santis out. Then take him down. Yeah, that might work.

There are alternatives to Olivia. You had some backup plans, remember?

But he didn't want the backup plans. He didn't want the alternatives.

He wanted Olivia and he was fucking going to have her.

And no one was going to get in his way.

Including himself.

"And you really didn't get a glimpse of him?"

Olivia met her father's intense blue eyes and slowly shook her head. "No. He put a hood over my head so I couldn't see anything. I tried, Dad. I really tried. But there was nothing I could do about it."

She wasn't quite sure why she was lying to her father about the reason for her disappearance from her room the night before, especially when she'd been so desperate to warn him about Wolf's intentions to take him down.

Yet when the moment came to say it, somehow she couldn't.

Perhaps it had been the date that had been the code to unlock the door.

When Wolf had finally fallen asleep and she'd grabbed his phone—cautiously picking up his big hand and pressing his thumb against the button to unlock the screen—she'd initially had trouble finding the app. He'd hidden it in an apparently innocuous folder, which had taken her a little while to figure out. Then, when she'd opened it, she'd keyed in a code that she thought would work—his birthday—only to find that it wasn't right and she was only allowed three tries before the app deleted itself.

Then she'd cursed herself because of course it wouldn't be his birthday. It had to be something less obvious. So she'd thought and thought, trying to figure out what number would have meaning for him.

She didn't know why the date of his adoption had occurred to her. Perhaps it had been the memory of the hug he'd given her all those years ago, and how he'd told her about his own mother, who wasn't dead but who was just as lost to him as her own mother was lost to her.

Whatever, the date had popped into her head and she'd put it into the phone with shaking fingers.

And heard the door unlock.

She'd felt a surge of some emotion she didn't recognize sweep through her in that moment, though it wasn't the triumph that she'd expected. It had been more like . . . regret. Which didn't make any sense.

She hadn't stuck around to figure it out though, moving quickly to the door and pulling it open. She'd moved fast, expecting him to wake up and come after her with every step, but the alcohol must have put him out completely because she reached the first floor without him appearing.

At the check-in desk, she'd made up some story about losing her room key and could she borrow the phone to call a family member. Then she'd paced nervously around the foyer, keeping an eye on the elevators, waiting for her father to send someone to pick her up.

Now she was back in the familiarity of the de Santis mansion, showered and changed out of that damn nightgown, sitting in one of the armchairs in the living room being interrogated by a furious Cesare.

And he *was* furious. She could always tell because his eyes went flat and cold.

He stood in front of the fireplace, his hands in the pockets of his dark suit pants, radiating an icy anger that frightened a lot of people, but didn't frighten her because she knew it wasn't her he was angry at.

He was angry at Wolf, even though he didn't know it had been Wolf who had taken her.

She still couldn't think why she hadn't told him. Why hadn't she mentioned that Wolf had been playing both of them all along and he was intent on taking her father down. That, at the very least, she should mention.

Yet she couldn't seem to get the words out. The code that had unlocked the door was stuck in her head, the date of his adoption, in memory of his mother who'd had to give him up, unable to afford to look after him, and all she could think about was the fury in his eyes as he'd told her that Cesare was the reason his father had died. Cesare had had him killed.

Family had always been important to Wolf, and even more so because the family he'd had was so dysfunctional. She knew how she grieved for the one he should have had, because she'd sensed it. Had heard it in his voice the few times he'd spoken about it.

No wonder he'd been so furious. He'd lost that family and clearly blamed her father for it, believing completely in the lie that Cesare had had his father killed.

The day he'd told her about his mother, when he'd put his arms around her and held her as she'd grieved for the loss of her own, she'd put her head on his chest, feeling the reassuring strength and warmth of him ease the pain inside her. And he'd talked about his mom. He'd only been three when he'd been adopted, so he had no memories of her.

She'd heard the grief in his voice, heard his pain, and maybe that's when she'd fallen in love with him. Or at least, what she'd thought then was love. She never got to talk about her own mother—her father had forbidden all mention of her—but Wolf had asked about her and so Olivia told him of her mother's unhappiness. Of how she'd hated leaving her home in Wyoming to come to New York, but had tried to make the best of it for her husband's sake. How she'd become an alcoholic and how desperately Olivia had tried to make her happy. Because her father and brothers ignored Olivia, but her mother never had.

Except nothing had worked, and in the end her mother had taken an overdose of sleeping pills and alcohol and had been found dead in her bed the next day.

Wolf had told Olivia it wasn't her fault, and there had been such conviction in his voice that part of her even believed it.

Yes, maybe then she'd loved him. And even though he'd somehow taken on board some lies about her father—lies that Noah Tate had clearly fed him—she couldn't bring herself to tell her father.

Grief and anger had clearly been driving Wolf, and even though it was obvious he'd meant what he'd said about

taking down the de Santis empire, maybe he'd change his
mind later.

Maybe she should leave off telling her father right now,
give Wolf some time to calm down. He'd reflect on it, see
it wasn't a good idea. And maybe she could even help, find
some evidence that Cesare had nothing to do with Noah
Tate's death.

*Why? Afraid of what Dad might do when he finds out
Wolf wants to hurt him?*

Of course she wasn't afraid. Her father was a cold man
who'd done some shady things in the past, but all of that
was behind him. He'd never do anything to hurt Wolf, not
even if he knew that Wolf wanted to bring him down.

But still. Maybe it would be better to wait. At least until
there were some signs that Wolf was indeed moving to
take down the de Santis empire.

"You're sure he didn't harm you?" her father asked.
"Not in any way?"

It was obvious what he really meant, and Olivia felt her
cheeks get hot. "No. Like I said, he didn't touch me." No,
she was the one who'd touched him.

And then lost your nerve.

She ignored that.

Her father remained motionless, staring at her, his gaze
oddly sharp. "And he didn't tell you what he wanted?"

"He didn't say a word to me. I assumed you would get
a ransom demand or something."

Cesare was silent a moment. "I find it very odd, Olivia.
That someone would kidnap you out of your bedroom,
hold you blindfolded and tied up in a hotel room, then
vanish."

Her father was adept at sniffing out a lie—as a business-
man it was a useful skill, and over the years he'd honed it.
But she too had her own strengths, and hiding things she
didn't want him to know about was one of them. Usually

it involved never letting her feelings show since he didn't like emotional displays, but it certainly came in useful when she didn't want him to know that she was lying to him.

She met his gaze guilelessly. "I'm not sure what to tell you, Dad. I know it's strange and I can't explain it, but that's what happened."

His icy blue eyes flicked over her again. "There was no ransom demand. No nothing. And you said he didn't touch you, so what the hell could he possibly want from you?"

There was something in the words that Olivia didn't like, though she wasn't sure what it was. Smoothing her hands over her skirt, she shook her head. "I don't know. I really don't. But I'm okay, I wasn't hurt, and isn't that the main thing?"

The cold, hard expression on his face didn't change. "Someone took you from my house. *My* house, Olivia. I have the best security detail in Manhattan and yet whoever it was, was able to snatch you away without anyone seeing. I'm struggling to understand how that was possible without whoever it was having some kind of inside knowledge."

Okay, so maybe her not being hurt wasn't the main thing after all.

A familiar anger twisted inside her, but she made sure it didn't show. "Maybe it was an ex-security staff member?" She tried to sound concerned. "I don't know. I was drugged at the time so I'm afraid I can't help."

"You're taking this extraordinarily well, I have to say."

She clasped her hands together, her palms inexplicably damp. "I was terrified if you must know. But I'm safe now, so there's no point getting all worked up."

Her father's eyes narrowed a moment, as if trying to work out whether she was telling the truth or not. Then he gave a grunt and glanced down at the floor. "I'm not taking this to the police. I'm going to investigate this myself, because no one kidnaps my daughter out of her goddamn bedroom. Anyway, security will be doubled and for the next couple of days, you'll be staying here."

Olivia squeezed her hands together. "Are you sure that's necessary?" She normally had a security detail whenever she went out—her father made sure she was protected at all times—and she didn't mind that. But not to go out at all? That seemed . . . excessive.

"Don't question me," Cesare snapped. "Your safety is of paramount importance and if I say you're to remain here, then here you'll remain, understand?"

Keeping her expression neutral, Olivia nodded, accepting his orders the way she normally did. There was no point arguing, not when he was in this kind of mood. He was rattled, that was obvious, and it was always best to tread carefully when he was rattled.

"Also," Cesare went on, "I'm going to have a doctor check you out, to make sure you're okay."

Olivia frowned. "I don't need a doctor, Dad. I told you, I'm fine. I wasn't hurt."

"Just say, yes, Olivia. I'm not the mood for an argument."

"Yes, sure." She tried to make her voice calm, because he liked it when she was calm. "No problem."

The tension went out of his shoulders then and he looked at her, the cold expression fading from his eyes. "I was concerned for you."

Her father wasn't one for words of praise or encouragement, and he certainly never said "I love you." But every so often, he'd let her know, in his own way, that he cared.

She smiled, warmth sitting in her chest, because she lapped up his praise whenever he chose to bestow it, like a hungry plant laps up sunlight. "I know you were." She wanted to say more, but prolonging the moment tended to make her father irritated, so she left it at that.

He gave another grunt then looked at the floor again. "Yes, well, let's leave this issue for the meantime. I need to talk to you about something else, Olivia."

"Oh?"

"Daniel May called me a couple of days ago."

The name sent a small electric shock down her back, Wolf's voice suddenly in her head.

"He told me that he'd promised you to Daniel May."

"I see." She kept her tone measured. "What did he want?"

Her father lifted his head. "He wants to go on another date with you."

Another electric shock, more intense this time.

Olivia fought to keep her expression neutral. "Really? I thought the last date I had with him was a complete failure."

"Apparently not. He likes you. Very much. You remind him of his late wife."

Cold nestled in her chest and she couldn't think of a single thing to say.

"It's more than that though," her father went on, not waiting for her to speak anyway. "He's an old-fashioned man and asked if I would give him leave to court you."

This time she couldn't stop the shock from leaking out. "Court me?" she repeated stupidly, staring at her father's still-handsome face.

"Yes. Like I said, old-fashioned. But I like that he asked." Cesare stared back at her. "What do you think?"

Olivia blinked, the shock reverberating through her, not processing what he was saying. "What do I think about what?"

"What do you think about him courting you? I know he's older than you, but I have no objection. He's a powerful man too. Rich. He'll be able to look after you quite well."

She blinked again, Wolf's voice and what he'd told her echoing in her head. No, her father hadn't promised her to Daniel. Daniel had asked for permission to court her and now her father was simply passing along some information. She didn't *have* to see the man if she didn't want to.

"I don't know if I'm ready for that," she said, pleased with how calm she sounded. "I'm quite happy being on my own at this stage."

She thought he might shrug and that would be the end of it, but he didn't. Instead he frowned, pinning her with that sharp, blue stare. "Yes, but you can't be on your own all your life, Olivia. It's lonely. Believe me, I know."

Taken aback, because he didn't normally share his feelings with her, Olivia could only blink yet again. "Dad, I know you—"

"I think you should say yes," he interrupted. "You'll need someone to protect you if anything happens to me, and May can do that quite well."

She stared at him, bewildered. "But I don't need protection."

"Of course you do. You're my daughter. You'll always need protection."

Olivia thought about pointing out that he hadn't protected her very well the previous night when Wolf had stolen into her room and kidnapped her, but she decided that wouldn't go down very well. "Then beef up my security. Or better yet, *I'll* beef up my own security. Daniel doesn't have anything to do with this."

Her father's frown only deepened. "It's a good business move. You and Daniel, I mean."

The cold thing in her chest got colder. Doubt. Because her father had never shown any interest in her love life or lack of it before. Oh, she knew what was expected of her in terms of being a de Santis daughter, and he'd told her once that he expected her to act with dignity when it came to members of the opposite sex, which was code for "you're not allowed boyfriends unless I say." Which had been fine since the only man she'd ever even conceivably wanted like that had been Wolf.

But for him to suddenly be persistent about Daniel May? It didn't quite make sense.

Unless Wolf was telling the truth.

She shook her head to get rid of the thought. Best to let her father know right now that she wouldn't be going on any more dates with Daniel May.

"I like Daniel, believe me." She met her father's gaze steadily. "But I'm sorry. I have no interest in him as anything more than a friend."

Cesare said nothing for a long moment, but she didn't miss the burn of an icy blue flame in his eyes. "Think about it," he said, and this time she heard something that sounded an awful lot like a warning in his voice. "There are lots of advantages to an alliance with May."

"But Dad, I—"

"Like I said, think about it." He glanced down at his watch. "We'll talk more about this later. Right now, I have a meeting and you have a couple of issues I'd like you to take care of for me. The details are on your desk."

Olivia knew better than to push, so she simply shut her mouth and nodded.

Her father couldn't possibly want her to start seeing May. He couldn't.

But the cold kernel of doubt in her chest didn't go away.

It got colder.

CHAPTER EIGHT

Wolf felt his phone buzz in his pocket, but he ignored it. He knew who it was going to be. Van yet again. He'd had quite a few phone calls from his oldest brother the past two days, and he'd ignored all of them. No doubt Lucas would join in too, at some point. Or considering the look on his face when Wolf had pulled the trigger on the asshole who'd been threatening Grace Riley, maybe he wouldn't. Maybe he'd be too busy fussing around after her. Fussing, aka banging.

Wolf shifted against the window frame, keeping his attention on the old stone mansion across the street. The de Santis mansion.

He'd been watching it for the past two days now from the safety of an empty apartment he'd discovered on his initial casing of the area before he'd kidnapped Olivia. Getting inside the apartment had been relatively easy and so far no one had discovered him.

Which was good, because he hadn't discovered much about Olivia's situation since he'd gotten here. She hadn't left the house, not once, at least not that he'd seen—and since he'd kept the place under pretty heavy surveillance, he'd seen quite a bit.

So, it either meant she wasn't there at all, or that she

was hiding in case he came after her. And since she didn't have anywhere else to go, he'd bet the Tate billions that she was hiding. Smart girl.

Or else de Santis isn't letting her leave.

Yeah, there was that. She'd been kidnapped from under her father's nose and he'd hate that. He'd want to make sure it wouldn't happen again, so it was conceivable that he'd want to keep Olivia close.

And that was the other weird thing.

Wolf had expected to see some evidence that de Santis was mobilizing to find him, since he'd assumed Olivia would have told her father all about Wolf and his plans to take down the de Santis empire. Making him number one on de Santis's shit list.

But he'd seen no signs of any such activity in the past two days. There had been no contact from de Santis either, and that was weird because the guy really liked making threats, especially to the people he was going to hurt.

So either de Santis was planning to go after Wolf on the quiet, playing his cards close to his vest, or he didn't know it had been Wolf who'd taken his daughter. Which would mean Olivia hadn't told him.

He couldn't work out why she hadn't, couldn't think of one single reason. Yet he didn't know how else to explain the lack of activity at the mansion.

There was one way to check for certain, though it came at the risk of giving away his position.

Wolf slid his phone out of his pocket and stared down at the screen. Yeah, fifty million missed calls from Van, plus at least twenty all-caps texts. None from Lucas. He should let his brothers know he was okay, but he didn't want to have any more depressing conversations about his duty as a director of Tate Oil and Gas. In fact if he never heard about that ever again it would be too soon.

He had plans. And they didn't include any fucking directorship.

Punching in the number he'd memorized, he waited for it to be answered, his heart beating oddly fast.

He had complicated feelings about de Santis, always had. Even before the bombshell of his father's letter telling him de Santis was likely to have been the one who'd murdered him. But there had been times when the man had been supportive in his odd, cold way.

Wolf had been under no illusions it was because de Santis actually liked him. No, it was only because Wolf was a Tate, a chance of a strike at his old enemy. So it didn't matter that de Santis had finally found out the truth, that Wolf had been playing him all along. He certainly didn't care about the old prick, not when his intention was to put a bullet in his brain.

But his heartbeat still wouldn't settle as the phone rang, and when the old man's voice came down the line, demanding to know who was calling him, Wolf at first couldn't bring himself to say anything.

"Who is this?" de Santis asked again, his cold voice sharp. "How did you get this number?"

"It's me," Wolf finally forced out and braced himself.

"Christ," de Santis muttered. "About time you called. I need an update on your progress with those plans."

Wolf turned his back to the wall and leaned fully back against it, conscious of an intense rush of relief sweeping through him. So, Olivia hadn't told her father it had been him who'd kidnapped her, or warned him that Wolf was coming for him. His secret was safe. Thank fuck. Unless de Santis was pretending, but no, Wolf couldn't detect anything other than mild annoyance in the man's tone.

"They're progressing," he said. "May take a little longer than planned, though." The plans were a mission de Santis had given him, hoping Wolf would retrieve them from

Noah's private records. The original title deeds to the two Wyoming ranches that his father and de Santis had bought as young men, back when they'd still been the best of friends. Before his father had changed the boundaries on his ranch to include the oil strike that had initially been on de Santis land.

Yeah, Noah had told him all about that way back when and had sworn Wolf to secrecy about it. He'd told Wolf he'd done it so he could create something special, something worthwhile. A legacy he could hand on to his sons.

Cesare had never wanted a family, not the way Noah had, and so Noah had told himself Cesare didn't need all that oil, not if it was only ever going to be just him.

Wolf understood that his father had been wrong, but he'd excused him. It had happened years ago and there was nothing to be done about it now. But if there were indeed plans in existence that would prove that Noah altered those boundaries, then Wolf was quite happy to find them.

Then he'd destroy them.

Finding them had been his primary mission from de Santis, and since Noah's death, de Santis had become more insistent that Wolf locate them. Probably because all his other schemes for taking back what was rightfully his kept falling apart.

"I don't want it to take longer, I want them as soon as you can find them," de Santis said flatly.

"Yeah, well, I would, but my incentive isn't what it was. Know what I'm saying?"

There was a silence. "If this is about Olivia again, I'm sorry, but my hands are tied. May wants her and I need him on our side. He can make life very difficult for us."

Meaning the illegal-arms sideline that de Santis had going on.

Wolf grimaced, not liking the way de Santis kept saying

"us," like he was involved in it too. Because he wasn't, even though de Santis had tried to draw him into it on a number of occasions. Wolf had always refused. He would never be a traitor to his country or to the men of his team. His loyalty was to them and to his family, that was all.

Everything else came second. Everything.

"Yeah, and you can stop saying 'us,'" Wolf said. "I'm not part of that shit."

"Your loss. That doesn't change the fact that I promised her to May."

Wolf's jaw hardened. "She's not your property, Cesare. You can't give her away like a piece of furniture."

"Don't presume to tell me about my relationship with my daughter, Wolf. You know nothing about it. She's perfectly happy with May if that's what you're worried about. And that's the end of the subject."

Wolf bit back the urge to tell de Santis that no, Olivia *wasn't* "perfectly happy" with May, and no, it fucking wasn't the end of the subject. Instead he said, "Then you'll have to wait for your fucking plans then, won't you?" and before the other man could say anything, he disconnected the call.

"Christ," he murmured to the empty apartment. So de Santis was hell-bent on giving Olivia to May. Not that it was going to change his own plans. Hell, if anything, it only made him even more certain that taking her back was his only option.

Sliding his phone back into his pocket, he turned back to the window

Then went still.

The front door of the mansion had opened and a couple of bodyguards came out, flanking a small woman wearing a form-fitting blue dress, her dark brown hair neat and shining down her back. Olivia.

Fucking finally.

Something surged in him and he wasn't sure what it was, maybe relief that she was okay. But no, it wasn't quite that. There was another element to the feeling that made his blood start to pump a little harder. But he didn't want to examine that too closely, so he didn't.

A limo waited at the curb, but Wolf didn't wait to see her get into it, he was already moving for the door.

Time to get kidnap mission 2.0 underway.

"Dammit. I told them I wasn't to be disturbed." Daniel flashed Olivia a polite smile as his phone buzzed yet again. "I really need to take this. Would you mind?"

She gave him the same polite smile back. "No, it's fine. Go ahead."

Not that he was listening to her anyway, since he'd already started to reach for the phone before she'd even opened her mouth.

As he answered, half turning in his chair so he faced away from her, she sat back and smoothed the napkin over her knees to give her hands something to do.

It was the middle of the day and the swanky restaurant Daniel had taken her to for lunch was full of people. It was one of Manhattan's more exclusive lunch spots, with big skylights over the dining area that let in lots of winter sunlight. The room was full of the buzz of voices and the clink of cutlery, and she could see a few famous faces dotted here and there among the crowd.

Daniel had brought her here to impress her. She knew that because he kept mentioning how difficult it was to get a table since it was so popular, but luckily he knew the maître d' so it was no problem for him to get a booking.

Like that sort of thing had mattered to her.

Olivia reached for her glass of iced water and took a sip. She hadn't wanted to go to lunch with Daniel. In fact, it had been pretty much the last thing she felt like doing, but her father had insisted, telling her to give May a chance. She could, of course, say no and he would never force her into doing anything she didn't want to do, but if she could do this one thing for him, then he would appreciate it.

She hated it when he manipulated her, and he *was* manipulating her. But when he put it like that, she felt like she couldn't refuse.

It was only lunch. Not much of a big deal.

She had no idea why May was so fixated on her, but she could sit through a lunch for her father's sake. Cesare had had a great many things taken from him by people he'd trusted, and she didn't want to be one of those people. She didn't want to let him down.

So she'd been a good girl and had met Daniel at the restaurant, had been polite and smiled a lot and made small talk. Not that there had been much of that since even though he'd apparently told people he wasn't to be disturbed, he kept getting calls on his phone all the same.

And answering them. They all appeared to be important.

She sipped at her water, staring at the man sitting across from her. His voice was quiet but firm, and she guessed it was okay. Didn't have that gravelly roughness that made Wolf's so attractive though. And Daniel wasn't bad looking. Yes, he was pushing fifty, but he was still trim, and although there was white in his dark hair, it could reasonably be called distinguished. His features were pleasant enough, though he had a rather mean cast to his thin-lipped mouth, yet maybe given time, she could warm to them.

He wasn't built tall and broad though, nor did he have that intense, physical charisma that . . . say . . . Wolf Tate had.

Why are you comparing him to Wolf?

Olivia shifted uncomfortably in her chair. She *shouldn't*

be comparing him to Wolf. She shouldn't be thinking of Wolf at all. At least, that's what she'd been telling herself for the past two days as she'd busied herself with work.

But telling herself not to think about him didn't stop her brain from returning to him again and again. To the heat of his body under hers as she'd sat astride him, and the smoothness of his skin as she'd touched him. To the concern in his uneven gaze as he'd asked her what was wrong. To the way he'd brushed her hair behind her ear, his fingers grazing her skin.

To the regret she'd felt as she'd opened the door and walked out of that hotel room.

Not forgetting all the lies he told you, the way he used you, showing you exactly how much your friendship meant to him.

No, she wasn't going to think about those things either. They hurt too much.

What she should be thinking about now was Daniel. He wasn't what she wanted, no, but then no man was.

Except one.

Olivia put her water down and ignored the thought, smiling yet again as Daniel finally ended his phone conversation.

"Now," he said, sitting to face her again as he put his phone down. "Where were we? Ah yes, I was going to talk to you about something your father and I have been discussing." His smile was thin, and she thought he probably meant it to look friendly, but it didn't. "Something that concerns you."

Her stomach lurched. "Oh?"

"Don't worry, it's nothing bad." He gave a laugh that sounded forced. "At least, not that bad."

Not reassured, Olivia wished she'd gotten a glass of wine instead of the water. "What is it?"

Daniel picked up his own wine glass and took a sip.

"Well, I think you know I'm interested in you, Olivia. Very interested. And I'd like to take our relationship to the next level, so to speak."

Her stomach lurched again. Hell, she really didn't want to talk about this, not now. Moving her fingers restlessly on her napkin, she tried to keep the smile pasted to her face. "Our relationship?" She was careful not to make it sound too sharp. "I wasn't sure we had one. It's only been a couple of dates."

"Exactly. Which is why I want to make it more. I want to keep seeing you, Olivia. Get to know you better." Another flicker of that thin-lipped smile. "And who knows? Maybe it'll lead to something deeper?"

Something deeper . . .

Daniel wasn't a bad man, at least not that she'd seen. Plus, her father had given her some reasons as to why it would be useful to get to know him better, so it couldn't hurt, could it? Besides, there were worse things than dating him.

Sleeping with him?

She blinked. That *would* happen if she kept dating him, wouldn't it? And if she said yes to him courting her, then the natural conclusion of that was marriage. And marriage would lead to sex and then it would be Daniel's hands on her skin. Daniel's mouth on hers. Daniel brushing her hair back behind her ear . . .

Ice gathered in her gut, a shiver of revulsion moving over her skin. It irritated her. Dear God, it was only sex. It didn't mean anything. Not when the benefits of allying herself with May would outweigh her own distaste.

Yes, keep telling yourself that.

Well, she *had* to keep telling herself that. What other choice did she have? It wasn't as if she could have the man she truly wanted.

You could have. You ran away.

"Well?" Daniel was looking expectantly at her. "What do you say?"

She opened her mouth to reply, to say what she didn't know, but at that point a man walked into the restaurant and her awareness of everything else completely vanished.

Tall, broad, insanely muscled. Walking in like he owned the place and everyone in it. He was once again in jeans and boots, a dark blue shirt and that battered leather jacket thrown over the top. Aviator shades covered his eyes, his wide mouth curving in a smile that was only a hair short of arrogant.

Wolf.

People turned to look at him as he passed because a six-foot-five gladiator of a man was something most of them didn't see every day, plus the animalistic grace with which he moved made him pretty damn mesmerizing.

At least, *she* was mesmerized. Frozen completely to her seat.

What the hell was he doing here? Had he come for her? And if so, how had he known where she'd be?

Of course he's come for you. Who else would he come for?

She was being an idiot. She'd escaped him before he'd gotten that information, and now he was here to get it. To get her.

The ice in her gut melted clean away and the shiver that went through her wasn't revulsion at all, not this time. It was excitement, along with a thrilling fear that had her clutching her napkin in her fists, her whole body gathering itself to run. But whether she'd run away from him or toward him, she couldn't tell.

He didn't move in her direction straightaway. Instead he aimed for the table where the two bodyguards her father had insisted come along sat. Obviously he knew them because he greeted each of them with a high-five before leaning down to speak to them.

She stared. What was he doing?

"Olivia?" Daniel was looking at her strangely. "Anything the matter?"

Dragging her gaze away from Wolf, her heartbeat loud in her ears, she forced yet another fake smile. "Oh, I'm fine."

"Really? You seem distracted."

"No, no. Just . . . thinking about something Dad said to me earlier."

"Oh? What was that?" Daniel's eyes gleamed. "Something about me I hope?"

But she couldn't answer, because out of the corner of her eye, she could see Wolf finish up his conversation with the bodyguards, then turn and head straight toward their table.

She swallowed, reaching for her glass of water, the strange combination of excitement and fear turning over and over inside her. Not to mention a sneaking admiration for the sheer gall of him. To come for her right here, in the middle of a crowded restaurant, making no effort to hide his identity. Seemingly not caring that her bodyguards were right there.

He must want her very badly indeed.

No. He wants that information. Don't forget that.

Daniel was frowning at her, and she realized she should have answered his questions. But by then it was too late, because Wolf was there, coming up behind Daniel, that easygoing, lazy smile turning his mouth. "Hey, there," he said in a friendly tone, the familiarity of his rough voice making her hands clench tighter on her napkin. "I hate to interrupt your romantic little lunch, but would you mind if I had a word with Olivia?"

Daniel's frown deepened as he twisted and looked up at the man standing beside his chair, towering over him.

"Excuse me?" Daniel's tone was *not* friendly. "Who the hell are you?"

"Oh, my bad." Wolf reached up, took his shades off, and grinned. "Wolf Tate." He put his sunglasses in the pocket of his jacket then held out his hand. "Pleased to meet you . . . ?"

Daniel stared coldly at Wolf's outstretched hand but didn't take it. "Actually, I do mind. We're in the middle of something."

Wolf didn't seem at all offended, his lazy grin widening. "Chill out, bro. I'm just a friend of Olivia's and all I need is five minutes of her time." Then he looked at her. "What do you say, Liv?"

The impact of his gaze was almost physical and she didn't know why it hit her so powerfully right in that moment. But she could feel it, a shudder moving through her, all the way down to her toes. The sapphire-and-emerald gleam of his eyes was inescapable and in them she could see something glittering, but she didn't know what it was. She only knew that it made the shivering excitement inside her even worse.

"Olivia's not going anywhere," Daniel said. "She and I are in the middle of—"

"Yeah, you know I think Olivia can speak for herself," Wolf interrupted lazily, his gaze still on hers. "Can't you Olivia?"

David looked furious. He opened his mouth to say something and Olivia knew that whatever it was, it would only make this situation worse. Which gave her two choices. She either refused Wolf and alerted her bodyguards to the fact that she was in danger—and then Wolf would leave or he'd have to fight the bodyguards off and snatch her in the middle of the lunchtime rush.

Or she agreed to his five minutes.

It's not going to be five minutes. And he's not going to let you get away.

She should stay. She should tell him politely but firmly she wasn't going to go anywhere with him, all the while alerting her bodyguards.

Yet when she opened her mouth, that wasn't what came out. "It's okay, Daniel," she said instead. "It'll only be five minutes. I'll be back, I promise."

Wolf's expression didn't change, but she saw the flare of triumph in his eyes all the same.

"Olivia," Daniel began. Only to stop as his phone once again started ringing.

"It's fine." She pushed her chair back, her heart thundering. "Answer it. You can talk while I'm gone."

Wolf's smile was very white as she got to her feet. Then he jerked his head toward the restaurant's exit. "Come on. I won't keep you long."

She didn't dare look in the direction of her bodyguards, following Wolf as he threaded through the tables, heading for the door.

She still couldn't believe she was doing this. Because she knew with certainty that he wouldn't let her come back to the table. That once they'd gotten out of the restaurant, she would be his captive.

His willing captive.

Olivia took a shaking breath, a complicated mess of emotion tangling inside her. The pull between what she wanted to do for her father and her own intense longing for her friend. Because the two were incompatible, she knew that as surely as she knew her own name.

Outside the restaurant was a foyer area with a corridor that led to other offices, plus a bank of elevators right in front of the restaurant door itself.

As soon as the doors shut behind him, Wolf turned and

reached out, his strong, warm fingers wrapping around her elbow.

She stiffened at the touch, not ready for the surge of heat that went through her as he did so. "Wolf, wait," she said, trying to pull away.

But he only held on tighter, moving away from the restaurant doors and down the corridor a little way before turning and pushing her up against the wall. He let go, but since he was standing right in front of her, his height and his build essentially blocking her from getting away, it didn't mean a hell of a lot.

The easygoing smile that had turned his mouth was gone, the beautifully sculpted lines now hard, and there was no doubting the glitter in his eyes. Anger, pure and simple.

Yet all he said was, "I was right, wasn't I?"

Bracing herself for an interrogation about how she'd escaped him, all she could do was blink up at him for a second. Then it penetrated what he was talking about. "What? About Daniel?"

"Yes, of course fucking Daniel."

"No, you're not right," she snapped, annoyed with his tone all of a sudden. "Dad hasn't promised me to him. All he said was that Daniel was interested in me and that he wanted to court me."

"Court you?" Wolf gave a harsh laugh. "Is that what they're calling it these days? No Liv, he doesn't want to court you. He wants to marry you so he has leverage against your father. And your father has no choice but to let him have you, because he wants the alliance with May. That's how it works."

She didn't want to believe it, not one word. But she couldn't forget that conversation she'd had with her father, about how beneficial it would be for her to start seeing May, couching it in business terms, making it sound like a business merger.

"Well, and so what if I'm okay with marrying him?" The words sounded wrong as soon as she'd said them, but she went on anyway. "Perhaps it would end up being a good thing for me. It'll certainly be useful for our family."

Wolf scowled and brought up his hands, placing them flat to the wall on either side of her head, leaning down so his face was inches away from hers. "Is that the kind of bullshit he told you? You didn't hear a word of what I said about how you're just leverage?"

"But I—"

"And a warm body in his bed to fuck."

Again, that word in his harsh voice went straight through her, making all her awareness zero in on how close he was standing. How he'd surrounded her with hard muscle and heat and that dark, intoxicating scent. Making it so difficult to think. Hell, even stringing words together was difficult.

"You think I'm stupid?" She had to force herself to speak. "You think I don't know any of that? That I haven't thought about it?"

"What I think is that you're naive." He dipped his head even lower, so all she could see was the glitter of sapphire and emerald. "Your father isn't who you think he is."

She didn't like it. She didn't like *any* of it. The way he kept picking at her doubt, making it sharper, more certain. Undermining the comfortable shell of denial she'd surrounded herself with.

"You have no idea who my father is," she said, defensive. "And anyway, what if I want Daniel to court me? What if marrying him *is* what I want?"

"You don't want him, Liv. I know you don't."

"Yes, I do." It was a lie, but she couldn't help it. She had to protect herself somehow. " He's exactly what I need."

"No, he's not."

"And how the hell would you know?"

The hard glitter in Wolf's eyes intensified. "Because what you need is me."

Then before she could say another word, he closed the last remaining inch between them and covered her mouth with his.

Olivia went completely still, but her lips under his were so fucking soft he could hardly breathe. He could smell her, strawberries and musk, and he knew he should pull back, let her go, but he couldn't.

She was lying to herself. He'd seen the look on her face the moment he'd walked into the restaurant, and it hadn't been the look of a woman having lunch with a man she was ecstatic about. He knew a genuine Olivia smile when he saw one, but the one curving Olivia's mouth as she'd looked at May was as fake as they got.

She hadn't wanted to be there, he would have laid money on the fact.

He hadn't been able to put a name to the thing that had surged in him right then. Possessiveness maybe, but he'd never been possessive about a woman before, so it couldn't have been that surely? So maybe it had simply been protectiveness. She hadn't wanted to be having lunch with that asshole and so he was there to make sure she didn't have to.

He'd already spotted the de Santis security team, because of course de Santis wouldn't let her go out without some kind of protection. Luckily he knew both men and had detoured to their table to say hi and to let them know he was going to take Olivia out for a quick five-minute conversation, no biggie. And because they knew him and knew he was best buddies with de Santis, they were more than fine with it. He wanted them to know who'd taken her, too, especially if he wanted his bait plan to work.

After that, he'd headed straight for Olivia's table, keeping a firm hold on his temper, because what he'd really wanted to do was smash that asshole May straight in the face. But that kind of thing wouldn't exactly make it easier to get Olivia away, and so he'd managed to hold himself back.

At least until he'd gotten out of the restaurant and she'd started talking bullshit about how she'd wanted to be there with May. How an alliance with him would be good for her family and that it was exactly what she needed.

It wasn't though, and they both knew that, so why she had to keep lying to herself and to him, he didn't know. He *did* know that she was wrong. And that there was only one thing he could think of to do to prove it.

He felt the shudder that ran through her as he deepened the kiss, opening his mouth on hers, touching his tongue to the insane softness of her bottom lip, tracing the line of it.

She remained quite still, and since she didn't pull away, he stepped closer to her, so that their bodies were almost but not quite touching.

He was a pretty straight-up guy. When he wanted a woman and she was into it, he went ahead and got right down to it. In other words, kissing was nice but he preferred a woman's mouth to be wrapped around his cock.

Yet kissing Olivia was different. He could feel the tension in her body, as if she was on the point of pushing him away, and some deep instinct told him that if he wanted this kiss to keep going, he was going to have to go slow.

"Slow" wasn't in his vocabulary and really, he shouldn't be kissing her at all, especially since kissing Olivia wasn't high on his list of mission objectives. But now that he was, he couldn't seem to stop.

Pressing his hands flat to the wall on either side of her head, he ran his tongue along the seam of her lips, coaxing gently, encouraging her to open to him, because he was suddenly desperate to taste the sweet heat of her.

She gave a little tremble as he did so, then sighed, mouth opening up under his, letting him deepen the kiss.

Christ, she tasted so fucking good. She had back in the hotel room a couple of days ago too, but she tasted even sweeter now, though he had no idea why. Her mouth was hot and when he touched his tongue to hers, encouraging her to respond, she made a soft sound in the back of her throat.

His cock got suddenly insanely hard and before he could stop himself, he'd closed the distance between them, pushing her up against the wall so all her soft heat was pressed the length of his body. Then he gripped her chin and tilted her head back, sliding his tongue deeper into her mouth, taking the kiss from gentle to something hotter, more demanding.

His blood was pumping hard in his veins and all he could think about was tasting her deeper. Then maybe undoing all the buttons that fastened the front of her dress and opening it up, touching her skin, perhaps sliding his hand between her thighs, feel how wet she was for him. God, he wanted to get inside her.

He wanted her heat and her softness. He wanted her sweetness. Everything female about her that excited everything male in him. And maybe it was simply because she was a woman and he hadn't had a woman in six months, or maybe it was more than that. Whatever it was, he wanted her. Like, now.

At that moment, Olivia made another sound, this time one of protest and her hands were against his chest, pushing at him. He didn't want to stop, but he made himself, lifting his head, struggling to catch his breath.

She looked up at him, her eyes wide and dark, her cheeks flushed. Her hands weren't pushing now, her fingers curling into the fabric of his shirt as if she wanted to keep him close instead. "I can't leave," she murmured. "I can't."

At first, his head was so full of the taste of her that he couldn't work out what she was saying. "Leave? What do you mean?"

"I can't leave with you."

Of course she'd know he wasn't here to question her about her apparent preference for that asshole May. She'd escaped from him a couple of days ago and had realized that he wasn't going to let that stand.

He tried to steady his breathing, but it was difficult with her standing so close, filling his head with her sweet scent. "You don't have a choice," he said, his voice huskier than he wanted it to be. "I'm taking you whether you want to go or not."

Her fingers curled tighter into his shirt, her head shaking. "I can't, Wolf. Dad needs me. He needs me to do this with Daniel. And I can't let him down, I just can't. Everyone left him, everyone took things from him. His wife committed suicide and then his sons took his company away from him." She took a breath. "He's got nothing and no one anymore. No one but me. And I can't let it happen. Because I know what it's like to . . ." She stopped and looked away, biting her lip.

Wolf knew he should be letting her go and getting her in that elevator, that the minutes were ticking by and sooner or later someone was going to come looking for her. But he couldn't make himself move.

The distress in her eyes made his chest feel tight. He'd never understood why she was so loyal to her father, why she felt she had to do all the things she did for him, but he maybe he did now. A little anyway. "What did you lose?" he prompted softly. "Tell me."

Her lashes fell and he could see the gleam of moisture on them, and it made his chest go from tight to sore. He had a hand beneath her chin, and it was instinct that made him stroke the line of her jaw to offer her some reassurance.

She shivered as he did so, but didn't pull away. "Dad wasn't the only one who lost something when Mom died." Her voice was so quiet he almost didn't hear the words.

Shit. Her mother. Of course. She'd spoken about her in those conversations in the library, but not a great deal. He almost wondered if she was afraid to for some reason. But he did know that Olivia had grieved for the loss and had grieved deeply.

Apparently she still did.

It left him with nothing to say, because what the fuck did he know about consoling anyone? No one had consoled him after Noah's death, not even his brothers. They'd all been struggling with their own issues and none of them had anything left for shit like reassurance.

He stroked her jaw, looking down at the top of her head, her glossy brown hair shining under the lights of the corridor. He had to fight the urge to bury his face in it, inhale the strawberry scent of her shampoo or whatever the hell it was that made her smell like that.

"Shit, I know it's hard," he said, trying to think of something better to say than that and coming up with nothing. Words weren't his forte and never had been. "But . . . Liv, you can't sacrifice living your own life because of what happened to your Dad." That her father wasn't worth her sacrifice he didn't add, even though he wanted to. "None of that is your fault." And it wasn't. Whatever had happened to Cesare de Santis, he'd brought it on himself.

A breath went out of her and she leaned forward, putting her forehead on his chest, holding onto his shirt, and his heart raced, thundering in his head. The slight weight of her against him was making him lightheaded and all he wanted to do was put his arms around her, crush her against him. But she was so small and fragile, and upset.

"I know." Her voice was muffled. "I know it's not my fault. But there's no one around to help him but me."

Wolf's jaw ached and he had to lower his hands to his sides, because he couldn't trust himself not to keep on touching her. "It doesn't have to be you. Why do you need to help him anyway? What has he ever done for you?"

She shook her head, the slight movement of it against his chest making him wish he wasn't wearing his goddamn shirt because he wanted to feel her silky hair against his skin. "He's my Dad," she said simply. As if that explained everything.

And it did. Loyalty to someone, even as flawed as her father, was something he understood and understood well. He'd done many things for his own father, things he wasn't proud of, but he'd done it because Noah was his dad. And Wolf loved him, despite everything.

He prized loyalty too, and Olivia was loyal to a fault. Even if the person she gave her loyalty to didn't deserve it, and God knew her father didn't. Come to think of it, neither did he, not after he'd lied to her so completely and for so long. Yet here she was, letting him kiss her then resting her head on his chest like he was the friend he'd once been to her.

Shit, they really needed to get out of here. This wasn't the time or the place for heart-to-heart chats.

Glancing toward to the restaurant doors, he checked to make sure the coast was still clear, then said, "Yeah, well, whether you want to marry that son of a bitch for your father's sake or not, I'm not letting you. We gotta get out of here."

She started to shake her head again, but he grabbed her

chin again and held her tight, looking down into her eyes. "You've got two choices, Liv. Either you come with me right now or you scream and make a fuss and I take you anyway. What's it to be?"

An expression he couldn't read flashed across her face. "I have bodyguards."

"Which I could take out in ten seconds."

"Daniel has a couple too."

"You think I don't know that? I'd take them out in five."

She swallowed and this time her indecision was clear. "Wolf . . ."

So he made the decision for her. Taking her arm, he walked with her to the elevator and hit the button.

She made no move to get away from him, only glancing once toward the restaurant. She didn't scream or cry out. Didn't yell for help.

"If anyone asks, you did your best to escape me, but I was too strong for you," he said as the elevator chimed. The doors opened. He lifted his hand and pointed two fingers at her. "Also, I had a gun. Which I used to force you into the elevator."

She glanced down at his fingers then lifted her gaze to his again. And he was sure he saw her mouth curve very slightly. "Okay."

He gave her a smile, because it was clear she needed one, and gestured with his fingers toward the elevator. "You'd better get in. I don't want to have to shoot you."

Her mouth curved a little more and this time she didn't look toward the restaurant, getting into the elevator instead. He joined her, hitting the button to close the doors.

Okay, the clock was going to start ticking right now, which meant he had to move fast if he was to get her away without anyone following them.

The past couple of days he'd debated a lot about where

to take her, whether to go back to that hotel or find a place outside of New York City. But the hotel had been compromised when she'd escaped, and if he was out of New York, he couldn't keep tabs on de Santis. Which left him with little choice.

There was the Tate mansion that was currently vacated since Van was in Wyoming, but the place was a giant target and the last place he wanted to hide Olivia away in. He could call Lucas and hit up his brother for the keys to his apartment, but involving his brothers in this mission wasn't what he wanted either.

Which left him with only one option. He'd have to take her to his secret bolt-hole.

The 79th Street Boat Basin.

The elevator doors opened and Wolf grabbed her hand, hustling her out of the building and onto the sidewalk. The cab was waiting for him just as the driver had promised—Wolf had paid him extra—and when he opened the door, she got into without a protest.

As he got in after her and closed the door, settling himself in the seat, she said, "Are you angry at me for escaping?"

The taxi pulled away into the lunchtime traffic, the driver already knowing where to take them.

"I wasn't exactly thrilled." He glanced at her. "How did you guess my code?"

"I didn't guess." She folded her hands in her lap. The blue dress she wore, with a lot of little buttons down the front and a narrow belt around her waist, made the color of her eyes look more intense. "I thought about what kind of code would be relevant to you and that date just . . . popped into my head."

He still didn't know how he felt about the fact that she'd remembered. "Uh-huh. And all that alcohol was to get me drunk enough to pass out?"

She colored and looked down at her delicate hands. "It worked."

Another thought occurred to him. Had her offer of a blow job been part of that too? Because if it had . . .

His earlier anger, still simmering, boiled up again, though he had no idea why. He'd been telling himself all along that he didn't want her. So it shouldn't matter to him why she'd offered to suck his dick. Yet . . . all he could think about was what if it had been a lie? What if it had all been part of her escape plan?

That kiss doesn't lie.

He could still feel her lips against his, hot and soft, the sweet taste of her mouth and the way it had opened up beneath his. No, fuck, that hadn't been a lie. Or the way her fingers had curled into his shirt as if she hadn't wanted to let him go.

But he couldn't resist asking her all the same. "So was that blow job all part of your escape plan too?"

The flush in her cheeks deepened and she glanced toward the driver then back at him. "I . . ." She faltered. "I'd heard that it can make some men sleepy . . . afterward."

Holy shit.

Wolf stared at her, inexplicably pissed but also kind of impressed. Because it was a decent plan. She couldn't physically fight him, so her only option had been to render him unconscious. Which she had, without even the aid of an orgasm.

Still . . .

"Did you lie?" he asked even though none of that should matter. "About wanting me then?"

Her eyes widened as if the question surprised her. Then she looked down at her hands again, her lashes veiling her gaze, and no matter what he'd tasted in her kiss, he wanted to hear the words. He wanted to know whether she'd lied to him or not.

No, it shouldn't matter what she felt about it. It shouldn't matter whether she was into him or not, because it wasn't like there could be anything between them. He'd pretty much destroyed their friendship when he'd told her about being a double agent, and despite those kisses and her response, he didn't think a physical relationship was likely either. Not given how quickly she'd leapt off him when the moment to get down and dirty with him had come.

So why he wanted to know whether she'd lied was anyone's guess. That didn't make him any less desperate to know.

Her gaze stayed on her hands, and he thought she wasn't going to answer. And he was debating grabbing her stubborn little chin and turning her to face him again, making her answer anyway, when she said, very quietly, "No. I didn't lie."

A jolt of electricity shot straight down his spine.

Well, okay then. Good to know.

Not that you're going to do anything about it. Not after the way you used her.

His jaw clenched. He wasn't going to do anything about it *anyway*. Olivia had once been his friend, not to mention that he was pretty sure she wouldn't be on board with his assassination plans for her father. And then there was the fact that once he'd dealt with de Santis, he had to go get his mother.

He wasn't looking for any kind of relationship now even if she still wanted him after all of that.

He shifted in the seat next to her, conscious that her thigh was very close to his and all he'd have to do was move slightly and it would be pressed up against him.

Jesus.

"So you lost your nerve then," he said. "That's why you pulled away."

She looked at him finally, her gaze guarded. "Yes, I did."

"Why?" He should drop the subject, he really should.

"Because . . . I'd never done it before."

"No. That's not the reason." Because why would she have offered it in the first place? No, she'd looked . . . upset. And then she wouldn't tell him what was wrong.

Why are you pushing?

Christ he didn't know.

Lifting a hand, he scrubbed it through his hair. "Look, you don't have to answer that—"

"Because you matter to me, Wolf." The words were very quiet, cutting through his statement and blowing everything else he'd been going to say clean out of his head.

It didn't make any sense. He'd lied to her. For years, he'd lied to her. About everything. About the reason he'd been friends with her in the first place, and yet, here she was, telling him that he mattered to her?

"What do you mean I matter?" He could feel his chest getting tight again, the way it seemed to lately whenever she was around, and he didn't like it. "How can you say that after everything I said to you?"

She'd gone pink, but she didn't avoid his gaze this time, staring back at him, a glint of defiance in her eyes. "Yes, it hurt to find out that you only got close to me to get to my father. And yes, I'm really angry with you. But you were my friend for ten years and I can't turn my feelings off just like that."

He found himself rubbing at his hair yet again, a nervous tic he'd never grown out of. "That's got nothing to do with the BJ, Liv."

"Yes, it has. You matter to me and I . . ." She stopped, her hands twisting in her lap. "I knew that if I went ahead with it, I might not ever be able to get you out of my head."

But he didn't understand. "What does that mean?"

"Nothing will ever happen between us, Wolf. I know that. But I didn't want to start anything that would make living without you even more difficult than it is already."

CHAPTER NINE

Olivia knew she shouldn't have said it, shouldn't have given away so much. But she'd had to give him the truth. In letting Wolf take her out of the restaurant, she'd walked away from her father, and once she'd crossed that line there was no crossing back.

Wolf had sown the seeds of doubt inside her about her father's motives and even if she'd gone back to her awkward lunch with Daniel, those seeds would still have been there. And they would have continued to grow.

But she hadn't stayed. She'd gone with Wolf and, in doing so, she'd chosen him.

She still wasn't sure why she had. Maybe it had been that desperate, sweet, overwhelming kiss he'd given her against the wall. Caging her with the heat and the strength of his body, giving her something to lean against and hold onto. And she had held onto him. Because not only had that kiss had made her legs feel like rubber, it had also stripped away her cozy blanket of self-denial. Simply torn it out of her grip. Leaving her with nothing but the bare truth.

That all the justifications in the world about how she was doing this for her father didn't make her want to go back and sit down with Daniel May. Didn't make the thought of going out with him, marrying him, sleeping

with him any easier. Didn't make the revulsion she felt at
the thought of him touching her go away.

She didn't want to do it. The only man she wanted was
Wolf, and he'd proved it to her.

She'd protested having to go with him, because she felt
she had to, but when he'd told her she didn't have a choice,
that he was going to take her anyway whether she wanted
to go or not, something inside her had been so relieved. She
hadn't wanted to make the decision herself, and he'd taken
it out of her hands.

That had added another layer of complication to her already complicated feelings for him, but maybe a bit of truth
would make things less complicated. Not the truth that she
actually loved him and still did, despite everything, but he
had to know that she cared about him.

She didn't want that to be a secret.

His gaze narrowed, as if he was suspicious of what she'd
said. But then the taxi pulled in to the side of the street
and the driver was informing them that they'd reached
their destination.

Wolf gave her an intense look, then he turned away to
deal with the driver.

A minute later they were standing on the sidewalk with
the Hudson River glittering in the late-afternoon sunshine,
and a marina right in front of her, with lots of yachts and
barges and houseboats all pulled up to the docks.

Wolf took his phone out and discarded it in a nearby
trash can. Then he grabbed her hand and she had no choice
but to follow him as he led her along the sidewalk to a gate
in the tall fence that separated the sidewalk from the docks.
Digging into his pocket, he brought out a key that he used
to unlock the gate, swinging it open and gesturing for her
to go through.

She frowned as she stepped through the gate. "Are we
going sailing?"

He shook his head, pulling the gate shut behind him. "No. We're going into hiding." Then he took her hand once again and moved to the steps that led down to the docks.

The docks were floating, making her feel unsteady in her dark blue pumps, her footsteps echoing on the wood as he guided her down a dock that projected out into the river.

She stared at the different boats, one a huge barge that looked big enough to be a house in its own right, and then a long, sleek-looking one probably worth millions, some rich man's toy.

Wolf stopped beside an older yacht with a couple of masts that lay low in the water. There was a small gangplank that led from the dock to the yacht, and he gestured at her to cross first.

Deciding to keep her questions to herself for now, Olivia put her hands on the rails of the gangplank and walked gingerly across to the side of the yacht and climbed onto the deck. Then Wolf came after her.

He gave her one of his wicked grins as he took out another key and moved over a small set of stairs that led to a door that presumably opened onto a cockpit or berths, or whatever it was that you called rooms on a boat.

Opening the door, he gestured again and she found herself moving unsteadily down some steps and into a tiny corridor that led to what she was expecting to be some cramped below-deck quarters but turned out to be a surprisingly roomy space.

In one corner was a tiny galley, with a gas hob and a fridge, a sink, and a small pantry, while in the main area was a round, curving bench strewn with cushions, built around a similarly curved drop-leaf table.

The other end of the tiny corridor led to what probably was the bedroom/bathroom area.

Wood gleamed as the sun poured through small port-holes in the side of the hull, the air heavy with the scent of wood polish, salt water, and engine oil.

"Welcome to the *Shady Lady*." Wolf's deep voice came from behind her. "Go sit down. I'll make you some tea."

Olivia made her way, wobbling slightly because of the movement of the boat, to the curved bench and sat down. "The *Shady Lady*?"

"Yeah, that's what she's called. The yacht I mean. I didn't name her. She came like that." Wolf moved into the galley and she watched, amazed, because she hadn't thought there would be room for a guy as big as him. But, apart from having to incline his head a little, he didn't seem fussed by the small space, pulling out a kettle and filling it with water without any problems, his movements economical and fluid. Obviously he knew this boat and he knew it well.

"This yours?" A stupid question. Then again, he hadn't told her he'd gotten himself a boat, so maybe it wasn't.

"She is." He flicked the gas on the hob on and put the kettle on it. "I got her a few years ago. I thought having a bolt-hole that no one would guess at would be useful. Plus, I can move it if anyone finds out I'm here."

"I never would have picked you for a . . . boat person."

He grabbed a couple of mugs out of a tiny cupboard then put them on the minuscule counter, giving her another of those lazy smiles. "Hey, I'm a sailor. Of course I'm a boat person."

A sailor. Right.

He slid aside the door of the small pantry and took out a packet of tea. "Did you know that I'd never seen the ocean until I got to Coronado for my training?" He ex-tracted a couple of teabags, then dumped them in the cups. "I thought it was the most beautiful thing I'd ever seen. Until we were forced to sit in the fucking thing for hours on end, freezing our nuts off."

"Sounds like a great introduction to the sea." She took another look around the cabin. "You can sail her then?"

"Yeah. But I don't take her out very often. Got too much other shit to do normally." He put his hands on the counter and leaned on them, his gaze sharpening as he looked at her.

Her breathing quickened and she found her hands had curled into fists in her lap.

There was a porthole behind him, the sun making his short, black Mohawk look glossy, and sending the rest of his face into shadow. It made him look dangerous all of a sudden, and the size of the boat didn't help.

He was so big. It felt like he was taking up all the space, sucking up all the air.

"What?" she asked, resisting the urge to smooth her hair.

"Explain what you said to me back there in the cab."

Damn. She'd been hoping he might have forgotten all about that. The way she'd said it had made it sound . . .

Like you're in love with him? Well, you are.

Maybe. She'd been in love with the idea of him certainly, but now? In love with this very real, very present man? She really didn't know anymore, just like she really didn't know him.

Olivia glanced away, gazing around the cabin instead. On the table in front of her was a sleek silver laptop, plus a stack of papers and a pen. It looked as if he'd been in the middle of some work.

"Didn't you want that information from me?" She straightened the pen so it sat neatly beside the stack of papers. "That's why you turned up at the restaurant all set to kidnap me again, isn't it?"

"Sure, but that can wait. I want to know why you said living without me was hard."

Well, she hadn't meant to say it like that. She'd simply wanted him to know that she'd cared about him. That she'd thought about him a lot all the years he'd been away. Living without him hadn't exactly been hard because she'd never had him to live with in the first place.

So why did you say it?

She gritted her teeth, ignoring the thought. What the hell was she going to say to him? She had to give him something, because he was never going to let this go. And it had to be something she could explain. That wasn't fraught with all these complicated feelings.

"Okay." Letting out a long breath, she made herself meet his gaze. "So the truth? I wasn't lying back in the hotel room, when I told you that I wanted you. I have since I was fifteen. But yes, since you were a Tate and you never showed any interest in me, I never said anything to you about it. I thought it would fade over time but . . . it didn't. I still want you and I probably always will."

The kettle began to whistle, but Wolf made no move toward it, only stared at her.

"Kettle," she prompted, resisting the urge to wipe her damp palms against her dress.

Wolf scowled, muttered a curse, and grabbed for the kettle, flicking off the hob and pouring out the boiling water into the cups.

She swallowed, her mouth gone dry, aware of the tension that now filled the cabin.

Couching her feelings in terms of want was far easier and less revealing than talking about love. And maybe "love" wasn't the right word for what she felt for him anyway. Maybe she'd been mistaken, because how could she really be in love with a man she didn't know?

Yes, maybe she'd been wrong all this time. Maybe it

was simply plain-old lust that she'd mistaken for something else. Like she'd been mistaken about a whole lot of other things.

Dad, for instance . . .

Her gaze dropped to the computer as Wolf clattered about in the galley getting the tea ready.

There was a way she could check to confirm Wolf's suspicions about her father and what he'd intended with regard to Daniel. But it was a step she didn't know if she wanted to take. Because once she did, there would be no coming back from it.

You already took that step when you walked out of the restaurant with Wolf . . .

Crap. She was going to have to do this, wasn't she?

Olivia let out a breath and before she could second-guess herself, reached out and pulled the laptop toward her, opening it up and waiting until the screen flashed on. Then she opened a new tab on the browser and quickly typed in the web address she'd memorized. A password prompt appeared and she put it in, watching as the window to her father's private intranet appeared. She'd set up remote access to it months ago, in case she needed to access a file when she wasn't at home.

Quickly, she navigated through to his diary and began to sort through all his appointments, looking for any references to Daniel May. Her gut lurched. Because there were plenty of references, and a pattern. Every Monday, dead on at nine a.m., he had a meeting scheduled with Daniel. There were emails associated with those meetings too, private emails that would be easy enough to open up and read.

She sat back against the seat, her fingers cold as they dropped from the keyboard, and shaking slightly.

You should look at those emails.

But she didn't want to. She didn't want to see if her

father had discussed her with Daniel. Discussed her like she was nothing more to him than an asset he wanted disposed of in the right way.

No. She didn't want to know that. Did she?

She reached for the keyboard again anyway, clicking on one of the emails from her father.

"Don't worry," one paragraph began. *"I'll talk Olivia round. She may not like the idea initially but I can make her see reason. 'No' will not be an option. You can leave that to me—"*

Olivia pushed the laptop shut abruptly, an icy feeling settling down inside her, her heart trying to pound itself out of her ribcage.

" 'No' will not be an option."

"Hey." Wolf's voice came from near her elbow. "What were you doing with my computer?"

A mug of tea appeared on the table in front of her and she stared at it as he slid into the circular bench, taking up a position opposite her.

"Liv?" he asked, sounding puzzled. "Are you okay?"

But there was an odd roaring in her ears.

Wolf had been telling the truth. Her father had been going to give her to Daniel May after all. And not in a "go on a few dates, see how it goes" kind of way. In a "no will not be an option" kind of way.

Oh God. What if she had refused? What would he have done? Forced her to see Daniel? Forced her to marry him? To sleep with him?

Everything in her recoiled.

Why the outrage? You weren't going to say no anyway.

Yes, even as she'd sat at the table with Daniel, she'd been telling herself it wouldn't be so bad. Talking herself into it. Her father had seemed so genuine, telling her he wanted someone to protect her after he'd gone and that it would also be a good business decision. Using words guaranteed to make her stop and think and consider.

Manipulating you.

The walls of the cabin felt like they were closing in. Her hands were cold and her breath was short, and she wanted to get out, get some air. Get some space. Find somewhere to think, to sort through what she'd learned.

She got up jerkily, bumping the table and spilling the tea.

"Liv?" Wolf's gaze narrowed. "You better fucking tell me what's going on. You've gone white."

But she wasn't listening, already blindly moving on shaky legs out of the living area and down the tiny corridor. She pushed open a door and found herself in a surprisingly spacious bedroom, with a giant bed right in front of her, bathed in light from the portholes.

This was not the way out. Dammit. She must have missed the stairs back up to the deck.

She turned. Only to come up short as Wolf appeared right in front of her, his massive, broad-shouldered form taking up the entire doorway.

His green-and-blue gaze was laser sharp, moving over her. "Are you gonna tell me what the hell is going on with you or are you gonna make me have to guess?"

She sucked in a fruitless breath, feeling like she was suffocating. He was too close. He made this room too small. He made everything too small. Taking up all the space and all the air. Filling it up with his scent and his heat and his huge, muscular presence.

A surge of adrenaline went through her, breaking through the feeling of suffocation and the roaring in her ears.

This was all his fault.

He was the reason she was here and not with Daniel. He was the reason she was feeling this way. He'd put that seed of doubt inside her. And that doubt was why she'd looked at that email. Now there wasn't any doubt, only certainty.

Things were not what she thought. Her father wasn't what she thought. And now it felt as if the foundations of her life had been undermined and eroded away. Her safe little life, where she worked for her father who loved her. Who needed her. Who was a good man.

It had all been fine until Wolf had come through her bedroom window and taken her away, telling her things she didn't want to hear, making her see truths she didn't want to see. That maybe her father wasn't the man she thought he was after all. And that if Wolf had been telling the truth about her father giving her to May, then maybe he was telling the truth about other things as well.

Such as the fact that Dad killed his father?

"Get out of the way." Her voice came out far louder than she wanted it to.

His gaze narrowed. "What happened, Liv? You were okay and then suddenly you went white. What did you see on that computer?"

He'd lied to her. For ten years Wolf had told her he was her friend and he wasn't. He'd been playing her.

Just like Dad was playing you.

Anger flared, white hot, and before she could stop herself, she'd lifted her hands and slammed them against his chest, shoving at him to make him get out of her way, to give her space.

He didn't move.

It enraged her. She never lost her temper, certainly never hit anyone. But now she relished the burn of anger running through her, shoving him again. Harder. Yet it was like pushing at a big block of stone. He stayed exactly where he was.

Her anger became fury, fueled by the deep hurt she'd been ignoring and trying to deny. Hurt at the way he'd lied to her, at the way he'd made her believe that it was her he was interested in when he'd become her friend. Hurt at the truths he'd exposed about her father. Hurt at the doubts he'd uncovered within herself. Doubts she'd ignored and refused to listen to. Doubts about her father. Doubts about herself.

You were never precious to him, just useful.

Olivia's hands curled into fists and she slammed them into Wolf's chest, wanting to hurt him the way he'd hurt her, wanting to do *something* because she didn't know how to deal with the complicated rush of pain and doubt and fury that was filling her, consuming her.

Wolf said nothing as she drove her fists into him. Didn't make a sound. Didn't even move. He only stared at her, the expression in his eyes impenetrable.

Hitting him was like hurling stones at a mountain. It had no effect whatsoever.

That didn't stop her from launching fist after fist into his chest, hurting herself because hitting all that dense muscle was like hitting a brick wall over and over.

Then Wolf grabbed her, wrapping his long fingers around her wrists and holding them still. "You done?" he demanded, his gravelly voice even rougher than normal.

The restraint only made her madder. "No!" She tried to pull her hands away from his. "Let me go, asshole!"

But he didn't. He simply held her as if he could stand there all day while she pulled and raged. Watching her impassively as if all of this meant absolutely nothing to him.

It made her rage go from burning to incandescent.

How dare he stand there unaffected? Like he had been for the past ten years, while she'd burned for him. Longed for him. But of course he was unaffected. He didn't want her. He never had. And that kiss outside the restaurant had been just another lie.

She had no idea what she was doing. She only wanted

to get a reaction from him any way she could. So she stepped right up close to him and rose up on her tiptoes, bringing her mouth to his.

Then she sunk her teeth into his bottom lip.

He grunted and jerked his head back, his eyes thin slits of emerald and sapphire, glittering down at her. "What the fuck was that for?"

She was trembling, her anger not ebbing but changing, alchemizing into something hotter. More desperate. Suddenly becoming aware of the pressure of his fingers around her wrists, the heat of his massive, chiseled body inches from hers, the intoxicating scent of him going straight to her head. And all she wanted to do was to fling herself at him, break herself on him, channel all of her rage and all the years of loneliness and lies into him. Emotionally exhaust herself so she didn't have to think anymore. So she didn't have to hurt.

She didn't answer him. Instead she rose up on her toes again and this time she didn't bite him. She kissed him instead, inexpert and clumsy, not knowing what the hell she was doing and not caring. Not caring about the line she was crossing either. She pressed her lips to his desperately, pushed her tongue inside his mouth and tasted him, some dark delicious flavor she couldn't name, but made her instantly a thousand times hungrier than she'd ever been in her life.

She made a helpless sound in the back of her throat, wanting more.

"Liv," Wolf said harshly against her lips, but she didn't stop.

Instead she wrenched her hands from his grip, touching him again, pulling at his shirt as she kissed him, fingers trembling as she yanked open the buttons and found his skin. As hot and as smooth as she remembered.

She groaned. He felt so good. Hard and perfect. Invulnerable. Like rock, like a mountain, as if he would be there forever. Nothing wearing him away, nothing wearing him down. A constant, enduring presence who would never leave.

The harsh sound of someone's breathing filled the confined space of the cabin. Hers. But she didn't care about that either. Desperate to touch even more of him, she ripped his shirt from his massive shoulders, jerking it down his arms and away from him.

He didn't move as she spread her hands on his bare chest, stroking and touching, pressing kisses to his throat and down further, licking the salty heat of his skin.

Her heart was raging and her own skin felt too tight. She was so desperate she didn't know what to do. She pressed herself against his hard body, the chain of his dog tags cool against her fingertips as she explored the sculpted muscle of his chest, tracing the ink of his eagle and trident.

It wasn't enough. But she didn't know how to ask for more. And he was standing so still. As if her touching him had no effect whatsoever.

Tipping her head back, she looked up at him, fear curling in her heart.

But it wasn't indifference that glowed in those beautiful eyes of his. It was heat. And it set her on fire.

"What do you want?" The words were guttural.

"You," she said raggedly, because there was no point in pretending otherwise, not even to protect herself. "Now."

He didn't hesitate, gripping her hips and walking her back until the edge of the bed was against the backs of her knees. Then she was down on the mattress and he was with her.

Excitement took her by the throat as his big body surrounded her, and she expected to be pulled beneath him. Instead he rolled onto his back, taking her with him so she found herself straddling his lean hips. Exactly the way she'd been sitting that morning in the hotel.

"You wanna drive, baby?" The words were full of rough, lazy heat. Yet the hunger in his eyes was anything but lazy. "Take me out for a spin?"

Lying back there, shirtless, all powerful muscle, tanned skin, and ink, he was so hot she couldn't think. Couldn't even speak. All she could do was nod.

His mouth curled and he lifted his hands to the fabric of her dress, beginning to slide the hem up her legs, holding her gaze with his as he did so.

He went slowly, making her shudder as his hot palms brushed over the bare skin of her thighs. Oh God, he was so hot she was going to have to check herself for scorch marks later.

She tried to breathe normally, but it was impossible. Not when every nerve ending she had was achingly aware of his hot palms on her skin. Aware too of the raw heat and power of his body beneath her, and the hard length that was pressing insistently against the inside of her thigh.

There was no mistaking that. He wanted her. He was hard for her. And men couldn't lie, not about that.

She felt dizzy looking down at him as he drew the hem of her dress up to her hips, his gaze dropping down between her thighs. "Wolf . . ." Her voice was shaking and she didn't know what she was asking for. Maybe just to say his name.

This was happening. This was real. And she didn't know if she could handle it.

"It's okay." His eyes gleamed from beneath long, black lashes. "I'm gonna make you feel so good, Liv." Then he pushed all the fabric of her dress to the side, his finger drawing a slow, hot line right down the center of her sex, tracing her through her panties.

She gasped, the gasp turning into another groan as he

stroked his finger back up, lingering to circle her clit, before tracing another line back down again.

No one had touched her like this before. She'd never even touched herself like this before. It made her feel as if she'd been plugged into a power socket, electricity surging through her veins, pleasure lighting her up. He stroked her again, then once more, and she shook, her breathing starting to get faster, harsher.

"You like that?" His voice was rough velvet and heat.

"Y-Yes. God . . ." His finger circled her clit through the fabric of her panties again, lazily, as if he had all the time in the world. And the pleasure it gave her was . . . indescribable. It made her restless and needy. It made her ache.

She shifted against his hand, wanting him to touch her with more pressure. "Wolf . . . please . . ."

"Impatient, huh?" He gave her another long, slow stroke that left her gasping, then his hand dropped away. "Hang on." Without moving position, he reached over to a drawer inset in the smooth wood that made up the headboard and pulled it open, taking something out of it.

She watched him, dazed, her hands in fists, her nails digging into her palms because she didn't know what else to do with them. She didn't know what to do with herself. She'd never thought about this moment, or let herself imagine it, and now it was happening. Now it was real.

Wolf had taken out a condom and soon he would be inside her.

She couldn't handle it, the thought overwhelming. Yet she couldn't move either. Something was holding her there, making her watch as he unzipped his jeans and reached down beneath the fabric, his fingers curling around something long and thick and hard.

Her breath caught, a shiver moving over her skin.

If you're going to leave, leave.

But then it was too late, because he was drawing out his cock and she couldn't look away. And she'd been right about the long and the thick and the hard. He was all that and probably more.

Her heartbeat was deafening as he ripped open the packet and took out the condom, rolling the latex down with a lazy, practiced motion that she somehow found unbearably erotic.

Then he reached for her, those big, warm palms settling on her hips, drawing her up his body a little.

She was shaking, her mind struggling to process what was happening.

He reached to pull aside the fabric of her panties, keeping his gaze on hers as he stroked lightly through the slick folds of her sex, drawing a gasp of agonized pleasure from her. Then he did it again, grazing her clit with the pad of one finger, making her toes curl and sending a shudder through her.

"You look scared." The words were soft and gravelly, the intensity of his gaze inescapable. "Are you sure you want this?"

She couldn't speak. The slow, firm pressure of his finger on her clit seemed to drag all the air from her lungs and all the words from her head.

No she wasn't sure, at least not emotionally. But her body was desperate. Her body had waited years for this moment, and now that it was here, it didn't want to be denied.

She gave him a jerky nod.

Emerald and sapphire flared in his gaze, a flash of heat that scorched her soul. Then his fingers were parting her wet flesh and the head of his cock was pressing against her entrance, spreading her open, stretching her.

She made a helpless, inarticulate sound, shuddering as he pressed harder against her. His hands gripped her tighter, tilting her hips, and then she was sliding down onto him, and it hurt enough to make her cry out, her vision blurring with sudden tears.

He didn't move. "Breathe," he murmured. "Breathe, baby. It'll be okay. Only lasts a second, I promise." His hands shifted from her hips to her thighs, stroking up and down, a calming, soothing motion.

She stared down at him, shivering all over. She felt stretched apart, invaded. Impaled. He was there, inside her. So hard and hot, filling her up so completely she couldn't even breathe, no matter how many times he told her to.

"I can't . . ." Was that her voice? All cracked and broken? "I can't, Wolf . . ."

"Yes, you can." His palms were on her hips again, settling her down on him, and unbelievably, the pain and the full feeling began to fade, leaving behind it a maddening, aching pressure.

She sucked in a ragged breath and found him watching her, unmistakable hunger in his eyes. "You wanna move?"

And she did. Oh God, she *really* did. "Yes," she croaked. "But how?"

His mouth curved in a smile that made her heart slam hard against her breastbone. "Let me show you." His hands tightened on her hips, guiding her, moving her in a slow, undulating motion, up and down.

It felt weird at first, but pretty soon there was nothing weird about it. No, it was the opposite. It felt right, natural, and the way his cock slid in and out of her, the friction of it, was incredible. She couldn't stop staring at him, at his long, hard body stretched out underneath her, at the play of his muscles, tensing and relaxing as she moved on him. A big, powerful, dangerous animal and she was in control. She was riding him.

His eyes gleaming hot through his lashes, the lines of

his face drawn tight with hunger. With lust. He wasn't immobile now and he definitely wasn't indifferent, and she was the one who had done this to him.

It was so unbelievably sexy to realize that at last, at last, she wasn't the only one feeling this way.

"Does that feel good?" His drawl was ragged round the edges, threaded through with heat. "Do you like it?"

"Yes." Her own voice didn't sound much better. "Yes . . . God . . . *so* good."

His gaze dropped down to where they were joined, lingering there, the glow in his eyes flaring. "Yeah, so do I . . ."

The pressure inside her was building, the pull of the pleasure becoming stronger, deeper. But it wasn't enough—she wanted more. She wanted faster. Harder. Putting her hands flat on his chest, her fingers spreading out to touch as much of his hot skin as she could, she leaned forward, shifting her hips, trying to intensify the angle.

His gaze flicked back up to hers and she was caught by the beauty of the jewel-bright colors once again. So different. So special. Just like him.

She shifted again, pressing herself down harder on him, and he hissed.

"*Fuck*, yes . . ." His mouth twisted in a snarl. "Do it again. Fucking ride me, baby. Harder."

She was desperate to, but she'd never done this before and couldn't find the rhythm, so he showed her again. Holding her tight, lifting her up on him and slamming her back down, over and over.

The pressure inside her rose to intolerable levels. She was shaking, trembling all over, and suddenly terrified for reasons she didn't understand. Her fingers dug into the hard muscle and warm skin of his chest, desperate to hold onto him, to anything that would keep her grounded, because when this pressure blew, she didn't know what would happen.

She kept saying his name over and over, and somehow he must have understood her wordless panic. Because the next time he brought her down hard on him, he held her there and rolled, and she found herself on her back beneath him, his huge, rock-hard body over hers, covering her. Surrounding her completely.

Driving into her deep, his fingers between her thighs, stroking her clit as he thrust, and that aching, intolerable pressure finally burst apart, shattering her.

She screamed, scratching her nails heedlessly down his back before digging into the heavy, dense muscle of his shoulders, feeling herself coming apart beneath him. Only dimly aware of his rhythm getting faster, wilder, out of control.

Then he stiffened, turning his head against her neck, and groaned. "Oh, fuck, *Olivia* . . ." All four syllables, harsh and desperate. Her name in his mouth the way she'd never heard it before.

She lay there beneath him, trembling with the aftershocks as this big, powerful man came apart just as she had not seconds earlier. And she held onto him as the shudders rocked him, feeling like she'd been torn apart and then put back together in a way that was unfamiliar. Too new and strange to take in.

Wolf Tate, the man she'd been in love with since she'd been fifteen years old, had taken her virginity and it was too much.

Everything was too much.

Olivia closed her eyes and burst into tears.

CHAPTER TEN

Wolf heard her sob, half muffled against his shoulder, and felt the shudder that went through her small body tucked up under his. A lot of chicks cried after sex, especially when the sex had been mind-blowing, and it had never bothered him before. He simply held them and stroked them until whatever emotional storm had passed.

But the sound of Olivia's sobs hit him in a completely different way.

He didn't like the sound, for a start. It made his chest feel tight, made him think about whether he'd made a mistake, that he shouldn't have given her what she wanted after all.

It made him feel like he'd hurt her—and that thought, in turn, hurt him.

He shifted his body so he wasn't lying directly on top her, because she was very small and he wasn't. Then he did what he normally did and kept his arms around her, tucking her head beneath his chin, stroking the long silky brown strands of her hair.

She gave another sob, burrowing into his neck, and began to cry in earnest, her breath warm and damp against his bare skin.

Wolf stared up at the low wooden ceiling, at the long bar of afternoon sunlight that came through the porthole and stretched over the wood. The familiar movement of the boat at the dock was soothing. Olivia weeping, not so much.

Fuck, had he made a mistake? Had he taken what he shouldn't have?

He'd had no idea what had set her off, what had made her get up from the table and head straight for the bedroom. She'd clearly been trying to get off the boat, which he couldn't allow, not when her father would no doubt by now be mobilizing his forces to find her.

He'd simply wanted to make sure she didn't blow their cover, plus find out what the hell she'd been so upset about. He hadn't expected her to suddenly start laying into him, her small fists battering against his chest.

She'd been angry about something, that was for sure. No, not simply angry, she'd been furious. And for some reason she'd turned it on him. He'd let her hit him, because it hadn't hurt and she clearly needed to get rid of some of her rage. But then he thought she might hurt herself, since he wasn't exactly a soft target, so he'd grabbed her wrists and held on.

She'd looked at him then and he'd seen the moment the anger had turned into something different. He hadn't expected her to act on it though. To step up to him, bite him. Kiss him.

Perhaps if she'd left it after the bite, he'd have been fine. He would have been able to resist. But she hadn't. She'd kissed him again, awkward and hesitant, her fingers shaking as she clawed at the material of his shirt. Shaking as they'd touched his skin, her breath coming in short, hard pants.

He'd never had a woman be so desperate for him before. So desperate that her hands shook. Women liked him, and when he had sex, he made sure they went away happy and satisfied. But there was something about the way Olivia had touched him. As if she couldn't get enough of him.

She'd wanted him so long. Longer than he'd ever expected. And now she was touching him . . .

That touch of hers did things to him, traced fire all over him, and he'd thought he'd let her explore for a bit and then gently but calmly push her away. Because having sex with her hadn't featured in any of his plans.

Their relationship had already gotten complicated after he'd told her the truth about his friendship with her. Sex wasn't going to make things any clearer.

But . . . he'd found he couldn't breathe, that his heart was going as hard as if he'd been on a twenty-mile ruck march, and that he ached. Not only his cock either. There was an ache inside him, somewhere deep, that wanted her hands on him. That wanted more of her shy, hesitant kisses. Her shaking, trembling touches.

He shouldn't have asked her what she wanted. Shouldn't have looked into her eyes, seen the hot blue flame burning there.

You. . . . Now.

He'd never been a man who'd been good at resisting temptation, and Olivia in her little blue dress, her eyes full of heat, her rosebud mouth full and red from the kisses she'd given him, was his biggest temptation yet.

He'd told himself that refusing her would hurt her and he knew that rejecting her advances definitely would.

But that wasn't the whole story. Something inside him wanted her just as badly, and right here, right now had seemed liked the perfect time.

So he hadn't thought. He'd simply given her what she'd wanted. Him.

And it had been . . . incredible.

Virgins weren't his thing, he didn't have the patience. But with her, he found he had a boundless supply. Taking her down onto the bed, feeling her slight weight rest on him, the heat of her pussy seeping through his jeans, driving him insane.

He'd wanted to flip her over, tear her panties off, sink inside her immediately, then fuck them both into oblivion. But he'd held himself back, letting her sit on him so he could see her face, studying her reactions as he'd drawn her dress up, as he'd traced her hot little pussy through the material of her panties.

She'd been so wet, so slick. And when he'd touched her, he'd seen the bright flare of reaction that had crossed her face, heard her soft, shocked gasp.

Yeah, somewhere deep inside himself, he'd found that patience for her. Had taken it slow, had kept himself under control. Watching her, touching her, feeling the tight, wet heat of her sex close like a fist around his cock, had been . . .

He'd had a lot of women. Done a lot of things with them. Sometimes he'd had two at once and on a couple of memorable evenings, three.

But for some reason the sight of Olivia de Santis, her dress pulled up above her hips, her blue eyes black with desire, her panting gasps filling the room as she'd moved on his cock, had been the most erotic experience of his life.

And when the orgasm had broken over him it had been like an IED exploding right near his head, blowing him to bits and taking his consciousness with it.

Yeah, he'd never had that happen to him before. An orgasm so intense it had blinded him.

His body tightened, more than ready for another round, but Wolf ignored it for the meantime, turning his head and checking on Olivia. Her sobs had quieted and she now lay beside him, breathing softly, her breath warm against his neck.

If this had been like any normal sexual encounter, he'd have pushed her onto her back and gotten her ready for round two, but this wasn't a normal sexual encounter. And this wasn't some chick he'd picked up in a bar.

This was Olivia. Who'd been a virgin. Who'd need some special handling after this.

Moving her gently, he got himself free then got off the bed and went over to the door that led to the tiny bathroom, stepping inside to get rid of the condom. Then he ran some warm water in the basin and found a clean washcloth, soaking it before wringing it out.

He undressed completely after that, leaving his clothes in a heap on the floor, before coming back to the bed with the damp cloth.

Olivia lay on her back, one arm thrown over her face. The buttons of her dress were open up to her waist, exposing the luscious curves of both waist and thighs, her pale strokeable skin.

She looked absolutely fucking delicious.

He came down onto the bed, reaching for her panties and slowly easing them down her thighs. She made a soft noise and took her arm away from over her eyes, revealing her tearstained, flushed face.

So fucking delicious. So fucking beautiful.

Her blue gaze dropped to the cloth in his hand. "What are you doing?"

"Figured you might be sore. This will help." Gently he nudged her legs apart, noting the small spots of blood on the fragile skin of her inner thighs.

Yep. Definitely a virgin.

"Wolf . . ." She made a small embarrassed sound as he brought the washcloth between her legs, her hand half reaching to push his away as he stroked the cloth gently over her.

"Hey," he chided. "Let me do this. It'll feel good okay?"

She pulled a face. "I can do it myself."

"Sure, you can. But I want to, so you're going to let me."

She made a sound of disagreement, but didn't move away or try to stop him. Instead she threw her arm back over her face again, tensing as he brought the cloth to her skin. But it didn't last long, the tension easing out of her as he stroked her, cleaning away the last remains of the blood, soothing her.

She sighed. "I'm sorry." Her voice was still muffled behind her arm. "I don't know what happened to me."

"Sorry? Sorry for what?"

"For crying. I didn't mean to. It just . . . came out."

"It's okay. You've got nothing to apologize for." He got rid of the cloth down beside the bed, then reached up and pulled her arm away from her face so he could look into her eyes. "It sometimes happens, especially when the sex happens to be mind-blowing."

She blinked. "Mind-blowing?"

He gave her a slow smile, letting her see just how incredible he'd found it. "Hell, you certainly blew *my* mind, baby."

Olivia looked away, adorably flushed. "Yes, well, I shouldn't have hit you either."

He reached out and began to undo the little buttons that held the front of her dress together, taking it slow because the way the fabric parted, giving him a glimpse of her pale, silky looking skin, was something he wanted to savor. "You want to tell me what that was about?"

Her gaze dropped to watch his hand sliding the buttons out of the buttonholes, but she made no move to stop him. "I've got access to Dad's intranet, so that was what I was doing with your laptop. Having a look at his diary. I just wanted to check . . . about Daniel. You know . . ." She stopped.

He did. She'd wanted to check to see if he'd been telling her the truth.

He said nothing, easing the rest of her buttons open,

then pushing aside the blue fabric. As he'd suspected, she was gorgeous. Full breasts cupped in white lace, the pink of her nipples visible through the material. Beautifully rounded hips and the prettiest little thatch of dark curls between her thighs.

She was all soft and womanly, and his palms itched to touch her.

"I know," he murmured, unable to drag his gaze from her body. "You wanted to see if I was lying. And I wasn't, was I?"

She shook her head. A flush stained her skin, creeping up her neck. "I don't know what to do, Wolf. I don't know what to think. I thought at least I'd get a choice about Daniel, but I read one of Dad's emails to him and it said"— her eyes were huge and dark—"it said that no wasn't an option."

The tightness in his chest that had gripped when she'd cried, gripped him again at the distress in her face. No matter how he felt about Cesare de Santis, the prick was Olivia's father. And she loved him. And finding out that he wasn't the man she'd thought he was, was always going to be hard for her.

She might not be ready to face the whole truth about him yet, but the seeds of doubt had been planted.

If you handle this right, she'll give you want you want the way you wanted it to happen all along.

Him seducing her. Her willingly handing him her father's head on a plate. Yeah, a couple of days ago that's exactly what he'd been hoping would happen.

And now . . . it kind of was happening, wasn't it? She had access to Cesare's intranet, which meant he could get her to look at his schedule from here. He wouldn't even need to leave the yacht. He wouldn't need to use her as bait.

Then again, Cesare would know by now that Wolf had taken his daughter. Which meant that Wolf's element of surprise was gone. De Santis would be armoring himself with whatever security he could get, making a hit impossible. Using Olivia as bait was still Wolf's best option.

In which case, why didn't he feel more triumphant about it? Or at least relieved? Because he didn't feel either of those things. All he could see was the distress in her blue eyes, knowing that this discovery about her father would hurt her and hurt her terribly.

And that he did *not* like. Not one bit.

But it was too late to do anything about it now. She'd seen the emails, the doubt would be settling down inside her, and as for the seduction . . . he hadn't planned that. She'd made the decision for him. But he wasn't sorry about it, not at all, and now he had her lying half naked in his bed, he wasn't going to give her up.

Not yet at least.

He couldn't take away all the lies he'd told her, or the betrayal of what her father had done to her. After all, the only things he was good at was fighting and blowing shit up. But there was one other thing he could do and do well.

Fucking. He was *really* good at fucking.

Gently, he stripped away the fabric of her dress, taking her bra with it so she was left lying entirely naked on the white sheets. She remained quiet as he bared her, saying nothing as he pressed her back against the pillows, kneeling between her spread thighs before leaning forward, his hands resting on the pillows beside her head so he could look down at her.

"I know it's hard," he said, offering what he could. "He's your dad and it sucks. You gave him your loyalty, worked your ass off for him, and he shouldn't treat you like that."

She turned her head on the pillow, avoiding his gaze. "I thought he cared about me." Her voice was husky. "I thought it mattered to him that I hadn't left him, that I hadn't betrayed him like everyone else had. But I guess he didn't care about me after all. I was just another tool for him to use."

Just the way you're using her right now.

Wolf looked down into her pale face, seeing the hurt she made no attempt to hide. Feeling the hurt himself. He didn't know how that worked, that he felt her pain as acutely as she did, but he did.

He had shit he had to do and he needed her to get to de Santis. But something inside him told him that his bait plan sucked. That he couldn't use her to do it. For the past ten years that's all he'd been doing, using her friendship to get close to de Santis. Using her the way her father had used her, as a tool, a means to an end.

And he couldn't do it. That would make him no better than de Santis and fuck that. He wasn't going to use her and he wasn't going to lie to her, not anymore. Their friendship might have started out fake on his end, but that hadn't stopped him from liking her, from coming to care about her. Sure, it was the weakness his father had warned about, but it was too late. It had happened.

He didn't want to hurt her anymore, and so he wouldn't.

It would play havoc with his already shitty plans, but too bad. He'd have to figure out some way around it.

Wolf reached down and took her chin in his hand, turning her head back to face him. Her eyes were very dark as they met his and the hurt in them made him want to growl.

"What do I do, Wolf?" she whispered. "What do I do now? When he finds out I went with you willingly, he'll never forgive me. He'll never forgive me anyway if I don't marry Daniel. If he even lets me refuse in the first place."

He stroked her chin, the musky, feminine scent of her messing with his restraint. But he held on to his insistent libido, because that could wait. Right now, she was more important. "We'll cross that bridge when we come to it, okay?"

But the distress in her eyes didn't lift. "He won't let me come home, I know it. And then I'll have nowhere to go and no one . . ." She stopped, swallowing.

"You don't have no one." He stared down into her eyes, willing her to understand. "You have me, Liv."

She blinked. "How can I have you? You lied to me. You weren't ever my friend, not really. God, you don't even want me. All of this is just . . . I don't know. Pity sex, maybe."

If she hadn't looked so hurt, he would have laughed. Pity sex? Jesus.

"I don't do pity sex, and as for wanting you . . ." He paused, because this was important and he wanted no more lies between them. "You're right. I didn't want you at the start. Dad told me that I should seduce you, because then you'd be more likely to tell me stuff. But I told him no, that you were too young. And then, by the time I'd gotten to know you, I'd realized that you were . . . so much more. " He held her gaze, letting her see the truth in his. "You were too bright, too sharp. Way too fucking smart for me. You always knew what to say and not only that, you listened too. You made me feel like I wasn't stupid, Liv. That I could do more than just break stuff, hit stuff. You were too good for me, and so I made sure I never saw you as anything more than a friend."

Her eyes had gone wide, her lips parting like she wanted to say something, yet nothing came out.

He let his fingers trail from her chin down her throat, feeling her soft silky skin beneath his fingertips. "I was going to seduce you in the hotel, use sex to get that information out of you, but it wasn't going to mean anything. And then I kissed you and . . ." He stopped. "I'm shit with words, Liv. You know that. I can't describe how it changed for me, it just did. But here . . ." He reached for her hand and brought it to his chest, pressing her palm flat to the skin above his heart. Stared into the deep midnight blue of her eyes. "Feel what you do to me." Keeping her hand there, he lowered his head and brushed his lips over hers. Once. Then again. And then he slid his tongue deep into the heat of her mouth, exploring her slowly, tasting her. Letting his heartbeat race as the kiss deepened, got hotter.

He never kissed like this. Never went slow like this. But he wanted her to know he wasn't lying. That this time it was true, he wanted her. And not *for* anything, or because she would give him something. He wanted her for her.

After a moment, he lifted his head and looked at her.

There was wonder in her eyes. "Your heart is beating so fast." Her palm rested on his skin like a small, hot coal. "Is that . . . me?" She sounded shocked.

He smiled. "Yes." Taking her hand from his chest, he guided it further down between their bodies, to where he was already hard and ready for her, closing her fingers around him. "This is you too."

Her eyes went even wider, searching his face.

"I'm not gonna lie to you anymore, Liv," he said. "It's gonna be nothing but the truth from now on. I promise."

Her gaze dipped to his mouth, her fingers around him squeezing slightly, making his breath catch. "We probably shouldn't do this. I mean, it can't be a good idea, can it?"

"Do you want to stop?" Fuck, *he* didn't want to, but if she did, then he'd have to. "Because if you do, just tell me and I'll stop."

Silky dark lashes came down, veiling her gaze for an instant. Then slowly they rose again, her blue eyes wide and dark as the midnight sky. "No," she whispered. "I don't want to stop."

A surge of desire went through him, making him catch his breath. Making him go very still in case he lost his grip on his restraint, and simply pounded her into the mattress there and then. He didn't want to do that. She deserved more. He wanted to go slowly, touch her the way she'd touched him, gently and carefully, as if she was a work of art. Savor her.

But if he was going to do that, she needed to take her hand off his dick.

Reaching down, he pulled her hand gently away, relishing the small sound of protest she made as he pressed her wrist into the pillow beside her head. "Uh-huh, baby. You've had me on my back with your hands all over me twice now. It's my turn."

"Wolf, I—"

He stopped her words with his mouth, giving her another long, deep kiss, before moving down, trailing kisses down her neck, tasting the salt and sweetness in the hollow of her throat. He hadn't known there could be pleasure in this for him as well, that the flutter of her pulse beneath his tongue could be exciting, feeling it begin to speed up for him. It made him hard, made him breathless to feel her sigh and shift beneath him.

He kept on going, moving down her curvy, delicious little body. Finding her full breasts and cupping one, feeling the soft weight of it in his palm. Fucking perfect.

She shuddered as he touched her, then shuddered again as he bent and licked a slow circle around one hard, pink nipple, teasing her. No one had ever done this to her before, no one had tasted her like this before. He was the first and he fucking loved that he was. And if that made him a primitive Neanderthal, then he was a goddamn primitive Neanderthal.

He flicked his gaze up her body as he touched his tongue to her nipple, watching shock and pleasure ripple over her expressive features. Then he closed his lips around the stiff peak and sucked on her, hard.

Olivia gasped, her cheeks flushing. And there was

something intensely erotic about the way she kept watching him, as if she couldn't help herself.

Her eyes were so dark, he'd never imagined blue could look black. Never imagined he'd ever lose himself in a woman's gaze. But he was beginning to lose himself in hers.

He shifted his hips, pressing his aching dick to the soft heat between her thighs. She was all wet and slippery, and he couldn't help grinding himself against her, loving the slide of his cock through her pussy.

She shuddered, and he could see the pleasure he was giving her glow in her eyes as she stared at him, felt the echo of it inside himself too. They were sharing it, a bright, shining line of sensation joining them, connecting them.

It was new to him, this feeling of connection. It shocked him, awed him.

He didn't want to lose it.

Releasing her nipple, he murmured, "Keep your eyes on me, baby. Don't look away." And she didn't as he began to kiss down her stomach, maintaining eye contact as he licked a circle round her belly button, and then further down.

She began to shake then, as he spread her thighs wider, holding them apart and keeping them there with his palms. "Wh-What are you doing to do?" she asked thickly, raggedly.

"What do think?" He gave her a wicked smile. "I'm going to eat you out." He could have prettied it up for her, but part of him wanted to shock her, make her blush again. Make her stammer. She always seemed to know what to say, so making her at a loss for words was particularly sweet.

Her mouth became a perfect O of surprise, then opened further as he used his thumbs to spread the slick folds of her pussy open, a husky sound escaping. He didn't look away from her as he lowered his head, or when he ran the flat of his tongue directly up the center of her sex.

She gasped his name, her hips jerking, but he pressed down on her thighs, pinning her to the bed as he circled her clit with his tongue, taking his time and being lazy with it. Watching her face go pinker and pinker, her eyes glowing.

She tasted as fucking delicious as he thought she would, so he lingered on her clit, teasing her, feeling her writhe beneath him, the cabin filling with her soft, husky cries of pleasure.

But he wasn't done yet. Even though he was hard as a fucking rock, he kept his grip on his patience, spreading her open even wider, licking down her pussy to the entrance of her body, and circling there too.

She jerked again, shuddering in his grip and panting.

He shifted, sliding his hands beneath her butt and lifting her, angling her hips, then pushing his tongue deep inside her.

Olivia cried out then put her hand over her mouth as if to silence herself, her breasts rising and falling fast and hard. There was a sheen in her midnight eyes, but he knew it wasn't because she was in pain or distressed.

It was because of the pleasure he was giving her and how overwhelming it was for her. But he didn't stop what he was doing, licking her deep and slow. Instead he reached out and took her hand, guiding it his head. "Hold on to me," he murmured. "Hold on tight."

He didn't need to tell her twice, her fingers instantly threading in his hair, holding on as he began to explore in earnest.

He shoved his shoulders beneath her thighs, so her knees were near his ears, her heels pushing hard into his back. And he licked her deeper, using his fingers on her clit, working her until her thighs began to tremble uncontrollably and she was writhing and crying his name over and over.

She pulled at his hair, and that and the taste of her pushed him nearly to the edge of his control. But he didn't move until her cries became screams and her thighs were clamped around his ears, her fingers gripping him so tight it felt like she was going to pull his hair out by the roots.

Then she abruptly collapsed back on the bed, panting, all the tension gone from her body.

Yeah, he wasn't done.

He let her lie there as he reached for another condom in the drawer by the headboard. But his hands were shaking as he ripped open the packet, and as he rolled the latex over himself, he felt her watching him.

He glanced at her, meeting her dark eyes, seeing behind the glaze of pleasure, satisfaction too, as if she liked the fact that his hands were shaking. It made him even harder and he wanted to say something wicked to her about it, about how hot she made him. But he was too close to the edge.

Instead, he flipped her over onto her front then shoved a pillow under her hips, pulling her back up so her butt pressed against his aching groin. She turned her head to the side, her body trembling.

He'd always liked this position, liked the power of it, but it felt even more intense now. The past couple of times he'd been at her mercy as she'd run her hands all over his chest, but now she was at his.

He slid a hand beneath her, spreading his fingers out on her stomach to hold her still, and then he flexed his hips, easing into her tight heat. Going slow, not only because she might still be tender, but also because slow seemed to be his new modus operandi and he was enjoying the hell out of it.

She took a sharp breath as he pushed into her, sliding as deep as he could get before pulling back, relishing the feel of her pussy clenching around every inch of his dick. Then again. The long, slick glide inside her, in and out, slow and deep.

Her lashes fluttered closed, her mouth open, soft sighs escaping as he moved.

The pleasure was beyond words. He stroked her hip, the curve of her ass, her soft, rounded thigh, something raw surging in him. The edge of desperation. Possessiveness. Need. She was lying on her front with her dark hair everywhere, her body clenching tight around him as he pushed in and out of her.

But there was too much space between them. Too much distance. He needed her close, her skin against his, not just at the point of their physical connection.

He shoved himself inside of her and then leaned forward, putting his hands down on either side of her head, covering her completely with his body. She gave a moan and now he could feel her pressed up against him, every inch of her, and that was so much better. So fucking *good*. Her tight little pussy gripping his cock, the softness of her ass against his groin, her elegant spine to his chest. Her hair smelled like heaven itself, and he buried his face in her neck, thrusting harder, deeper.

She moved beneath him, her hips in time with his, and she had the rhythm now, his beautiful Olivia. It wasn't just him driving.

But fucking hell, it was too good and he was losing it.

So he whispered her name, bit her shoulder, pushed one hand beneath her and found her clit with his finger, rubbing it over and over in time with his thrusts, until she went stiff beneath him, crying out against the pillow.

Then he moved harder, deeper, feeling savage and feral. Like an animal with a potential mate. Wanting to claim her, mark her. Make her his so completely she'd never want anything different. Never want anyone else.

He'd never felt like this before, and perhaps he should have fought it. Olivia de Santis wasn't his and never would be. But he didn't fight it. Because right now, right here, she *was* his. She'd given herself to him, he'd been her choice, and that meant something. He didn't know quite what, but something. Something important.

The pleasure began to release in an astonishing, annihilating wave, rolling over him, crushing him, and he cried her name against her neck, holding tight as he thrust one last time deep and hard into her.

And let the climax drag him under.

CHAPTER ELEVEN

Olivia woke to find that the bed was moving. In fact, the whole room seemed to be moving, and it took her a moment or two to remember why.

Lunch with Daniel. Wolf coming for her. The yacht. Her freak-out and then . . .

A wash of heat went through her as memory hit, making her groan and fling an arm across her face.

Wolf's hands on her, Wolf's mouth on her. On her breasts and between her thighs. His cock inside her. Lying on her front with his massive body pressing her down onto the bed, anchoring her as he moved in her. Surging into her, powerful and inexorable as the tide itself . . .

There was an ache between her legs, insistent, nagging. She felt tender and a bit sore, and she would have said it was impossible to want him again, yet somehow she did.

Keeping one arm over her face, she reached out with the other, but after groping around a bit, it was clear that she was alone in the bed.

Disappointed, she moved her arm from her face and blinked around.

The cabin was, indeed, empty. The light coming through the portholes was fading, which meant she must have slept a good couple of hours. Strange. She never went to sleep during the day. Then again, she never had emotional break-downs, followed by the loss of her virginity either.

Sighing, she sat up, looking around for her clothes. Her blue dress was damp and scrunched up into a ball at the end of the bed, and she didn't like the idea of forcing her-self into it. It was tight and she didn't feel like wearing something tight. She felt . . . oddly light. As if there had been a stone sitting on her chest that had been taken away, and now all she needed to do was push off with her toes and she'd float right up into the sky.

It was weird.

Ignoring the dress, she found the shirt Wolf had been wearing on the floor and picked that up instead. It was far too big, the arms ridiculously long and the hem coming to just above her knees, but it wasn't tight and it smelled of him, and she liked the idea of being surrounded by his scent.

Slipping off the bed, she did the buttons up, then pushed open the door to the tiny corridor, moving toward the gal-ley and the living area.

Wolf was sitting on the funny circular bench, his atten-tion on the laptop placed on the table in front of him.

He was shirtless, all his incredible muscles and tattoos on display. The roughly handsome lines of his face were drawn into lines of intense concentration, his straight black brows pulling down. Through those long black lashes, she could see the glitter of his eyes, green and blue.

He was so beautiful.

He made her heart kick. Hard.

But not in the same way as before. Because now she knew things about him that she hadn't before. She knew what it was like to touch his skin and to have him touch her in return. To come with that hungry, avid gaze on her. To hear the sound of his own climax as he thrust deep and hard inside her. To have his tongue on her, in her . . .

Rough, physical, heated things. Things she'd never known and never imagined.

Things that changed the feeling in her chest in ways she didn't understand.

She must have made a sound, because he looked up suddenly, his gaze catching hers, making her instantly breathless.

He smiled and it felt as if the summer sun had flooded the small cabin with light and warmth. "Hey, baby. Want something to eat?"

She wanted to go and sit down, but that smile of his was making her feel unsteady, so she leaned against the doorframe instead. "Maybe. I never got my tea."

"Come sit. I'll make you a fresh one." He slid off the bench with all that fluid, athletic grace, and she thought he was going to move into the galley.

But he didn't. He came straight for her, and then his big palms were cupping her face, turning it up to his as his mouth came down on hers. Kissing her with such tenderness, she felt tears start behind her eyes.

Good God, crying? What was wrong with her? It was just a kiss.

With an effort, she blinked them away as he lifted his head and looked down at her, that gorgeous smile playing around his mouth. "Think you can make it to the table?"

"What do you mean?"

"You look a little unsteady on your feet. I mean, it's okay, I have that effect on women."

She laughed, half embarrassed, half thrilled that he'd noticed. "I think I can manage."

He ran a thumb over her cheekbone, making her shiver. "Dammit. There goes my excuse for picking you up and carrying you over there." His gaze dropped to her mouth. "Alternatively, I could just carry you back to bed. Your tea will have to wait though."

The nagging ache between her thighs liked this idea, liked it very much indeed, but her heart felt raw, the feeling inside her too different and new, making her think that a bit of space was what she needed, not more sex.

"Tempting." She touched his chest. "But I really need my tea. Plus . . . I'm a little sore." Not a lie, though not quite the truth either.

His gaze flickered and she had the impression he knew exactly how much of an excuse that was. But he didn't call her on it. Instead his smile warmed. "Hey, you're wearing my shirt."

She flushed like an idiot. "I hope you don't mind."

"Hell no. I like it." His hands dropped from her face and then she was in his arms, held against his broad, naked chest. "But if you're gonna wear it and nothing else, I can't be held responsible for anything that might happen to you."

For a second she thought she was going to be carried back to bed anyway, and part of her was thrilled at the idea, no matter what she'd decided about space.

But he didn't, turning instead and taking a couple of steps toward the bench, then depositing her on it.

Telling herself she wasn't disappointed, she watched him go back to the galley and start the tea-making process.

A strange silence fell, one that shouldn't have been awkward and yet somehow was.

Damn. Had her refusal to go back to bed hurt him? She couldn't think why it would.

"So," he said, his deep, rough voice breaking the silence. "Your father has started pulling the city apart looking for you."

A shock went through her. Oh God. She'd entirely forgotten about the fact that Wolf had supposedly kidnapped her. Again. And this time her father was under no illusion about who had done it.

"Oh," she said faintly. "And I guess he's looking for you too?"

"Yeah."

Fear began to curl icy tendrils through her. She stared at him. He was moving calmly, taking out a tea bag and dumping it in a cup, making her tea as if it was no big deal.

"How do you know?"

"I've got contacts keeping an eye on things. They let me know what's happening."

Olivia clasped her hands together to stop them from shaking. Her father would be *so* angry once he found out that Wolf had been lying to him all these years. So very, very angry. "Does he know that you've been—"

"No." Wolf poured hot water into her cup then added some milk, stirring. Then he dumped the tea bag, picked up the cup, and brought it over to her, placing it on the table in front of her. "All he knows is that I interrupted your romantic lunch with May, took you out, and disappeared."

She looked up at him, not wanting to pick up the tea yet since her fingers still weren't steady and she didn't want to spill it. "You shouldn't have come into the restaurant. You should have sent a note to me or something, kept your identity secret."

He gave her another of those heartbreaking smiles, touching her cheekbone lightly. "You worried about me?"

There was no point in denying it. "Yes, of course I'm worried about you. Dad will be furious and I don't know what he'll do if he catches you."

But Wolf only shrugged. "I'm a SEAL, Liv. I'm not exactly helpless. Plus, I'm not planning on having him catch me."

Her hands twisted in her lap. "But what if someone followed us from the restaurant?"

"No one followed us from the restaurant." He moved around the other side of the table and sat down, pushing shut the laptop. There was something sitting next to it, something long and lethal looking, metal gleaming in the last rays of the sun coming through the portholes.

A gun.

The icy tendrils of fear deepened.

Wolf picked it up and began checking over it, each movement practiced and certain and capable, as if he'd done this a thousand times. "I made sure we weren't tailed in the taxi, that's why I got him to drop us off a little way from the boat basin. I also made sure we avoided any security cameras. The *Lady* isn't registered under my name, neither is the berth here, so even if somehow someone suspects we're on a boat, they're going to find it damn near impossible to track us down." He flicked something on the gun that made a clicking sound, then placed it back down on the table and met her gaze. "As long as we stay here, we're safe."

Olivia looked into his eyes. He looked so calm. Strong and steady, that mountain enduring. It should have reassured her. But inexplicably, all she seemed able to concentrate on were those icy threads of fear.

Maybe it was the gun. The way he held it . . .

"Okay," she said, trying to ignore the cold feeling. "I understand. But how long do we have to stay here for?"

He didn't look away. "Until I've figured out how to take your father down."

Oh. Yes. She'd forgotten about that.

Deciding this was a great time to try that tea, she took her hands from her lap and picked up the cup. The ceramic was hot against her chilly fingers, almost burning, but she didn't let it go. Instead she raised it to her mouth and sipped.

"I told you I wasn't going to lie to you anymore," Wolf went on quietly. "And I meant it. When I told you I'm taking your father down, I meant permanently."

Permanently.

It took her a second to process that because he couldn't mean what she thought he meant. Because permanent meant . . .

"Yes." Wolf's gaze was unflinching. "I'm going to kill him, Olivia."

The icy grip of fear spread out inside her, making her fingers go numb, and she almost lost her grip on her teacup. Putting it down, the cup rattling against the saucer, her heart beginning to race, she started at him in disbelief.

There was nothing but hard certainty in his beautiful eyes.

"Why?" The word sounded breathless and shocked. "Because he supposedly killed your father?"

"Yes." His voice was harder than granite, clipped. "And because he's not gonna stop until he's crushed Tate into the fucking ground."

"No, he wouldn't—"

"Did you know he kidnapped my adoptive sister a couple of weeks ago? That he was going to use her to get his hands on Tate Oil and Gas?"

Olivia blinked. The words made no sense to her whatsoever. "Kidnapped your adoptive sister?" she echoed stupidly. "That's insane."

"Yeah well, he did. Took her back to his own mansion and held her there for a whole night." There was something cold in Wolf's eyes now, all that tender warmth gone. "And I bet you never heard a fucking thing about that, right?"

No. She hadn't.

"Two weeks ago . . ." Her lips felt numb and nothing was going to warm up her hands. "I heard nothing. I didn't see—"

"No, of course you didn't. He's protecting you." Wolf's gaze was so sharp it felt like it was cutting strips off her "He made sure you never knew anything about this. Or maybe you just didn't want to know."

Her brain tried frantically to catch up, to process what he was saying. "I never . . . I didn't know. . . ."

"I told you he's been selling experimental weaponry on the black market and getting the military to help him. I told you back at the hotel, but you didn't believe me. You need to believe me now. That's treason, Liv. And the penalty for treason is death."

She didn't know what made her hand flash out all of a sudden, what made her fingers close around the hard metal of that gun. What made her lift it, pointing it straight at the man sitting opposite her. The man who was telling her things that she didn't want to believe, but that somewhere deep in her heart, she did.

The man she thought she loved, but maybe didn't after all.

For all that her father had been a weapons billionaire, she'd never touched a gun before, because she didn't like them. The metal didn't feel cold like she thought it would, but warm and heavy. Her numb fingers tightened, firming her grip. The barrel was shaking as she kept it pointed at Wolf's broad chest, at the tattoos she probably wouldn't ever find the stories behind now.

He didn't move, merely stared at her, and she knew it hadn't been speed or surprise that had stopped him from grabbing at her hand as she'd snatched the gun. He'd let her take it.

"You gonna shoot me, baby?" His voice was soft, full of that roughness she loved. But cold too.

"I don't believe you." Her heart was beating too fast and her hand was shaking, but she kept it pointed right at him. "I don't believe any of this."

"Yeah, you do. I think you know I'm telling the truth."

"You can't kill him, Wolf. I won't let you."

"So, what? You're gonna stop me?"

She struggled to get a breath. "Yes, if I have to."

"Why? What's he ever done for you except use you?"

It hurt, catching something raw deep inside her. Tears filled her eyes and she had to blink them away hard. "I know that. But that doesn't mean he deserves to die, and it certainly doesn't mean you have to be the one to kill him."

Wolf tilted his head. "Doesn't it? What do you think I've been training all my fucking life for? I'm Dad's weapon. And my target is de Santis. It always has been."

"Always has been . . ."

She took a ragged breath, her stomach lurching. "Wh-What? But I thought you were supposed to get close to Dad. To get secrets—"

"Yeah, sure. And then, when the time came, I would be in place to deliver the coup de grâce." As he said that, he raised his hand, pointing his fingers at her, miming aiming a gun and pulling the trigger.

Her throat closed, her hand continuing to shake. He looked so cold now, so distant. Not the warm, affectionate man who'd touched her in the bedroom, but someone else. Someone hard. Implacable as a judge.

He's a SEAL. This is what he looks like when he goes to war.

The realization hit her hard, in a way she'd never fully appreciated before. Because, of course, he was an elite warrior and he'd been to war. He'd done things she couldn't even imagine. Hard, violent things. Killing to protect his country, his team. And now he was going to kill to protect his family.

Family had always been important to Wolf. How had she forgotten that?

"I can't let you," she forced out, more a croak than anything else. "This isn't a war, no matter what you might think, and you're not judge, jury, and executioner. You don't get to decide these things. And you certainly don't get to take someone's life, purely as revenge for someone you didn't even know."

Wolf said nothing for a long time. Then very slowly he leaned forward, extending a finger toward the gun in her hand. She tensed, ready to pull the trigger, even though she knew it would be futile.

But all he did was flick something on the stock and then he leaned back again, one corner of his mouth lifting minutely. "The safety," he murmured. "*Now* you can shoot me."

God. So the safety had been on all this time.

She felt like a fool, but she didn't lower the gun. This was too important. This was her father's life.

"And you're wrong," he went on, never breaking eye contact. "I did know my father."

No, he had to be lying. That didn't make any sense. "But you told me your father died."

"He did. But not before I was born."

"No," she said blankly. "You told me that your father died and your mother had to give you away. And that you were adopted by Noah Tate."

"Yeah and that's all true."

"How can it be true? If your father was alive?"

The expression on his face was taut, something glittering in his eyes she didn't understand. "Because Noah Tate was my father. My *real* father."

Olivia's face was dead white and her hand was trembling, the barrel of the gun dancing all around. Jesus, perhaps clicking the safety off had been a stupid idea. She was shaking so much she'd probably pull the trigger by mistake and end up shooting him.

You got a death wish?

Maybe he had. Maybe he simply wanted to give her the

opportunity to stop him while she could. Or to at least feel like she could have stopped him.

She wouldn't pull that trigger, though. She wasn't a killer.

Unlike himself.

"He can't be your real father." There was shock in her voice. "You told me he adopted you and the others because he couldn't have children."

"He had a low sperm count when he was young and it gradually decreased as he got older. But it was enough to give him one kid."

She shook her head. "You were adopted. You told me—"

"My mom left Dad before either of them knew she was pregnant. He only found out when I was given to the boys home, and his name was given to the caretakers as my father."

"I don't understand. Why did you pretend he was your foster father then?"

"Why do you think? Because of Cesare. Because of the threat he represented. Dad could never tell anyone I was his real son, because he was trying to protect me."

"No," she said again, continuing to shake her head as if that alone would negate everything he'd said. "He didn't want to protect you. He beat you, Wolf. I know. I saw the bruises on your face."

Another lie he'd had to tell. Another manipulation he'd had to pull off.

"He never hit me, Liv. He never beat me. The bruises were from a boxing tutor I had. Dad thought de Santis would be more likely to help me if he thought Noah was knocking me around."

This time Olivia didn't say a thing, just stared, that gun still pointing directly at his heart.

"He thought it would also generate sympathy from

you," Wolf went on, unable to stop now that he'd started. "And it did."

There was pain in her expressive blue eyes, a deep, abiding hurt that he felt deep inside himself too. It didn't seem fair that he was always the one hurting her. That he kept delivering blow after blow.

He hadn't wanted to tell her any of this, but he'd promised himself there would be no more lies. He would tell her the truth about his mission, about what he intended to do, and he'd keep nothing back.

It would change things between them, probably irrevocably. Any feelings of friendship or the sense of connection he'd experienced while in her arms would be gone. He knew that.

But the truth was important, even if it was painful. Even if it hurt him too. And it was certainly a damn sight more important than his impatient dick, which only wanted to get back to bed with her, not spend hours talking.

"Why are you telling me this?" Her voice was cracked and hoarse. "What do you think is going to happen? That I'm suddenly going to say 'Sure Wolf, my father was bad, you can kill him, no problem'?"

"No, I don't think that." He held her gaze. "I'm telling you that because I don't want to lie to you anymore. You deserve the truth."

Something trickled down her cheek, a tear. "If the truth is what I deserve, then I must have been a really, really awful person."

The sight of that tear and the thread of hurt in her voice made pain twist inside him, an animal tearing at his flesh. Yes, he knew this wasn't what she wanted to hear. He *knew*. But all those lies. . . . He couldn't keep telling her those either.

He wanted to reach out to her, take the gun from her hand and pull her into his arms, kiss away her tears. Touch her, stroke her until all the pain was gone and there was nothing but pleasure in those beautiful blue eyes.

But he couldn't do that. Not after he'd just told her that he was going to kill her father.

"You're not an awful person," he said, because he couldn't think of anything else to say. "And you deserve so much more."

Her lashes fell, veiling her gaze. Then she lowered the gun, putting it carefully back down on the table.

"Not going to use that after all?" he murmured.

"I can't shoot you and you know it."

There was a tense, awful silence.

Olivia looked up at him, her eyes full of pain. "Please don't kill him, Wolf. For me. Please."

Ah fuck.

It felt like she'd reached right inside him and grabbed onto his heart, and was now squeezing it very carefully between her hands. "I have to," he forced out, his jaw gone tight. "It's my mission. Dad's death has to be avenged. This stupid fucking feud has to end and it won't until your father is dead."

Olivia shook her head again, slowly. "How do you know he killed Noah? You have no proof. The coroner said he died falling off his horse."

"I'll find proof. It'll be there."

"No, Wolf. No. Killing Dad isn't the answer. I know you don't care about him, but if you feel anything at all for me, please . . . Don't do it."

Those delicate fingers around his heart squeezed tighter, deepening the pain. He'd never thought that when it came down to it, it would be her who'd get in his way. At least not like this.

He'd never thought that it would be painful. That he'd end up doubting himself. That he'd end up doubting his own father too.

He reached out for the gun and put his hand over it, drawing it toward him and clicking the safety back on. But he kept his hand on it, a reminder of what he needed to do. A reminder of his father's promise.

"My mom is still alive," he said, staring down at the table, because that was easier than looking into her wounded eyes. "Dad spent years trying to find her, because after this thing with de Santis was all over and done with, he had plans. He was going to acknowledge me as his son, get Mom back, be a family again. But he died before that happened." He rubbed his thumb over the butt of the gun, the metal warm under his hand. "That letter I got from him, the one that told me I had to kill de Santis, also said that he'd finally found Mom. But he couldn't go get her until de Santis was dead because it was too dangerous for her otherwise. He said that it was now up to me to bring our family back together again. That once Cesare was dead, I'd receive information about where Mom was and I could go get her." Wolf lifted his gaze. "I need to find my mom, Liv. I know there's not much left of my family now, but I want it. I *need* to have it."

"So you're going to kill Dad just to find out where your mom is?" She blinked hard. "Did you ever think you could go find her without doing that?"

He grimaced. "I tried." Because he had. In the two weeks after receiving that letter, he'd tried his hardest to look for some sign of where his mother might be. How his father had found her, he had no idea, because every lead Wolf had followed had been a dead end. "I don't know where she is, but she's hidden so well, I couldn't fucking find her."

Olivia folded her arms around herself, as if she was cold, and he wanted to close the distance between them, wrap his own arms around her, but he stayed where he was. Having him touch her would be the very last thing she'd want, and besides, he was pretty sure that if he did touch her, he wouldn't want to stop. Then she really *would* shoot him.

"We should try to find her." Olivia's tone was flat and there was a cast to her jaw he recognized. Determination. "If your father found her, then we can."

Wolf shook his head. If it had been that simple, he would have done it already. "No, I can't get her until the feud is over. Cesare uses people, you know that, Liv. And if he knew that my mother was alive and that she was important to Noah, do you think he'll leave her alone? Christ, this has to end once and for all." His father had been very clear. The only way any of this would stop would be if Cesare was dead.

"The way to end it is not to kill my father." Anger was burning in her eyes now and part of him was glad, because anger he could deal with. Pain only made him want to howl.

He didn't look away, letting her see that this was the path he was set on and there would be no deviation from it. "I'm sorry, baby. But this is the way it's gotta be. There's no other option."

She stared at him a long moment, saying nothing, her gaze hot as a gas flame. "If I found your mother *and* proof that Dad didn't kill Noah, would you change your mind?"

Wolf shook his head. "He's been running guns and using the military to do it. Like, I said, that's treason."

"Jail then," she said without hesitation. "Let the authorities decide what to do with him. Like you were going to do with Daniel."

Prison wasn't what he'd envisaged for Cesare, he had to admit. And it was difficult to change focus, especially when in his head, de Santis's death had been the only option. But he made himself try the idea on for size, because this was Olivia and he still hated the thought of her hurting her.

"What about Dad's death?" he asked.

"What about it? If my father didn't kill him then there's nothing to get revenge for, is there?" She leaned forward, putting her palms flat on the table. "Did it ever occur to you that killing Dad wouldn't end this feud anyway? A life for a life doesn't work, Wolf. If my brothers found out you'd done something—"

"Your brothers won't find out, because no one will know it was me. I'll make sure of it."

"*I* will know it was you."

Another tense silence fell and he didn't break it, because suddenly it was there between them, the unspoken threat. That she now knew all his secrets and that if she was free, she could take him down.

But he would never let her go.

She went still, as if she'd only just realized that herself. And he could see by the way her muscles tensed, that she was preparing to run.

He reached out before she could do so, across the table, closing his fingers around her wrists. She tried to make a move then, but it was too late. He had her.

Holding on tight, he hauled her across the bench and into his arms, not knowing what he wanted to do with her, only that he had to stop her from running. Stop her from getting out and ruining his plans.

Stop her from leaving him. She wouldn't escape him, not again.

But he should have remembered that Olivia, though physically weaker than he was, wasn't at all a pushover.

She twisted in his arms, jerking her wrists from his grip. Then she shoved against his chest with all her strength, bringing her knees up at the same time, no doubt to drive them somewhere sensitive.

Letting her go was not an option, but he didn't want to physically hurt her either, so he simply wrapped his arms around her and held on as she struggled. As she hit him and kicked and kneed him in the balls. Stars burst behind his eyes, because it fucking hurt, but physical pain was something he'd long since overcome as part of his SEAL training, so he ignored it, holding onto her tighter.

She didn't make a sound as she fought to get free, silent as she struggled, the way she'd been when she'd driven her fists into his chest in the yacht's stateroom earlier.

He hadn't thought she'd have had any energy left after that and all that time spent in bed together, but apparently she did.

She must have known it was pointless to struggle, that he couldn't and wouldn't let her go, but she kept on struggling anyway. Then he caught a glimpse of her flushed face and saw the tears streaming down it, and this had to end. He had to stop it. Now.

So he grabbed a handful of her glossy brown hair, closing his fist around it and pulling her head back against his shoulder. Then he wrapped his other arm right around her body, hauling her into his lap with her back to his chest and holding her there tightly. She fought him, trying to pull away even though with the grip he had in her hair it must have hurt.

Christ, she was a little warrior. She couldn't win and yet still she fought.

"Stop," he ordered, putting every ounce of command he had into the word. "Just fucking stop, Liv. You're going to exhaust yourself."

Her body was trembling against his and the feel of her bare skin, the scent of strawberries and musk, and even the way she fought making him hard. He wanted to bite her neck, shove his thigh between hers, get her to ride him. Rub his cock against the soft curve of her ass. Jesus, so many things he wanted. But after everything that had gone down just now, that was impossible.

"So what are you going to do?" she demanded, fury running through the words, even though they were hoarse and broken sounding. "Kill me like you'll kill Dad? Shoot me in the head? Because I know too much now, don't I? I know your plans. You can't ever let me go. You'll have to keep me forever or—"

Wolf put his free hand over her mouth. Not hard, only enough to stop the flow of words. The words that burrowed into his chest, hurting far worse than any bullet.

She felt so fragile against him. So small and defenseless. Yet every word she said was right. This was always going to be his choice at the end. After her father was dead, she would know exactly who'd killed him. And Wolf couldn't have that. She'd go to the police, she'd tell them everything she knew.

She's right. You can't ever let her go.

Something deep inside him shifted, heavy with certainty and a kind of satisfaction.

No, he couldn't let her go. He wouldn't. She was his now. She'd chosen him the moment she'd walked out of that restaurant; and in the stateroom just before, she'd chosen him again.

And he was fucking taking her.

She'd gone quiet, her breathing fast against his palm. She wasn't fighting him now and her eyes were closed. There were tears on her cheeks and as he looked down at her flushed face, he saw more tears seep slowly from underneath her lashes.

He'd hurt her, he knew that. He accepted it. And if he'd been a different kind of man, maybe a better kind of man, he would have let her go. Would have allowed her the chance to go to the authorities or maybe even have changed his mind about killing Cesare.

But he wasn't a different kind of man.

He was the man his father had made him, a weapon. And he was locked onto his target.

You understand that she'll never forgive you, don't you?

She wouldn't. But once this was over, he'd certainly spend the rest of his life trying to make it up to her.

"I'll never physically harm you, Olivia," he said, making each word a vow. "Never ever. But you're right. I'll never let you go either." He lifted his hand from her mouth and looked down into her night dark eyes. "You're mine now, baby. Understand?"

Her gaze was black with storms and a thousand other emotions he couldn't identify. Then he felt her hand move, her palm covering the front of his jeans, finding his cock hard and ready beneath the denim. The breath went out of him in a hiss and he almost snarled, because it felt too fucking good.

"I loved you once, Wolf Tate," Olivia said, never taking her gaze from his, her thumb running the length of his aching cock, stroking him. "But I don't think I love you anymore."

CHAPTER TWELVE

His heat was familiar by now and his strength, well, she already knew all about that. She could feel it in the way he held her, as if there was nothing she could do to make him let her go. And some part of her liked that. Some part of her loved it even. That she could hit him and kick him and cause him pain, struggle against him, and he'd be that mountain. He wouldn't move.

He'd hold her till the end of time.

She didn't know what had made her touch him. What made her keep her palm on the hard ridge beneath his zipper. What made her squeeze him.

Maybe it was the way she could feel every muscle in his body tighten as she did so, the hiss of his breath in her ear. The knowledge that right now, with her hand right there, she had some power over him.

She was desperate for some power over him.

He wouldn't hurt her, she believed that implicitly. Wolf Tate might want to kill her father, but he'd *never* hurt her. Yet he wasn't going to let her go either and she believed that too. She knew too much now and she'd made her position clear.

He might not let her go, but she wasn't going to let him kill her father.

No matter if what Wolf had told her was true—and

clearly he believed it totally—he didn't get to be the law. He didn't have the right to take someone's life simply because he'd been wronged.

The treason was a different story and she still refused to believe that, but even if it was true, it should be brought to the authorities. It wasn't Wolf's job to dispense justice.

And that wasn't even considering what else he'd told her, that he hadn't been beaten after all, like she'd always thought. Or that Noah Tate was his real father.

No, those things didn't matter.

What mattered right now was that she use what little power she had over him to change his mind about killing her father.

And save him from himself . . .

His big body was still beneath hers, his fist in her hair painful, the arm around her waist crushing. She had her head back against the hard slab of muscle of his shoulder, could hear the beat of his heart, the slow rhythm of it gathering speed.

"You loved me?" There was shock in his rough voice.

She shouldn't have said it, but she'd wanted to hurt him. And she had so very little to hurt him with. "Once," she whispered, and she couldn't tell whether it was a lie or not, the emotions inside her confused and tangled. "Not anymore." Then she squeezed that hard ridge under the denim again, testing her power.

He gave a low rough laugh that ended on a hiss. "Keep doing that and I might decide to change your mind."

Beneath her hand, she could feel him getting harder, his heartbeat slowly accelerating. Good. This was a way she could reach him, she was certain of it.

You're getting off on it yourself, don't lie.

No, she couldn't lie about that. There was a pulse between her thighs, heavy and slow, and she wanted to spread her legs and lean forward, grind herself against the muscle of that powerful thigh, use him the way he'd been using her all this time

And why not take him? Why not use him? Everyone else had no qualms about using her, so why shouldn't she take something for herself too?

Olivia squeezed him again, even harder this time, relishing the sound of his breath catching, feeling his muscles tighten, shifting and flexing beneath her. She rubbed her thumb along the length of him for good measure, pressing down on the sensitive tip.

"Fuck," he hissed, his hips jerking. "Little tease."

He shifted, releasing her hair and taking her hips in his hands, moving her so that her butt was more fully settled against his cock, shoving a thigh between hers.

Then he rolled her hips forward, gripping her tightly, grinding against her ass as that hard thigh of his pressed between her legs and the wetness there.

She wasn't wearing anything beneath his shirt, the denim rough against her tender flesh, pushing on her clit, sending that insane ache into the stratosphere.

The breath went out of her and he must have heard, because his fist was in her hair again, dragging her head back, his mouth near her ear. "You like that, baby?" The question was all gravel and heat. "You wanna ride my thigh, get yourself off like that?"

God, if she wasn't careful she was going to lose her advantage, fall under his spell instead of him falling under hers.

Gasping as he rolled her hips again, grazing her clit, she fought the need to simply lie back in his arms and let him do whatever he wanted with her. This was too important for simple pleasure. This was a power game and one she had to win.

She moved her hand again, fumbling with the button on his jeans, finding the tab of the zipper and pulling it jerkily down. The she pushed her fingers under the fabric, grazing what felt like an iron bar covered in hot, velvety skin.

This time it was his breath that caught, a harsh rush in her ear as she closed her fingers around his cock.

"Oh . . . *fuck* . . ." The curse was hoarse, his massive body shuddering as she ran her thumb around the head. "Baby, that's so good."

Her mouth was dry, her own heartbeat thundering in her head. She was bitterly conscious of his thigh and the way he was moving it, subtly, against her. Making her want to rock and grind, forget the power play and simply lose herself in pleasure.

But she wasn't going to. She needed this. She had to have it.

"If I find your mother," she forced out raggedly. "You leave my father alone."

His breathing was fast and hot against the back of her neck, his mouth grazing the sensitive skin under her ear. "Is that what we're doing here? You're using my dick against me?"

"Yes." She slid her thumb around the head of his cock, his skin slick and hot. "Well, do we have a deal?"

He groaned. "Hell no."

Dammit.

She gripped him tighter, moving her hand up and down awkwardly, not knowing what she was doing, but judging from the growing harshness of his breathing and the way his hips were moving, it was having some effect. "I'll find your mother and you give me some time to find proof that Dad didn't kill Noah."

He made another rough sound and the hand on her hip slid forward, his fingers pushing between her thighs, slipping over her slick flesh.

She shuddered, pleasure igniting along every single

nerve ending she had, a raw gasp escaping whether she wanted it to or not.

"Yeah, you like that, don't you?" Wolf's voice was a rough caress. "Maybe I'll just get you off like this. No need for all this fucking deal bullshit."

No, she wasn't going to lose this one, she refused.

She let herself melt back against him, spreading her thighs wider, letting him feel how ready she was for him. How wet she was for him. But she kept her hand on his cock, slowing down her movements, squeezing him hard. "Two hours," she said thickly. "I'll find your mother and you give me two hours to find proof of my father's innocence."

He was panting now, his hips moving, pushing himself against her hand. "Little bitch," he murmured, and despite the harshness of the word, she could hear what sounded like admiration in his voice. "You think you can get what you want just because you've got your hand on my dick?"

"Y-Yes." Her own voice was ragged, breaking up as his fingers circled her clit then eased down, finding the entrance to her body, sliding inside. Her whole being shuddered in reaction, and she couldn't stop another moan from escaping her. "Two hours and I'll let you f-fuck me like this." The word came out surprisingly easily, and for good measure, she wrapped her whole palm around his cock and pumped hard.

A groan broke from him, his hips lifting beneath her. "Ah, Jesus Christ . . . You fucking tease." He sounded like he was at the end of his patience. Good. "Two hours . . ."

His finger pushed deep inside her and she had to close her eyes, struggling to keep herself together and not simply let go. "Y-Yes."

"Okay . . . two hours." He was panting. "Now get on my fucking cock."

"I . . . want your word, W-Wolf. Promise me."

He growled and she felt his teeth against the side of her neck, delivering a nip that only added to the fire he was stoking between her thighs with his clever fingers. "I promise." His thumb slicking over her clit, making her gasp. "Happy now?"

Relief and an intense satisfaction swept through her. Yes, she'd managed to get a concession out of him. Thank God. "V-Very happy, yes."

"Good. Now get the fuck on my cock. I'm not going to ask again."

So demanding. There wasn't any reason to like it, but she did. It made her want to keep teasing him, keep using her unexpected power over him. Make him burn, make him hurt.

"Condom," she murmured, moving her hand then leaning back on him, pressing the curve of her butt against the rigid heat of his erection.

He cursed roughly and she felt him shift, his breathing wild against her hair. He must have found one from somewhere, maybe his back pocket, because she heard the rustle of foil, and then, a second later, his hands were clamped to her hips. "Lift up for me," he ordered thickly.

But she wasn't done. She undulated against him, shifting her pelvis so she could feel his cock rubbing against her sex, giving him the heat and the slick feel of her flesh but nothing more. "Say please."

Another growl broke from him and he gripped her harder. "You are, you're a goddamn tease . . ."

"Say it," she demanded, grinding herself against him, shivering as the movement sent sharp, electrical shocks through her.

He groaned. "Jesus Christ, baby. You're gonna kill me. *Please*."

The word was harsh and raw, but it made everything inside her clench hard.

She leaned forward, putting her hands on the table in front of her, lifting herself up, the head of his cock pushing against her entrance. And this time they groaned together as she slid down onto him, her already tender flesh burning as she stretched to accommodate him.

He began to move almost immediately and she found herself scrabbling at the table, trying to hold onto something, his pelvis lifting as he thrust up into her, hard and deep. She tried to move too, to set her own rhythm, but it was clear her moment of being in charge was over.

Those large, warm hands were clamped to the bare skin of her hips, holding her absolutely still, so she could do nothing but take whatever he had to give her.

He began to talk, rough, dirty words that made her shiver. That made her break out into a sweat. That made her want to shift around on him, ride him, grind herself down on him to get some satisfaction.

But he was obviously set on punishing her for making him wait, because he wound one powerful arm around her waist and jerked her back against the intense heat of his body. Crushing her to him. Pinning her in place as he began to thrust up into her. Harder. Deeper.

She squirmed, because it felt so good but she needed more friction. Craved it. And this time it was *her* panting, *her* saying please, trying to move, hot and restless and aching.

He turned his mouth into her ear again, those hot, erotic, dirty words whispered against her skin, and she had to close her eyes. It was too much for her. He was too much for her.

But there was no escape. He'd slowed right down so she could feel every single inch of that long, hard cock inside her, the deep slick glide as he thrust in, the pull and drag as he slid out.

She couldn't move. Held immobile against him. Gasping and trembling. And just when she thought he was going to deliver the ultimate punishment by not letting her come, he took one of her hands and guided it down between her thighs, to where they were joined. Then he pressed her fingers to her clit. "Touch yourself, baby," he ordered. "I want you to come all over my cock."

So desperate she didn't even hesitate, Olivia did exactly what she was told, stroking herself as he thrust into her, her mouth opening on a scream as the orgasm gathered inside her, the pleasure crushing, exploding in a wild burst of jagged white light behind her closed lids.

"Good girl," she heard him whisper.

Then both his hands were on her hips, lifting her up and slamming her back down, over and over, until those filthy, dirty words turned into a wordless roar and his massive body went rigid beneath hers.

Afterward there was silence, broken only by the harsh sounds of their combined breathing and her own wildly careening heartbeat.

She didn't want to move, didn't think she could anyway, not while he was holding her so tightly. His mouth was in her hair and he made no move to loosen his grip on her, keeping her hard against him.

For a second she simply let herself relax. He was warm and he smelled so familiar, and the sound of his slowing breathing was somehow reassuring. And she wished, suddenly, that all there was, was this.

That her father didn't exist—and his didn't either. That there had never been a feud, and no one had ever gotten hurt, and no one had been lied to. No one had been stolen from.

That there was only his arms around her, holding her.

Them, together.

But there wasn't only this. And she knew the dangers of letting herself want more than what she had.

So after a minute she said, "Two hours, Wolf. You promised."

He didn't want to move. He would have been quite happy to sit there forever with her in his lap, feeling the wet, velvet heat of her pussy ripple around his cock as she came. Listening to her hoarse gasps of pleasure. Listening to her saying *"Please, Wolf, please"* in that soft, serious voice of hers.

He definitely didn't want her reminding him of the concession he'd granted her, those two fucking hours she'd wanted. He still didn't even know why he'd said yes, because it wasn't going to make any difference. She wouldn't find evidence proving de Santis hadn't killed Noah. Because it wasn't there.

And even if it had been, it wouldn't have mattered.

De Santis had to die. End of story.

Granting her a couple of extra hours was no skin off his nose, though. He was going to need the time to get together his plan to lure de Santis somewhere out of the way, where he could ice the guy with minimal fuss.

Olivia shifted, sending sparks of electricity through him, making him shiver. Christ, she was so fucking hot. He'd never realized, never understood. He'd never looked at her that way and maybe that had been his brain protecting him. Because if he'd known how good it would be between them, he might done something sooner with her, and maybe have gotten even more attached than he was already. Which would have really screwed everything up.

She might have been a virgin, but she knew what she'd been doing when she'd put her hand on his cock. When she'd squeezed him and told him she wanted two hours to find proof of her father's innocence.

It might have annoyed him that he'd let himself be so

easily manipulated, but the orgasm had been totally worth it. Hers too.

"Yeah, yeah," he muttered, easing her off his lap and onto the bench beside him. "You can have your two hours. As long as you find my mother first."

He didn't look at her, getting up to dispose of the condom in the galley trash, before doing up the zipper on his jeans. Only then did he turn around, and it was a good thing he'd put some distance between them, because she was sitting there, leaning back against the seat. The shirt she'd been wearing had come half unbuttoned, the fabric parting to reveal the lush curves of her breasts. Her glossy brown hair was in a tumble down her back and her face was flushed, her eyes dark and sultry as she gazed at him.

That just-fucked look suited her. It made him hard. Again.

And clearly she was aware of it, because her gaze dipped to the front of his jeans then back up to his face again. One corner of her gorgeous mouth turned up in a smile that didn't quite reach her eyes. "Okay, I'll find your mom. Then I get my two hours. And then if there's anything I can help you with, I will."

His dick, she meant. Obviously.

Yet the way she said it and the slightly distant cast to her smile, needled him. It looked calculated, and he didn't like it.

What do you expect? You're going to kill her father while you keep her your prisoner. She's not exactly going to be happy about it.

That heaviness in his chest, the one he'd felt as he'd made the decision to keep her, grew heavier.

"I loved you once . . ."

Shit. He didn't want to think about that or the soft thread of pain in her voice as she'd told him she didn't love him anymore. Didn't want to think about the way that had made him feel. Angry. Sad. Regretful.

They were all weaknesses he couldn't afford. Not now.

"Maybe it won't take two hours." He reached down to adjust himself, not being shy about it. "Maybe you'll hurry it up so you can get back to the important stuff."

Like he'd hoped, her gaze dropped to his hand where it rested on the front of his jeans, and the flush in her cheeks deepened. "Maybe," she murmured. "Well, why don't you make me some more tea?" She nodded toward the cup he'd placed in front of her before. "This one's cold." Half of it was spilled on the table too, probably from when he'd been fucking her. She'd been holding onto the table for dear life initially, until he'd pulled her back against him, the soft curve of her ass pressing against his—

No. Jesus Christ. He wasn't going to let himself get carried away yet again. There would be time for that later. For now though, if she wanted her goddamn two hours, she could have it.

He looked away, out the portholes, noting that dusk was creeping over the river, the lights coming on. "Yeah, little late for tea, baby. How about a beer instead?"

Olivia had sat up and was refastening the buttons on his shirt—sadly. "You know I don't like beer."

"Christ. That's three teas in a row you haven't drunk."

"Not my fault." She reached for the computer. "You need to give me your mother's name so I can do some searching."

He frowned, a thought occurring to him. "Wait up. You're not doing any searching unless I'm sitting right next to you."

She flashed him an irritated blue glance. "Why?"

"Just in case you go tipping your daddy off."

"I won't—"

"Oh and just so you know, you need a password to open

the email program on that laptop, and I've blocked web-mail sites too."

She gave a him a flat, direct stare. "Then how exactly am I supposed to contact my 'daddy' to tip him off?"

"You're a smart girl, Liv. I'm sure there are a hundred ways to do it." He bent and pulled open the small galley fridge, taking out a couple of beers. "Soon as my back's turned, you'll be letting him know somehow."

Her gaze flickered. Of course he was right.

Taking the caps off the bottles with a twist of his wrist, he came back over to the table and put them down. Then he grabbed a cloth and cleaned up the tea before sitting back down beside her.

She inched away, putting some distance between them. "I told you I don't like beer."

Resisting the urge to put his arm around her and close that distance, he grabbed his bottle instead and took a sip, relishing the cold liquid as it went down. Hell, nothing like a cold beer after fantastic sex. "Then don't drink it."

She pulled a face, but didn't answer, opening up the laptop instead. "Your mom's name, please."

Wolf gave it to her, watching as she began to plug the name into various search engines. He could have told her it would be useless. He'd looked already after receiving his father's last letter to him, spending hours in front of the computer searching various different public records to see if he could find any trace of her. Then various other records, which were not public and not even legal, that a contact of his had given him access to. But he'd turned up nothing.

It was like she'd vanished off the face of the earth. God only knew how his father had found her, because he sure as hell couldn't.

After fifteen minutes of watching her stare at the computer screen and typing his mother's name endlessly into different searches, Wolf began to get bored. He'd finished his beer and was considering drinking hers, even though he shouldn't considering what had happened the last time he'd had too much alcohol.

He didn't want to leave her alone for a second. She was way too smart for him, leaving him to rely heavily on his considerable physical skills if he wanted to stop her from doing something she shouldn't. They were effective when used against her, he had to say, but only if he moved quickly.

Sadly, that left him with having to watch her like a hawk.

"I promise I won't do anything to contact Dad," she said coolly, not looking up from the screen. "So if you want to go away and do something, then by all means go away and do it."

He scowled. "I don't want to go away and do something."

"Then stop doing that thing with your leg. It's making the table shake."

Shit. Wolf stilled the restless bounce of his heel, which he hadn't realized he'd been doing.

"Go on," Olivia murmured. "You promised me two hours. I promise you I won't do anything to warn my Dad."

He probably shouldn't leave her, but he *did* have a whole lot of crap to organize. And he was finding it very difficult being in the confined space of the cabin, with the scent of strawberries and sex all around him and her so very close and wearing so very little.

He wanted to touch her too much. He wanted more than the quick fuck on the bench. He wanted to take her back to the stateroom and take that shirt off her, use his hands and his mouth on her, find out what she *really* meant when she'd said she'd loved him once.

But there was no time. He could do that later, after all this was over.

And it would be over very soon.

"Fine." He pushed himself out of the seat. "But you're to stay in here, understand?"

She merely lifted a hand and made a flicking gesture with her fingers.

He wanted to take that hand and nip those delicate fingers, suck each one into his mouth. Suck them like she'd no doubt suck his cock.

Hell. He needed to get out of here.

He left the living area, pulling shut the door that separated it from the small corridor with the steps up to the deck, locking it with the keys in his pocket. No fancy fucking codes today. She wasn't going anywhere.

Then he went into the stateroom and pulled open a drawer in the built-in dresser, finding a spare hoodie and tugging it on. In another drawer he found an unopened burner phone, which he broke out of the packaging, inserting a new SIM card into it. There was enough charge in it to send a couple of texts, which was all he needed.

Going outside was tempting fate, but he was as certain as he could be that no one would have tracked them to the *Lady* just yet, so he could probably risk going above deck. And if anyone did happen to be watching, all they'd see is a guy in a hoodie checking his phone. They wouldn't know who he was and they certainly wouldn't know who he had tucked up safe in his galley.

Wolf took the steps up to the deck, sucking in a deep breath as soon as he was outside. Clearing his head of the scent of Olivia with the sharp smell of cold, engine oil, and salt, and the thousand other scents the city produced.

Darkness was sliding over the river, the lights of Manhattan flicking on.

It was peaceful with the water all around him. Gave him some distance from the city itself, making him feel like he could simply stand there and observe it.

De Santis would be going out of his mind by now, that was for sure.

Wolf smiled in the darkness, then reached for the new phone.

He debated calling his brothers yet again, to see what kind of shit was going down with de Santis, because no doubt they'd be keeping tabs on what was happening. But then he decided against it. He'd have to explain what he was trying to do, and neither Van nor Lucas would understand. They'd try to stop him, which wasn't happening either.

He'd call them later, when de Santis was out of the picture and he had his mother back. When he could get that birth certificate and show them the truth of what Noah had been to him.

First up though . . .

Opening the browser on the phone, he accessed a web-based text messaging service, then entered the number he wanted to text, plus a message.

Yes, I have her. Yes, she's safe. But if you want her back, you're going to have to meet me to talk.

That should do it. De Santis wouldn't be able to track the new burner from the text since he'd used a web service, but he'd understand. Wolf would give him an hour or two to sweat before sending a follow-up text. He could also use the time to think about where he wanted to meet with de Santis.

He lingered on the deck for another twenty minutes or so, pacing up and down to get rid of the restlessness that had gripped him down below decks, inhaling more of the sharp night air.

Then he went back down the stairs to the galley/living area, grabbing his keys to unlock the door.

As he pushed it open, Olivia jumped, as if his sudden entrance had given her a fright.

"Hey," he murmured, grinning. "It's only me. Your friendly neighborhood kidnapper."

She didn't smile, staring at him with a white, stricken look on her face.

Something in his gut dropped away. "What's up?"

She shook her head then slowly turned around the laptop on the table so it was facing him.

He couldn't see it clearly from where he was standing, and suddenly he didn't want to. Because he knew without a shadow of a doubt that something had put that look on her face, and whatever it was, it wasn't good.

"Tell me yourself," he ordered harshly.

"It's better if you look—"

"Just do it, Olivia."

Her blue gaze came to his, horribly direct and full of what he suspected was sympathy. Which didn't make any sense, because why would she be sympathetic?

"I found your mother, Wolf. There's a reason she was so difficult to find, why there was no trace of her. Because you were looking for someone who's still alive." Her voice cracked. "I'm so sorry. Your mother is dead. She died twenty-seven years ago. Six months after you were adopted."

He frowned, his brain refusing to deal with the information. That was wrong. Very, very wrong. His mother was alive, his father had said. He'd been searching for her for years and then he'd found her just before he'd died.

She couldn't be dead. That wasn't possible.

A tear ran down Olivia's cheek and he wanted to laugh, because why was she crying? It was just another lie. She must have gotten his mother mixed up with someone else or something.

"No," he said, smiling and shaking his head. "That's not true. You got the wrong woman." He took a few steps over to the computer sitting on the table, glancing down at the screen.

The image blurred as if his brain refused to accept it, and he had to blink hard to focus. Then he had to blink hard again, because it couldn't be what it appeared to be, it just couldn't.

But it was. A death certificate with her name and the date of her death clearly typed.

Olivia had been telling the truth.

His mother was dead and had been all this time.

His whole life his father had lied to him.

CHAPTER THIRTEEN

Wolf had gone bone white, his whole body stiffening. And Olivia felt her heart crack in her chest. She wanted to look away, not see the realization dawn over those roughly handsome, familiar features, but she made herself do it anyway.

She didn't take any pleasure in destroying his world, even though it hadn't come as a shock to her to discover that Wolf's mother had died. She'd searched for a while without turning anything up and had wondered if perhaps the reason for that was because his mother had died recently without him knowing it. So she'd searched among the death records instead.

What *had* come as a shock was finding out that his mother had died twenty-seven years ago in an institution in Wyoming. Six months after giving Wolf up for adoption. The cause of death was listed as an overdose, but Olivia knew what that meant. Suicide.

Grief had gripped her then, because not only had it meant that Wolf had been holding onto a hope that had never existed, he'd been holding onto a lie.

A lie his father had told him. A fiction his father had created and maintained all those years. Using it as an incentive to get Wolf to do what he wanted him to do. Crafting his son into the perfect weapon.

Olivia watched that weapon now and saw the agony that

stripped those jewel bright eyes of any remaining warmth. That twisted his mouth and hollowed his beautiful face, a flare of grief so intense it made her heart not only crack, but nearly shatter.

She got jerkily to her feet and started around the table toward him, no thought in her head but to go to him, not caring about the fact that he was determined to kill her father. The only thing that mattered was that he was in pain and she wanted to help.

"*No.*" The word vibrated with shock, and it wasn't pain in his eyes now, it was rage. "Don't you fucking touch me."

Her throat closed up and she froze. "I don't know why your father lied. I don't know why—" She broke off, as he turned without another word and stormed out of the galley, slamming the door behind him.

The key turned in the lock, the way it had before when she'd told him to go, to get that restless, impatient energy of his out of the cabin, because she couldn't think with him there, taking up all the air and all the space.

Couldn't think with his hard, muscled body half naked and so close.

Now, all she could think about was how she wanted to put her arms around him, do something, anything to ease the hurt.

But he was angry. In shock. And now he'd locked her in here and she couldn't even go after him.

She moved back to the curving seat and sat down, her eyes feeling dry and gritty, her chest tight with grief.

Wolf had done nothing but hurt her since he'd kidnapped her from her bedroom, and yet seeing him hurt also hurt her. He was as wedded to his own fictions as she'd been to hers, in many ways. Why else hadn't he thought to search for his mother among the dead? It wouldn't have taken much. But he'd so firmly believed that she was alive, that he hadn't even considered the possibility.

Olivia eyed the beer he'd gotten for her for a second, then she reached out and took a large swallow. It wasn't cold anymore and there was a bitterness to it that made her pull a face, but she didn't put the bottle down.

He'd only wanted a family. That's what he'd told her. That's what he'd always wanted. He'd lost his father, and now his mother. His mother who'd been dead for years. There would be no chance of a family for Wolf Tate, not anymore.

The family he wanted was gone. Perhaps it had never really existed in the first place. And not only that, the father he'd adored had been lying to him for years.

Olivia took another sip of the beer, trying to ease the ache in her throat.

She could well imagine why Noah had lied. He'd wanted a weapon, aimed at the heart of his enemy. And Wolf—loyal, passionate, protective—was perfect for the job. Yet, Noah had needed something extra to make sure Wolf would do what he'd asked him to and there was no doubt he'd used Wolf's need for a family to get him to do that.

He'd told him his mother was alive and that after de Santis was dead, he'd get her back. That Wolf would be acknowledged as his son. A powerful incentive for a man who'd only wanted to belong.

Because that's what it was about, wasn't it? He'd been given away and then adopted by a man who'd been cold and distant by all accounts, and who'd kept that distance between them, no matter that Wolf had been told he was Noah's real son. That may be the case, and Noah may not have beaten him, but keeping someone like Wolf at arm's length? Someone who felt that deeply and passionately? It must have been devastating for Wolf. It must have hurt.

You know how that feels.

Oh yes, she knew. How desperately she'd wanted more from her mother. More hugs, more kisses, more time. But there had never been any time, not when her mother spent half her life "sleeping" in her room, out of her mind with drink and depression.

Then that time had simply run out.

She blinked fiercely, sympathy and pain turning over and over inside her.

She realized that Wolf had never gotten any time at all, and all these years he'd thought he would.

Damn fathers. Damn fathers and their fucking secrets. Their lies. Their manipulations.

Olivia drained the bottle, but the pain in her chest didn't go away.

Her gaze fell on the laptop and certainty shifted and settled inside her.

She'd been avoiding this for too long, been afraid for too long. Wanting to preserve her safe little world, all the fictions she'd believed in. Creating identities around people because she was too afraid of the reality. Creating identities around Wolf, around her father.

Well, she was still afraid of the truth. Still afraid that the people she cared about weren't the people she thought they were. Weren't the people she loved.

But she couldn't be afraid any more. Couldn't hold onto love for the sake of it because she was afraid of being alone. Afraid of being unloved. She was stronger than that. If nothing else, being with Wolf had certainly taught her that much. There were many things she could bear.

She wasn't fragile like her mother. The truth hurt, but that was better than believing a lie.

Only once you knew the truth, could you move on.

Olivia reached out and pulled the laptop over.

Time to find out the truth about her father.

It was a bad idea to leave the yacht, a bad idea to go out into the city, but all he knew was that he had to move. He had to leave. Had to get away from the terrible sympathy in Olivia's blue eyes. From the glaring lie that was staring up at him from the computer screen.

His mother's death certificate.

He walked, didn't run. Pulling the hoodie over his head so no one saw his face. He moved quickly, going nowhere in particular, needing the sensation of doing something, needing something to occupy his tense muscles.

Eventually he broke into a jog, because walking was too slow and there was too much adrenaline inside him.

Too much anger. Too much grief.

His mother was dead. She'd been dead for twenty-seven years. There had never been a chance for them to be a family. Never. And all those promises his father had made him . . .

They were nothing but lies.

He ran harder.

People paid him no attention—there were always idiots out running at night in the middle of winter—and he ignored them. He just kept on going.

He could fucking do this all night. Run right around the entire length of Manhattan. Whatever it took to ease the agony in his chest.

His father had lied to him. His father had made him a promise, knowing how much it meant to Wolf, knowing how badly he'd wanted his family back again. The family he'd never gotten a chance to have.

"We'll find your mother, Wolf, I promise. As soon as de Santis ceases to be a threat to us. And then you can finally be my son."

His feet pounded the pavement. Lies. Lies. Lies.

Why had Noah said that to him? Why had he promised him that, knowing all that time that Wolf's mother was dead? Why had he said he'd found her when he would have had to know she was dead? Noah wasn't a man who left

anything to chance, and he would have wanted to know
what had happened to Wolf's mother the day he'd adopted
him. Especially if she was the mother of his only child.

Wolf kept running, going harder, faster. Trying to outrun the voice in his head that kept whispering that if Noah
had lied to him about his mother, what other lies had he
told?

Are you even his son?

Another bolt of agony twisted in his chest and it had
nothing to do with how fast he was running. Not when he
could run fifty miles without a break.

He tried to go faster, because he didn't want to think
about that, didn't even want to consider the possibility, but
it stuck in his head like a splinter and he couldn't get it out.

You have to know. You need to.

He came to a stop, the dark city on one side of him, the
river flowing endlessly on the other.

He couldn't outrun this. And he needed to know. He
had to.

Turning to face the water, he dug into his pocket and
grabbed his phone, punching in a number.

"Wolf?" Van answered instantly. "Jesus Christ, that better be you on another burner, because I've got something
to—"

"Did Dad ever lie to you?" Wolf interrupted harshly. He
didn't want to hear whatever it was his brother had to say.
This was too important.

"What?" Van sounded taken aback. "What do you mean
did Dad ever lie to me?"

"You heard my fucking question."

Van must have heard the desperation in his voice too,
because there was a brief silence and then he said, "Yeah,
of course Dad lied. In fact, that's what Lucas and I need
to talk to you about. There's a few things you don't know
that—"

"I know them." Another interruption, but he didn't give a shit. "I know that Dad changed the boundaries on the ranch to include the de Santis oil strike. I know Dad stole de Santis's fucking oil."

There was a shocked silence down the other end of the phone.

"I knew about Chloe too," Wolf went on before his brother could speak. "Before you did. I knew all along she was de Santis's kid."

Another long silence.

"He told you?" Van's voice had gone flat. "He told you all of that?"

"Yeah. I knew right from the beginning."

"Wolf," Van began.

"No, I don't want to fucking talk about it right now." He could hear his own voice, getting harsher, rougher. *You're cracking up.* "What I wanna know is did Dad ever lie to you about your parents?"

"My parents? No. They were crack addicts. That's it. End of story." Another pause. "Why?"

His throat had tightened and he had to force out his next question. "Are you in Wyoming?"

"Yeah, but—"

"I need you do to something for me. I need you to go into Dad's study and find my birth certificate. The original."

More shock. Wolf could virtually feel it oozing down the phone line.

"What the fuck is going on, Wolf?" Van growled. "You won't answer any of my calls—"

"For once in your *fucking* life just do what I say," Wolf ground out, barely hanging on to his patience. Barely hanging on to himself.

Jesus Christ, if Van was going to get into an argument about this, he didn't know what he would do.

But Van must have heard the cracks in his voice, signs of his barely leashed fury, because after yet another long silence, he said, "Okay. Hang on."

In the background Wolf could hear footsteps and a door opening.

"You still on base?" Van asked neutrally.

"Yeah." He'd been telling his brothers the same lie for a couple of weeks now, that he'd cut short his bereavement leave and gone back to Virginia. But he hadn't. He'd been staying in Manhattan on the *Lady* all this time.

More sounds. Drawers being opened, then shut; the rustle of papers.

"Got it," Van said at last. "What do you want to know?"

Everything inside Wolf drew into a hard, tight knot.

Do you really need to know this?

His jaw ached, his teeth clenched together hard, and again, he had to force out the question. "My mother's name should be there. But I need to know if my father's is too."

There was a silence and in it he could hear his own heartbeat, louder than fucking thunder.

"No," Van said. "The box is blank."

Blank. The box was blank.

He lied about that, too.

Wolf stared at the river, at the dark water going by, at the lights shining across it. Van was saying something in his ear, but he couldn't work out what so he hit the disconnect button to shut him the fuck up.

Noah had promised him his name was there. He'd promised. Noah Tate, father of Wolf Tate. And then when de Santis was dead and his mother had been found, Noah would let the world know who Wolf really was.

Who Wolf *really* belonged to.

But there was no name in that box, despite Noah's promises.

What did it mean? What the *fuck* did it mean?

It means you don't belong to anyone.

Wolf lifted his phone again, punched in another number, his hand shaking. And this time it rang for longer before Lucas's cold voice came down the line. "Who is this?"

"It's me." Wolf couldn't keep the rawness from staining the words. "I wanna know something. Did Dad ever lie to you?"

"What? Has Van gotten in touch with you—"

"Just answer the fucking question!" Wolf roared, not caring who heard him. "Did Dad ever lie to you? About your parents?"

There was the slightest pause. "No. Dad didn't lie to me," Lucas said. "He told me the truth."

Wolf gripped so tightly onto his phone, the plastic creaked. "What about?"

"My parents died in a fire. Everyone told me that Mom died of smoke inhalation. But she didn't. Dad found out that she'd burned to death instead." It was very faint, but Wolf heard it nonetheless, the sound of pain in his brother's otherwise emotionless voice. "He told me when I was thirteen."

Wolf's chest had gone tight and sore, squeezed in some massive, inexorable vice. "Why? Why the hell did he tell you that?"

"Because I was too volatile. I set fire to the stables and nearly killed all those horses, so Dad told me about my mother, to teach me the value of control."

Oh Jesus Christ. The tightness in his chest got worse.

Unlike Lucas, he hadn't been given any lessons in the value of control. No, instead his father had done the opposite. He'd let him have his emotions, carefully cultivating his need to belong to someone, starving his hunger for love, his desperation for family. Encouraging loyalty and then Wolf's righteous anger at how de Santis was targeting the Tate family. Promising Wolf he'd get everything he wanted eventually, if only he did what his father told him.

Noah had wanted Lucas cold and emotionless. He'd wanted Wolf full of righteous rage. Because Wolf was the weapon. The sledgehammer he was going to use to break his enemy—and anger was the fuel he needed to fire it.

Anger and love.

Lucas's voice had turned tinny, and Wolf realized he'd dropped the phone from his ear.

"Wolf?" Lucas was saying. "What the fuck is going on?"

Wolf said nothing. Instead, he drew back his hand and flung the phone into the river with all his strength.

It disappeared into the water without even a ripple.

He stared at it, feeling as if the world around was full of cracks and was going to shatter at any moment. Or maybe that was just himself. He felt so fucking hollow he wouldn't have been surprised.

Noah had lied to Van, but he'd told the truth to Lucas. And he'd lied to Wolf about his mother. Had he lied about being Wolf's father too?

Jesus, what was the truth? What were the lies? And if he wasn't Noah's son, who the fuck was he?

You're no one's. You don't belong to anyone.

The ground under his feet felt unsteady, as if there were chasms and crevasses all around him and one misstep could take him down into a pit so deep he'd fall for days.

"Don't ask questions, Wolf," Noah had told him one day, after he'd been persistently asking about his mother. *"Your job isn't to think, remember? That's mine. Your job is to be strong and do what you're told. You're a soldier, that's what you are. You're* my *soldier."*

And he had been. He'd been Noah's good soldier. Not

thinking, obeying orders, doing what he was told. Believing everything his father told him, because he loved his father and his father was always right. His father also wanted him, needed him.

You were not always very smart.

His hands were gripping the rail that separated the river from the sidewalk, hanging on so tightly to stop the grief and formless rage that was tearing him apart from escaping.

All he wanted to do was go to a bar, find some drunks, pick a fight. Plunge his fists into someone's face. Break someone. Cause some pain.

But even now, even when he was dying inside, he had some sense left that doing that wasn't a good idea. The media, already lapping up the story of Van and his adoptive sister, would love it if the "wild one" of the Tate family got caught in a bar fight.

Wolf slowly, painfully, let go of the rail.

Who was he now? *What* was he now? He had no idea. For so long he'd believed he was Noah Tate's true son and that he had a mission to fulfill, and at the end of that mission, he'd claim his reward. That he'd be where he belonged, with people who loved him.

But that reward was gone now. And the people he'd thought would love him were both dead. One had given him away and one had used him. Neither of them had loved him.

All he had left was the mission.

Kill de Santis. That's what he'd been trained to do. That's what his whole life had been about. All those years spent honing his physical skills. All those years spent getting close to Cesare.

All those years spent lying to Olivia . . . hurting her . . .

Ah fuck.

The pain in his chest was bright and sharp, like knives.

It was all for nothing, wasn't it? All for a lying, manipulating man who'd done someone wrong once, and who was too greedy to make amends. Not that de Santis was innocent. No, he was as bad as Noah. He'd lied to and manipulated his own daughter, just as Noah had lied to and manipulated his own son.

If you're even Noah's son.

Wolf turned his back on the river and leaned against the rail, his hands in fists at his sides, furious, impotent rage whirling like a tornado inside him.

He didn't know what to do. He had nothing. No reward. Nothing to fight for, nothing to aim at. No one who needed him. No one to belong to.

His direction had been taken from him, his purpose lost.

You still have a mission. Are you going to let it all go to waste? Don't think—that's not your strong point. Just do what you're told.

Something savage turned over inside him.

Yeah, that's right. There was nothing to be gained by these endless fucking questions, because there were no fucking answers. Thinking only led to pain, to confusion. Thinking led to a whole lot of weak emotions he wasn't supposed to be feeling in the first place. Emotions like love, like loneliness. Like need.

Anyway, he wasn't a thinker, or a strategist. He wasn't a commander.

He was the weapon and he had a target. He had a mission to complete and he was going to fucking complete it.

It was all he knew. All he was. It was the only thing he had left.

Wolf shoved the pain and the grief to one side, concentrating only on the anger, then he pushed himself away from the rail and began to run back the way he had come.

He ran and ran hard, stopping only to pick up a new burner phone and get a new SIM. He wouldn't check to see if de Santis had replied to his text yet or not, he'd let the fucker sweat a bit longer. Maybe even leave it till the morning.

And in the meantime?

Normally when he had a whole lot of rage to burn off, he went to the gym, worked out till his muscles screamed. But he couldn't do that here, and running would only heighten his chances of being seen.

He was fucking lucky he hadn't been spotted as it was.

No, he couldn't work out, and since drinking himself insensible was out of the question, there was only one other option.

Olivia. He may have lost everything else, but he hadn't lost her.

His heart rate began to pick up as he reached the boat basin, and suddenly he couldn't think of anything else.

He didn't have to explain anything to her. She knew everything already, all his secrets, all his lies. She knew how badly his father had lied to him. She knew what he'd been promised and what he'd been denied.

She knew everything and she was the only person in his entire fucking life who did, and he hadn't realized until now what that meant to him.

He may not belong to her, but she certainly belonged to him.

He ran harder, thumping down the docks to where the *Lady* was moored, then over the gangplank and onto the deck. Gripping the handrails on either side of the stairs, he slid down them without even touching a step, landing in the corridor. Then he grabbed the key out of his pocket and unlocked the galley door.

Olivia was sitting where he'd left her, on the bench with the laptop open in front of her. Two empty beer bottles were beside her and when she looked up at him, her eyes were red.

Those fucking feelings twisted and knotted in his chest, reminding him of everything he'd shoved aside. All the grief and the pain, and the sudden, intense realization that in doing what he'd done to get closer to Cesare de Santis, in using her to further that end, he was no better than his goddamn father.

"You were right," she said before he could speak. "You were right about Dad. While you've been away, I tried to get into his intranet, but he's changed the passwords. And I'm sorry, but I found a way around the blocks you had on webmail. I really wanted to look at my own email records, to see if I could find that link between Dad and May, because he'd get me to send through things for May sometimes, or forward things."

Wolf had never wished he hadn't been right before. But in that moment, seeing the pain in her lovely eyes, he wished he had been. He wished he'd been wrong about Cesare de Santis. He wasn't even mad that she'd found a way around his blocks.

"I discovered a few emails in my sent box with heavily encrypted attachments. They were from Dad to May, and I don't know what the attachments are. But I do know the encryption is one that DS Corp uses in its labs, for anything that's highly classified or commercially sensitive. And anything at all to do with weapons developments." Carefully, Olivia reached out and closed the laptop. "I can't decrypt the files, but whatever they are, Dad didn't want anyone to know about them. And since he stepped down as CEO of DS Corp, I can't think of a single reason why he'd use encryption that strong for anything." She put her hands on the table and slowly stood, as if in pain. "Except I suppose there is a reason, isn't there?" Her gaze met his. "Those weapons deals you told me about. That . . .

would definitely be something he'd use that level of encryption for."

Wolf stared at her, not saying a word. What was there to say? Words were useless. They meant nothing. And nothing was going to make the betrayal any easier.

"Dad used me to send those files for him," she went on, moving around the table, coming toward him. "He knew I would never look at them. He knew I'd never even think to look at them."

Wolf's whole body tightened as she came closer, her warm, familiar scent surrounding him. Her hair was hanging around her shoulders and she was still wearing his shirt, her legs bare, her skin pale and silky. But there were dark circles beneath her eyes, and her jaw was tight, and in those deep blue eyes there was nothing but weariness. Disappointment. Grief.

"He used me," Olivia said, coming to stand right in front of him. "He lied to me. Both of them did, Wolf. Both of them lied to us, betrayed us. And for what? For greed. For some stupid fucking black stuff coming out of the ground." Her voice broke on the last word, but there were no tears in her eyes now, just a burning blue flame.

He had nothing left in him to give her. No words to make things right. His own rage and grief took up every part of his heart, and yet somehow, there was room for her pain as well. And he was grateful for that, because he knew he didn't deserve her. Didn't deserve to have her give herself to him the way she had.

Not when nothing had changed. He still couldn't let her go and he was still going to use her as bait to lure her father. He was still going to kill that fucker first chance he got. And he'd still hurt her with his lies.

He couldn't do anything about that, but at least he could help them both forget. For a little while.

Wolf lifted his hands to her face, cradling the delicate

line of her jaw in his palms. She leaned into him, the warmth of her skin both easing the ache in his chest at the same time it made his dick hard. "I think I want you to touch me now," he said roughly. "And I think I want to touch you. You okay with that?"

Her hands came up to rest on his chest. "Yes." Her gaze had darkened even further. "I don't want to feel this anymore, Wolf. I don't even want to think about it."

"I know." He stroked his thumbs along her jaw, watching the shadows move in her eyes. "This changes nothing, though. You understand that, right? I'm still on a mission. And I'm gonna do what I have to do." He had to get that out there, so she was under no illusions about him. So they were clear. There were already too many lies clouding everything, he wasn't going to add to them.

Her gaze didn't flinch. "I understand. As long as you know that I'll do what I have to do to stop you. Dad might have lied to me, but he doesn't deserve death. That kind of judgment isn't your call to make."

Despite everything, the pain and fury, the betrayal and the grief, and the ache of shame he felt whenever he looked into her face, he felt his mouth curl in a half smile. Even with what she'd been suffering too, she wasn't lying down and taking it. She was still determined to challenge him.

He fucking loved that about her.

You probably fucking love her, too.

The thought came and went, bright as summer lightning. But he couldn't take it in, and he didn't want to think about it, so he didn't.

Instead he murmured, "You can't stop me, baby. But feel free to try."

Then he held her tenderly as he covered her mouth with his own.

CHAPTER FOURTEEN

Wolf's mouth was hot and his hands on her jaw were gentle. It was a slow, aching kiss, like the one he'd given her in the hotel that first time, coaxing and tasting. His tongue touching the seam of her lips, encouraging her to open. And she did, because she was desperate to taste him.

It was wrong to want this, to give herself over to him. Especially after everything he'd told her and everything he'd done. Everything he still wanted to do, too.

But there was no one else in the whole world who knew what this kind of betrayal felt like. And he did. Sure, he'd betrayed her too, but he'd also been used. He'd been manipulated like she had.

It had hurt to find those files. Hurt to realize what they meant. And perhaps what had hurt worst of all was the fact that she hadn't even been shocked. As if a part of her had always known what she'd discover.

She felt stupid. Betrayed. Hurt beyond measure. That her father had not only lied to her about what he'd been doing, he'd also used her to cover his tracks. He'd used her love for him, her desire to please him, her desperation for his validation. And all she could think about was that it was true. She *had* been nothing but a tool for him. A means to an end.

He didn't care about her for her. Because if he had, then

surely he wouldn't have lied to her so completely and for
so long.

*It's true. You've never been precious to anyone. Not
your mother and not him.*

She'd cried a little about that, but then had decided she
wasn't going to shed any more tears for Cesare de Santis.
She wasn't going to waste any more grief.

So she'd opened another bottle of beer and had drunk
it slowly, not even registering the taste as it went down, trying to decide whether or not she'd use Wolf's absence to
get a warning to her father. Even though he'd betrayed her,
she didn't want him to die. Answer for his crimes, yes, but
justice in the form of a judge and jury, not in the form of
executioner Wolf Tate.

There wasn't much point looking for evidence that he
hadn't murdered Noah, not now, so she didn't bother looking, drinking her beer and trying to figure out what to say.
Getting around Wolf's blocks had been tricky, but not too
difficult—she'd picked up a bit of coding experience here
and there in the course of working for her father—so obviously sending an email was the way to go.

She had to warn him. Because quite apart from the
fact that she didn't want her father to die, she also didn't
want Wolf to be the one to take his life. She had the feeling that Wolf had taken lives before, in the course of his
SEAL operations. But that was war. This wasn't. This
would be murder, pure and simple, and she didn't want
him to have to bear that as well as all the other things he
was dealing with. Because despite everything, she cared
about him.

Eventually, she settled on: *Dad. I'm safe. But he's coming for you. Protect yourself.*

She probably should have told him where she was, but
the moment she'd started to enter her location, she'd
stopped, a strange reluctance overcoming her.

If her father knew where she was, he'd sweep in and rescue her, and he'd hurt Wolf into the bargain and she didn't want that. She'd rather stay here, as Wolf's prisoner, than to have anything happen to him. And if that was twisted, then hell, it was twisted.

But he'd been her friend long before he'd been her kidnapper, and those feelings didn't go away just like that.

In fact, she'd thought she was maybe okay with where she was. That maybe she didn't want to be rescued at all. Because what else was there for her to go back to? Her father's house. Her father's job. Everything she did, her whole goddamn life, was centered around her father. And quite frankly, now that she thought about it, it was a narrow, limited kind of life. One she wasn't sure she wanted to go back to. At all.

Not that she had any idea what kind of life she'd have as Wolf's prisoner, but it had to be better than that, didn't it?

So she'd stopped short of giving away her location, leaving the warning as it was as she'd drained the rest of her beer. Sitting there with only the sound the water lapping at the hull.

She hadn't tested the door, she knew it would be locked. And all it had taken was a couple of minutes of silence for her to be fully aware that Wolf was still not back. That he'd left upset and in pain, and she didn't know where he was.

He was gone a while, leaving her to sit there, an ache in her heart, contemplating a third beer. Then she'd heard the key in the lock and everything in her had leapt as the door opened and he'd stepped into the cabin.

Tall, massively built, the dark tips of his Mohawk nearly sweeping the ceiling, those jewel bright eyes meeting hers. He was angry, she could feel it radiating from him like a physical force, and she could see the remains of pain and grief in his gaze too.

And all she'd been able to think of to say was to tell him

that he'd been right about her father all along. That he wasn't alone in being betrayed by someone who was supposed to love him, that she'd been betrayed too.

She hadn't known she'd wanted to touch him until he'd listened to what she had to say without a word. And she'd seen the wordless sympathy in his eyes. Then she'd found herself closing the distance between them, because she was suddenly cold and he was nothing but raw heat.

He'd told her not to touch him when he'd left, but when he reached out to take her face between his palms, she knew that wherever he'd gone and whatever he'd done, he'd come to some sort of decision.

Then he'd told her what it was and she hadn't been surprised. With his world collapsing down around his ears, he'd held on to the one thing that made any sense to him. His mission.

She was glad he'd been clear with her about that, because it had helped her make a decision of her own. She *would* stop him. Somehow, she would. She couldn't let him murder her father in cold blood. She just couldn't.

But until then, they had this moment.

This slow, deep aching kiss. Where neither of them had to think about fathers or missions or death. Where there was only the warmth of another person's lips and the sweet taste of them. The slick glide of tongues and the hot press of bodies.

His hands were so gentle, the way he kissed her so sweet. He was such a big man, contained the potential for so much violence, and yet he handled her as if she was made of fine china.

He handled her as if she was precious.

Tears prickled behind her eyes, her throat unexpectedly tight. She wasn't precious to him though, was she? Everything she'd thought they'd had between had been a lie.

You weren't supposed to be in love anymore. This isn't supposed to matter.

And yet it *did* matter. It did.

As if he'd sensed her distress, Wolf lifted his mouth from hers, those big hands cradling her jaw, his gaze searching her face. "What's up?"

She didn't want to tell him, not given what it would reveal. But the time for holding back had long since passed. "Was it ever real?" Her voice wasn't quite steady. "Our friendship, I mean. Did you ever care about me? Or was I just another means to an end?"

Something shifted in his face, a flash of pain, of shame. He didn't answer immediately, his thumbs moving on her jaw, stroking her. Making goose bumps rise all over her body.

"I remember you liked Hades and Persephone," he said, his voice soft. "Because you thought Persephone got everything she wanted in the end. The guy, the summer, seeing her mom. And when I told you that was great, but she still had to spend half her life in the Underworld, you said 'You're assuming she didn't want that.' I thought that was smart. I just liked Theseus and the Minotaur because he got to kill the monster." One hand moved to brush back her hair from her forehead. "And I remember you telling me about one of your tutors. And how he sniffed a lot and made a mistake marking one of your algebra tests. Then there was that day you talked about your mom. About how she used to let you into her closet so you could look at all her pretty dresses. Sometimes she'd let you try on her shoes too, and the thing you really missed about her was her hugs. So I gave you a hug, because you looked so sad I couldn't stand it." One finger eased a lock of hair behind her hair. "I remember once we had an argument about *The Lord of the Rings* and *The Hobbit*. I preferred *The Hobbit* because it had a dragon in it, and you tried to argue that

The Lord of the Rings was better and quoted some Elvish poetry at me, like that was supposed to make me change my mind."

He remembered. He remembered everything.

Her throat constricted even further, so she could barely breathe. Had to force the words out. "And you just said, 'Yeah, but dragons.'"

"First time I'd ever seen you speechless." His mouth curled in a smile that made her heart race. "You always had something to say, always had an opinion and were always ready to argue for it. You were so smart. I was so in awe of you. But the really great thing about you, Liv, was that you never talked to me like I was stupid. You always talked to me as if I was as smart as you were. I liked that. I liked that a lot." His thumbs stroked over and over on her jaw, gentle movements, caresses. "I liked that you always wanted to know what I thought about something and you always listened to what I had to say. I remember once trying to sell Nine Inch Nails to you, because the lyrics were so cool, just as good as the folky chick stuff you listened to. I could tell you didn't want to, but next time I visited, you started into this great fucking diatribe about one of their songs."

She couldn't stop it this time, the tear that slid down her cheek and she couldn't speak, not when he was holding her like that, touching her like that. Telling her about all the things they'd talked about in the library of her father's house all those years ago.

"I don't remember that," she croaked.

He gave a soft laugh. "It was quite something. You were so pretty when you got wound up—I remember thinking that too." The smile faded from his face. "I don't remember much about your emails after I joined the Navy. I had too much stuff going on, I think. But there were a couple that stuck in my mind. When you told me that you weren't going to study history after all. That your Dad wanted you to study business instead. I felt pissed about that."

She didn't know what to say, couldn't have spoken anyway, and then all possibility of speech vanished altogether when he ran a gentle finger down the side of her cheek, tracing the path of her tear.

"I tried to tell myself that being friends with you was just a job, that I couldn't get too attached. Dad warned me that it could happen and that I had to keep some distance. But I couldn't. Not with you. I liked you. I liked you a lot. I liked sitting in that library talking with you. Back in the hotel, when I told you the truth, I kept telling myself that it wasn't real. That I didn't care." His fingers tightened fractionally on her jaw. "But I was just trying to protect myself. Because no matter how many times I told myself it wasn't real, that you were only a means to an end, it didn't feel like it. And in hurting you, I was hurting myself."

Another tear slid down her cheek. She wanted him to stop talking and yet never stop.

Intensity glittered in his eyes, the force of his will suddenly palpable in the air around them, violent and strong, totally at odds with the way he held her. "You were my friend, Liv." His voice had gotten hoarse, but she could hear the hard edge of certainty in it. "I cared about you. And I still do. It was real, baby. It was all real."

Her heart knew then. Her heart recognized the boy in the library. He was still there, shining in the eyes of the man, the boy she'd fallen in love with. Which made the man standing in front of her, holding her, not the stranger she'd thought he was.

He was and would always be Wolf.

And she loved him.

She should never have doubted herself.

The distance between them felt too great, so she lifted

herself up on her toes, closing the gap, pressing her mouth
to his. But that wasn't enough either, so she wrapped her
arms around his neck, arching her body against all that
heat, trying to kiss him harder, deeper. His hands cradling
her jaw slid gently down her neck to her shoulders, then
further down in a long, slow caress to rest on her hips.

Then in a casual display of strength, he picked her up
as if she weighed nothing at all. She spread her legs in-
stinctively, wrapping them around his lean waist, arching
again against his rock-hard torso.

The warmth of his palms cupping the bare skin of her
butt lit up every nerve ending she had, his kiss turning demanding and raw. And she returned it, desperation beginning to pull tight.

He was so strong he could probably take her like this,
holding her without any support. She could slide right
down on him, grind herself against him, ride him. . . .
God, she wanted to.

Her hands reached down to the button on his jeans,
fumbling with it, getting it open, sliding her fingers over
the taut plane of his stomach and down to curl around the
rapidly hardening length of his cock.

He groaned against her mouth, a shudder going through
that massive, muscled body as she got his zipper down, tilting her pelvis so she could grind her clit against his erection, craving some relief. Wanting him so badly she could
barely think.

She pulled away a little, kissing his jaw, the side of his
neck, tasting his skin. "Like this," she whispered. "I want
you like this."

He gave another deep groan, the sound rumbling in his
chest. "Believe me, baby, so do I. But I need a condom and
unless you've got one somewhere handy, we're gonna have
to move."

She didn't have one, but by then she didn't care how he

took her. She just wanted him inside her as quickly as possible. So she didn't protest as he turned and walked with her out of the galley, moving through to the stateroom, taking her down on the bed.

She lay there on her back, her breathing wild as he very carefully began to open the buttons of the shirt she was wearing, peeling it off her shoulders and away, leaving her naked. Then he knelt there, straddling her hips, and simply looked at her.

His gaze burned, made flames lick her skin, made her feel restless and demanding, but she let him look because the heat in his eyes, the desire, filled up a part of her she hadn't known was empty.

"You're so beautiful," he whispered. "So fucking beautiful."

Only Wolf could make a curse word sound like the sweetest thing she'd ever heard.

She reached out her arms to him. "Come here. I want you."

"Wait." He pulled his hoodie up and off in a single fluid movement, chucking it down beside the bed, revealing the sculpted, muscled lines of his chest. His dog tags hung between his pecs and she couldn't resist sitting up and reaching to touch them, grip them. She met his gaze. "I said, come here." Then she used them to pull him down so she was on her back and he was braced above her, the heat of his body so close to hers it was almost torture.

"You think you can order me around, huh?" His voice was deep and dark with heat. But there was a smile turning one side of his beautiful mouth. "I might have to punish you for that."

Electricity shot down her spine and her fingers tightened on his tags. "Do it. I can take anything you give me."

Flame leapt in his eyes, and suddenly her mouth was

crushed under his, and he was kissing her hard and desperate and rough.

It was thrilling, exciting, and she gave as good as she got, biting his bottom lip as the kiss became consuming, one hand gripping his tags, the other digging into his shoulder.

He cursed then broke away, reaching over for the drawer in the headboard and getting out another condom packet. Seconds later he'd gotten rid of his clothes and was kneeling over her again, his hands shaking as he rolled the condom down.

She tried to help, but he wasn't having any of it, knocking her hands away and then pulling her beneath him, pinning her to the bed as his weight came down on hers.

He didn't wait, gripping her hips tightly as he thrust hard into her, but by then she didn't want him to wait. She gasped at the sweet burn of him inside her, arching up as he began to move, the delicious friction making her tremble.

Digging her fingers into his shoulders, she held on tight, because he wasn't going slow this time and he wasn't holding back. Deep. Hard. Fast.

The metal of his tags dragged over her skin, brushing against one nipple, sending another arrow of heat to join the fire building inside her.

He didn't kiss her, merely looked down into her face as he slammed himself into her, his own features drawn tight with desire, with hunger. Pinning her in place with his gaze as surely as he pinned her with his cock.

God, he was amazing. So intense. So beautiful.

She wrapped her legs around his waist, her heels pressing hard against the tight muscles of his butt, moving with him, trying to match his pace. But he was wild and she couldn't do it, shaking as he slipped his hand between her thighs and stroked in time with his thrusts.

The orgasm broke over her without warning, making her shut her eyes and cry out, her thighs quaking and her heart feeling like it was going to pound its way out of her chest. And before she'd quite recovered from that one, he slid his hands beneath her butt and lifted her hips, tilting them back before shoving his shoulders beneath her knees and her thighs now up around his ears. She groaned as the position let him slid even deeper inside her, trembling in reaction as his movements became sharper, harder.

It was so good. It was too much. She couldn't handle it.

"Wolf . . ." Her voice was little more than a whisper. "Wolf . . . I can't . . ."

"Yeah, you can." He drove inside her, over and over, stoking that fire until it blazed again. "You can take anything I give you, right?"

And she did.

He rode her hard and deep and long, the agonizing friction and the weight of him on her, grinding down on her, tearing a second orgasm from her. It made her scream, the sound echoing around the cabin, and only then did he let himself go, his breath coming in short, hard pants in her ear. His movements got jerky and out of rhythm before he thrust one last time, so deep it was nearly painful, then went still, his body shuddering. A low, tortured sound escaped him and his teeth closed on her shoulder, making her shake right along with him.

And like she had before, that last time in bed, she wrapped her arms around him. And brought him home.

Wolf couldn't move. It was like every single one of his muscles had lost the power to function properly. Except he was going to need to move, because Olivia was under him, and if he didn't, he'd probably suffocate her or crush her, or something equally as hideous.

Forcing himself into motion, he rolled to the side,

gathering her up in his arms and taking her with him, reluctant to give up the simple joy of having her bare skin against his. Then he groaned, because he had a condom to get rid of and he didn't want to do that either.

Olivia folded her arms on his chest then rested her chin on them, smiling at him. "What's that noise for?"

"Fucking condom." Gently he nudged at her to move. "Gotta get rid of it. Don't go away, though, okay?"

"Are you kidding me? I'm not going anywhere."

He grinned then made himself shift, going into the tiny bathroom to get rid of the stupid condom, before coming back to the bed. He propped himself up with some pillows against the headboard this time, pulling Olivia into his arms and adjusting her so she was lying down the length of his body, her sweet warmth and soft curves against every part of him.

Yeah, that was better. So much fucking better.

She put her hand out to touch the dark lines of his eagle-and-trident tattoo, tracing them, her fingertip the merest brush against his skin. "Tell me about your tattoos. Like this one. Is it a SEAL thing?"

"Yeah. It's our emblem."

Her fingertip moved to the tribal tattoo he had on his right arm, touching the skeletal frog at the center of it. "And this one too, yes?"

"Yeah, that too."

"What about . . . this?" She moved onto the pattern around it, sharp black lines and jagged edges.

He smiled. "The tattoo guy was a real artist, thought it would look better as part of an entire design. So he drew one up and I liked it."

Her mouth curved. "Me too." She traced another line up his arm and back over to his chest again, and he had to repress the urge to shiver at the delicate touch. Christ, he liked her hand on him.

"This one?" She'd moved to his left shoulder and arm this time, looking down wide-eyed at the Chinese dragon sleeve that covered it.

He had to laugh. "It was in Shanghai. Got drunk on some rice wine with some buddies, and of course getting some more ink was a good idea."

"Of course," she echoed, amusement in her blue eyes. "But it's a lovely tattoo."

"I was lucky. One of the other guys wanted some Chinese characters on his neck and the tattoo guy's English wasn't great. He ended up with a tattoo that basically says 'dog place record.' "

Olivia laughed. "Oh my God, you *were* lucky. So why the dragon?"

"Why do you think?"

She gave him a sidelong glance. "Please don't tell me that's an homage to Smaug."

He grinned and lifted his arms, putting his hands behind his head. "I can neither confirm nor deny."

Her smile made his heart sing, and then she made it sing even louder as she bent and kissed the dragon on the top of its head where it crested his shoulder.

"You do love your monsters." Her wandering fingertip came back to his chest, stopping over his left pec, above his heart. Then she frowned. " 'The world breaks everyone,' " she read slowly, " 'and afterward, many are strong in the broken places.' "

He didn't move, only watched her. Would she remember? She hadn't remembered some of what he'd told her back there in galley, about their conversations, but he hadn't minded that because it hadn't been about him.

It had been about that sound in her voice when she'd asked him whether any of it had been real, and the pain in her eyes. It had been about him realizing that he'd been lying to himself all this time, believing that it hadn't been a real friendship and that she'd never meant anything to him.

It had been about him wanting to tell her the truth, even though it made him ashamed of his own behavior. Even though it hurt him to acknowledge that he'd hurt her. Even though he was worried it would put his mission at risk.

He wanted her to know that yes, it had been real. And yes, he'd cared about her. Cared about her enough to remember their conversations, to remember them in detail. Every little thing.

"That's familiar." Olivia looked up at him, a crease between her winged brows. "Where have I heard that before? It's beautiful."

"It's something from a book you read parts of aloud to me once, because you were convinced I'd like it. But it was by Ernest Hemingway and was considered a classic and I thought it would be boring."

A wave of color swept over her skin, making her eyes glow. "*A Farewell to Arms*," she said quietly. "You remembered that too?"

"Of course I remembered. That quote you read out, I liked it. And you know what else? I was on a mission in Central America a couple of years back, and we ended up hiding out in an abandoned house. And in one of the bedrooms there was a copy of *A Farewell to Arms* in English. I shit you not."

Her eyes went wide. "Don't tell me . . ."

"Yeah, I read it, because there was nothing else to do. And you know what?"

Olivia bit her lip like she was trying not to smile. "You hated it?"

"No, I fucking loved it. You were right. It's an awesome book, even if the ending sucked. Anyway, I liked the quote. So I had it inked in so I'd remember."

Her gaze dropped back down to his chest, her fingertip tracing over the words again, and there was a small
silence.

"I missed you when you left," she huskily. "The library was so quiet and there was no one to talk to anymore. You were the only one who was ever interested in
talking to me, Wolf. My mom was gone, Dad was too busy,
my brothers were all older than me and didn't much care. I
think you were the only friend I had."

The thought of her all alone was painful. "No, come on.
You must have had someone else, Liv. Not even one girl-
friend?"

She shook her head. Her finger had moved onto his dog
tags, tracing his name engraved on them. "I didn't go to
school, I only had tutors, so I never really met anyone. I
had a few friends in college, but Dad always got really suspicious of them. He didn't like anyone getting close to
me. I didn't mind all that much, not when no one talked to
me the way you did."

There was a small hot coal inside him, one that glowed
warmly at her praise. And his instinct was to throw cold
water on that shit, keep his distance. But right now, with
her lying on top of him and her hand moving on his skin,
distance was the last thing he wanted from her. "Really?"
He tried to sound casual, as if it didn't matter to him. "Bet
it was the first time you'd actually had any intelligent conversation."

Her gaze flicked to his, unexpectedly sharp. "I don't
know why you keep thinking you're not smart. Or that I'm
smarter than you are. Because it's a lie, you know that,
right?"

His jaw tightened and he shifted under her, uncomfortable. "Well, you *are* smarter than me, that's a fact. But . . .
I'm the muscle, not the brains. Someone tells me who to
hit and I hit it, that's it. That's all."

She didn't move, still staring at him. "You're more than that and you know it."

The softly spoken words were difficult to hear though he didn't know why. "It's okay," he said, trying to take it down a notch. "I don't mind. My marks were never as good as Van's or Lucas's, but Dad said he didn't care about that. He said my job wasn't to think anyway. My job was to be strong."

But there was a look in her midnight eyes. A steady look that seemed to see all the way through to his soul. "Don't believe it, Wolf. Don't believe that for a second. You told me you liked the way I treated you as smart, and you know why I did? Because you *were* smart."

He couldn't think of what to say, because you could only deny something so many times before it started to look like you were fishing for compliments. Yet he wanted to deny what she said all the same.

Because maybe if you accepted it, you wouldn't have any excuses for swallowing Dad's bullshit, hook, line, and fucking sinker.

"You talked to me about a lot of things," she went on slowly, her fingertip moving from his dog tags back to his skin again, tracing little patterns on his chest. "And I was always interested in what you had to say, because you were interesting. You weren't stupid in any way. You thought about the things you were passionate about very carefully." Her tracing finger dipped lower, drawing a curving pattern over his abs, making them tighten. "Anyway, a stupid man wouldn't have kidnapped me right from under my father's nose and taken me somewhere he couldn't find us. Not only once, but twice."

Desire was starting to build inside him again, the warmth of her body and her scent and that maddening touch of hers driving him slowly insane. And he really wanted to ignore what she was saying, because he didn't like hearing it. Yet that hot coal in his chest burned to hear more.

"A stupid man wouldn't have cared about our friendship," she went on, her finger moving out to his hip and then back again. "And he wouldn't have cared about hurting me. It wouldn't have occurred to him to remember those conversations we had in the library, and he definitely wouldn't have cared enough to have an Ernest Hemingway quote tattooed on his chest." Her finger moved lower, making his breath hiss as it headed toward his groin. "A stupid man wouldn't have thought the truth would be important." Her fingers curled around his already achingly hard dick, gripping him, the look in her eyes absolutely inescapable. "But most of all, I wouldn't have fallen in love with a stupid man, Wolf Tate."

He wanted to say something. About how she was wrong, that she couldn't have fallen in love with him, because he *was* stupid. He was just a dumb meathead who didn't belong to anyone or anything. Who didn't have anything else in his life but his mission. Who couldn't let that go. Even if it would hurt the only person in his life who, as it turned out, had never lied to him.

She's not lying now, either. So why not believe her?

Oh, Christ, how he wanted to. But that word and that look in her eyes, they made that fucking coal in his chest burn so bright it hurt. It just fucking hurt. If he crossed the line, believed what she'd told him, it would bring everything down.

It would make him question everything, and he couldn't afford to.

Because you know the mission is a lie.

No, he had to believe it was worth it. He had to believe that all these years of following orders and doing everything his lying daddy told him was for something. Even if all it was, was ending this fucking feud that had caused so much harm and hurt so many people.

Never quit—that was one thing a SEAL *never* did, and so he couldn't.

So he didn't say anything. Instead he sat up and took her face between his hands, kissed her hard and long and deep. Then he said, "Remember what you promised me in the hotel? How about you give it to me now?"

Yeah, you fucking tool. Answer her declaration with a request for a blow job. Excellent response.

Something shifted in her eyes, a fleeting sadness that made him wish that he was a different person, a different man. A man who deserved her instead of a man who was quite frankly the worst person in the entire world for her.

"No," he said, changing his mind as a hot kind of shame filled him "Forget I said that. You don't—"

Olivia laid a finger across his lips, stopping the rest of his sentence. "It's fine," she murmured. "I want to. But you're going to lie back and think of England while I figure out how to do it myself, okay?"

He should refuse, he really should. But he wasn't that good.

Lie back and think of England. Holy fuck.

So Wolf lay back, but he didn't think of England. He only thought of her.

Impossible not to when she gripped him in her fist and her hot mouth finally wrapped itself around his dick. And he thought he was going to lose it right then and there, like a goddamn virgin. But he held on and let her play, let her lick and explore, let her tongue circle the sensitive head of his cock then graze it with her teeth.

His hands fisted in the sheets and he couldn't stop himself from giving orders, telling her to put it in her mouth, suck him harder, just fucking *suck* him.

But she didn't. She continued playing around with licks and nibbles, only occasionally rewarding him with the wet, velvet heat of her mouth.

It began to be clear to him then, that she wasn't simply giving him a blow job for his pleasure. It was actually a subtle punishment. A reminder of what she could do to him, how she could make him shake and gasp. A reminder that she had power here and that he was as powerless when it came to this as she was when she was under him.

He knew what the punishment was about. He'd seen that fleeting sadness in her eyes when she'd told him that she loved him after all and he hadn't said a word in return.

But that was the problem. He couldn't say it.

Love didn't mean anything, that was what Noah had told him the one and only time he'd said, "I love you, Daddy."

It was only a word, his father had said. And he didn't need words. Love was a weakness, and he didn't need that either. Only action mattered. Only loyalty. Only duty.

That's all he could give Olivia de Santis. Loyalty, duty. And death. She needed more than that. She deserved more than that.

So he kept his mouth shut and he let her punish him with the most indescribable pleasure. Let her push him to the edge of his strength, his endurance, his patience, testing him in a way he hadn't been since he'd earned his trident in Coronado.

It was so sweet, so painful. The pleasure, indescribable.

He hadn't had a woman concentrate on him like this since forever.

You've never had a woman concentrate on you like this at all.

Fuck, he probably hadn't. Certainly not one he cared about the way he cared about Olivia. Not one who mattered to him the way she did.

He had to move his hands in the end, had to shove his fingers into the soft silk of her hair to keep her head right where it was, thrusting his hips up into her mouth. It was either that or go completely fucking insane.

She let him do it, didn't fight him. Only sucked him in deeper, turning him inside out, making him forget his own name.

When the orgasm hit, it was like a bullet direct to his brain, blowing him completely away. And as he fell into the white light of complete ecstasy, he was aware of only one thing. That there was only one person he'd been lying to consistently all this time, and that person wasn't Olivia.

It was himself.

CHAPTER FIFTEEN

Olivia woke from an incredibly deep sleep to the sound of
splintering wood and men's voices shouting at each other.
The bed seemed to be shaking too, or rocking at least.

Still not really awake, she sat up, shoving her hair out
of her eyes to see Wolf at the door to the cabin. He was
naked and seemed to be struggling with a man dressed all
in black who was waving . . . a gun.

Adrenaline burst in her head at the same time as the gun
went off with the muted percussive sound of a silencer.

Fear followed hard on the heels of the adrenaline, slamming into her brain, making her go absolutely cold. She
opened her mouth to scream Wolf's name.

But the bullet must have missed him because he didn't
fall. Instead he drew back one massive arm, punching the
guy in the face with a short, hard jab, before bringing up
his knee and driving it into the man's stomach. The man
groaned, slipping to lie still on the ground. Wolf didn't
pause. He swiped the man's gun, then grabbed his own
jeans from the floor and tugged them on.

Olivia made her mouth work. "What's happening?
Who's that? Why are they—"

"Stay here," Wolf ordered, cutting over the top of her,
his words vibrating with a hard authority she'd never heard
from him before. He moved over to the side of the bed and

before she knew what he was doing, he'd put the gun he was holding in her hand then bent to kiss her, hard.

"Don't make a fucking sound," he murmured, lifting his head, the look on his face fierce. "Understand? I'll deal with this."

The metal of the gun felt heavy in her fingers, deadly. "But don't you need this?"

He lifted his other hand, something sleek gleaming. Another gun. "Already got one."

"But . . . I don't know how to use . . . this."

"With any luck you won't have to. Just in case."

Heavy footsteps sounded on the deck above them.

Wolf cursed. He kissed her again and without another word, went to the door of the cabin and stepped through it, closing it behind him. He didn't make a sound.

Fear curled like an animal in Olivia's chest.

What the hell was going on? Who were these people?

Something in her gut was telling her she knew exactly what was happening, but she didn't want to accept it.

She'd only told her father that Wolf was coming for him. She hadn't let him know her location.

Yes, but obviously he's tracked you somehow.

Olivia slipped out of bed, scrabbling around in the darkness for her clothes. Her panties and bra were screwed up on the floor, as was her blue dress, and she didn't particularly want to wear any of it. But she certainly wasn't facing what she had a horrible suspicion she was facing naked.

Once she was dressed, gripping the gun firmly in her hand, she crept over to the unconscious man on the floor near the door. It was dark in the cabin, but there was a bit of light, enough to see the guy's features as she tilted his head toward her.

The fear inside her clenched tight.

She knew the man. He was one of her father's security team.

Of course her father had found her. He always found her.

The boat rocked and she heard more hard, heavy footsteps on the deck above her, then there came the sound of a splash. She took a frightened breath, rising up from the unconscious body beside her and going over to the closed door.

Her fingers tightened on the gun.

Wolf had told her to stay here, but her heart was throwing itself against her ribs, urging her to go and find him. Help him somehow. Not that she'd be much help, since she had no idea how to fire a gun and would probably only get in the way.

Your father might be here. Wolf might kill him.

She swallowed, dry-mouthed with fear, her palms damp.

Whatever was happening, she couldn't stay here. She had to do something.

Lifting her hand, she began to turn the doorknob, only to hear more footsteps above her, and then a massive thump, the boat rocking more.

Then silence. Stillness.

Her heartbeat was a terrified rhythm in her head, the metal of the gun slipping in her sweaty palms. What the hell was happening? There had been no gunshots, but if all the weapons were silenced, she wouldn't hear any.

Had something happened to Wolf? Had her father found him? Or had Wolf found her father?

Unable to stand it anymore, Olivia pulled open the door to the cabin, only to come face-to-face with a familiar figure. His face was shadowed in the darkness, but she knew who it was anyway.

"Miss de Santis," Clarence, her father's head of security said. "Come with me please."

She couldn't find enough air to breathe and her pulse was going insane.

"Where's Wolf?" she had to force out the words. "What have you done with him?"

"Mr. Tate has been taken care of." He reached out to take her arm. "Now, Miss de Santis, please. Boss wants to speak to you."

But Olivia didn't move. "What do you mean 'taken care of'?"

"Miss de Santis, please. I won't ask again."

Her hand was shaking, but she raised the gun and aimed it squarely at Clarence's chest. "Tell me."

A small silence fell.

Clarence glanced down at the gun, then back at her. "He's alive, if that's what you want to hear. Now you need to come with me. Boss told me to extract you with whatever force necessary."

"He's alive . . ."

The words echoed in her head over and over again, her knees feeling weak.

She gripped the gun harder. "Take me to him."

"Miss de Santis, we really can't—"

"I said take me to him." She couldn't think of anything but seeing Wolf for herself, checking that he was actually breathing.

Why would your father leave him alive?

She ignored the thought. That could wait until she'd seen Wolf.

Clarence was looking impatient, but she ignored that too. "I will fire this, make no mistake," she said succinctly. "Once I've checked for myself that Mr. Tate is still breathing, I'll go with you."

She didn't want to go with him, but she knew her father. If he wanted her back, he'd take her back, kicking and screaming if he had to. The thought of being hauled over Clarence's shoulder and dragged back to the de Santis mansion didn't thrill her and it wouldn't exactly help the situation either.

It would be better to pretend to be the good daughter and go quietly. That way she'd be able to find out how he'd managed to find her and what he intended to do about the threat Wolf posed.

Clarence merely shrugged. "Fine. Follow me then." He turned and went up the stairs to the deck.

Olivia forced herself into motion, climbing the stairs after him.

It was still dark outside, but there was a faint light in the sky, which meant it was close to dawn. The air was frosty and she shivered in her thin dress.

Until she saw the dark form of a massive man lying still on the deck and all thoughts of the temperature went straight out of her head.

It was Wolf.

She almost ran to him, only to be brought up short by Clarence's hand on her arm. "Don't get too close," Clarence said flatly. "Boss doesn't want you anywhere near him."

Olivia opened her mouth to argue, then closed it. Again, arguing wouldn't get her anywhere and it wouldn't help. Neither would continuing to threaten Clarence with that gun. She wasn't going to pull that trigger, and he probably knew it too.

So all she did was nod and stay where she was, looking at Wolf's still form on the deck.

There were three other men lying around him, all of them unconscious. A fourth was sitting on the edge of the boat, dripping wet, his hand on his jaw and moaning something about it being broken. A fifth stood nearby, his gun trained on Wolf's head. He was cradling his hand close to his chest, as if it was injured too.

God. Looked like Wolf had taken down nearly five men all on his own.

Taking a shaky breath, she looked at him.

He was lying on his front, his head turned away, the arrows and lines on his back dark against his skin. She hadn't asked about that tattoo yet. He was breathing, she could see the slow rise and fall of his chest.

Tears filled her eyes. She didn't want to leave him and she was afraid. Both of what her father was going to do and what Wolf might do when he woke up.

Swallowing back the tears, she glanced at Clarence. "What are you going to do with him?"

Clarence's expression was a mask. "You don't need to concern yourself with such things."

Oh no, she wasn't having that. Not now. Not here. "Don't treat me like I'm stupid, Clarence," she said coldly. "I know the kind of man my father is." *Yes, now you do.* "Killing one of the Tate heirs would be a very short-sighted move right now."

If killing Wolf had been on the agenda, Clarence gave no sign, his face impassive. "Boss has other plans for Mr. Tate. He's waiting for you, by the way. And you know how much he doesn't like waiting."

Olivia's jaw felt so tight it ached. Still, it didn't look like any retribution was going to rain down on Wolf's head right now, which was a relief. Of course, now she wanted to know what those "other plans" of her father's were, and maybe he'd tell her. If she was biddable enough.

Straightening her shoulders, she reversed the weapon she was holding and handed it to Clarence. Then she turned and moved around the deck to the gangplank, walking across to the dock. She didn't look back as she made her way out of the boat basin, Clarence following along behind her, but her heartbeat hadn't slowed. And she didn't know whether it was raw fear or deep fury that went through her as she spotted her father's limo waiting for her at the curb.

Perhaps it was both.

She gave a nod to Angus, her father's driver who was holding the door open for her, and climbed inside the car.

It was warm and the leather of the seat was soft as she sat back against it, but as Angus shut the door, she couldn't shake the feeling that it sounded like the door to a tomb closing.

Her father was sitting opposite her, his expression as impassive as Clarence's. But his blue eyes glittered coldly as he surveyed her.

Olivia met his gaze without flinching.

Fury. It was fury she felt, not fear.

"You went with him," Cesare said, his voice heavy with accusation. "You went with him willingly."

"And you lied to me." She made her voice as cold as his, because after all, she *was* his daughter. "You lied to me about everything."

His expression flickered then and she caught the slight widening of his eyes, as if he was surprised. "And what exactly did I lie to you about?"

"Daniel May. You were going to give me to him."

"Yes," he replied without hesitation. "But I thought you knew that. I told you what the advantages were and you seemed to be in agreement."

" 'No' wasn't going to be an option, though, was it, Dad? You were going to give me to him whether I wanted him or not."

Her father said nothing for a moment. Then he leaned forward and pressed the button on the intercom. "Take us home, Angus."

The car pulled away from the curb and she had to resist the urge to look back, to find the *Lady* in the darkness of the boat basin. To see if she could get one last glimpse of Wolf.

But she didn't. She stared at her father, the man she thought had loved her. The man who'd simply been using her all these years.

"Explain to me, Dad," she said when he didn't break the silence. "Explain to me how you were going to make sure 'no' wasn't an option. Would you have forced me up the aisle with a shotgun held to my back? Or would you have simply manipulated me the way you've been doing for the past ten years? Made it seem like it was a good business decision? That I'd be doing it for your sake, to make you happy?"

He tilted his head, his cold gaze moving over her, staring at her as if she were something new, a stranger he'd never met and yet found intriguing. "What kind of lies has he been telling you?"

"Who? Wolf? No lies at all. He told me the truth. And I found the evidence of it in some emails you sent to May." She held his stare, finding a strength inside her she didn't know she had. A fury that burned white hot. "You must have been thrilled with me all these years. How perfectly I fitted the role of the good daughter. Who never questioned you, who only wanted to please you. I was the perfect tool for you, the perfect cover." She didn't let the fury show in her voice. Kept it completely cold. She would fight fire with fire. "How long were you going to use me like that, Dad? Tell me, I'd really like to know."

Her father's expression didn't change. "You said he was coming for me. Care to elaborate?"

Ah, so he wasn't going to talk to her about any of that. He was going to pretend it didn't exist. But that was okay, he knew that she knew. Perhaps it would have been better to keep playing the perfect daughter, but the fury inside her wouldn't let her. She'd been playing that role for the last ten years, hiding from the truth. Afraid of it. Needing the lies to protect herself, to make herself feel like she wasn't alone. That she was loved.

Well, that time was past. She knew the truth and she wasn't afraid anymore. And she wasn't alone either.

Wolf Tate might not love her, but he did care. He was still her friend after everything that had happened between them, and that mattered.

"First of all, tell me how you found me," she said. "I didn't tell you where I was."

"No, but we were able to track down the IP of the laptop you used," her father answered casually. "Easy enough to do if you have the right person with the right skills."

Ah, so that's how he'd done it.

Your fault.

Yes, well. She'd have to deal with that when the time came.

"He's coming to kill you, Dad," she said flatly. "He's been a double agent for Noah Tate all this time. His mission was to insinuate himself into our family, pass information back to Noah, and then, when the time was right, kill you."

Her father leaned back against the seat and let out a breath. "Yes, I know."

Olivia refused to let her shock show. "You know?"

"Of course." He lifted his shoulder. "An obvious and foolish ploy on Noah's behalf, but it was useful for me. I gave Wolf information to take back to Noah to make it look like he had secrets of mine and in return I got secrets from Wolf. It was all bullshit, but even bullshit information is still information." Her father's mouth curved in a cold smile. "He had Chloe and so I thought I'd try and get Wolf."

Chloe, Wolf's adoptive sister.

She frowned. "What's Chloe Tate got to do with Wolf?"

"Chloe Tate is my daughter, Olivia. I have two, you see."

More shock pulsed down her spine, her fingertips going numb. Chloe Tate was . . . her half sister. She couldn't even start to process that one.

"Noah took her as a baby after her mother died," her father went on. "I thought it prudent to leave her with the Tates. My very own inside man, so to speak. Then Wolf appeared at my door one day with some obviously made up story about Noah knocking him around. And I thought why not take him too?"

She fought to keep still, staring at the man opposite her, fury beating inside her like a prisoner trapped in a room and screaming to get out. "Why Dad?" she heard herself ask, even though she hadn't meant to. "Why are you doing this? You and Noah Tate, hurting each other and not caring who you use to do it."

Cesare's eyes glittered in the streetlights outside, sudden fury passing over his face. "You know why. He stole from me, Olivia. He stole *everything* from me."

"No. He stole your oil. That's all." Her voice wasn't cold now, it was full heat, full of the fury she couldn't keep inside her any longer. "You had a wife. You had children. You had a family who loved you and you used them all, alienated *all* of them, and for what? Thirty years of pointless plotting and manipulation, and all because your friend stole some oil off you."

Her father's expression twisted. "You don't understand—"

"No," she cut across him, not waiting for him to speak. "I don't understand and I never will. You had everything. A huge company you created out of nothing, money to burn. A wife who loved you, children who adored you. And yet it wasn't enough. You couldn't let go what Noah did, could you? So you sacrificed everything you had, your company, your wife and your children, and for what? For money? For your hurt feelings?"

The brief flare of rage had disappeared from her father's face as if it had never been there. "You don't understand," he said, continuing as if she'd never spoken. "Noah never admitted fault. He never admitted he'd done wrong. He stole from me, stole my future. He betrayed me, Olivia. And I will never forgive him for that."

No, she could see that.

He will never change his mind.

All the fury suddenly bled out of her, leaving her feeling hollow and sick. There was no point arguing with him. No point talking. Nothing she said was going to make any difference to him.

Like Wolf, he had a mission and he would not deviate from it.

You know what you have to do then, don't you?

This feud would never end until her father was dead, she knew that now. But she couldn't kill him, neither would she let Wolf do it. He had to be stopped some other way, put in prison for a very long time where he wouldn't be able to hurt anyone ever again. Where he had time to reflect on what he'd done and maybe find some peace with it. Or maybe he'd never find peace. Maybe all there would ever be was fury.

That was fine. At least he wouldn't be around to take that fury out on anyone else.

Her mind made up, Olivia sat back against the seat and folded her icy hands in her lap. "What are you going to do with Wolf?"

"Why?" Her father's gaze was sharp. "You care about him, don't you?"

"Yes. He's my friend."

"And more, judging from your appearance right now."

She almost put her hand to her hair to smooth it, then didn't bother. It would be obvious. Which also made lying to him pointless. "Yes, you must know that."

Cesare only nodded. "If you want him, I can arrange some things. It could be useful for you to be allied with a Tate."

"He wants you dead, Dad."

"So you told me. But there are always ways around these things. Always ways to change people's minds."

She held his gaze. "I won't let you kill him."

Cesare gave a short, harsh laugh. "What makes you think I want to kill him? What would the point be? He's useful. And if he wants you, then he's more useful still."

Ah, so that was what he intended. He was going to use her to get to Wolf.

It should have worried her or at the very least called back her fury, but she felt neither. Only . . . oddly reassured. Because this was expected behavior from her father. Of course he'd use whatever was between her and Wolf to his advantage, but at least he wouldn't hurt him. And that also meant that perhaps she could use his own predictability against him.

She wasn't sure how yet, but she was sure she could come up with something. Two could play at that game.

She was nothing if not her father's daughter.

Wolf came to with a cracking headache and feeling like he'd been dumped in a deep freeze for a couple of hours. Which given that he'd been lying half naked on the deck of his boat in the middle of winter for at least that long, was pretty much literally what had happened.

He was also deeply and completely enraged.

The last thing he remembered was laying two assholes out cold on the deck, while he'd punched a third in the face then picked him up and flung him into the river. He was just starting onto the fourth, when someone had hit him very hard over the back of the head. Dazed, he'd spun around and wrenched the truncheon he'd been hit with from the prick's hand, hopefully breaking that mother-fucker's fingers in the process, but someone else had then hit him again. And this time he'd gone out like a light.

Normally he could take five guys on and beat the pants off them. But these guys had been military trained, the one who'd hit him the first time likely special ops, which meant they were a grade above the usual security asshole.

He might be a SEAL, but he wasn't superhuman, and as galling as it was to admit he'd been beaten, they'd certainly managed to knock him out.

The really weird thing though was that they'd left him alive. He couldn't think why that would be. Because he'd known from the second the inexplicable rocking of the boat had woken him up, that de Santis had somehow found them, and had come for him.

Still, killing a Tate and leaving him dead on his boat in the middle of Manhattan wasn't exactly an intelligent move. There were more subtle ways to kill a man and ones that wouldn't leave a trail.

Which had to mean that de Santis wanted him alive for some reason.

Aren't you forgetting one other thing?

Under the boiling heat of his fury, something icy gripped him.

Olivia.

Ignoring the cold, the pain in his head, and his blurred vision, Wolf stumbled from the deck and down the stairs, tearing aside the door to the stateroom.

But it was empty.

Olivia wasn't there.

He leaned back against the doorframe as his stomach dropped away.

She was gone. Fuck. Fuck. *Fuck.*

He closed his eyes, gritting his teeth as an aching emptiness swept through him. Ridiculous. It wasn't as if she'd

vanished off the face of the planet. It wasn't likely she'd be
in any danger, either, because it was clear her father had
taken her and he wouldn't hurt his daughter, that much
Wolf did know.

How did they find you?

Good. Fucking. Point.

De Santis had found him and made a preemptive strike,
taking Olivia away, leaving Wolf with nothing with which
to lure him out again.

Holy shit, how many more times was he going to fuck
this up? All he had to do was kill the bastard. How hard
could that be?

*Yeah, yeah, quit whining and figure out what you're
going to do now.*

Growling, he shoved himself away from the doorframe
and walked over to the dresser, opening the drawers and
pulling on some clothes to get warm. A thermal, leather
jacket, boots. Then he fiddled with the loose bottom on the
drawer and pulled out the Sig Sauer 9mm he had secreted
in the base of it, sliding the gun into the waistband of his
jeans at the small of his back.

There was no question about what he was going to do
now. The mission objectives hadn't changed. Yes, it was
now going to be harder, but he'd had that problem when
Olivia had escaped the first time and had overcome it.

He'd overcome this too. And he had an idea about how.

Moving from the stateroom back into the galley, he
went over to the table where the laptop sat and pushed the
power button. A blue glow instantly illuminated the cabin
as the laptop came on.

There were a number of files already open and as he
cycled through them, he smiled as the one in particular he
wanted came up. One of Olivia's emails, with the encrypted files attached. She'd obviously downloaded them
in the hope of being able to decrypt them.

His smile turned feral as he hit forward on the email and typed in Van's email address. Then in the subject line he put: *Decrypt these ASAP.*

He wasn't certain if Van would be able to, but if anyone could, it was him.

Pressing send, Wolf closed the laptop and stood for a moment in the gradually lightening darkness of the galley.

There was only one way to play this and that was to go big or go home.

No more sneaking around. No more watching and coming in the dead of night to steal the asshole's daughter away. No more hiding.

He would take this directly to de Santis's door.

Getting the prick to let him in might be a problem— then again it wasn't as if he didn't have any leverage. No, he had plenty. Enough that he was pretty sure that if he knocked on de Santis's mansion, the guy would not only open it wide, he'd invite him inside.

Which was exactly what Wolf wanted. Once he was in, that would be that. De Santis was his.

What about getting away without anyone knowing it was you?

Yeah, well, that was going to be the tricky part, wasn't it? Grabbing Olivia and getting away would be difficult, escaping a murder charge even more so.

Maybe you'd have to stay and take the rap. Maybe it would be worth it just to have everything end.

It wouldn't be fair. Not to his brothers, who'd have to deal with the fallout of one of the Tates being arrested for murder, especially when they already had more than enough on their plates. And not to Olivia either.

You're looking for reasons not to do it now?

No, he wasn't. It was necessary. There would be no end to this until Cesare de Santis had joined Noah Tate, dead and in the grave. Too many people had been hurt, and too many lives had been ruined to allow it to continue.

Olivia would never come with him after this, but maybe that was something he'd have to live with.

"Nothing worthwhile comes without sacrifice, Wolf. Nothing worth fighting for is taken without blood."

Yeah, that's what that fucking old prick had kept telling him, and shit, Wolf knew all about sacrifices now, didn't he? He'd sacrificed his own needs and wants on the back of Noah Tate's dream of vengeance. He'd shed blood turning himself into the weapon his father had wanted him to be in the hope of being the son Noah had needed. But it had all been lies.

Noah hadn't needed a son after all.

Of course. This is all about you being angry at Dad, nothing else.

Wolf snarled into the dark.

Yeah, he was angry at Noah. He was fucking furious. But his father was dead and there was no satisfaction to be had from him. There was only de Santis left to take some justice from, and if that made him a selfish bastard, then too bad.

Didn't he deserve to take something from all of this? Didn't he deserve some goddamn reward? It wasn't the reward he'd always wanted, but it would be so fucking satisfying all the same.

And Olivia? What about her?

His heart clenched tight in his chest.

Sacrifices. It was all about sacrifices.

Olivia would be just one more.

Decision made, Wolf turned and strode out of the galley. He made his way off the *Lady* and out of the boat basin. The sun was coming up, the city waking, and the ice on the streets was sparkling in the sunrise.

It was going to be a perfect winter's day.

He found a cab and got it to take him direct to de Santis's front door. He'd debated waiting a few hours before charging right in so he could think up a better strategy, but he was sick of thinking. Sick of arguing with himself. Sick of the tight feeling in chest. He wanted this to be over and done with once and for all. Anyway, he already knew he wasn't a strategist. He acted and then dealt with the consequences accordingly—that's just how he rolled and always had.

There was no security on the door of the mansion, but Wolf didn't make the mistake of thinking the place unguarded. In fact, de Santis was probably waiting for him.

There had to be a reason he'd been left alive after all.

Getting out of the cab, he didn't hesitate, heading right up the steps to the imposing, double front doors and pressing the buzzer. He stared up into the camera above the door and grinned at it. *Yeah, it's me, asshole. But you knew that already, didn't you?*

He didn't know what it was that de Santis wanted, whether it was simply to one-up him after he'd grabbed Olivia not once but twice, or whether he had a punishment in store for him, but whatever it was, Wolf didn't care.

As long as it got him inside, he was okay with it.

The door clicked and swung open, one of the de Santis security team in the doorway. It wasn't one of the guys he'd taken out earlier, sadly.

"Good morning, Mr. Tate," the asshole said expressionlessly. "Mr. de Santis is expecting you."

"What, already?" Wolf grinned. "But I haven't even had time to freshen up."

The look on the man's face didn't change. Instead he merely turned, obviously waiting for Wolf to follow him.

Wolf obliged, letting the asshole lead him into the house and gesture toward a door on the right that was off the main entrance hall.

Not that Wolf didn't know what that room was. He'd been here many times before and knew it was the formal sitting room, where de Santis entertained people he didn't particularly like.

Giving the security dick another grin, Wolf went to the door, opened it, and strode right in.

The room was white and stark, uncomfortable couches and chairs covered in white linen, the only color from some abstracts on the wall painted in dark, threatening hues.

Cesare was standing beside the white marble fireplace, leaning one arm on the mantelpiece, smiling as Wolf entered. Yet his blue eyes were colder than the winter's sky outside.

On an armchair near the fire sat Olivia.

She'd obviously showered and changed, her long glossy brown hair no longer in a sleepy tangle down her back, but lying smooth over her shoulders. She'd ditched his shirt in favor of a plain white blouse and a neat, dark blue pencil skirt that fitted over her gently rounded thighs like a dream.

He preferred her wearing his shirt with nothing on underneath, but he approved of the pencil skirt. He wanted to see more of it, even.

Olivia's face was expressionless, her hands clasped together in her lap. She looked distant and very contained, though her gaze wasn't in any way as cold as her father's. No, there was a heat to it, the flames leaping high as their eyes met.

She said nothing, but then she didn't need to. Those flames in her blue eyes told him all he needed to know.

Yeah, she's glad to see you now, but how long will that last? Until you kill her father?

Wolf ignored that thought, looking at de Santis and spreading his arms out. "You're not even gonna get some asshole to pat me down?"

"Of course not. That wouldn't be very polite of me, would it, Wolf? Especially after you've been part of our household for so many years." The smile that had turned his mouth faded. "Then again, kidnapping my daughter wasn't very polite of you."

"The first time it was definitely a kidnapping," Wolf amended. "Second time, though, she came with me." He flicked a glance at her. "Didn't you, baby?"

She was staring at him, and he was suddenly aware of the tension in her body, as if holding herself braced for an attack.

Made sense. Since he was here and she knew what he intended. But . . . had she told her father about it?

"Yes, Wolf," Cesare murmured, as if he'd read his mind. "She did tell me. Who do you think let us know where to find you and your charming yacht?"

A jolt of something sharp went through him.

She'd promised him she wouldn't contact her father until she'd found the evidence she needed that he hadn't killed Noah. The need for that evidence had faded after what had happened with the discovery of his mother's death certificate, but she'd still made him that promise.

He gazed at her, knowing that Cesare had likely only said it to get a reaction and yet being unable to help himself all the same.

Olivia didn't flinch. "I warned him that you were coming for him," she said quietly. "I didn't tell him where we were."

She might not have, but the end result was still the same. Well, she'd always been up front about the fact that she was going to stop him.

Not that it mattered.

Not seeing any need to drag this out more than he had to, Wolf reached around and grabbed the Sig from the small of his back. Cesare made no move to stop him, merely watching with apparent interest as Wolf pointed the gun at him.

Olivia stiffened.

"I don't care what she did," Wolf said, staring into the heavy, still-handsome face of Cesare de Santis, his father's enemy for over thirty years. "You're still going to die."

Cesare's gaze dipped to the gun then back up again. "Interesting. So this is my repayment after ten years of support?"

Wolf gave a short laugh. "Support? Like a janitorial position at DS Corp type of support? Thanks but no thanks."

"Honest work, though," Cesare said. "And it would have led places. Better than where you are now, wouldn't you say?"

"But I'm happy with where I am now." It wasn't a lie. The Navy was his life, though after this, maybe not. Maybe he'd be looking at a jail term instead. "The military's been a better family to me than the rest of you bastards."

"A family," Cesare murmured, those cold blue eyes seeing right into him. "Yes, that's what you wanted, wasn't it? To be part of a family."

The words hit Wolf square in the chest, unexpected and painful, digging in deep.

He couldn't remember—had he said those things to Cesare? He must have, on one of those evenings in Cesare's study, when the old man had listened to him list his made-up litany of grievances about Noah. He'd been given a tumbler of whiskey because at seventeen he'd been a man, and Cesare had sat there and listened to Wolf talk. He hadn't interrupted, hadn't told him his opinions weren't asked for and weren't required. He hadn't told him that he was thinking too much, talking too much. He hadn't told him to shut up and do what he was told.

No, he'd simply sat and listened. Then when he was done, Cesare had asked him what he wanted more than anything in the whole world, and Wolf, drunk for the first time in his life, his inhibitions lowered, had given him that answer before he could think better of it.

Because you're stupid.

"I can give you that family, Wolf," Cesare went on, his voice low. "I can give you what you wanted. No, I'm not your father and I know I can't take his place, but I can be like a father to you. And I have Olivia. I know you want her. She could be yours, you could have a family with her. I'd be proud to call you my son."

Something hot and desperate coiled in Wolf's chest. A longing, an ache. "I don't want to be part of your family," he said through clenched teeth, denying the feeling. "I'm a Tate."

"Are you sure you don't want that?" Cesare tilted his head, and was it Wolf's imagination that those blue eyes softened a little? "A father to love you, to stand at your side? A father to support you, to be proud of you?"

"Dad." Olivia's voice was low, warning.

"What? You think after all these years I don't have feelings for the boy?"

"He knew, Wolf," Olivia said, ignoring her father. "He knew all along that you were only trying to get close to him for Noah's sake."

It should have surprised him, maybe shocked him. But it didn't. Of course Cesare had known all this time. The fucker was smart and Wolf, as a seventeen-year-old, hadn't been. He'd been a lonely boy looking for a father figure.

They used you. Both of them used you. Because you were too stupid to know any better.

His fingers tightened on the gun. "You think that changes anything? It doesn't."

Olivia got up suddenly.

"Olivia," Cesare murmured, a warning note in his voice.

Pull the trigger now.

Yet he didn't. And then Olivia was standing in front of her father, facing Wolf. Blocking his line of fire completely.

You fuck-up. You can't even kill a man properly.

The terrible frustrated anger that had been simmering away inside him knotted and tangled in his chest. But all he could see were her blue eyes staring at him, seeing inside him. Seeing everything he was.

Cesare was saying something, but Olivia was talking and that was all he could hear.

"Don't listen to him, Wolf. You know he's only trying to manipulate you. But you don't need to kill him either. There are other ways to end this. There are always other ways."

Somehow he'd moved, though he wasn't conscious of doing so, taking a few swift steps so he was right in front of Olivia, towering over her as she stood between him and her father. Towering over Cesare too, though the guy didn't move, didn't look away either.

She'd put her arms out to the sides, trying to block as much of her father as she could. And then the gun was pointing at Olivia's chest, as if he might shoot through her to get to the prick behind her.

His heartbeat was far too fast and the knot in his chest was pulling tighter and tighter. The barrel of the gun was pointed right between Olivia's breasts. If he pulled the trigger now, it would take out her *and* de Santis.

"Nothing worthwhile comes without sacrifices, Wolf. Nothing worth fighting for is taken without blood."

She didn't even look at the gun. As if it wasn't important in any way. As if pulling the trigger at point-blank range wouldn't kill her. She only looked into his eyes, steady and calm. As if nothing was wrong.

"You don't need to do this." Her voice was level and unafraid. "You're not a machine, Wolf. You're not a mindless soldier. You're not a weapon. You're smart, remember? You're so goddamn smart. *Think*."

He should be concentrating on the man behind her, the man who had somehow become a symbol for everything that had fucked up in his life. His mother's death. His father's lies. All the years he'd spent thinking he was doing good, that he'd managed to gain de Santis's trust. When that bastard had known all along.

Both of them, Noah and Cesare, had known all along. They hadn't needed him. They'd only needed a knife to stab each other with.

"No." His voice was gravelly, rough. A broken version of his own. "You're wrong. I'm a fucking weapon, that's all I am. That's all I'll ever be. And you know what the point of a weapon is? It's to kill people."

He reached out, grabbed a hold of her and shoved her forcefully out of the way, because if nothing else he could move faster than anyone when he wanted to. Then he jammed the barrel of the gun against Cesare de Santis's chest, forcing the older man up against the mantelpiece.

The only sound Cesare made was a slight indrawn breath, but Wolf didn't miss the flicker of fear in the asshole's eyes.

"Yeah," he growled. "About fucking time you started taking me seriously, motherfucker."

"Wolf!" Olivia called his name desperately. "You're smarter than this. You're better than this. I know you are."

He ignored her, staring into a different set of blue eyes. Colder and much more guarded. Full of secrets. "You never liked me, you fucking prick. You never wanted me. You only wanted to use me, like Noah fucking Tate." He jammed the Sig harder into de Santis's chest. "Just like you want to use me now. Admit it, fucker. Admit that's what you want to do."

Cesare was silent. "You could have been so much more," he said quietly after a while. "You could have been the best of them if you hadn't been so desperate. You reeked of it, did you know that? You wanted validation so badly, wanted praise. Wanted love. It made using you so easy. No wonder you were Noah's pet. You were the perfect tool just waiting for someone's hand."

Someone was pulling at his back, tugging hard and shouting at him. But he wasn't listening. All he could see was Cesare de Santis's blue eyes and the truth in them.

So easy to use. So easy to manipulate. That's all you ever were to any of them, you dumb fuck.

The anger blossomed inside him, going nuclear, a fucking mushroom cloud. De Santis was right. That's all he'd been to both of them.

That's all he'd ever be.

"Yeah, I am," he said, low and guttural. "Tell Dad I said hi when you see him."

Then he pulled the trigger.

CHAPTER SIXTEEN

Olivia screamed as the gun went off, horror unfurling inside her.

She'd been so certain that if the worse came to the worst in this stupid meeting that her father had insisted on having, despite her warnings, she'd be able to stop Wolf. That he'd listen to her. But he hadn't and she knew why.

Even after all this time, he was still listening to the lies his father had told him.

And now it was too late. Too late for her father. Too late for Wolf.

Too late for her.

Wolf stumbled back as her father collapsed onto the floor, and suddenly the room was full of her father's black-suited security staff. People were shouting, guns were all pointing.

At her.

She blinked, unable to keep up with what was happening. There was a powerful arm around her waist and a rock-hard body at her back. Something hard was sticking into her side, burning through the material of her blouse.

The gun. And the barrel was still hot.

Grief and horror turned over inside her, making her feel sick, and she was conscious that she was shaking.

Wolf had killed her father and now he was using her as a shield to protect himself.

She really had lost him.

"Come any fucking closer and I'll kill her like I killed your boss," he shouted to the men gathering around them. "Now get the fuck out of my way. Let me go and nothing bad will happen to her."

Her heart was racing and nothing made any sense. She was crying, tears running down her face and down her neck.

She'd spent all morning quietly gathering evidence on her father's activities, because weirdly, she was still able to access all her files. Her father hadn't blocked them from her, which he really should have done.

Apparently he still trusted her, which had caused her a few moments of grief. But she'd shoved them all aside, doing what had to be done. Contacting a DS Corp R&D staff member and asking for help with some encryption. Turned out decrypting files was easy when you had the key and the right instructions.

The files she'd decrypted had turned out to be a list of merchandise. Illegal merchandise. Experimental weapons that should never have left the lab, let alone the country. And her father had sent them to Daniel May.

It was all the evidence she needed.

She'd sent the list off to her brother Rafael, CEO of DS Corp, with instructions that it go to the correct government official, and to be careful because she wasn't sure who was in her father's pocket and who wasn't. But Rafael would know, and if he didn't, he certainly had the contacts to find out.

He would handle it.

Her father was going down.

Turned out that was all for nothing though. Because Wolf had killed him.

She tried to stifle the sobs as Wolf walked her out of the living room into the hallway, moving fast toward the front doors. Her father's men were following, guns pointed, looking for an opportunity. Not finding one.

Wolf walked backward to the front door, keeping her in front of him, his hot body like a furnace against her spine. He opened the door then paused in the doorway. "I want a car. Now."

One of the men—Clarence, Olivia saw belatedly—put a hand to his ear and said something into it.

A minute later a car screeched up outside.

"Nice work," Wolf growled. "Now you can give me half an hour. Anyone follows me, she's dead. Understand?"

He didn't wait for a response, dragging her outside and pulling her down the steps. The car's engine was still running as he bundled her into the passenger's side then basically slid over the hood to get in the driver's side.

An impact sounded, then another, but by the time she could figure out what they were, Wolf was pulling away from the curb in a screech of tires.

"Seat belt," he instructed curtly, turning down one street after another, reminding her of the night that felt like a lifetime ago when he'd kidnapped her from her room and driven her to that hotel.

Her hands were shaking as she reached for the belt, automatically obeying him. She should simply open the car door and leap out, but they were moving so fast and she wasn't that stupid.

You are pretty stupid though. You thought you could change his mind. That you would be enough.

But she wasn't enough, was she? She never had been, not for anyone.

"You killed him." Her voice was thick with tears. "I'll never forgive you for that."

"He's not dead," Wolf said shortly.

At first Olivia couldn't quite take it in. "What? What do you mean he's not dead. You pulled the trigger—"

Wolf's gaze was firmly on the traffic ahead of them, his hands gripping tight to the wheel. "There was no fucking blood. None at all. He was wearing body armor."

Body armor . . .

Olivia stared at Wolf's strong profile, her brain replaying those last few horrific seconds after he'd pulled the trigger. Her father had collapsed onto the floor, but . . . there hadn't been any blood. And she would have seen if there had been, because the mantel was white marble.

Oh God. No wonder her father had been so calm, insisting on no pat-downs. Seemingly not at all concerned that Wolf was likely to be armed and hell-bent on killing him.

No, he'd wanted to "talk" face-to-face. And he'd wanted Olivia to be in the room. She'd agreed, because she'd thought she'd be the only thing standing between her father and certain death.

But no. Her father had been wearing body armor. Even then, he hadn't really needed her. The only reason she'd been there at all was so he could use Wolf's feelings for her against him.

Her heart squeezed tight, pain of a different sort filling her, and along with it, anger. "Did you know that?" she demanded. "Did you know he had armor on before you pulled the trigger?"

Wolf's mismatched gaze flicked to hers then back to the traffic in front him, weaving through the cars. "No."

She clutched onto the seat belt as the car lurched. "So none of what I said made any difference at all, did it?"

He said nothing.

"I told you," she said, her voice scraped raw. "I told you who you were. I told you how I saw you. But you didn't believe me, did you?"

A muscle jumped in his hard jawline.

"You didn't listen. You didn't hear. You didn't want to. Because you've still got your father's voice in your head. You're still trying to prove yourself to him even now."

Abruptly Wolf pulled hard on the wheel and the car lurched again as he screeched to the curb, jamming his foot on the brake, making her jerk against the seat belt.

Then he turned, his gaze on hers, full of fury and heat, the strength of it filling the car so much that it felt like she couldn't breathe. "You're wrong," he said hoarsely. "You're just fucking wrong. I don't want to prove myself to him. You know why? Because I found out that Dad never put his name on my birth certificate. He promised me it was there, but it wasn't. He was never gonna acknowledge me as his son. He was never fucking gonna do it. And it just came clear to me now, why. Cesare's right. I was desperate for all those things he said, and Noah knew it. So he used me. He told me I was the perfect weapon, and I thought it meant because I was strong. I didn't have the smarts, but I sure as hell had the fucking strength." His mouth twisted, pain stark in his eyes. "It wasn't that at all, though, was it? I was the perfect fucking weapon because I was weak. Because I could be used. Because I didn't question and I didn't think. I did whatever he said, like a good soldier boy, because I wanted to be his son. Because I loved him. Because he was my fucking dad and all I wanted was for him to love me back!"

He was clutching the wheel, his knuckles white, and despite everything, her heart ached for his pain. She wanted to put her hand over those white knuckles and stroke him, soothe him. Tell him he didn't need that man's twisted love, that he deserved so much more.

But he was never going to listen to her, was he?

She would never be enough.

"He never did though, did he?" Wolf's voice was ragged

and full of anger and pain. "He never loved me. He didn't give a shit. He used the fact that I wanted a family against me so I'd do exactly what he wanted. I was just a tool to him, a weapon. And what else can a weapon do, but find a target?" The grief in his eyes leapt high. "That's all I am, Liv. That's all I'll ever be."

Her eyes filled with helpless, stupid tears. "So you've made your choice then. Sounds like a great decision to me, to be your father's loaded gun even when he's dead."

"It's not my fucking decision—"

"Yes it is!" Her voice rang in the car, bouncing off the surfaces, but she didn't care. She stared into his beloved face, so angry with him she could barely think straight. "You're still doing exactly what he wants even now. You had a choice, Wolf Tate. You had a choice to be someone different, to *not* be Noah's weapon. But you didn't take it, did you? You believed everything he said about you. Everything Dad said about you. And you're still believing it now. You're still letting both of them use you." She took a breath, clutching on to her seat belt. "Why? What the hell do you think you'll get from this? His approval? His love? He's dead, Wolf. He's *dead*."

Fury leapt in his gaze. "Don't you fucking dare—"

"I fucking dare everything!" She leaned forward, getting in his face, so they were nose to nose. So close she could see the glittering sparks of sapphire and emerald in his eyes. "I loved you then and I love you still, and I told you what you were. I told you that you were better than that, that you were smarter than they ever gave you credit for. I told you that you didn't have to do what they said, but did you listen to me? No, you didn't. You believed everything Noah said, and you're still believing, still listening to him and Dad. You're still letting them use you." The words were spilling out of her and she was helpless to stop them, fury pouring out along with them. "Maybe your father was right, Wolf Tate. Maybe I was wrong. Maybe you're too stupid to understand after all."

An emotion flickered across his face, bright and brilliant. Pain. And for a second the anger in his eyes was gone and there was nothing but heat, nothing but something that looked terribly like sadness.

She'd hurt him, but she didn't feel bad, no, not one shred. He'd done nothing but hurt her all this time and even now, he was still hurting her. And though her heart was breaking into tiny little pieces inside her chest—because it was obvious that there couldn't be anything between them, not now, and that a part of her had been desperately hoping there could be—she couldn't let him go without some scars. Not when she would carry the ones he'd given her for the rest of her life. She had to leave her own mark on him in some way.

"Olivia," he said hoarsely, her name jagged with pain, and he reached out to touch her face. But she jerked back, jabbing at the button of her seat belt then pulling it free.

"No," she whispered. "Don't touch me. Don't come anywhere near me." Loss was choking her, grief aching like an open wound in her chest. "You wanted a family, Wolf. You wanted someone to love you. *I* love you. And I could have been that family. You could have belonged to me."

Agony flared in his eyes. "Liv—"

"It's too late," she cut him off. "It's too late for us. You made your decision and so I don't want to ever see you again, understand? You don't come to my house, you don't knock on my door, you don't call. And the next time you try to use me as a means to an end, whether it's to get information or lure my father out of hiding, or as a goddamn human shield, I'm going to scream. And if I manage to get your gun, then God help you, because I'll pull that fucking trigger."

The agony in his eyes deepened, and as she grabbed the

door handle and opened the car door, he half reached for her, as if he wanted to grab her and pull her back inside.

But she looked him straight in the eye, fury and grief shaking her apart. If he stopped her now, she didn't know what she would do.

He didn't stop her. His hand closed into a fist inches from her arm and his expression closed up like a door shutting in her face, the pain in his eyes dying, leaving them nothing but cold, glittering chips of glass.

"Okay," he said in a dead sounding voice. "If that's how you want it."

She didn't reply. She didn't even look at him as she slipped out of the car and slammed the door after her.

And she didn't turn to watch him leave as she heard him pull away in yet another screech of tires, so he wouldn't see the tears streaming down her face.

It wasn't what she wanted, not at all. But this was the way it had to be.

He was a man, and yet he refused to see himself as anything but a weapon.

And he was the man she loved.

Which meant there could be no future for them. None at all.

Wolf drove, though he had no idea where the hell he was going. He kept randomly turning down streets and driving, not paying attention to anything but making sure he didn't crash.

It felt like he'd been the one shot at point-blank range, and not with a handgun, but a shotgun. And he wasn't wearing body armor so there was a huge hole in his chest and nothing he could do to stem the flow of blood.

He was bleeding out, getting weaker, paler, the pain making him insane.

"Maybe you're just too stupid to understand . . ."

That shot had come from the one person he'd never expected it to, hitting a place he was already vulnerable, and like the coup de grâce, it had killed him.

Eventually he had to pull over in an abandoned lot by the river, and simply double over because the pain in his chest was so bad it was physical.

She's only telling you what you already know. Why are you being such a fucking pussy about it?

He didn't understand that. Because it was true, wasn't it? He'd accepted all this time that he was a dumb fuck and everything he'd done up until this point had proved it. The botched kidnappings and then the shooting that hadn't even happened, because that prick had been wearing body armor. And he hadn't seen it because he'd been so consumed by rage, by his own agony.

His hands gripped the wheel, holding on so tight the metal creaked.

He'd shot a man in cold blood, right in front of that man's daughter. It didn't matter that Cesare had been wearing body armor, the intent had been the same. Wolf had been determined to shoot him regardless, and for what?

"What the hell do you think you'll get from this? His approval? His love? He's dead, Wolf. He's dead . . ."

She was right. She'd been right all along.

He was still clinging to the role his father had given him, still desperate for his approval. For his love. For anything that would fill the gaping hole in his soul. But nothing ever would, he knew that now.

Noah was dead, and he shouldn't have pulled that trigger.

What you should have done was fallen on your sword the moment you knew Cesare was still alive.

Yeah, fuck, he should have. He should have let de Santis's security shoot him where he stood. But he'd taken one look at Olivia's horrified face and known he couldn't let her watch him be gunned down. She already thought he'd killed her father and to have him be *actually* killed right in front of her was just too much.

So he'd grabbed her, using her to draw attention away from Cesare's unconscious body so he could leave alive, it was true. But he'd wanted to explain. Except that hadn't gone so well, had it? He hadn't been able to do that properly, either. She'd been so furious, so angry. And every word she'd said had been like a hammer on a nail, driving that nail through his skin and deep into his flesh. Into his heart.

You're too stupid to understand . . .

Now she'd gone. She slipped from the car and he'd made only a cursory attempt to stop her. He'd had to let her go though, because she was right about everything. The decision to shoot Cesare, to become what his father had made him, had been his. It had been a choice.

"I could have been that family. You could have belonged to me . . ."

The hole in his soul grew wider, deeper. Aching with loss, with grief.

Yeah, he'd made a choice and the choice hadn't been her. He'd literally turned his back on her, refused to hear what she was telling him—what she'd been telling him all this time—in favor of satisfying his own rage.

He could have chosen her, belonged to her, and he hadn't.

He'd chosen his dead father instead.

Wolf slammed his hand against the steering wheel, a low moan of anguish escaping him.

"Earn your Trident everyday," was the part of the SEAL code and yet what had he done? Every day he'd made wrong decision after wrong decision. Bad choice after bad choice.

If he didn't deserve Olivia de Santis, then he certainly didn't fucking deserve his trident.

Forcing himself to sit up, Wolf made a decision and started the car again, pulling back onto the street.

Some time later, he pulled up outside a familiar building and got out, stalked up the steps to the front door. He pressed the buzzer and a second later the door was pulled wide. But it wasn't Noah's old butler standing on the doorstep of the Tate mansion, or even the housekeeper, but his brother Van.

Van's hazel eyes narrowed. "About fucking time you arrived," he said gruffly. "Come on. Lucas and I have got something to say to you."

Shock pulsed down Wolf's spine. "Why are you here? You weren't supposed to be in New York."

"Got here this morning. Heard some shit on the grapevine about how my youngest brother had kidnapped Cesare de Santis's daughter. Thought I'd better come and check it out." He stood to the side. "Are you going to come in or not? And the answer had better be yes, just saying."

"How did you know *I'd* come here?"

Van shrugged "Knew you'd have to turn up eventually. Especially given the de Santis situation."

Wolf hadn't expected this. He'd expected to see an employee, to give whomever it was the message, and then go back to Virginia, back to base, and hand his fucking trident in.

The last person on earth he wanted to see was his goddamn brother, who apparently had "something to say."

Van's gaze narrowed even further. "Wolf. Don't make me ask again."

He didn't have the energy for this all of a sudden. It was like all the fight had simply drained out of him, so he shrugged and stepped into the hallway.

"Good decision," Van muttered, moving past him and toward the door that led to the sitting room. He pulled that open too and jerked his head.

Wolf went through, moving on autopilot, coming into the warm, comfortable sitting room with the familiar photos on the mantel and the tasteful art on the walls. It was decorated in shades of cream and full of soft edges, in stark contrast to the hard white and sharpness of the de Santis sitting room.

Lucas was standing near the fireplace, his hands thrust in the pockets of his jeans, his silver-blue eyes clear and icy. Though, maybe now that Wolf thought about it, they weren't quite as icy as they once had been.

"All right," Van said from behind him. "Now we're all here, you'd better fucking explain what the hell is going on, Wolf. Because I'm sick of you sneaking around and being vague and generally a pain in my fucking rear."

Lucas said nothing. Obviously his middle brother agreed.

Fuck.

Wolf didn't sit, he turned and went over to the windows, trying to collect his thoughts, figure out what the hell he was going to say. There was no point hiding anything now, or making excuses about not having the time to explain. Not that he had the energy for more subterfuge anyway.

His brothers deserved to know the truth, because in many ways he'd failed them too.

He kept his gaze out the window, his hands in his pockets. "You know I had a close relationship with Dad. Well, there was a reason for that. He told me that I was his real son." There was nothing but silence behind him, so he went on. "He said that he and my mom were going to get married, but she left him, and didn't tell him she was pregnant. He only found out three years later when he was contacted by someone at a boys home. Apparently a kid had been handed in, and he'd been named the father. So he went to find out about this kid, and there I was. He told me he'd had tests done and that, yes, I was his son. I had to keep it secret, because de Santis was a real threat and he didn't want anything to happen to me."

More silence from behind him, but he could feel his brothers' shock all the same.

"He said that he was going to try to find Mom, and that one day, when the threat of de Santis was gone, he'd acknowledge me as his son and we'd be a family again, like we should have. But in order for that to happen, I was going to have to do a job for him. He wanted me to infiltrate the de Santis household. Get close to the old man, gain his trust. Be a double agent. He wanted information about what de Santis was doing, plus, when the time was right, I would be in position to take out the prick whenever Dad was ready."

"Fuck," Van muttered at last. "You serious?"

Wolf didn't turn around, didn't want to see his brother's face. No doubt they thought he was stupid too, for believing all those lies, because he himself could hear now that he'd said it out loud, just how ridiculous they sounded.

Christ. How had he *ever* believed them?

Ignoring Van, he went on. "So I did. I did what he told me to. I got close to de Santis and to Olivia too. I did jobs for him, passed on information, made myself useful. All that kind of shit." He paused. "That's why I was around to save Grace, Luc. De Santis wanted that asshole taken out, so I took him out."

"I thought you were back on base," Lucas said, sounding a little rough. "That you'd cut short your leave. That's what you told us."

"Yeah, well, I lied. I've been in New York all this time."

"Why?" Van this time, the question barked out. "To stick around for de Santis?"

At last Wolf turned around, looking both his brothers in the face. "You want to know what was in my letter from Dad? He told me he'd finally found out where Mom was. But he couldn't get her out while de Santis was alive, which meant my final mission was to finish the job we'd started together. I had to kill him. Dad said in his letter that once de Santis was dead, I'd get the information about where Mom was. He also said he'd be sad he wasn't here to finally be the family we'd always wanted, but that his name was on my birth certificate. I could get Mom and tell the world that Noah Tate was really my father. It wasn't exactly the way we'd always planned it, but it was something."

Van muttered a curse, vicious and soft. "His name wasn't on your birth certificate."

Wolf slowly shook his head. "No. And Mom? Turned out she died years ago."

Shock rippled over both his brothers' faces.

"What?" Lucas demanded. "What do you mean she died?"

"I mean, Dad told me exactly what I wanted to hear. I wanted a family and so he promised me one. All I had to do was kill his enemy."

"Christ," Van muttered, scowling. "That prick has a lot to answer for."

Lucas was staring at him, his sharp gaze inescapable. "So is that what you've been doing all this time? Planning on how to take de Santis down?"

And failing. Always failing.

Wolf tried to give his usual fuck-you smile, but it didn't work. "I tried," he said roughly. "I fucking tried. In fact, that's where I've just been. I confronted him at his house, even had a gun. Even pulled the goddamn trigger. But he was wearing body armor, so all I did was knock him flat on his back."

Van's expression darkened. He flicked at glance at Lucas, who frowned, then looked back at Wolf. "You shot him?"

Wolf heard the condemnation, felt it like a knife in his chest. But he refused to look away, meeting his brother's green-gold eyes head-on. "Yeah, I did. You gonna tell me I'm stupid too?"

"Of course you're fucking stupid," Van growled. "I wouldn't have picked you for a cold-blooded murderer, though."

The knife twisted, an intense, burning pain. "Turns out I'm a lot of things." He tried to make it sound casual and not like he was falling apart on the inside. "I'm a weapon, Van. That's all I was brought up to be. Dad fed me all those lies just to make me the bullet in his fucking gun."

"Oh bullshit." Lucas's cold voice was heavy with derision. "You're a goddamn Navy SEAL. You're no one's fucking weapon."

Wolf shook his head. They didn't understand, neither of them did. "I'm not even that, Jesus Christ. Where do you think I'm going now? I'm going to Virginia to hand in my goddamn trident. Because yeah, you're right. I'm a murderer. I'm a coward. I'm a dumb fuck who didn't know any better, and I don't deserve to have it any longer."

Lucas's chilly gaze glittered. "Why? Because you nearly killed a man? Because your Daddy lied to you and didn't love you after all? Jesus, he told me that my mother burned alive because of a fire *I* lit. But do you see me running off to Virginia to hand in my trident? No, you don't. I accept what I did, but I'm not letting it define me. And I'm not letting Noah and the way he manipulated me run my life, either."

Wolf took an involuntary step forward, his hands in fists at his sides, anger and pain feeling like they were tearing him apart. "I shot him, you fucking asshole. I shot him right in front of her and now . . ." He stopped, Olivia's white face and the tears in her eyes as she got out of the car all he could see.

You'll never be hers.

He couldn't stand it then, being here in this room with the only two people he'd known for most of his life, the two men he'd looked up to and tried to be like, who were looking at him like he was a stranger and one they didn't particularly like, either.

Without a word, he headed straight for the door, only for Van to reach out, grabbing at Wolf's arm. Wolf was taller than Van and a touch broader, but the strength in his oldest brother's fingers brought him up short.

"Wait." Van's voice was flat with authority. "This is about Olivia de Santis, isn't it?"

No, Christ no. He didn't want to talk about Olivia and what he'd lost, not now. Not in front of these two men. "Let me fucking go," he growled, trying to pull away.

But Van held on. "It is, isn't it? What did she say to you? Christ, if she hurt you—"

"She didn't," Wolf lied, cutting straight across his brother. "She's the only person in my whole fucking life who ever told me the truth."

So why don't you believe her?

The thought fell into a hole in his mind, dizzying him, and for a second the room faded away. There was only that question. And there was only one answer.

He hadn't believed her when she'd told him he was smart, that he was more than simply a weapon in his father's hand. And he hadn't, because he was afraid of the truth.

He was afraid of being weak. Afraid of that hole inside him that wanted his father's approval so desperately. That wanted so much to belong. So afraid, that he'd let himself believe his father's promises, his lies, because belief was all he had. And then it had been turned against him.

So how could he believe her? When everyone else had done nothing but lie to him?

Van was staring at him, his gaze so sharp it was like he'd been taking sniper lessons from Lucas. "Jesus," he said at last. "You're in love with her."

Of course you are. You've been in love with her for years.

"No," Wolf said, though he could hear the lie in his voice as soon as it came out.

"You fucking are." Van let go of his arm. "Then you shot her dad. Good for you."

His fist was cocked, ready to punch Van in the face before he'd even realized what he was doing. "Don't you fucking talk about her," he growled. "Don't even say her name."

But his brother didn't look at the fist aimed at him. "What happened? She walk out on you?"

Wolf said nothing, trying to resist the urge to punch him.

You don't want to punch him. You want to punch your own stupid face. Because you made the wrong decision. You should have believed her and you didn't.

"Yeah," he ground out. "Funnily enough she didn't like me shooting her father."

"Then why did you?"

"Because apparently I'm fucking stupid."

It was Lucas who answered. "And you'll be even stupider if you believe that bullshit."

"Fucking A." Van didn't take his eyes from Wolf's. "Jesus Christ, Wolf. You're volatile, but you're not dumb. And if you let the woman you love go because of it, then you really do have shit for brains."

Wolf's fist wavered, wanting to drive forward into his brother's face.

They didn't understand, they just didn't.

Or maybe it's you who doesn't understand. She saw something in you and you're still looking for every excuse in the book not to believe her.

But if he did believe her, what then? Who would he be? Who would he belong to?

You could belong to me . . .

Longing swept over him, so intense he could hardly stand it. Oh God, if there was anyone in the entire world he wanted to belong to, it was her. But he'd refused her, made the wrong choice. He couldn't take it back. . . . Could he?

His fist slowly lowered.

"I have to let her go," he said hoarsely, even though he hadn't meant to say anything at all. "I made the wrong choice. You can't come back from that."

Van's gaze flicked to Lucas's then back again. "Of course you can. You fail and then you get back up and try again. Didn't you learn anything at Coronado? Never quit, Wolf. You should know that."

"Never quit . . ."

His breath caught.

If he gave her up, let her go, he'd be quitting, no two ways about it. He'd be letting himself be defined by his father, by Cesare de Santis. Letting himself believe that he was simply the big dumb asshole who was weak when he should have been strong, who wasn't worthy to be anyone's son.

Or he could make a different choice.

He could choose to be the man *he* wanted to be, if only he knew what kind of man that was.

You know what kind of man you want to be.

Of course he did.

He wanted to be the man Olivia thought he was.

He wanted to be the man she loved.

"Holy shit," Van muttered, eyeing him. "What's wrong now?"

"I just thought of something." Wolf jerked his arm out of his brother's grip. "There's someone I need to see."

Van opened his mouth to say something, only to be interrupted by his phone going off. Scowling, he held up his finger, indicating that Wolf was to wait, then pulled his phone out of the pocket of his jeans. His scowl deepened. "I have to take this. Looks like some shit is going down."

"What shit?" Lucas asked.

Van only shook his head and hit a button, raising the phone to his ear.

But Wolf was already turning away, heading for the door.

He couldn't wait.

He had to see Olivia. Right the fuck now.

CHAPTER SEVENTEEN

Olivia perched on the edge of the couch in the sitting room, her hands in her lap. Her father had been taken to a private hospital straightaway, before she'd managed to get back after Wolf had taken her, but everyone had assured her Cesare was alive. That it was true what Wolf had said, he'd been wearing body armor underneath his shirt. He'd probably have a broken rib or two, but he'd recover.

After Clarence had asked her whether she wanted Wolf Tate taken down for what he'd done to the boss and she'd declined firmly, he'd called Angus, her father's driver, assuming that Olivia would want to get to the hospital straightaway, and had been very surprised when she'd refused.

Ignoring him, Olivia had gone straight to her father's office and booted up his computer. Then she'd proceeded to copy every single one of his files onto a small hard drive that she'd then stuck in the pocket of her skirt.

When the Feds came, de Santis staff would no doubt try to destroy his computer and make sure all those files were erased, but now she had them.

Her father wasn't going to be able to escape what he'd done, not this time.

She didn't know what to do after that, so she'd gone

downstairs, thinking to wait in the sitting room, though what she was waiting for she had no idea.

She was still so angry and hurt at Wolf. At his refusal to accept what she kept telling him, his refusal to listen to her. Proving to her that her love didn't matter to him, not one goddamn bit.

Then again, her love had never mattered to anyone, had it? It hadn't saved her mother and it hadn't saved her father.

All it had done was hurt her.

She got up in the end and walked out of the room, pausing only to grab a coat, and then, after another idea struck her, making a detour into her father's study yet again to grab something else from his desk.

A gun.

After slipping it into the pocket of her coat, she went back downstairs and let herself out the front door.

She walked down the sidewalk, not having any direction in mind, just needing to move, her brain going over and over what had happened. Wolf pulling that trigger and her father falling.

"I'm a fucking weapon. That's all I am. That's all I'll ever be."

Tears slipped down her cheeks and she let them fall. She'd already cried a lot today, so what was a few more?

She had no idea what she was going to do now. It all seemed so pointless. The Feds would come and they would pull apart her father's life, and they would pull apart hers too. With any luck they'd believe her that she had no idea what her father had done and she wouldn't be named as an accessory, but she had to accept the fact that she might be.

She'd tell them the truth whatever happened.

The sidewalk was still icy so she kept her head down, watching her step, so she didn't see the man in front of her until it was too late to avoid him.

It was like cannoning into a tree.

Her hands came up to steady herself against a rock-hard chest and she was looking up, an apology already coming out of her mouth, "Oh God, I'm so sorry. I didn't see—"

Whatever she'd been going to say died in her throat.

The man was looking down at her and one of his eyes was green and one was blue. He had a short, black Mohawk, and his hands were large and warm, and they were gripping onto her arms, holding her still.

"Olivia," Wolf said, his gravely voice rough round the edges.

She stiffened, a flood of fury and pain erupting inside her and she reached into the pocket of her coat for the very small, DS Corp handgun. It was tiny, experimental, and she had no idea why she'd even slipped it in there in the first place, it had just seemed like a good idea at the time.

She knew now.

Her fingers closed around it and she'd whipped it out of her pocket and pressed against Wolf's flat stomach before she'd even thought about it. "Remember what I said if you came back?" she said softly. "If you even thought about touching me?"

His eyes widened, but he didn't move or let her go. "Do it," he said. "I deserve it."

And she knew all of a sudden that if she was to pull that trigger, he wouldn't avoid the shot. He'd take it and he wouldn't stop her.

Pain closed her throat. "What are you doing? Why did you come back?"

"Because I had to tell you something."

"Tell me what?" She pressed the barrel harder against his gut, his abs tensing as she did so. He was so close she could feel the heat of his body and the warmth of his palms soaking through her blouse. It made her ache.

"That I should have listened to you," he murmured

roughly, searching her face. "That I shouldn't have pulled that trigger. I should have believed you when you told me I didn't have to be a machine, I didn't have to be a weapon. But I didn't listen and I didn't believe you, because I'm a fucking idiot and I was afraid. Because choosing to believe you're stupid was a better excuse than choosing to believe a lie." His fingers gripped her harder. "You were right. I was still doing what Dad wanted, still being what he wanted me to be, and I told myself that's what *I* wanted to be too. Because he's my Dad and I loved him, and I wanted him to love me back. I wanted to be his son." His voice turned hoarse. "But he didn't love me, Liv. He lied to me. Everyone fucking lied to me. And so . . . I couldn't let myself believe you."

Her throat constricted and she had to swallow in order to breathe.

"But you've never lied to me," he went on, hoarsely, raggedly. "You've never lied, not one time. So I've got no fucking excuse now, have I? I've got no choice but to believe you. That I'm not just a weapon. That I'm smarter than I thought I was." He was tugging her close, and it had to have hurt to have the barrel of the gun sticking into his stomach, but if it did he gave no sign, those brilliant eyes holding hers, full of something fierce that reached inside her and gripped her tight. "I've got no choice but to believe that I'm the man you seem to think I am. I've got no choice but to *become* that man." His massive chest heaved as he inhaled raggedly. "I want to, Liv. I want to be that man. I don't want to be a weapon anymore. I don't want to be another fucking tool all those bastards use to hurt each other. I want to belong to you. Because you're the woman I love."

Her heart felt like it was being squeezed in a vice, and it hurt. There was a flame in his eyes, hot and bright and fierce, and she was afraid to let herself hope that it was what she thought it was. "I thought I wasn't enough," she croaked. "I thought you didn't want to listen to me. That me telling you I loved you wasn't good enough. That I wasn't good enough."

He shook his head, a violent, sharp negation. "No, fuck, you know the truth? I'm the one who's not good enough. I'm the one who doesn't deserve what you were trying to give me. I kidnapped you, used you, lied to you. Then I shot your goddamn father right in front of you. I'm no better than them and I know it."

"Wolf, you're—"

"No, let me finish." That look in his eyes was burning bright, no mistaking it now. Determination, all the power of his considerable will behind it. "I want to make a different decision, a different choice. I want to be worthy of you, Olivia de Santis. I want to deserve you. I want to be everything you think I am. And you can fucking bet I'm going to spend the rest of my life trying to."

Tears trickled slowly down her cheeks, all her anger draining away, and all the pain flowing out along with it.

She'd never ever thought, not in a million years, that she would ever get this from him. That she would ever hear those words.

"You don't have to do anything to deserve me," she said thickly. "You don't have to do anything to be worthy. You already are."

His expression became even more fierce. "If your father hadn't been wearing body armor, I would have killed him. How can you forgive that?"

She shook her head. "It's not me you need find forgiveness from for that. It's yourself." She reached up and touched his face. "I think deep down you know who you are and you don't need a name on a birth certificate to prove it."

"Yeah, you're right." He lifted his hands from her arms and cupped her face between his large, warm palms. "I know who I am. I'm the man who loves Olivia de Santis and that's all I ever need to be."

She wanted to say something, but then he kissed her and not gently. There was nothing but raw demand in the kiss, nothing but heat and passion. When he finally lifted his mouth, he said, "You can take the gun away now. Unless you still want to take a shot?"

A hiccupping laugh escaped her, that somehow turned into a sob, and she let him take the gun away. He put it into his pocket and then he put his arms around her and crushed her against him. And she didn't protest, she simply opened her mouth and let him devour her completely, heedless of the people walking by.

"I want to take you to the *Lady*," Wolf murmured against her mouth. "Lay you out on the bed, make you mine. Right the fuck now."

She shivered. "I want that too, but I think I might need to stay here. I think I might be receiving a visit from the FBI at some point."

Wolf raised his head and looked down at her, his eyes wide. "What did you do, baby?"

"I had those files decrypted and then I forwarded them on to my brother to take to the FBI. Oh and I also copied all the rest of my father's files onto a hard drive. Which I've got in my pocket."

"Holy fuck," Wolf murmured approvingly. "You're more of a genuine badass than I am."

She grinned, his praise setting up a warm glow inside her. "I guess that means we genuinely can't go back to the *Lady*, though."

The expression on his face changed. "I think we can find the time. They're not here yet, right?"

Wolf took her back to his boat and did as he promised. He laid her across his bed and stripped her naked, then he explored every inch of her beautiful body, worshipping her the way he needed to. The way she deserved. Loving her the way he'd promised her he would, because he wasn't a weapon of destruction anymore. He was a man, and his mission wasn't to kill, it was to make her feel good, make her feel loved.

So like he did with every one of his missions, he gave it a hundred and ten percent. Maximum effort.

Her phone went off before he was ready and of course it was the FBI wanting to have a word with her about her father—or at least that's what they realized when they finally listened to the message—because they had other more important things to do than answer phone calls.

At some point she would have to go back to the de Santis mansion and confront the consequences of her father's crimes. But he'd already decided she wasn't going to do this alone. That he would be at her side, and he would muster all the power of the Tate name to help her.

For once a Tate was going to help a de Santis, not kill them.

But all that could wait at least another half hour.

Because although Wolf's favorite things were fighting, fucking, and blowing shit up, loving Olivia de Santis was his most favorite of all.

EPILOGUE

The day Cesare de Santis went to jail for a very long time, the Tate brothers met at Leo's Alehouse to celebrate. Because that's where all of their family's dramas had started.

Though this time, it wasn't just the three of them.

Chloe, his adoptive sister and now his sister-in-law, was nestled against Van's side, talking about the new stable complex or some such bullshit, while Grace, sitting in Lucas's lap, was listening attentively. Lucas was not listening attentively. He was winding a lock of Grace's fire red hair though his fingers and obviously thinking about something else.

Wolf glanced at the door, impatient for the latest addition to their family to show herself.

This was going to be a difficult day for Olivia. The trial had been long and exhausting for her, and watching her father be put away for years wasn't going to be easy either, but she'd told him she'd wanted to come to Leo's. She just had a few things to do first.

He really hoped those few things weren't going to take too long, because he hated being apart from her, most especially when he knew she was going to need him.

Eventually though, the door to the bar opened and there

she was, dressed in his favorite "hot secretary" outfit. Pencil skirt and demure blouse and pumps.

Fucking delicious.

Except as she came toward him—drawing not a few male gazes as she moved through the crowd of largely military men—there was a crease between her brows.

His gut tightened. Something was wrong.

He pushed his chair back and got up, not bothering with making excuses, simply heading straight toward her.

They met in the middle of the bar and he couldn't resist the urge bend his head and kiss her in front of everyone in the whole place, staking his claim.

Her hands came to his chest and she leaned briefly against him, returning the kiss. Then she pulled away. "Wolf, there's someone outside to see you."

His gut tightened even further. "Who is it?"

Olivia's blue gaze came to his. "Your father's lawyer. He was coming in right when I was, and asked me if I knew you and whether you'd be inside or not. I thought it would be better if he didn't come inside. He has something he wants to give to you."

Oh, fuck, that wasn't good. It never was.

Wolf glanced back at his brothers—they weren't even looking at him—then back to her. "Good thinking. Come on. Show me where he is then."

Threading her fingers through his, she led him outside, and sure enough, some asshole in a suit was standing there, looking very lawyer-like. As Wolf approached, he asked, "Wolf Tate?"

"Yeah, that's me."

He took an envelope out of his pocket and held it out. "Your father wanted me to deliver this to you six months after his death."

"Shit," Wolf muttered, not wanting to take it, but doing so anyway.

The lawyer gave a brief nod then turned around and walked away, leaving Wolf standing there holding the envelope, foreboding winding threading through him; the last envelope his father had given him had torn his life apart.

Warm fingers tightened around his.

It also led you to Olivia.

That was true. So, not all bad then.

He looked down into Olivia's worried blue eyes. "Any ideas what this is all about?"

"No. Do you want me to open it?"

"Hell no. I can do it." Then he gave her another light kiss. "But thanks for the offer, baby."

She gave him a smile. "Open it, Wolf. Let's handle this together."

So he ripped open his father's last message and looked down at the piece of paper he held in his hands. It was old and creased, and looked like a property title.

Realization hit him then, like a mortar shell.

"It's the Tate ranch's plans, isn't it?" Olivia breathed. "The originals."

It was, and with the original boundaries. Proving that the Tate oil strike had originated from Cesare de Santis's land.

"That's the proof your Dad wanted," Wolf said, staring at the plans, not knowing how he felt about it. Because this could topple the Tate empire.

Six months ago, he would have used it to do just that. Destroyed Noah's empire in return for all the lies he'd told him.

But he was a different man now and revenge no longer interested him.

Wolf folded the plans, put them back into the envelope and handed them to a surprised Olivia. "This is yours. This is your inheritance. And it's your decision to make what you do with it."

She stared at him, a suspicious glitter in her eyes. Then she blinked, looked down, and quite carefully tore the envelope into halves, then quarters, and kept on going until she had nothing but confetti in her palms.

And then, because she was Olivia, she went over to the nearest trash can and disposed of the paper.

"There," she said, when she came back to his side. "It's over."

And just like that, the Tate/de Santis feud was done.

Who would have known that it would end up being that easy?

Wolf lifted his hands to her face, tilting her head back, looking down into her beautiful eyes. He should have thought of something to say for this moment, something meaningful and eloquent. Like the Hemingway quote he'd had tattooed on his chest. But he wasn't Hemingway and he'd never been a particularly eloquent man, and besides, he didn't give a shit about the feud.

There was only one thing in the whole damn world he gave a shit about and only one thing he wanted to say.

"I love you, Olivia de Santis," he said, because the thing that mattered was her. And love.

All the tension left her face and all the worry too, her smile filling up the empty hole in his soul. She lifted a hand to his face. "I love you too, Wolf Tate."

He'd wanted to belong to someone all his life and it was only now, staring down into her beautiful blue eyes, that he realized that all this time, he'd already belonged to someone.

He'd belonged to her.